Climbing to the Sun

a novel

SHELLEY BURCHFIELD

Climbing to the Sun

By Shelley Burchfield

Published by BeanPress

Copyright © 2024 Shelley Burchfield

All rights reserved.

ISBN: (Paperback) 979-8-218-29271-3

This is a work of fiction. Names, places, characters, conversations, and events are fictitious. Any similarities to actual events and persons, living or dead, are purely coincidental. Any trademarks, service marks, product names, or named features are assumed to be the property of their respective owners and are used only for reference. If any of these terms are used, no endorsement is implied. Except for review purposes, the reproduction of this book, in whole or part, electronically or mechanically, constitutes a copyright violation. Address permissions and review inquiries to www.shelleyburchfield.com.

Editor: Shelley Holloway
hollowayhouse.me

Front cover image by Daniel Flagel

Front cover image: iStock "Peruvian Passion Flower" by duncan1890 and Antique engraving illustration: "Passiflora sanguinea" by ilbusca

Back cover image: Adobe Stock "Frame of passion flower plant watercolor seamless pattern isolated on white" by katyalanbina@gmail.com

Second Edition 2024.

To My Mother.

The Sovereign Lord is my strength; he makes my feet like the feet of a deer, he enables me to go on the heights.

Habakkuk 3:19

Prologue

January 7, 1901

Kizzy Beecham knew it was time to call for the old granny woman. She'd never known such pains—strong and regular, hard muscle clenched tight around the baby, pushing downward with every contraction. She grimaced and held her breath as her abdomen tightened yet again. She blew out a low moaning breath between pale lips and willed the inescapable process to slow down, before leaning over and bracing herself against the back of a chair.

"Mr. Beecham?" she called weakly. She swiped tendrils of dark hair from her damp cheek as another contraction began to twist her insides in knots. She waited for it to pass before she crossed the room and peered through the dirty window, scanning the yard for her husband. Despite lengthening shadows, Kizzy saw her husband heading toward the fence line, a coil of barbed wire held away from his body. A day's worth of tree limbs and stumps from the newly cleared patch of land smoldered behind him, a pasture for the new milk cow almost complete.

Searching for her coat, she glanced around the shabby room, dim in January's twilight. The aging wood stove struggled to heat the space in the cold South Carolina winter, so Kizzy already wore nearly everything she owned. She grabbed her moth-eaten coat, plunged her arms into the sleeves, and waddled toward the door.

As she wrenched it open, a bitter blast swept into the room. She cursed under her breath before pulling the door shut behind her. The shack shuddered its disapproval.

"Mr. Beecham!" she moaned from the porch. "Go get Miss Seeta. It's time! Hurry!" She doubled over, clutching her belly.

The rail-thin man stood still for only a moment as the news registered. Suddenly he dropped the coil of wire and jogged across the bare yard toward the barn. Kizzy watched expectantly as he reappeared on horseback. He waved his hat toward his wife and the old mare trotted down the long, muddy drive toward the main road.

Kizzy leaned against the porch post. A cold nose snuffled her hand, and she patted the soft brindle head of their Plott hound. "I don't know if he'll make it in time, Buck. An' I'm not sure I want him to." She turned to go back inside, tears welling in her eyes.

She slowly sank to the threadbare sofa and closed her eyes as another contraction began to overtake her. The knife under the sofa wasn't working to cut the pain, so she grabbed her mother's worn family Bible and opened it to the book of Matthew before lying back with the open book on her chest, a charm sure to work.

But it was no use. Soon, the granny woman would deliver this baby, and whether it lived or died, she prayed to God that it would favor Jim Beecham. She ran her hands through her damp hair and cried out, the pains gripping her like a vice once more.

Jim Beecham. Her husband of only eighteen months. Fifty-one years old to her fifteen and a half. He had mooned after her since she was twelve or so. He'd had nothing to offer her except freedom from her own abusive father, Leslie Jakes, who was mean as a rattlesnake half the time and falling-down drunk the other half.

Kizzy's daddy worked first shift as a loom tuner at the cotton mill. The money was poor indeed, and he spent most of it on corn liquor, instead of on his three little girls, soon motherless after the last one's birth. Their ramshackle house close to the edge of colored town was a shameful sight, she knew, but it had kept them mostly dry in the wet and mostly warm in the cold. Kizzy should have been in school, but Jakes had pulled her out on her eleventh birthday to care for her younger sisters, Viola and Rose.

Paid every Friday, Jakes usually drank his entire paycheck away by Sunday. He'd send Kizzy into the company store on Mondays to beg another week's grace period for payment on the grocery bill. Kizzy would try to ignore the catcalls and dirty talk from men streaming out of the mill at the end of a long shift. She'd pull her shawl tight across budding breasts and hurry into the store as soon as Lottie Gilstrap put out the "Open" sign.

Sometimes, the woman would sigh and nod to Kizzy's request for leniency, allowing her to shop for groceries on credit to keep the little girls from starving. Leslie Jakes was a poor excuse for a father, she knew. Other times, she would give the girl a few heads of cabbage and tell her to get gone until her daddy's accounts were caught up.

Jim Beecham had occasionally lingered outside the company store after his shift ended on Mondays, hoping to catch Kizzy on her daddy's errand. He was what they called an overlooker, and he was her daddy's boss. Kizzy hadn't minded him so much. He didn't use dirty language like the others, but she'd still backed away as he smiled a gap-toothed smile, his eyes traveling up and down her body.

"Afternoon, Miss Kizzy," he'd offered the first time he spoke to her, lifting his hat and nodding as if she were a fine lady. His watery blue eyes and long gray whiskers made her think of Santa Claus in her teacher's Christmas book.

The second time Beecham spoke to her, she had just come out of the store empty-handed. "I can he'p ya, girl." He'd offered her a string bag of carrots, onions, pole beans, and yellow squash, which she took gratefully.

"Thank ya, Mr. Beecham," she muttered, head down. She hurried home quickly that day, bolted the door, and made a pot of vegetable soup for herself and her hungry little sisters. When Leslie Jakes stumbled home close to midnight, no trace of the soup remained, and their only cook pot was cleaned and stashed away near the hearth.

By the time Kizzy was thirteen, her bottom was crisscrossed with scars from her daddy's belt, and she'd lost a tooth to his angry blows to her face. Viola and Rose were sent away to live with a great-aunt somewhere near Aiken. Jakes sent Kizzy to work in the mill as a spinner and pocketed every cent she earned. Kizzy ached for her baby sisters and began to look to Jim Beecham's attention and his proffered groceries as a mild enough diversion from her loneliness.

When Mr. Beecham approached her father soon after her fourteenth birthday and asked if he could marry Kizzy, Jakes laughed and uttered a string of profanities, to which the old man blushed deeply. Leslie Jakes had grabbed his daughter by the wrist and fairly flung her down the steps into her future husband's spindly arms. The ceremony took place at the county courthouse, and Mr. Beecham instructed Kizzy to say she was sixteen if the Clerk of Court asked her age.

Compared to the rotting lean-to that she had called home for fourteen years, Jim Beecham's two-room house near Pumpkintown was a castle. The split shake roof was secure. The pine floor was swept clean. Colorful jars of preserves lined the shelves above the sink, and a kerosene lamp hung near the wood stove. An 1899 Coca-Cola calendar hung from a nail near the door and amazed Kizzy with its promise of a mysterious drink that was both "delicious and refreshing."

The tiny bedroom off of the kitchen had a wide bed, the tick filled with soft, fragrant straw. There was a red handpump at the well in the yard for water. The chickens were fat and happy. The clean privy was only steps away from the back porch, not a maggot-infested hole yards away at the tree line. It wasn't town living, but it was a far cry better than her daddy's place.

Kizzy hadn't known what to expect on her wedding night, but Mr. Beecham had been patient and fairly kind to her. The first time, it had hurt quite a bit, she remembered. She had lain quite still as he moved on top of her. She'd watched his rheumy eyes go wild, and a small silver line of drool dropped onto her cheek. He shuddered and slumped heavily, making her wonder if he was dead. He'd finally rolled off of her, apologized, gotten up from the bed, and gone to sleep in the main room, for which she was grateful.

She'd closed her eyes, wiped her face with her palm, and tried to imagine her new life as a married woman. He hadn't hit her or called her foul names, two things she had come to expect back at home. If he would let her keep her mill wages to buy fabric and notions, and eat as much as her growling stomach would hold, she could put up with his pushing between her legs of an evening, she mused. But she just couldn't bring herself to call her new husband by his Christian name. He was old enough to be her grandfather. He would always be Mr. Beecham.

A loud noise woke Kizzy from her remembering as both her husband and Seeta burst into the dim room.

"Mr. Beecham, you best wait outside now. This here women's work," Seeta barked. Kizzy was surprised to see him nod and back out of his house, in deference to the tiny colored woman staring up at him.

Seeta Young crossed the room quickly and knelt next to the sagging sofa where Kizzy lay prostrate. In the flickering firelight, Kizzy watched Seeta's bright red turban bend low over her abdomen. The woman ran her palms over the rolling infant.

"It's head down, thank the good Lawd. You haven't started boilin' water, Mizz Beecham?" she asked crossly, lifting the Bible from Kizzy's chest.

Kizzy grabbed the Bible. "It's for to ease the pains!" She shook her head pitifully. "They came on sudden. I wasn't 'spectin' the baby for another month," she lied.

Seeta yanked the Bible away firmly and laid it on the table. "That don't cut the pains any, child. Where you get such nonsense? Better to read it than leave it draped across yo' body," she muttered. "You been taking the raspberry leaf tea I brung ya?"

Kizzy nodded. She watched as the midwife bustled around the room for several minutes, moving old seed catalogs and piles of unfolded laundry before unpacking her supplies. She set the kettle to boil and washed her hands before drying them on a clean towel from her kit.

"Judgin' by the size o' yo' belly, this baby is right on time. About seven pounds. Best take off your underthings and stretch out on the bed. Jes' keep breathin' regular."

Kizzy moaned again and lay back on the sofa. She felt a sudden urge to expel the thing inside her. "Miss Seeta, I can't get to the bed. I got to push," she hissed. "Now."

Seeta crossed the room in three steps and leaned over her patient again. "Bend yo' legs, darlin', and I'll have a check. Little breaths, sugar."

Kizzy registered Seeta's surprise at finding the baby's head right at the edge of the birth canal. "Lawd, I'm glad Mr. Beecham came fo' me when he did. It's time. Alright, Mizz Beecham. You lean on me an' push."

Kizzy exhaled a groan and felt a flood of relief as the baby slipped smoothly from her body and into the new year. Before Seeta could say a word, the girl asked in a whisper, "Is it white?"

— • —

Seeta ran her index finger around the inside of the baby's mouth and then wiped the tiny face with a warm, wet cloth. The infant began to howl her protest, and Seeta smiled. She looked up at Kizzy and was not surprised to see tears running down both cheeks.

"You in it now, ain't ya?" Seeta leaned closer. "But dry yo' eyes. You think you the onliest white woman in this county ever asked me that question?" For a moment, her mind wandered. A white doctor had saved her own life at birth, and she would never forget it.

Kizzy wiped her eyes with the back of her hand. "Boy or girl?"

Seeta cut the cord cleanly with small scissors and wrapped the infant in a piece of clean cotton sheeting before swaddling it inside a warm blanket. She held Kizzy's daughter up for inspection. "It's a girl, healthy mostly. Looks a bit yeller in the eyes, though," she said, peering closely into the baby's big brown eyes.

Seeta remembered helping a white woman ten years back who had taken one look at her dark-skinned baby with a full head of black hair and demanded that Seeta smother it. The midwife had learned since then how to increase the odds that a white mother would keep her mixed-race infant.

Seeta placed the mewling newborn in her mother's arms. The baby quieted. "Look at how she already knows you her mother. You her world." She watched as Kizzy tentatively stroked the baby's cheek with one finger. "You gonna tell me who is this girl's daddy?"

Kizzy inhaled sharply as her abdomen contracted hard. She looked at Seeta, worry etched across her young face.

"That's jes' the afterbirth bein' born," Seeta said. "As long as it come out whole, we in good shape." She leaned over and massaged Kizzy's abdomen, until the rush of fluids produced what she was looking for. The woman peered closely at the deep purple mass and finally proclaimed, "It all here. We bury it in the yard for good luck. I 'spect you be needin' some o' that." She looked at Kizzy. "But I'm waitin' for an answer to my question."

— • —

Kizzy gazed at the infant in her arms. Swirls of dark hair and brown eyes like her own. But skin the color of coffee with a good splash of cream. She thought of the one time nine months before.

Marcus. Hired alongside a white man to reroof the old barn while Mr. Beecham was in Greenville tending his ailing mother. The white man didn't come back after the first day.

Marcus was young, like her. Well-muscled and tall, with large, expressive eyes and a ready smile. Each morning, he'd appear early, like a vision in the mist. He'd wave and climb up to his precarious perch on the old roof. It was slow going, with only one man to do the job. Each evening, as the sun set low in the woods, Marcus would climb down. He'd remove his shirt and pump a bucketful of water, douse himself with the cool contents, and then drink freely from a tin cup hanging at the pump handle.

She found herself sitting on the porch each day, whether snapping peas or darning socks, watching Marcus from under lowered lashes. She flirted with the idea of making one of her poppets, a small doll she'd stitch up and fill with bits of Indian tobacco and yarrow to attract love. But he was colored, and she was married. Still, when he left each evening, she found herself at the pump, the tin cup he'd drunk from still warm in her hands.

Kizzy watched Marcus up on the roof for six days. Swinging a hammer, he bent to his work with enthusiasm and precision, no doubt eager to collect the compensation due two men, Kizzy thought. Mr. Beecham had left behind a fat envelope of cash, with instructions to pay the men if he was delayed in Greenville beyond a week.

Marcus finally finished the job on a warm spring afternoon, the kind of day that made Kizzy feel all new and fresh. She was lonely. She offered Marcus a chance to rest before he headed home. Just a glass of sweet tea on the porch. He stepped up onto her porch and sat down next to her on the bench. They'd talked into the early evening hours.

He was from north of town and did odd jobs to help support his mother. He dreamed of one day owning his own business. At one point, his hand brushed her own, and she felt a stirring she hadn't experienced before. One thing led to quite another. When he stood to leave, she'd leaned forward and kissed him outright. When he kissed her back, she thought she'd died and gone to heaven. She hadn't known it could be like that. They'd shared a few hours together in Mr. Beecham's bed before Marcus went away. She'd forgotten to give him the envelope of cash, and he'd not asked for it.

Shaken back into the present by the baby's mewling cry, Kizzy ran a finger across her damp hair, tight with curls. "This baby might not be Mr. Beecham's," she whispered.

Seeta sighed. "Her daddy's brown as me, ain't he?"

Kizzy nodded, shame-faced.

"Did you an' yo' husband have relations anywhere near the time you was with the colored man?" Seeta asked pointedly.

Kizzy blushed and shook her head. "By the time Mr. Beecham came home, I knew I'd missed my monthly." She looked hopefully at Seeta. "So I walked over some graves in his family plot. Ain't that supposed to mark the baby to be born pale and ghostly?"

Seeta snorted. "I don't hold with them old stories—an' why you want to put a curse on a child?"

Kizzy's eyes widened. "I ain't wantin' to do such a thing. I put a twist of yarrow over the head of the crib, an' Mr. Beecham drove a nail into the crib post," she said defiantly.

Seeta shook her head and chuckled. "Law! Yarrow ain't gonna do anything just hangin' over a crib."

"It's to protect her from haints. From the evil eye," Kizzy replied. She swallowed hard. "Miss Seeta, will—will she pass?"

Seeta sighed and groped around in her bag. "She fair enough. When we get her cleaned up, she be right-lookin'. You both have dark eyes. Her hair has a kink to it but it might jes' show as curls. If I had to cross my heart and swear she looked all white, I'd be lyin' . . . but she pale enough to pass. You treat her white, and she be white. What you gonna name her?"

A wave of relief swept over the new mother. Kizzy stroked the baby's cheek. "I like the name Callie. Callie Viola Rose."

Seeta nodded. "That's real pretty. Now, I got some sugarcane juice in my bag. An' a liver tincture. That's why her eyes is yeller. Liver ain't right yet. I'll give her one teaspoon now. You do the same three times a day. I'll leave some lemon oil to rub on the soles of her feet twice a day. Once her liver cleans up, she won't look so high yeller." Seeta chuckled. "We treat this child, an' then you put Mizz Callie to the breast. Mama's milk is real good for liver ailment."

She pulled a small paper sack from her bag. "I'll leave you a tea that'll he'p your contractions, so's you don't have too much bleeding. You drink it twice a day for a week. I be back next week to check on you. And don't let Mr. Beecham near you for six weeks, you hear me? A woman's got to heal."

"Miss Seeta, what if Mr. Beecham can tell?" Kizzy trembled. "He'll beat the snot outta me. Or throw me out. Or worse."

Seeta glanced toward the door and pointed a bony finger at Kizzy. "Girl, you a mother now," she whispered. "You do anything you need to—to protect this child. Anything. You hear me? That's what mamas do," she snapped. "Don't you remember your own mama at all?"

Kizzy shrugged. "Mama died when my sister Rose was born. I weren't but six. But Mr. Beecham—you don't think he'll know?"

Seeta's expression softened and she said, "Don't put thoughts in anyone's mind. She's Mr. Beecham's daughter." The woman lifted each of Callie's tiny, curled feet and massaged a dropperful of lemon oil into her wrinkled soles.

Kizzy nodded shame-faced and watched as Seeta pulled a clean towel and a rubber syringe from her bag. She filled the syringe with liquid and slowly dribbled sugarcane juice between little Callie's pursed lips. Then she took a dropper and gave the baby one dose of dandelion root tincture. And thus it was that Callie Viola Rose Beecham experienced the divine healing of plants before her own mother's milk.

Chapter One

Callie gripped the pestle in her fist and ground the chopped root in the mortar until the slurry became a small amount of thick paste. She spooned a tiny amount of salve into a brown glass vial, placed a cork stopper in the opening, and handed it over.

"Mrs. Davis, this is truly potent stuff," she warned. "Remember, you'll dab just the tiniest bit on that sore every three days and then leave it be. Wash your hands afterward. Come back in two weeks and let me have a look."

"Callie, thank you so much, dear. This blemish is ever so unsightly." The woman touched the ulcerated spot on her cheek. "Who'd have thought that in 1928 I would be using an old-wives' remedy to cure a growth . . . Then again, I am an old wife," she joked.

Callie shook her head. "Bloodroot is strong medicine. It's not just a folk remedy. Follow my written instructions. It will get real ugly and form a dark scab, but it'll push out the cancer, and then your skin should be good as new."

"Thank you, dear." The woman pushed a dollar bill across the table.

Callie quickly palmed the money and slid it into the pocket of her white apron. She nodded her thanks as Mrs. Davis stood.

"It's a shame that my husband won't use your medicines in his practice, but you know Dr. Davis. He thinks of your herbs as pure snake oil." The woman shrugged. "He wanted to cut the growth out, but I didn't want a hole in my face. And besides, I like to help you—you being a spinster and all."

Callie forced a smile. "Thank you, Mrs. Davis. You know, snake oil actually worked. It was an old Chinese remedy. They'd press oil from water snakes and—"

Mildred Davis backed away, her gloved hand over her mouth.

"I'm sorry. I get carried away." Callie chuckled. "Follow my instructions on using the salve, and come back if you have any problems. I'll see you in about two weeks."

The woman nodded and left through Callie's front door. A chill autumn breeze blew into the small room, and Callie shivered and closed the door. She flipped the hanging OPEN sign to CLOSED, slid the bolt across the door, and heard the satisfying *click* of the lock.

She sank to the sofa and wearily pulled bills and some change from her pocket. *Is it enough?* "Eight dollars and seventy-five cents today," she murmured. A good day. She ran her hand through wild black curls, held back with a red bandana.

"Callie Beecham. You've done it!" she said out loud. There was enough money saved to finally buy the little cottage outright. She had been renting the place from Grady Wilcox for five years, fixing it up at her own expense. Each month she had dutifully walked the fifteen-dollar rent to the bank, putting most everything else into the mattress ticking, earmarked for the house. *Mama would've been so proud.*

She had wallpapered the rooms, scrubbed the warped heart pine floors until they gleamed, and planted a large garden in the backyard. She had repaired a broken window sash and replaced a door latch. Her front room now appeared comfortable, but professional. She had arranged a small sitting area with two chairs and a sofa near the fireplace. A doctor's examination table that had cost her two weeks' wages stood in the middle of the dining area. A large maple breakfront was all that was left of her childhood. It held her tinctures, potions, and salves.

Callie's heels clicked on the wood floor as she crossed to the breakfront. Pulling open a cabinet door, she grabbed the mason jar filled with the week's earnings. Holding it close, she walked into her small bedroom, knelt by the bed, and untied the mattress ticking. She felt around until her fingers touched the small leather satchel and eagerly pulled it out. Settling back against the bed frame, she unscrewed the jar lid and pulled out the thick roll of cash.

The smell of paper money wafted up from the curled ones, fives, and ten-dollar bills. She proceeded to count the week's pay once more before adding it to the rest. Writing the number down in a small ledger pulled from the satchel, she leaned back, a satisfied smile on her lips. Nine hundred dollars. It was a fortune. From selling her herbal formulas and tending to postpartum mothers, she had amassed enough to make the cottage her very own.

Callie glanced at her bedside clock, stood, and pulled the bandana from her hair, twisting her wild mane into a chignon. Tugging her gray cloche firmly over the mess of hair, she picked up the leather satchel, grabbed her coat, and headed out the front door.

— • —

Downtown was busy that afternoon, and the fresh breeze from the mountains in the distance brought the feel of autumn with it. Maple trees along the road had changed their colors seemingly overnight, chameleon-like. Summer green had been replaced by brilliant orange. Callie walked quickly down the sidewalk, refusing to look into Mabel Keith's tantalizing shop window that displayed new fall suits and stunning hats. She was eager to get to the bank before closing time.

But maybe now, she thought, she could afford a trip to the beauty parlor. Hairstyles these days were cropped and sleek, not long and curly. She shook her head. There would be little in the way of fun money after today.

Callie soon spied the imposing facade of Mountain Ridge Savings and Loan. She paused to adjust her hat, inhaled and exhaled a long breath, and waited for her pulse to slow before pulling on the heavy oak door to enter the busy lobby. Callie scanned the room, looking for Grady Wilcox, the bank president.

"May I help you, Miss Beecham?" A cheerful woman's voice behind her made Callie turn. The secretary smiled politely. "Are you here to make your rent payment?"

"Hello, Mrs. Ames," Callie said. "Today, I need to see Mr. Wilcox." She smiled proudly.

Mrs. Ames's eyebrows went up. "The big man himself? I see. Well, follow me. He was with a customer, but the gentleman just left."

Callie followed the woman toward the large office. A glass wall partitioned the space from the rest of the bank. Mrs. Ames knocked perfunctorily.

Red-faced Mr. Wilcox looked up from his desk and peered at the women over his bifocals.

"Miss Beecham to see you, sir." Mrs. Ames turned to go, but leaned toward Callie and whispered, "Good luck!"

"Mizz Beecham," boomed the man. He stood slowly, revealing the enormous belly he'd been hiding behind the large mahogany desk. "Come in. What can I do for you today? You bringin' me rent or are you finally going to open a little savings account with us?" He extended his arm toward a small leather chair on the other side of the desk, and Callie sat quickly.

"Not today, Mr. Wilcox," she beamed. "I'm here to buy the cottage."

With some effort, Mr. Wilcox resumed his seat behind the desk. He shifted his weight until he was comfortable and peered at her with small blue eyes. He reminded Callie of an enormous pink pig. She stifled the urge to laugh and continued.

"Yes, sir. I have the entire sum here. You said the cost to buy it outright was $900, and I have that today." She glanced down at the leather satchel in her lap. "Though I am hopeful that you will take into account the improvements I've made and the five years rent, and perhaps lower the price."

Mr. Wilcox chuckled and pointed a fat finger at her. "Mizz Beecham, I hardly think sewin' frilly curtains and polishin' floors is reason to lower an already low asking price. Any businessman in town will tell you that house is underpriced. It is right downtown. Running water and lights. It'd make a fine place to set up shop, run a retail business."

"Yes, sir." Callie cocked her head. "I know that. That's what I do—I live there and run my business from the front room."

Wilcox nodded his head and impatiently shuffled the papers on his desk. "What 'zactly is your business again, Mizz Beecham?"

Callie clenched her jaw in frustration. She had given the man details about her herbal medicine business several times in the past. "I run a business growing and selling medicinal herbs. I treat folks for what ails them—from plants. That, and I give a little bit of help to new mommas after their babies enter the world."

He wagged his finger at her. "You gone put Dr. Davis outta business? We can't have that, now," he joked.

"No, sir," Callie said. Impatient to transact her business, she opened the satchel and pulled out several bundles of cash tied with twine.

At the sight, Wilcox leaned forward. "Ah, you ain't kiddin' me now. You plannin' to stay. You got all $900 there?"

Callie registered the surprise on the man's florid face. "Yes, I do."

"What if your little business goes sour? I'm not sure you'd qualify for a mortgage. You should save some of that cash. Put it in my bank to earn interest. Save for furniture, a new stove . . . You yourself complain about that old stove every time you come to pay rent. An' I know how you ladies like to decorate."

Callie regarded the man quietly, her blood pressure rising. He was shrewd, she'd give him that. She had gone to great trouble to learn about the cottage. It was model 115 from the *Sears Modern Homes Catalogue, 1908*. It had cost $462 to buy the house as a kit. It sat on a wooden foundation, instead of an excavated one. The tax office showed that Wilcox had purchased it from the original owner in 1919 for $750. Its present value was right at $900. On Florence Street, it was downtown, and had electric lights and running water. A porcelain flush toilet even.

Grady Wilcox had already made his money back, over and over again, renting it out to folks over the years. She herself had already paid the man over one thousand dollars in rent money since moving in. The little house was a financial stretch, but being downtown was important to her small business. Pedestrians passed by all day long. She could walk or bike anywhere she needed to go.

"No, sir, Mr. Wilcox," Callie said firmly. "I would like to buy it outright here and now and walk out with the deed." Her hands trembled only a little at her temerity.

Wilcox leaned back so far in his chair that it groaned in protest. "Mizz Beecham, you've been a quiet tenant, I'll give you that. You came to me same time as the boll weevil, when no one around here had two pennies to pinch together. The Christian thing to do was let you rent that place for a song. You paid your rent on time. Didn't bother me to come fix this or fix that." His pig-eyes narrowed. "But now . . . I could sell that little place to the new doctor who came to work with Dr. Davis—for twice what you got there. He wants a place in town. Property values are up, so I need to do what I can with that little building."

Callie felt the heat rise in her cheeks, and she gripped her hands tightly together in her lap to keep them from shaking.

"With all due respect," she began, "we had a deal. It was a handshake deal to be sure, but a deal nevertheless. Why, every time I have come in to pay rent for the last few years, I've talked it up to Mrs. Ames and your tellers. And Stella Wright at the Five an' Dime . . . Mr. Duncan over at the butcher shop, and anyone else who'd listen."

She leaned forward. "Half the town knows I've been saving for that house! You said that it would be mine when I had saved $900, Mr. Wilcox. I have scrimped and saved. I have worked hard at what I know—making herbals—and now I have the entire amount. Right here." She slapped the satchel down loudly on the man's desk.

"Don't cheat me, Mr. Wilcox, just because I'm a woman. There's $900 right there. Write up the sale. Please, sir!"

Tellers and customers in the lobby had gone quiet, and Callie realized she'd been almost shouting. She leaned back and crossed her legs at the ankles. Noticing a long run in her cotton stocking, she crossed her legs the other way so it would not show.

Wilcox glanced through the glass partition at his lobby full of customers. He cleared his throat and spoke loudly enough to be heard at the teller windows. "Mizz Beecham, calm yourself. No need to get all hysterical. Of course we had a deal. I'll have the bank attorney, Mr. Jones, write up the sale. Wait in the lobby until he calls you back to his office." He stood with some effort and watched as his tellers and customers gradually resumed their business before coming from behind his desk, his enormous bulk blocking the office doorway.

Callie stood and smoothed her skirt. "Thank you, Mr. Wilcox."

Wilcox turned away from the lobby filled with customers and faced Callie. He leaned close and murmured, "If you ever embarrass me again like that, girl, I'll see that little shop of yours is closed up for good an' run you out on a rail. You hear me? An' I don't want to see you in my bank again." He brushed past her and left the office.

Trembling, Callie made her way to one of the chairs in the lobby. She sat down and tried not to notice the stares of other customers. Before long, Mrs. Ames quietly summoned Callie through a door near the teller stations and into a tiny office.

The young attorney was bent over a form in his typewriter and did not look up until he had completed it. He finally rolled the document out of the typewriter and shoved it across the desk impatiently. He slapped a fountain pen on top of it.

"Sign and date the bottom where it says 'Purchased By.' Press hard. The form is in triplicate," he said, without looking up.

Callie squinted at the copious fine print in the document. It did look to show the transfer of the home and half-acre lot at 909 Florence Street. That much she could see. "Some of it I don't understand," she said softly.

"Look, Miss Beecham." Mr. Jones softened. "It's a regular deed, proof of sale. After you sign it, he will sign it. No hassles. I promise. You'll own the place free and clear." He glanced past her toward the lobby. "I just don't want to get on the wrong side of the old man myself today. I was about to ask him for a few days off. Sign it and let me take it to him. Once he has signed it, the property is yours."

"I'd like it to be notarized," Callie said.

Jones sighed. He stood and crossed to the doorway, leaned toward the nearest teller, and said, "Dora, come in here with your notary stamp."

Callie quickly scanned the form again for the correct information as a young blonde teller entered the room nervously. She removed a heavy notary stamp from its leather case. Callie picked up the pen and scribbled her signature where Mr. Jones indicated.

The attorney picked up the form. "Wait here. I'll have Mr. Wilcox sign it. Dora will notarize the signatures, and we'll be done. Dora, come with me, please." The pair quickly left the room.

Callie watched as Jones handed the form to Mr. Wilcox at his desk. The man bent to scrawl on the form and then slid it away angrily. Dora leaned across the desk and pressed the document into the stamp, while Wilcox ogled her bustline.

Callie shook her head. *He really is a pig,* she thought, watching the two return from Wilcox's office.

Dora smiled at Callie. "Congratulations, Miss Beecham."

Mr. Jones tore off the top page and handed it to Callie. "You own a house. Mr. Wilcox is none too happy about it, but it's yours. Better clear out now before he blows his top."

Callie took the deed and stared at it a moment. With a wide grin, she looked up. "Thank you. And if y'all ever need herbal tonics and what-not, come by my shop. I'll give you twenty percent off."

Chapter Two

Weeks later, Callie lay prostrate under the kitchen sink, a wrench in one hand and a dishtowel in the other. She had identified the leak and was doing her best to tighten the joint and mop up the resulting mess. Sure enough, as soon as she became a homeowner, things began to break in earnest. First, the septic tank had backed up, then carpenter ants arrived. Now, the kitchen faucet. But it was hers to deal with, and it was exciting.

She turned the wrench one final quarter turn and wiped a tendril of damp hair from her face before easing out from under the pipes. "If one more thing breaks . . ." she muttered. Her orange cat, George, wound his way through Callie's legs and back again. "You're not helping me, George," she snapped.

The bell over the front door tinkled, and Callie heard customers in the front room. She stood quickly and glanced down at her stained apron and wrinkled skirt. "Blast it . . ." she muttered. She had no appointments scheduled for several hours. Whipping off her apron, she quickly tucked her blouse into her skirt waistband and, with a pat at her wild hair, called, "Coming!"

Callie rounded the corner and was surprised to see Mildred Davis standing next to a handsome young man, both of them intent on a chart tacked on the wall, depicting the human nervous system. "Oh," Callie said. "Mrs. Davis. Is everything alright? I wasn't expecting anyone."

Mrs. Davis nodded gleefully. "Yes, my dear. Look! The nasty growth is gone. And it's all because of you." She turned her pink cheek to Callie.

"Do you see how well it healed? I just had to bring Dr. Epstein to meet you!"

The young man turned from the chart and smiled, his blue eyes warm and kind. He was clean-shaven and wore a slightly rumpled brown suit under a fabulous navy coat, Callie noted. It was finished off with a jaunty paisley tie. His brown hair was slicked back, thinning at his temples, but he was altogether lovely, she thought.

He extended his hand. "Miss Beecham, I'm Sam Epstein. It is so nice to meet you. Mrs. Davis has been singing your praises since I came to town," the man exclaimed.

"Of course I have!" Mrs. Davis gushed. "Why, Callie, that paste is a miracle. A few days after I began using it, well, I thought I'd never seen such a horrid sight. My husband was simply furious with me for not having it removed. But then, the paste just ate the growth away, and it dropped off! I just had to get Dr. Epstein to come meet you. He is interested in natural treatments, even if Earl is not."

Callie shook Sam's hand, keenly aware of her disheveled appearance. "Welcome to town, Doctor."

"I am fascinated by your treatment of this growth, Miss Beecham," he said. "There isn't even much of a scar. Can you tell me what's in that paste?"

"Bloodroot." Callie looked from Mrs. Davis to Dr. Epstein, her defenses rising. She knew that Dr. Davis thought of her work as quackery, even witchcraft. But her deep and abiding affinity for plants and their medicinal uses was not quackery. She had cured too many toothaches with allspice berries, too many ulcers with cabbage juice and honey, and uncounted children's earaches with oregano oil. Her vervain tea concoction had soothed many a cough over the years.

"So that's a plant?" asked the doctor.

"Some people say that bloodroot can draw love or avert evil spells," she said eerily. "Others believe it'll protect you from haints if you place it around windowsills and doorways."

The doctor's shoulders sagged slightly, as if he'd expected as much and regretted being dragged to see her.

Callie laughed. "Black salve made from bloodroot is an escharotic—extremely useful in treating skin cancers and lesions," she said.

"Ah. Brilliant!" the doctor replied, his face once again animated. "I'd like to know how it's made."

Callie ignored the man's impudence and turned to Mrs. Davis. "May I look again at your cheek?"

The older woman leaned forward and grinned. "I could not be more pleased. I will certainly recommend you to my friends in bridge club."

Callie peered at the woman's cheek. "It does look good. I'm so glad."

Mrs. Davis gazed up at the doctor warmly and said, "Dr. Epstein has come to help my husband. The practice just keeps growing, and Earl simply has no time outside of the office. You know, he's practiced here by himself for more than thirty years." She shook her head, and the wattle of pale flesh at her throat jiggled. "But now Dr. Epstein is here all the way from New York City! And, after seeing how well my cheek healed, I knew he had to meet you."

Callie nodded. "I know your husband will appreciate another doctor in his practice. Dr. Epstein, what brings you from the big city to our little corner of South Carolina?"

"I grew up in Atlanta," he answered. "When I finished school up north, I hurried back down here as quickly as I could. My mother lives in the Atlanta area, as do my sisters. I wanted to be near them."

This information softened Callie a bit. "Ah, that's why you don't have an accent."

"Southern? Or New York?" he laughed.

Callie liked that his eyes crinkled when he smiled. She continued her interrogation. "And have you found a place to stay?"

"He wanted a place downtown but there is nothing to be had," Mrs. Davis said ruefully. "Even the hotel has no room for long-term boarders. He is staying in Sara Cane's boarding house out near Reese Mill for now." She frowned as if the thought were detestable.

Callie remembered Mr. Wilcox threatening to sell her little house to the new doctor in town and resented the twinge of guilt she felt. "Pickens is very small—but I am sure something close in will open up."

Dr. Epstein simply smiled and acted as if lodging three miles outside of town was not a huge issue for him. "I would love to talk with you about your practice sometime. Naturopathy is a field I am quite interested in." His eyes held her own and didn't look away.

Is this a test? Callie regarded the man warily. "If I remember my Latin roots, naturopathy is a system of treatment of disease that avoids drugs and surgery and emphasizes the use of natural agents."

"Yes, that's right," Dr. Epstein said, his eyes dancing. He glanced at the shelves of tinctures and teas. "Do you grow everything you sell?"

"I grow some of my own medicinal herbs, what doesn't grow wild. Some I get in Greenville. Some I have to order." She tried to change the subject. "You're an M.D.?"

He smiled again. "Yes. General Practice. I wanted to go to naturopathy school to study how the body can be healed with nutrition and massage, psychology, and complementary therapies—like herbal medicine. In a perfect world, I would have done both."

"The world is not perfect," Callie offered, surprised to hear that there was a school that taught some of the old ways.

"No. It's not. When Mrs. Davis told me about you, I just had to come meet you. I'm hoping you'll educate me." He shoved his hands in his pockets.

Mrs. Davis smiled up at him. "Isn't that a wonderful idea, Callie?"

Callie could see that the woman was slightly smitten with the young doctor. "I suppose I could give it some thought," she said.

Mrs. Davis patted Callie's arm and then looked at her own wristwatch. "Oh, Callie, I just knew you two would hit it off. Now, if you will both excuse me, my husband promised to take a lunch break and meet me at the diner." She leaned closer to Callie and pressed a five-dollar bill into her palm. "Thank you again, my dear."

When she pulled back, Callie was surprised to see the woman wink at her subtly. Callie frowned and put a self-conscious hand to her curly mop of hair.

After Mrs. Davis said her goodbyes, the two stood quietly. Callie was unsure of what to do or say next. *Why on earth would I want to help a doctor steal my patients?* She wasn't sure whether to leap about or crumble to the floor. If a new male doctor had all the knowledge about herbals that she did, would her clients rush to see Dr. Sam Epstein instead of Callie Beecham? *Of course.* Her clientele was already shrinking. And yet, how thrilling to learn that there was a school of medicine that recognized the old lore.

"What do you want exactly?" she asked. She realized that her tone was defensive, but she didn't care. Her back was up. "Are you asking me to teach you herbal medicine in thirty minutes or less?"

Dr. Epstein shook his head sheepishly. "Ouch. Now that you've said it out loud, it sounds like a lot to ask."

"I know how doctors feel about herbalists dispensing plant medicines. But they do work! Your American Medical Association gives its seal of approval to pharmaceutical companies based on the size of their donations—not the efficacy or safety of the medicines."

Sam's eyebrows went up.

"Yes," Callie said. "I do read. And I had a client come in several months ago just raving about her husband's high energy around the farm because Dr. Davis put him on amphetamines to raise his blood pressure. Then I saw her last week, and she was quite worried. She said he has developed stronger cravings for it and can't function without it. I could have offered a number of safe and effective teas, a tincture, and a list of healthy foods to raise blood pressure and provide energy. I am not some kind of witch doctor. I can vouch for the safety and efficacy of every remedy I make. Can you say the same?" As soon as Callie said the words, she reddened. "I'm sorry. That was rude of me."

The doctor seemed to understand Callie's trepidation. "Miss Beecham, I diagnose conditions and prescribe medications. Exams and prescriptions can be expensive. I read the local paper—I understand why half the print on each page is advertising products like Lydia Pinkham's tonic and liver pills. This is a rural area. Money is tight."

Callie bristled. "You know, Lydia Pinkham's tonic does contain plants that heal—like black cohosh and fenugreek."

"And a lot of alcohol." Sam chuckled.

"Doctors prescribe whiskey routinely," Callie snapped. "Every ten days a patient can get a pint prescription from your office, and you know it. I've seen jugs unloaded many times."

Sam threw up his hands. "I'm not trying to offend. We're taught in medical school that home-brewed medicine is pure quackery. And you're right, the AMA Journals are full of articles denouncing naturopathy. But herbal tinctures and ointments are familiar to people around here. They seem more likely to try a tincture or a salve made from something they are familiar with. And you are the herbalist. I know very little about plants for healing. I couldn't identify a healing plant if it was put right in front of me. I'm hopeful that we could strike up a partnership of sorts. Perhaps I could spend some time observing your work and buy your products outright? I am open to suggestions for whatever will heal patients."

A lock of his brown hair drooped onto his forehead, and he smoothed it back into place, which Callie immediately found quite endearing. "I'm not trying to take your business. But I'm willing to get my hands dirty, if you'll allow me to learn. You healed Mildred's lesion."

Callie inhaled and thought of her tangled garden in the backyard—the amaranth and red clover needing to be weeded. The wolfberry dropping its leaves. Elderberry had been devoured by birds, and St. John's Wort sat rootbound in pots. The lavender, sage, and peppermint would soon succumb to frost if not picked and dried. She exhaled slowly and found herself softening.

"Dr. Epstein, are you telling me that you don't know elderberry from purselane?"

The man's face relaxed and he grinned. "Please, call me Sam. And no, I don't even know what a purselane is."

She sighed. "Then, Sam, we'd better make you an appointment."

Chapter Three

Callie stooped to add a log to the fireplace and then prodded the fire back to life with a poker. The weather had turned cold, and the early November days were noticeably shorter. She liked nothing better than a hot cup of coffee in front of a fire on a cold morning. Outside, it was still dark, but she heard the first notes of birdsong in the chirp of a lonely Chuck-will's-widow. She hoped that George wouldn't present the headless bird to her later on the front stoop.

She sipped her coffee and gazed into the flames, cheered by the crackling and popping. As the holidays neared and families gathered, Callie always became melancholy. No husband. No children. No parents. If she dwelt on it too long, she would surely drop into her annual Christmas depression a bit early. She shook her head and swallowed the last of her coffee. There was too much to do.

Dr. Epstein would be stopping by later in the morning. She would show him her garden, the annuals decidedly limp and brown after the first frost, the perennials bare without leaf or berry. She'd let him ask questions, ask him to repot some perennials, and see how much he really intended to learn. While she doubted how much a medical doctor would really care about herbs in the garden, she knew that she had to play along. *And he's quite handsome*, she thought.

Mildred Davis was her biggest fan right now, and Mildred Davis would make or break Callie's success. The fact that she'd brought Dr. Epstein to meet her wasn't lost on Callie. He could be an important ally.

Times were changing. Dr. Epstein had said he thought the locals were more comfortable with the old country ways of treating illness and injury, but the truth of it was, folks were turning to modern medicine more and more. The small drug store in town did a booming business. New-fangled medicines were constantly being developed. Midwives could no longer practice in South Carolina without being registered by the state. She knew she was stretching things by seeing postpartum patients. Maybe an alliance with Dr. Epstein would help her keep her head above water.

The eastern sky outside Callie's window began to lighten, and she stood and stretched. She crossed to her bookcase and pulled a few volumes from the packed shelves. If Dr. Epstein wanted to learn about plant medicine, she had a number of books he could borrow. In the middle of her search, she startled when she heard a timid knock on her front door. Callie glanced at her watch. It was a little after seven, and Dr. Epstein wasn't due to stop by until ten. She heard the knock again, more urgent this time.

"The shop isn't open until eight," Callie called.

"Mizz Beecham? Help me, please," a man's voice said through the thin door. "My wife's havin' problems with birthin'."

"Blast," Callie muttered. She didn't recognize the voice. She pulled her dressing gown close around her and tied the waist tightly. "I'm not open for business this early—and I'm not allowed to attend births. I have no license."

"Yes'm. But my wife—she's bleedin' real bad. I got no one else to call on. The baby's done been born. My granny said to come ask fo' you."

Callie leaned her head against the door. Although she suspected the answer, she asked, "Have you tried calling Dr. Davis?"

Callie heard the audible sigh from the other side of the door. "Ma'am, he don't treat coloreds. An' we ain't got telephones up where I live. I got no car to take her to the hospital down in Six Mile that'll see colored people."

"Blast," she muttered again. She flipped the deadbolt and yanked the door open. A cold gust of air swirled into the room and sent sparks leaping heavenward in the fireplace. A tall, thin black man stood on her front porch, hat in hand.

"I come early so's no one would see me at your doorstep. Don't want to get you in trouble, ma'am. I'm Zeke Young. My granny said you the only one who can he'p my wife. Please." His eyes were red either from crying or lack of sleep, or both. Callie saw that he was desperate.

"Where is your wife?" she asked, stepping out onto the porch. The leaden sky was still lightening in the east.

"We live in Liberia, ma'am."

"I don't know where that is," Callie said warily.

"A bit north of Pumpkintown," the man answered hopefully.

Callie's eyebrows shot up. "That's more than ten miles away. I don't have a car. How did you get here?" She glanced up and down the dark street.

"Mule," he said, pointing toward two animals tied under Callie's large magnolia. "I brought an extry fo' ya. Subie's a ornery gal, but she's real fast. Please, ma'am. My wife could die."

Glancing around her, Callie knew that folks would likely be up and out soon. They'd surely question a colored man with mules tied out by the road. Already, the milk man had left a quart bottle on her front step. The paperboy would be around next. "You'll lead me out there and see me home?"

Zeke's face brightened. "Yes, ma'am! God's truth I will."

Callie hesitated only a moment. "Give me a minute to change and get my bag."

— • —

Callie felt like an idiot. She didn't even know if the man could pay her. And they had passed only one car on their way out of town, which meant no one would know where to look for her should she go missing. In her work, she had only ever gone as far as the outskirts of town. Her one bicycle and her two feet had always taken her wherever she needed to go. Until now.

The sky had turned gray and threatened a cold rain. She shifted in the saddle, her hip bones already rubbed to bruising. Although they were on a paved road, Callie had no idea where they were. They looked to be heading northeast to Pumpkintown, as Zeke had said. She knew that the Blue Ridge Mountains must be to the north, but even in November, the thick stands of roadside pines obscured the view on both sides. As her mule followed Zeke up the winding road, it would occasionally stop and drop its head to nibble on some tasty roadside greenery.

Despite Callie's lame attempts to pull at the reins, Subie wouldn't budge unless Zeke shouted out, "Subie—Heah!" At that command, the mule would lift her head and trot after her owner obediently. Until the next hedgerow.

I see where the phrase 'stubborn as a mule' comes from, Callie thought.

"Tell me exactly what happened with your wife," she called out, gripping the saddle horn tightly.

Zeke twisted to look at Callie. "She had our baby boy early this mornin' an' started bleedin' real bad after he was delivered."

"Did she have a midwife? Another woman to help her?" Callie asked.

"No, ma'am. Delia went into labor earlier than expected. Her mother lives a piece away. My granny used to deliver babies an' she talked me through it. Granny don't have none of the things she used to keep on hand for birthin' troubles, though. She's eighty-eight now. Guess she thought she was done with this. She too old to do much, but she told Delia when to breathe and told me how to cut the cord. Baby came out fast. A boy." Zeke beamed. "Our first child. But when it was time for the afterbirth, it didn't come."

He pointed to a split up ahead in the road and picked up his pace. "We almost to the turnoff. We leave the pavement an' goin' onto the dirt road from here," Zeke explained. He twisted around and said, "Thank you, Mizz Beecham."

She tried to soothe him. "These things happen. I'm sure she will be fine," Callie said.

Zeke shrugged and turned toward Callie again. "Had a good doctor in Pumpkintown area until '22. He'd see Negroes. He's gone now. We mainly doctor ourselves."

Callie shook her head. Segregation was still an ugly truth in America, she knew. She had hoped things would change after the war. Colored soldiers and white soldiers had fought and died in the trenches ten years ago against a common enemy, and yet, when the lucky ones came home, they found nothing had changed. She'd seen it firsthand in the Red Cross units. White men got good care while black men languished.

"How did your granny know to call on me?" Callie asked.

"Don't know, ma'am," Zeke said. "She just told me where to go to find ya."

Callie frowned. Her thoughts were interrupted when Zeke's mule rounded a bend and the tree line fell away. She gazed at the majestic wall of the Blue Ridge Mountains, spread out from east to west in the distance. The towering exposed-rock formation called Table Rock was to their left and the craggy face of Caesar's Head to their right.

"I'd forgotten how beautiful this is," she said. "I haven't been up to Table Rock since I was a schoolgirl and we came for picnics."

"It's mighty pretty, for sure. God's country," Zeke agreed. "This is the Liberia road."

Callie's eyes took in the pastoral scene before her. A green valley sat nestled between the enormous granite formations she remembered from a girlhood picnic. A stream meandered through the valley, dotted with small homes and farm fields. Morning mist swirled through the hollows and hills. She recognized what appeared to be the spire of a lone church in the center of the valley. At that moment, the clouds parted and bright sunshine fell on the little settlement below them. Liberia.

"I suppose Liberia got its name from the country? In Africa?" Callie asked, her free hand shielding her eyes from the sun.

Zeke shrugged. "Maybe so. Freed slaves settled here. It's a good place to be."

Callie could agree. Colored folks were not treated well in town. She knew they were not welcome in Grady Wilcox's bank. Could not step into Pat's Diner and expect to be served. Dr. Davis refused to treat black people. She'd heard rumors of violent Ku Klux Klan activity in the area, but doubted the stories. It was 1928, after all. Women had the vote, automobiles rumbled along paved roads, and times were good.

"We best hurry, ma'am," Zeke called. He snapped the reins, and his mule took off like a shot. Subie immediately followed after the man at a pace, leaving Callie to hold tight to her hat with one hand and the pommel in the other, while praying that she didn't fall off.

Zeke rode briskly down the hill into the small settlement. Callie tried to take in what she saw. Beyond the natural beauty of the surrounding mountains, the little community had much to offer. The homes and outbuildings were small and rough but well-tended. There were stubbled corn fields and gardens everywhere. Although it was early, Callie noticed several men and women out and about, working their land. Heads turned as the unlikely pair trotted past.

Callie self-consciously drew her coat close around her despite the warming day. At a closer view, the little wooden church appeared to sit in a field of boulders strewn everywhere. *Soapstone Baptist Church*, she read on the small sign out front. *All are welcome.*

Just past the church, Zeke turned off of the gravel road and onto a dirt track. He hopped off the mule and hurried to Callie's side to help her down. When Callie's feet touched the ground, she adjusted her hat and took her bag out of Zeke's hands.

Taking in the little whitewashed house before them, she felt somewhat better. A low boxwood hedge outlined the narrow front porch, and faded black shutters framed the windows. A wooden flagpole was bolted to a front porch post, and an American flag fluttered in the light breeze. "Come on in, Mizz Beecham," Zeke said.

She followed him past a few chickens pecking in the yard and up the steps into a small, overheated front room. A woodstove pumped out a furious amount of heat, and Callie quickly removed her wool coat. Zeke hurried through to a tiny, dark bedroom, motioning Callie to follow.

A young woman lay in the bed, her eyes closed. Her breath was shallow. Callie immediately smelled the iron-rich tang of blood and the foul odor of something burnt. She crossed the dark room and knelt by the bed. "Delia?" she whispered. "Delia, I'm Callie Beecham. I'm here to help you."

A low moan escaped Delia's lips as Callie flipped back the frayed quilts covering the woman's body. The sheets under her were soaked in dark blood.

Callie quickly reached into her bag for soap and a clean towel. She looked at Zeke. "Where can I wash my hands?"

The young man led her into the kitchen, and she spent a moment scrubbing under cool water. "Can you put the kettle on? This water is too cold. Bring it near to a boil and then pour it over my hands."

Zeke looked at Callie curiously, but did as he was told. Soon, the slow hiss of heating water told Callie what she needed to know. "Pour just a tiny bit at first. I don't want to scald myself."

"Ain't it gonna burn you?"

"Yes. But I have mule all over me," Callie said.

Zeke hesitantly tipped the kettle until Callie nodded. "It's nice and hot. Pour." As Zeke emptied the kettle slowly into Callie's open palms, she winced but continued to scrub her hands. She'd end up with some blisters, she knew. She finally rinsed and dried her red hands with the clean towel before rubbing a few drops of peppermint oil into her skin.

She returned to the bedroom and took Delia's wrist gently to feel for her pulse. It was faint and thready. "Zeke, I need more light. Can you open the curtains?" she asked.

The man drew back the curtains at the window and brought the oil lamp closer to the bed.

"Delia, I'm going to press on your tummy." The woman began to moan and writhe.

Callie bent over Delia and started to gently massage the woman's abdomen. "Zeke, did you pull on the cord? To deliver the placenta?"

Zeke shifted his weight from one foot to the other nervously. Callie turned to look up at the young man. "Be honest. I need to know."

"I told him not to pull on the cord," hissed a low voice from the corner of the dark room. "Boy, if you direc'ly disobeyed me... Afterbirth's got to come on its own!"

Callie startled and turned to see a wisp of an old woman sitting in a rocking chair behind her, snug in a brown housecoat, a red gingham turban wrapped around her head. She held the sleeping newborn in her arms.

Before Callie could acknowledge the old woman, Zeke blurted, "I thought I could tug a little and he'p it come out faster. She had a hard time, an' I wanted it to be over for her. I'd already burnt six chicken feathers under the bed."

"Zeke, that don't do nothin'," the old woman said sharply.

Callie knew of the old custom. It was said to stop possible hemorrhage during labor, and it explained the rank odor in the small room. She lifted and repositioned Delia's legs. "Your granny is right, Zeke," she said sharply. "The placenta—the afterbirth—will usually come on its own. We have to let it contract to stop the blood flow in its own time. Tugging on it can tear it. I'll massage Delia's abdomen to see if we can get it out in one piece. If the uterus will contract enough, it should expel the placenta on its own. You better wait outside now."

Zeke lingered in the doorway.

"Zeke, you heard Callie. Go on now," the old woman snapped. Chastened, Zeke slunk from the bedroom.

Callie rummaged in her bag and pulled out a small blue bottle. She glanced at the old woman and said, "Shepherd's purse tincture. A dropperful under her tongue stops the postpartum hemorrhage. Along with the chicken feathers." She winked playfully.

"That's right." The woman nodded in approval.

Callie turned to Delia. "Delia, open your mouth, dear. I need to give you something to help you."

The new mother opened her mouth obediently, and Callie dribbled the tincture between her lips.

Then Callie pulled a cake pan from her bag and placed it between the woman's bent legs. She concentrated on her task, while the old woman murmured prayers from the corner of the room. After a few minutes, Delia grimaced.

"Breathe easy, Delia. Long breaths," Callie cooed.

The woman gritted her teeth and, before long, Callie felt the hard knot of a contraction under her hands. Delia exhaled slowly, and soon the purple mass of afterbirth spilled between the woman's bent legs. Callie quickly caught the placenta in the pan and carried it over to the window. She peered at the organ closely.

"It all there?" the old woman asked.

Callie smiled. "I believe it is!" She began to set the pan aside but then paused. "Care to have a look?"

The old woman returned a gap-toothed grin. Callie brought the pan close and waited while the woman inspected the mass. "Yep. It all there. That's good to see. The Lawd is with us today," she said with a nod.

"My husband'll bury it outside later for good luck," Delia murmured.

Callie set the pan down and returned to her charge. Delia already had more color in her face, and her eyes were alert. Callie placed two fingers on the woman's wrist. Her pulse was nice and steady.

"How's my baby?" Delia asked weakly.

"He's a strong great-grandson. Got his finger wrapped around mine so tight." The old woman smiled.

"Thank you, Jesus!" Delia murmured, the emotion of the morning threatening to overcome the young woman.

Callie smiled. "Congratulations on your son."

"There's clean sheets in the closet there," the old woman said. "I'd he'p you, but I don't got the strength to get up outta the chair some days. Today is one of them days."

"You hold that precious baby. I can change sheets. I used to roll recuperating soldiers from one side of their cots to the other when I did beds in Camp Service. Delia is no problem." Callie pulled sheets from the closet and returned to Delia's bedside.

"Let's get you clean and get this bed changed. Then you can nurse your son. That'll help with contractions."

Delia opened her mouth to protest.

"Do what she says, Delia," barked the old woman.

Callie looked down at the newborn. "Have you checked the baby?"

"I have," the old woman said. "He got all his parts, an' we'll grease his naval cord with castor oil until it come off. He ain't yeller-eyed. His liver's fine. I'd say he's seven pounds."

Callie sighed. "Look at his expression. Almost a smile, like he's talking with the angels."

Seeta nodded. "We all born into this world knowin'—but then we lose the knowin'."

Callie pondered Seeta's words quietly. Soon, she had Delia in a fresh nightgown, clean sheets on the bed, and the baby nursing contentedly at his mother's breast.

"Thank you, Mizz Callie," Delia said weakly. "Zeke can pay you. He has a good job. An' he'll see you back to Pickens. I apologize if I was trouble. We ain't seen a white woman up here to birth babies."

Callie shook her head and put a finger to her lips. "If anyone asks, remember that I didn't birth him. Midwives are supposed to be registered by the state now." She reached in her leather bag. "I'm leaving some rose-petal cinnamon tea. Steep it until cool, and drink a cup once a day for your bleeding. And drink lots of water."

Delia nodded with heavy eyes and soon dozed off.

Callie spent some minutes packing up her bag, then washed her hands again and dried them with another clean towel. She pulled out a brown bottle and poured some of the contents into a vial.

"You gone dose her with castor oil?" the old woman asked her.

Callie nodded. "It helps the uterus contract. I'll let her sleep now, and you can tell her to take it when she wakes. She'll listen to you."

Gently lifting the sleeping baby from Delia's breast, she swaddled him tightly before handing him to his great-grandmother. "I think he needs a good burping, don't you?"

Seeta smiled and took the tiny newborn. She held him to her shoulder and patted his back gently.

Callie gazed at the old woman, whose rheumy eyes were fixed on Callie fondly. "How did you know who I was and where to find me?"

The woman smiled. "I know you, Callie. Girl, I brought you into this world nearly twenty-eight years ago. I'm Seeta Young."

Callie felt her knees wobble, and she steadied herself against the doorframe. "Miss Seeta?" she gasped. "Mama spoke of you so often! You stayed with us after Daddy died. When she had no one else..." She shook her head, amazed. "Are you really Miss Seeta?"

"I am. Yes, your poor mama had a real bad time of it. You was a colicky thing for months. Then Mr. Beecham died—an' your mama didn't have no one. Couldn't work at a mill job with a baby and no family near. She asked me to come watch you. I ended up stayin' for three years. I took in laundry to help with expenses. We had ourselves a time—for a while."

"I remember Mrs. Gilstrap who watched me," Callie said.

"You heard the story then." Seeta smiled. "I helped your mama out for a long time so she could work at the mill. After a few years, though, some people thought I was gettin' a bit too comfortable livin' in Mr. Beecham's house, an' made some noise. Your mama sent me away when you was three years old. After that, Mrs. Gilstrap watched you in her home while your mama worked her fingers to the bone in their cotton mill."

Callie felt her cheeks burn. "Mama always sang your praises. I asked her once what happened to you. She said you moved away to be with family and surely had died of old age."

Seeta cackled. "Did she now? I left y'all in '04 and moved back up here. I didn't wanna go, but it was for the best . . . I stopped midwifin' white people's babies and tendin' white people's sickness. Turned to healin' folks here."

"And you never saw my mother again?" Callie asked.

"No," Seeta said. "But I kept my ear to the ground. I was rightly fond of you both and wanted to know you was alright."

"You know where I live," Callie said.

Seeta nodded her head. "When I heard you was back home after the war, treatin' folks in town with herbals and such, why, I was fit to bust my buttons. You got yourself a storefront an' everything?"

"It's my home. I own it," Callie said proudly.

"Imagine that." Seeta stared up at Callie, her eyes bright. "You don't remember, do you? Well, you was only three years old. We'd walk in the woods near your house an' I'd show you plants for healin' and the roots for savin' lives . . . I spelled you to be a conjurer."

"A conjurer?" Callie looked down at the tiny woman.

"A conjurer—a healer. Someone who knows how to use plant medicine. That's you. You a root doctor. A granny woman." Seeta sighed. "When your mama decided to send me away, you cried an' cried. But I hoped you'd come to see ol' Seeta one day."

Zeke poked his head into the room. "Everything alright?" he asked, glancing at his sleeping wife and son.

"Everything is fine," Callie said quickly. "Delia needs to rest and drink plenty of water. The baby is perfect. I should be going." She rummaged in her bag. "I'll leave some skullcap. I want her to take it for two weeks. The directions are on the bottle. And here are some cumin capsules, to help with nursing. See that she takes one a day for the first week."

Zeke nodded. "I got Subie all ready to go. Whenever you ready, ma'am."

Callie turned to Seeta. "Miss Seeta, may I call on you some time? I would love to hear more about those days."

"Child, I would like that so much. Always welcome a visit from Callie Beecham."

— • —

Callie sat slumped on Subie's back, emotions welling inside her as the mule plodded along. Zeke had paid her three dollars cash and a quart jar of blackberry jam. She followed him now, their pace slower.

"Zeke, did you know your grandmother birthed me?"

Zeke chuckled. "Nah, I didn't know that. But Granny's full of secrets. She birthed a lot of white folks back in the day. Seen a lot of things. Some of her stories scared the hide off me when I was little."

"What stories?"

Zeke twisted around to look at Callie. "Things that happened while she'd be out midwifin' for white folks. The women needed her help, but sometimes the men didn't like that so much. She was a slave, too. She don't like to talk about it. But when I was a boy, she tol' me one tale about runnin' into a hungry Yankee soldier durin' the war. That story scared me to death!" Zeke shook his head.

Callie tried to imagine the wizened old woman as a young slave, facing off against a Union soldier. "She must have been very brave."

Zeke nodded. "She and my granddaddy found each other and that was that. But he died young. I don't know how she ended up here."

"Does she have living children?" Callie asked.

"No, ma'am. She had two sons—my daddy Jacob an' my uncle Marcus. My daddy an' mama both passed years ago. The story goes that my uncle ran off to Chicago as a young man. Got himself a job up north an' never looked back. My big brother, Willis, died of Spanish flu in '18. I'm Granny's only livin' kin—well, 'til now."

He turned again. "I can't thank you enough for comin' out here to see to my wife and baby boy."

"How many folks live in Liberia?"

Zeke pondered the question for a while. "Maybe sixty? My wife's kin mostly moved over near Dacusville. Ain't many things to keep folks here these days. The payin' jobs are closer to Greenville. But Granny won't move. I work in Dacusville myself—as a apprentice mechanic for Mr. Clements over that way," he said proudly. "It's sho' better than share-croppin' cotton."

"That's a long way by mule," Callie said. "Who will take care of Delia and the baby? Your grandmother isn't a young woman."

"Delia's mama will come stay for a while."

Callie glanced at her watch. 11:30. Dr. Epstein would have come and gone, probably irritated at being stood up for his garden tour. *Oh, well,* she thought. *I couldn't have imagined a more astounding morning.*

"Well, Mizz Beecham, I thank ya again. We comin' into Pickens. You want me to ride in with you or you rather walk?"

Callie snapped back into the present. Zeke had stopped on the outskirts of town where the sidewalk began. Eight blocks, and she'd be home. "I can walk. Subie has done a number on my sitting bones. Best for you to get home and take care of your family. What will you call your little boy?" She slid off of the mule, wincing only a little.

Zeke grinned. "Ezekiel Calvin Young. His middle name gonna be Calvin, after you. We'll call him Cal."

"I'm honored. Thank you, Zeke. Good luck to y'all!" Callie smiled as the man took Subie's reins. He nodded once and turned to go, both mules eager to get home.

Chapter Four

Callie woke with a start. She checked her pulse and registered the rapid pace of her own heartbeat. Dawn had yet to arrive, and only the embers of last night's fire flickered in the bedroom fireplace. She shivered and pulled the patchwork quilt up around her shoulders. George was still curled at the foot of her bed, fast asleep. She exhaled audibly and closed her eyes.

The dream had seemed so real. She had been wandering through the dark woods, looking for morels. Hearing noises behind her, she'd turned to see glimpses of shadowy figures following her. They ducked behind tall trees and moved on soft feet. She quickened her pace. Soon, there were catcalls and loud whoops and hollers. The crack of a branch. A towering, white-robed figure suddenly appeared before her on horseback, his face covered by a peaked white hood. Only ice-blue eyes were visible through slits in the fabric. Behind her, the others gathered, adjusting quickly-donned robes and hoods. Callie stopped, her legs trembling.

"Who are you?" she shouted with false bravado.

"It don't matter who we are. What matters is the message we came to deliver." With that, she felt strong arms pushing her down to the wet ground from behind. She struggled to stand, when the man on horseback tossed the limp and bloody body of her cat, George, onto the ground at her feet.

"This is just a warnin'," the husky voice drawled. "We know all about you, girl. Don't want you to get above your station now. Keep to your place or next time, it'll be worse." He wheeled the horse around and was soon lost in the trees. The men behind her also vanished.

She sat up in bed and reached to stroke George's silky fur, her heart pounding. He stretched and purred in response. Unable to sleep, she reached for her dressing gown and groped around with her feet for her slippers. She padded to the kitchen and put the coffee on to percolate. As she waited, she went over the details of the dream again. There was no way of knowing who the hooded men were, nor what their leader meant about a warning. But she knew what they stood for.

The burbling coffee pot brought her back to the present. She poured a cup and added a splash of cream before seating herself near the front window to listen to the world wake up.

The chirping of the early cardinal outside calmed her nerves a bit. The rattle of glass bottles on her doorstep told her that the milkman was making his rounds, and the hard thump of the newspaper against the front window told her that Billy Jones was making the deliveries this morning instead of his big brother, Nathan, who had better aim. She sighed into her steaming cup. It was just a bad dream, nothing more.

After her coffee was finished, Callie opened the front door and retrieved the quart bottle of milk and the rolled newspaper. The morning air was crisp and cool, with a breeze blowing down from the mountains in the distance—a perfect autumn day ahead. She quickly closed the door against the chill and stashed the milk in the icebox.

After a second cup of coffee, Callie bundled herself against the chill and dressed in her smart burgundy wool tunic dress and matching cloche. She checked the seams of her stockings in the mirror before donning her winter coat. The old and threadbare camel-colored wool coat made her feel dowdy, but a new coat was out of reach for now.

She made her way up the street toward the bus stop in front of Hilltop Baptist Church. She glanced at her watch. 7:55. In the distance, a short line queued up outside of the church's fellowship hall, men and women waiting for the 8:15 to Greenville. A morning of city errands awaited her. She shoved her hands into her coat pockets, lowered her head against the wind, and took her place in line.

A man in an expensive-looking navy-blue coat stepped up onto the nearby curb and crossed the busy sidewalk in front of her. Callie couldn't help but admire the cut of the man's coat, which looked vaguely familiar and yet quite over the top for Pickens.

"Dr. Epstein?" she called out.

The man turned around. He removed his fedora, and his face broke into a surprised grin. "Miss Beecham! How nice to see you. I wondered if you had decided not to have anything more to do with me," he teased.

Callie blushed. "Dr. Epstein, I'm sorry. I was called away yesterday morning. An urgent case. I couldn't get word to you at Dr. Davis's office. I was at a residence without a telephone."

"I see," Epstein said. "An urgent case. I certainly understand that. I'm glad it wasn't that you'd changed your mind." He stepped back as the line for the bus began to tighten. "Anything I can help with?"

She remembered her lack of a license for midwifery. "Oh no. All is well now."

Dr. Epstein smiled and his face lit up. "I hope that we can reschedule. I really would like to see your herb garden. And please—call me Sam."

Do his eyes really need to be that blue? Callie wondered. She heard the rumble of the old bus before she saw it.

Callie self-consciously toyed with the seam of her glove. "Of course, Sam," she answered. "I'd be happy to show you what survived the frost. I can lend you a book or two. And please, call me Callie."

A woman near them turned slightly and smiled, before moving forward in line.

Sam looked genuinely relieved. "I see you're headed out of town?"

"Morning errands in Greenville," she answered.

"Perhaps after your errands, let me buy you a late lunch at the diner?" His eyes crinkled again, and Callie felt her stomach flip.

The bus rounded a corner and pulled into view.

Sam smiled. "I'll save us a table?"

"Sounds nice," Callie said.

Sam stared at her for some time, and Callie felt the heat of a blush crawl into her cheeks.

Finally, he cleared his throat. "Well then, I should head to the office. There are always patients to see."

"True." Callie grinned. "Assuming the bus is close to on time, I look forward to lunch. How's 1:30?"

Sam smiled. "See you at 1:30."

— • —

Pat's Diner was bustling with customers when Callie pushed through the glass door. Even the lunch counter was full. She saw Sam standing guard over a vacant booth. He waved to her, and Callie threaded her way toward the table.

Two young women with rouged cheeks, bleach-blonde bobbed hair, and short skirts suddenly hopped off of their counter stools and intercepted Sam before Callie could get to the table. She overheard one of the girls praising "sweet Dr. Sam" to her friend. Callie watched the girl reach out to pat the lapel of his jacket affectionately and heard her label him "the bee's knees." The other girl giggled and batted her kohl-lined eyes. Both girls wore sheer stockings rolled below their knees, proclaiming their youth with wild abandon.

Even at a distance, Callie could see the color rise in Sam's cheeks as he tried to fend off the flirtatious young ladies who were dressed to impress. Callie self-consciously felt the hem of her long, pleated skirt brush her calves in their thick cotton stockings. She touched the coil of long brunette hair twisted into a chignon and felt positively aged in comparison. She quickly removed her drab coat and waited patiently for Sam to end his conversation.

Finally, Sam gave them calling cards and the young ladies reluctantly left, cards clutched to their chests. They waved furiously as they exited the building, and only then did Callie burst out laughing. Sam motioned her to sit, and then he sank into the seat across from her, rolling his eyes.

"Dr. Epstein, you've been here only a short time, and you already have such devoted patients," Callie teased. "I don't think you need to educate yourself on medicinal plants to get new business. You seem to be doing quite well on your own." She removed her gloves and laid them on the seat next to her.

Sam reddened and swept a hand through his hair. "Yes, well . . . that was Mary Kay Sweeney, a student at Women's College in Greenville, and her friend. She is back in town for a visit. Her father is—"

"The mayor," Callie finished his statement for him. "Yes, I know." She sat back and crossed her arms. "It's none of my business, but I don't recall ever seeing flappers in Pickens before. You're attracting new clientele, Dr. Epstein," she said.

She enjoyed seeing Sam so nervous. He might be a New York City doctor, but in Pickens County, she had the advantage. He adjusted his tie and cleared his throat. "Maybe we should order?" He picked up the menu and examined it closely. "What do you recommend?"

Callie smiled. "I always order Pat's meatloaf. She makes it with a blend of beef and pork sausage. You should try it."

Sam put the menu down and leaned in. "I try to avoid pork. I am beginning to think that might be a problem."

Callie shook her head. "Sam, Pat's serves BLT's, meatloaf, fried chicken, and pork chops—all cooked in lard. I think your best bet is to give up and just have dessert."

The waitress appeared and they ordered—meatloaf plate for Callie and a bowl of collard greens with corn bread for Sam.

"How was your morning of errands?" Sam asked.

"Oh, fine." Callie shifted in her seat.

The conversation ebbed, and Callie wondered if Sam regretted asking her to lunch. She wasn't one for small talk, and it didn't look like Sam was either, but the silence in the midst of a busy restaurant unnerved her. She gazed around the diner and noticed eyes on them, bent heads whispering. She nodded at a few folks she knew and returned their curious smiles.

She sipped her tea and then dabbed her lips with her napkin. "I don't want to pry, but may I ask why you took a job here? Why not Atlanta?"

"I thought I would like the slower pace," Sam said. "And I will get used to it. But I do miss Manhattan. I miss the people, the clubs, jazz festivals, the shows, and walks in Central Park. Have you ever been?"

"No," Callie said defensively. "But then again, I like the quiet of the country."

Sam nodded. "I'm looking for the positives. I can see the stars at night. Leave the office at a reasonable hour. Learn all of my patients' names. Those are the good parts. I had hoped that Dr. Davis would be eager to listen to my ideas. But I quickly realized that Earl Davis won't be swayed to alternative therapies."

"No," Callie said. "I could have told you to stick to traditional medicine with him. I think that's why he detests me—I practice the voodoo magic." She smiled mischievously.

Sam chuckled. "After you healed Mildred's lesion, he did seem peeved. He should have been elated. I should have known better than to try to explain naturopathy to the old man. His ego is fragile. He's been the only show in town for years."

"Shouldn't a doctor be interested in naturopathic cures?" Callie asked. "After all, aren't drugs derived from plants?"

Sam sipped his tea. "It's hard to convince someone who went to medical school in the last century that there is a different way, an older way, actually, to treat illness. Mildred may be on our side, but Earl . . ." He sighed heavily.

"I'm sorry, Sam," Callie said. "Not surprised, but sorry." His mood was dismal, indeed, but he wouldn't bring hers down. "So why didn't you stay up north? I'm sure you could practice medicine exactly the way you want up there."

He toyed with the straw in his glass. "After my New York residency, I headed home. I was to be married within three months and then back to New York with my bride. But my father died suddenly. Then my fiancée broke off the engagement. It seems that she found someone more desirable while I was up north—an established surgeon with a thriving career. And he is from a very wealthy Jewish family."

Callie's eyebrows went up, and Sam laughed. "Are you surprised to find out that I was jilted—or that I am Jewish?"

"Both," she answered honestly. "Although, with a name like Epstein, I should have known the Jewish part. Ah. Is that why no pork?"

"Is that—is that a problem?" he asked. "Can we still be friends?"

Callie blushed and toyed with her napkin. "Of course."

"Keeping kosher here will be a struggle," Sam answered sheepishly.

Callie smiled. "I do wonder how you'll get on here. Folks are either Baptist or Presbyterian. Lord help a Methodist! And there isn't a synagogue in the entire Upstate, I'd wager. But I'm more curious about the engaged part, past-tense."

The waitress appeared with heaping plates of food. "Here ya go, kids. Enjoy." She slapped the bill down on the table, and Sam slid it under his plate.

Callie's eyes darted from her plate to Sam's. Her slab of meatloaf was accompanied by a mound of mashed potatoes, cornbread, and a large serving of green beans. His bowl of collard greens seemed paltry in comparison.

Sam eyed her plate wistfully. "I could easily wolf down that fine-looking meal."

Callie began to nibble at her meatloaf. "A broken engagement? Was it—"

"Humiliating? Infuriating? Depressing? Yes, to all of those things," Sam said. "So, I wanted to get away from Atlanta. But I couldn't go back up north and leave my mother. She was a new widow. She'd met the Davises at a medical conference years ago. My father was a surgeon. Mother contacted Mildred Davis, and well, here I am. It was kind of Dr. Davis to take me on."

Callie watched Sam as he chewed his collards dejectedly, looking anywhere except across the table at Callie. She didn't know what she felt at that moment but supposed it was empathy.

She put down her fork. "I'll throw you a bone. You're not the only person in the world to have been jilted, Dr. Epstein."

Sam looked up, curious.

Callie nodded. "I was young. I was working with the Red Cross as a nurse's aide in Camp Service in 1917, outside of Washington, DC. There was a boy. He was a handsome, recuperating soldier from Charlottesville. Jerry Yancey. He was nineteen and wild about me. Classic story, right?" She paused to remember. "Anyway, Jerry proposed after ten days. I was over the moon. I don't know what I was thinking . . ." Her voice trailed off.

"What happened?" Sam asked.

"His girlfriend from home surprised him with a visit—and he remembered that he was spoken for."

"Oy," Sam said.

Callie smiled at the phrase. "Indeed. I dodged a bullet there. But I've learned to like being alone." Sam did not appear convinced, but she continued. "You're soon to be a successful doctor. Already you have fans. Enjoy your independence. You can always go back to Atlanta. Don't let an ex-fiancée stop you."

Sam regarded Callie as she resumed her meal. "Camp Service, huh? You must have been a child. How did you get in?"

Callie grinned. "Thank you for the compliment. I was sixteen. My mother had passed away and I needed a job, so I fudged a little on my age. I was bound and determined not to work in the mill."

"I'm surprised that you had only one proposal. Those boys were finally home from fighting—convalescing, grateful to be alive—and with a pretty nurse like you to tend them? You should have had dozens of proposals," Sam teased.

Callie felt herself blush. "Nurse's aide," she corrected. "I spent most of my time rolling bandages, emptying bed pans, and taking orders from my superiors. But I did pick up a bit of basic training, which I've used in my work here. Did you serve?"

"Being in college kept me stateside. Pre-med, the military wanted us to finish school. You can imagine my mother's relief. Then I picked up the Spanish flu, and by the time I had fully convalesced, the war was ending. I went off to New York for medical school a semester later."

Sam leaned forward and gazed at Callie intently. "You didn't want to go to nursing school after the war?"

"Of course I did!" Callie said. "I would have given anything to go to nursing school. But I was an orphan, the only child of deceased millworkers with not a penny between them. I'm lucky I found the Red

Cross. I saw what working in the mill did to my poor mother." She dabbed her lips with her napkin and laid it on the table near her empty plate.

"Sam, I ate an entire meal, and you've only touched your collards," she chided, anxious to change the subject.

Sam broke his gaze away from her and regarded the dish of limp greens. "You didn't tell me a bowl of collard greens would have chunks of ham floating in it."

Callie burst into laughter, her heart warm.

— • —

The next day, Callie stayed busy. She treated little Amelia Craft's diaper rash and Hal Smith's peptic ulcer, and then visited postpartum Sally Jenkins to see how she was healing up.

Callie earned just two dollars and a few jars of pickled okra that day. Business was decidedly down. The Roaring Twenties seemed to be roaring on—without her.

Late in the afternoon, she was brewing a female tonic for a client when the silver bell over her front door tinkled. "Hello, Callie? Are you open?" She recognized Sam's voice, and her pulse quickened.

"In the kitchen." She patted her wild hair and nervously smoothed her apron.

"Hmmm, smells wonderful," Sam said, lifting his nose to inhale the savory scent of rosemary. "Are you getting something ready for Thanksgiving?"

"No. And you don't need this particular concoction, Sam," she teased. "It's for premenstrual discomfort."

He put up his hands in mock surrender. "It did occur to me that I hadn't set up a new appointment to learn about plants from the town's resident herbal expert. I mean, you ditched me once, but I decided to drop by to see if you can fit me into your schedule."

Callie stirred the steeping tea and said, "There isn't much you can identify this late in the year." She glanced at her watch. "Still—I'm done with clients for today. Follow me." She turned off the stove, untied her apron, and led him through to the back door.

She opened the door to a display of nine raised beds in the large yard. A few straggler squash lay amid the tangle of late-fall debris in one bed. Another held the remnants of plants with dark berries still clinging to the withered stalks. A third seemed to be entirely made of upright sticks devoid of foliage. Callie knew that it was impossible for Sam to tell what was what. A heaping compost pile near the fence steamed in the late afternoon chill. Several young pecan trees at the back of the property stretched toward the sky.

"Other than the squash, the rest you probably wouldn't know." She leaned and yanked a dead tomato plant out of the ground roughly. "This is my little kingdom, Sam. For what it's worth. If I don't grow it, I forage for it—or order it. Plants are good healers."

"And have magic powers?" Sam asked with some humor.

"I don't know why you're so quick to dismiss ancient wisdom," Callie said softly. "Don't farmers still plant according to the phases of the moon? My own mama had willow divining rods pull down hard at the site of water. She planted birch trees near our house to ward off lightning and hung yarrow in the house for protection. She taught me the four spells."

"The four spells?" Sam seemed intrigued. "Oy."

"Fire. Water. Earth and Air." Callie chuckled. "Trust me. You're not ready."

She crossed the yard to withered vines crawling across the wooden fence and plucked a few yellowish-orange fruits from deep in the brown foliage.

"These are the last of the passionflower fruits. I don't know how they escaped the frost. Break one open and taste the pulp," Callie urged.

Sam tentatively took the proffered fruit and split one open with his fingers. He lifted it to his mouth and nibbled the pulp. His eyes widened. "It tastes like an orange!" he exclaimed. "What will these do?"

Callie shrugged. "I use passionflower for anxiety and calming. It's good for women's problems and for the heart. Truthfully, I just like the purple flowers in summer. Always have . . . The fruit is an extra benefit. I eat them out of hand."

Sam gazed around at the profusion of plant life in all directions. "All of these twigs and sticks have uses medicinally?"

"Well, actually, the bed closest to your feet is what's left of my vegetable garden," she said.

Sam squatted and looked at the raised bed, a tangle of withered vines, bent pea trellises, and brown stubble. "I do recognize the tomato plants and squash there. That's it. But I hate squash."

"Then how will you possibly get on at Mildred Davis's Thanksgiving feast?" Callie laughed. "She'll probably have six different squash dishes on hand. She may have even killed the fatted calf for you. She's your biggest fan," Callie joked. "I assume you're going."

"I am. Are you?" He stood and looked down at Callie. "She told me she'd asked you."

Her heart flipped. "I don't know. Mildred did invite me—although I'm not sure why. Her husband despises me. I should eat Thanksgiving dinner with my neighbor, Silas. He's all alone," she said.

Sam's face fell.

"But back to the reason for your visit." Callie gazed at the bare elderberry shrub, stray berries still clinging to the branches, before looking at Sam. "I can teach you a little bit. Lend you a book. But honestly, you have a shingle out front and the blessing of Dr. Davis. If I teach you what I know, the only leg up I would have is that my rates are far less. I barely make ends meet as it is, and you, with your medical degree . . ." The words trailed away. Callie shivered in the gathering dusk and rubbed her upper arms with her hands.

Sam looked around the yard for some time before speaking. The light was dimming quickly. "I would never do anything to negatively affect your work. I do have more than a passing interest in plant therapy, though. Perhaps you can act as my consultant. Or we could collaborate. I would pay you."

Callie pulled her moth-eaten sweater closer around her in the evening chill. She sighed. "You don't need me."

Sam smiled and his blue eyes crinkled. "I think I do."

Chapter Five

Callie jabbed the key to her post office box in the keyhole and opened her mailbox. She pulled out the contents and paused to sort through her mail. A *Sears* winter catalog, the light bill, two Christmas cards, and a small white envelope addressed to her in a spidery hand.

"Mornin', Callie," called a friendly voice.

Callie looked up to see her elderly neighbor, Silas Roberts, limping toward her with the help of his unique cane, a thick staff of twisted mountain laurel.

"Silas! You know I'm always happy to run errands for you. That hill is no picnic," she chided. "What brings you out and about on such a cold day?"

The old man grinned, showing tobacco-stained teeth. "I met with my attorney today. Redid my will," he said with a proud thump of his cane. "My daughter-in-law in Greenville thinks she's gonna take all my money when I go. But no sirree. She don't visit nor call. She got herself a new boyfriend last Christmas and thinks I don't know about it." His blue eyes narrowed. "I'm all by my lonesome."

Callie tilted her head sympathetically. "I'm so sorry." Roberts' only child, William, had died a war hero at Amiens. The old man had always seemed a little crazy in the head, but she listened to his strange stories and tried to help him out with grocery shopping and offerings from her garden. She had even mowed his lawn several times with his rusted push mower, more of a workout than she cared to repeat.

The man fumbled with his key. "Can you get this here key into my box?" He handed his key ring to Callie with a shaking hand.

"Of course!" Callie took the key and inserted it into her neighbor's post office box. She peered into the small space and pulled out one envelope. "I'm sorry. Just the light bill today." She handed over the envelope and key.

The man chuckled. "Don't know why I even keep a box. All I get is bills. Ain't likely I'm gonna get stacks of Christmas cards from well-wishers." He paused. "Say, you got any of that salve for joints? My knees and ankles have been acting up somethin' fierce lately." His long, gray beard quivered when he spoke.

Callie sensed the man's loneliness. She smiled. "I do. I'll bring some by this afternoon. And I won't take payment this time. You pay me way too much."

"Then I won't be takin' your salve!" Silas harrumphed. "I will pay for it, young lady. I can't walk straight nor tend my yard worth a darn, but I can pay for my medicines," the man said proudly. "An' maybe you'll stay and have a cup of Christmas cheer with me." He winked mischievously.

"Silas Roberts, shame on you. Have you forgotten Prohibition?" she teased. After glancing around the empty post office, she leaned closer. "Too many cups of Christmas cheer won't do your knees and ankles a bit of good. I'll drop the salve off this afternoon after my last client. I made Christmas cookies, so I'll bring a plate." She gave the man a cheerful smile and left the post office, tugging on her gloves as she walked.

Low, gray clouds hung over downtown and looked to threaten snow. A fierce wind whipped down the sidewalk, and Callie picked up her pace. When she passed Flora's House of Beauty, she slowed and peered through the glass at the bevy of women sitting inside draped in burgundy capes. Several had their hair in curlers, two were under dryers and chatting amiably. Flora and her assistant, Betty, stood over their clients, scissors in hand, chatting away. The scene was warm and cheerful. Tears welled in her eyes.

Callie touched a gloved hand to the twist of dark hair threatening to come unpinned in the steady wind. *I'm turning into an old maid. A spinster. And I look the part.* She swiped at her eyes with her handkerchief and resumed her walk. She wondered whether the gloom was due to her outdated hairstyle or her annual holiday melancholy.

She neared home and set about to cheer herself up. The little white house that she owned stood proudly. The front yard was neat, autumn leaves raked away into the compost pile, shrubs trimmed. She had painted the front door a cheerful green. A festive holly wreath hung there now and welcomed her home. She was blessed. Should be feeling grateful and not down, but the holidays always made her sad. This one, even more so.

She had gone to Thanksgiving dinner at the Davises, in part because Mildred refused to take no for an answer. And she had so looked forward to seeing Sam. She'd dressed her best. Worn a dab of perfume. A bit of lipstick. Even taken a loaf of homemade bread fresh from the oven.

Sam and two older couples had been in attendance, but something had felt wrong, off, as if she had been a hasty addition to even out Mildred's table. Dr. Davis had spoken only to Sam and the other men, pointedly ignoring Callie, while Mildred rattled on incessantly in the kitchen and would not allow the other women to help. The other women sat in the Davis parlor, discussing their children and their bridge club, while Callie quietly sipped her coffee. The warm loaf of bread sat forlornly on the kitchen counter, never making it to the bounteous repast.

Sam had barely said a word to her, even though Mildred had seated them together. A week later, she still hadn't heard from him and wondered what she had done to offend.

Callie snapped into the present. She opened the front door and the scent of Christmas greeted her. The small cedar Christmas tree stood proudly in her front window, decorated with clove-studded oranges, popcorn strings, and red glass ornaments. She inhaled and felt better almost immediately. Her homemade potpourri filled the room with fragrance. Her potpourris were always popular with clients, and this one, with pine and cinnamon, was usually quite profitable during the holidays. She hung her coat on the rack, tossed the mail on the sofa, and sat down wearily. George leaped up onto her lap and settled himself to nap.

"You're lucky you're a cat," she murmured, stroking his silky fur. She removed her gloves and hat and picked up the mail. There were two Christmas cards. The first was from Hilltop Baptist's pastor and his wife, inviting her to Christmas Eve services. The other was a glittery homage to winter from Dr. and Mrs. Davis, signed in Mildred's looping hand.

Callie pulled a small white envelope from the stack and studied it. No return address. She tore open the flap and pulled out a thin sheet of stationery. The spidery handwriting didn't look familiar. The letter was dated December 1—more than a week ago.

Dear Miss Callie,

Would you please call on me at your convenience? I would appreciate it very much. We have so much to talk about.

Sincerely, Seeta Young

Callie sighed. She wanted to hear stories of her mother, and to glean any sage advice on midwifery that Seeta could pass on. But the weather had turned colder, and she did not have a car. Her bicycle would not handle the distance nor rock-strewn dirt roads. And Pickens had no taxi service of any kind. She was sure that Seeta could not travel, and the thought of asking Zeke Young to come and get her for another damned mule ride was too much.

She set the letter aside and began to prepare for an afternoon of clients—Mr. Tanner with an ingrown toenail, Mrs. Roper with female complaints, a trip to Rita Lovell's to check on her at two weeks postpartum, before ending at Mr. Roberts' house. The visit to Liberia would have to wait until after the holidays.

— • —

Callie knocked on the front door of her neighbor's modest bungalow and waited. A cold drizzle peppered the bare trees, and she worried it might mean ice later. She huddled under the small porch overhang and waited. It always took Silas a while to get up from his chair and make his way to the door. After some minutes, the door opened, and he grinned.

"Callie, thank you ever so much. I knew you'd remember. Come on in, girl." He leaned on his twisted cane and led her into the dim interior. A fire blazed in the hearth, but it seemed to be the only source of warmth in the small house. A damp chill hung at the edges of the room, thick with cigarette smoke. Callie heard the radio on somewhere in the house.

"Have a seat. Visit a spell, won't ya? You like Jimmie Rodgers?" Silas asked, as he maneuvered himself back into his comfy chair. "This is his song—'T for Texas.'"

Callie sat on the edge of the stained sofa and glanced around her. At her last visit in early November, she had sorted stacks of papers, emptied overflowing ash trays, cleaned the small bedroom, and washed and dried the clothes draped on every surface. The little room was messier than ever.

"Is that what's playing? I do like it, actually."

"Oh, girl. Jimmie Rodgers is the real deal. When he comes on, my toes get to tappin'." Silas wiggled his feet and waved his cane in the air.

Callie smiled at the old man's antics. "I brought your salve. But if you continue to have so much pain, maybe you should see Dr. Davis. Just to be sure nothing is wrong." She placed the small glass jar on the table in front of him.

"I ain't visitin' that 'un. Hell no. No sirree." The man shook his head. He pulled several bills from his shirt pocket and slid them across the table.

"Silas, that's way too much. I see a ten in there." Callie scowled. "You need to save your money."

"Save it for what? My funeral? I do just fine with your medicine. It works every time. It's well worth the money, and I'll gladly pay. Now, can I offer you a small nip?" he asked slyly.

"I feel like I'm in a speakeasy," she said playfully. "Are you ever going to tell me where you get your liquor?"

The man cackled. "I ain't never gone tell no one nothin'. But it sure is good-sippin' on a cold evenin', and it do help the loneliness." He produced a bottle from behind his chair and pulled two glassed from under it. "Always prepared for company." He winked and poured the amber liquid into the glasses and leaned forward to hand Callie hers.

"Remember, girl, it ain't illegal to drink it. Just illegal to make it." He lifted a glass. "Merry Christmas, my dear," he said gallantly.

Callie held up her glass. "Merry Christmas to you, too, Silas." She tipped the glass back and drained the whiskey in a long swallow. "Whew!" she said, shaking her head with a grimace. "What's the proof on this batch? It burns."

Silas guffawed. "That'll be my good stuff. It's one-hundred proof."

Callie wiped her stinging eyes with the back of her hand. "That would make a fine menstruum."

"What's that now?" Silas looked embarrassed.

"It's not that!" Callie laughed. "A menstruum is the liquid I use in making tinctures. Grain alcohol works best, but with Prohibition, I've been stuck with using apple-cider vinegar. It's not the same."

"I'll say!" Silas laughed. "I can give you a bottle. For medicinal purposes." He made to stand up but Callie demurred.

"Silas, you know I can't accept. I could lose my business. Not that I don't like sharing a nip now and then with you on the sly." She smiled. "Now, can I expect you as usual for Christmas dinner this year? George and I would appreciate the company."

"Yes, ma'am," he said with a grin. "I thank ya. The holidays are hard for me. Knowin' I have someplace to go takes the ache away."

Callie nodded. "I certainly understand how you feel. I miss my mother terribly at Christmas."

Silas stared at Callie silently and sipped his drink. The music ended, and Callie heard the beginnings of a new program.

At that, the old man's blue eyes widened. "Oh! It's time for *Amos an' Andy*! You should stick around an' listen. These boys are hilarious. I got a pot of beans on the stove. Stay for supper?"

Callie stood and shook her head. "You enjoy your show and your dinner. I may stop in tomorrow and tidy up a bit. My Christmas present to you? Hmm?"

Silas tried to stand, and Callie hurried to stop him. "Don't get up on my account. You just sit back and listen to the music. Don't drink any more though, alright? And I'll see you tomorrow."

"You're a good gal, Callie," Silas said. "You must have way more to do on a Saturday night than visit an old man."

Oh, I wish that were true, Callie thought. She waved to her friend and let herself out into the cold drizzle.

— • —

The next morning dawned clear and cold. As Callie had suspected, the evening drizzle had turned into a night of freezing rain, and everything outside took on a silvery glaze. Trees groaned and cracked under the weight of the ice. The sun created glittering rainbow prisms in icicles dripping from the eaves. Callie found it quite beautiful. She made her way carefully down the sidewalk toward Silas's house, anxious to tidy up and then leave the afternoon free for reading and some baking.

She knocked on the door and waited, shivering in the sub-freezing air. She heard a mumbled voice from inside instead of the ubiquitous thump of the cane across the pine floor. Callie tried the doorknob and found the door unlocked. She turned the knob and opened the door.

In the dim light of a dying fire, Callie found the man laid out across the sofa, his socks off and his pants rolled up to the knees. The radio played its cheerful Christmas music from another room. "Blast," she muttered. "Silas? Are you alright?"

The man pulled his open shirt closed and began to fumble with the buttons. "I'm sorry, Callie. I'm feelin' poorly. Maybe today ain't a good day for visitin'." His breath reeked of liquor.

Callie took one look at her neighbor's extremities and crouched down on the floor. "Silas, you have severe gout. Your big toes are swollen. I can see your right ankle and knees are a mess, too. My salve won't touch this. We should call Dr. Davis."

"No!" said the old man sharply. "I won't see that man. An' he don't make house calls no more anyhow," he slurred. "Not for the likes of me."

"Drinking an entire bottle of whiskey didn't help," she chided, picking up the empty bottle. "Stop drinking to oblivion, Silas. You could have died," Callie said crossly. She regarded the bottle for a moment and then took Silas's pale right foot in her hand.

"Girl, what are you doin'?" he murmured.

Callie began to roll the bottle firmly back and forth across the sole of his foot. "It would work better if you could sit up."

Silas only sighed and threw a hand across his brow.

"I'm trying to improve the circulation in your foot. Your gout is severe—probably from the drinking. You'll want to do this with each foot for at least five minutes a day. I can run home and get dandelion capsules. I'll make up some apple cider vinegar tea, too . . . but you need a doctor."

She paused and switched to Silas's left foot. "Let me call Dr. Davis's new man, Dr. Epstein. I know him. He is a good one."

Silas glared at Callie from bloodshot eyes. "Ain't no way in hell Davis is comin' here. But if you vouch for the new one, I'll let him in."

Callie nodded. "He's staying at Sara Cane's. Hopefully, he can be found and can get a ride here quickly. Telephone's in the kitchen, right?"

"In the kitchen," Silas muttered.

Locating the telephone, she picked up the receiver and waited for the operator. "Yes, can I have Sara Cane's place?"

After a few rings, a voice connected on the other end. "Hello? Haven of Rest Boarding House," a woman's voice trilled.

Callie rolled her eyes. The name sounded more like a mortuary than a boarding house. "Sara, hello. This is Callie Beecham over on Florence. I am looking for Dr. Epstein. Is he still boarding at your place? I have a neighbor who needs seeing."

The woman paused. "The doctor is resting on his day off," she answered, a little possessively for Callie's liking. "His time is quite valuable."

"Perhaps you should let him know that there is a call, and he can decide whether it warrants his valuable time," Callie said firmly. "Please?" *Why does it seem that every woman who meets the handsome young Sam Epstein feels the need to claim him*, she wondered. First, Mildred Davis, then the coeds in the diner, and now, matronly Sara Cane.

The woman huffed and put the telephone receiver down hard

enough to give Callie a start. After some minutes, someone picked up the line. "Hello? This is Dr. Epstein."

"Sam, it's Callie Beecham," she said stiffly. "I have an elderly neighbor with pretty severe gout. Could you come take a look at him sometime today? I just want to be sure there are no underlying conditions. He can't travel. I know that it's Sunday but—"

"Of course," Sam said readily. "I'll get my bag and be on my way."

"Oh, thank you! Silas Roberts at 901 Florence. His house is two down from mine. Can someone there give you a ride?" Callie asked.

"I have a car. I'll be there in fifteen minutes." There was a click, and the line went dead.

Callie didn't know whether to be relieved that he would come or insulted at his curt manner. She hung up the telephone and returned to her patient.

"Silas, we have to air out this room before Dr. Epstein gets here. It reeks of liquor," she said, hands on hips. The man mumbled and turned over on the sofa.

Exasperated, Callie went to work. She threw open the front door and a gust of icy air entered the room. The man only groaned and shifted on the sofa. She stood for a few minutes, fanning the stale air. She added kindling and a few small logs to the fire and soon had it blazing away. Only then did she close the door. She opened the dusty curtains, and the sunshine spilled into the usually dark living room. She picked up the empty bottle and four or five glasses sitting around the room and rinsed them all out before placing them in the kitchen sink.

Grabbing a towel from the bathroom, Callie wet it and returned to wipe down Silas's face and beard. She buttoned his shirt correctly and then stood to scan the room. The predominant smell was back to cigarette smoke, and her patient appeared asleep instead of drunk.

She sat down wearily and dropped her head in her hands. The strains of the carol "Silver Bells" played from the radio. There was a tentative knock on the door and Callie jumped up. She opened the door to see Sam standing there, hat in hand, businesslike and stern. "How is Mr. Roberts?"

Callie stepped aside to let Sam into the room. "He's resting."

Before she could say anything, she knew that her attempts at covering up the smell of stale alcohol were futile. Sam's face registered the obvious, and he grimaced. He removed his jacket and scarf and laid them on a chair.

"Mr. Roberts. I'm Dr. Epstein. I'm going to listen to your heart." He crouched by the sofa and reached to take Silas's pulse without a word. He pulled his stethoscope from his bag and leaned to listen to the man's heart. Then he lifted an eyelid and let it drop back into place before moving to examine his swollen joints.

Callie watched nervously and waited for Sam's assessment. She noticed Sam's hair had gotten longer. It brushed across the top of his collar. His hands were gentle but thorough as he palpated the inflamed joints. His broad shoulders appeared well-muscled under his thin shirt. He stood up and jolted Callie back to reality.

"Other than aspirin powder for the inflammation, I think that whatever you have to offer him will be fine. His heart sounds good. He should drink more water and eat more fruits and vegetables, but I suspect you have been telling him that. I can leave aspirin powder though."

The sound of heavy snoring began to come from the patient. Sam gazed down at Silas and did not look at Callie. "No more alcohol for Mr. Roberts."

Callie felt her cheeks flame. "I think he drank most of a bottle. Thank you for coming, though. He has no family, and sometimes I think he's trying to do himself in. The holidays are . . . hard. He looks bad. I don't have a car or I'd have taken him to county hospital."

Sam glanced at Callie briefly. "What do you do for gout?" He leaned down and began to massage Silas's puffy feet with firm hands.

"Apple-cider vinegar and ginger teas. Dandelion or burdock as a blood purifier. Cherry juice when I can get it . . ." Her voice trailed off. "Things to lower uric acid."

Sam nodded. "Good. Bicarbonate helps to neutralize acidity. And try tissue massage." Sam picked up the empty bottle near Silas's feet and looked up at Callie.

Callie blushed even more deeply. "I used it to massage his feet."

Sam nodded with approbation and began to roll the bottle across the sole of one pale foot. He massaged his patient's feet and spindly legs quietly for some time before exhaling audibly.

"Well, I think I've done all I can for today." He handed the bottle back to Callie with the tiniest bit of a smile. "He will be fine—when he wakes up." He shoved his stethoscope roughly into his bag. "I'll check on him in a few days if you'd like."

"What do we owe you?" Callie asked. "For the house call?"

"No charge." Sam stood up and pushed his arms into his coat sleeves.

Callie searched her mind for something she might have said to offend the man but to no avail. "Thank you."

He buttoned his coat and wound the woolen scarf around his neck before finally looking Callie in the eyes. He crossed his arms. "Why didn't you tell me that you are engaged?"

Callie cocked her head. "Excuse me?"

"Dr. Davis told me. Before you arrived at their house on Thanksgiving Day. You have a fiancé. You're engaged to be married." Sam shoved both hands in his pockets. "Why weren't you honest with me?"

Callie gasped. "I don't even have a boyfriend—and why would you listen to what stuffy old Dr. Davis says anyway?" She put her hands on her hips, indignant. "That man has never given me the time of day. He was quite rude at Thanksgiving. How would he know anything about my personal life?" A tendril of her curly hair escaped from behind her ear, and she swiped at it angrily.

At the same moment, both Callie and Sam exclaimed, "Mildred!"

Sam's blue eyes crinkled in the way that Callie found so endearing. "The old hen was trying to make me jealous."

"Jealous?" Callie asked. "Is that why you said hardly a word to me at her dinner? Why you haven't so much as telephoned since? You were jealous?"

Sam looked at Callie and tenderly reached to tuck the stray lock of hair behind her ear. The shock of it sent electricity coursing through her. He let his hand linger on her cheek for a moment. Behind them, "The First Noel" began to play on the radio.

"Very jealous," he said softly. "I like you, Callie. A lot. I'm sorry. I should have asked you directly."

Callie crossed her arms defensively. "Yes, you should have."

Sam twisted his hat in his hands and stared at the floor.

"Well, I know how you can make it up to me," Callie said, her lips in a pout.

Sam looked up. "Anything. I'm at your service. You must know that by now."

"Can you give me a ride? I need to go to Liberia."

Chapter Six

The Ford bumped along the two-lane road at quite a clip, and Callie had to hold on to her hat with two hands. Sam had neglected to bring the side curtains, and every deep rut the front wheels hit sent a splash of mud into the air and very nearly on them both. Still, the afternoon was crisp and clear after the night's freezing rain, and Sam seemed eager to help.

Callie had only briefly explained her history with Seeta before they set out on their visit. To his credit, Sam was genuinely curious about the little town of Liberia and the woman who had summoned Callie.

He had not seen the undulating blue wall that was the Blue Ridge mountain range up close before. It stretched in front of them, ancient and regal. Callie pointed out the looming face of Table Rock Mountain. "Amazing, isn't it?" she said.

Sam nodded. "The views from town haven't done it justice."

Callie smiled. "The Cherokee words for the Blue Ridge mean 'Great Blue Hills of God.' I think it's the most beautiful place on Earth. And wait until we turn off into the valley."

Sam turned his gaze from the road to the young woman sitting next to him. "Beautiful," he said.

The car hit a deep pothole, and Callie bounced so hard her head hit the low ceiling.

"Sorry!" Sam said, over the whine of the engine.

Callie just smiled. "That was nothing. My first trip up this way was on the back of one very ornery mule. I feel bad for your lovely car, though. We're still on what passes for pavement. Soon it will be all dirt road."

"I bought it in Atlanta. Had I known the direction my career would take, I would have been better off with a horse and buggy," Sam joked.

Callie gazed toward Table Rock in the distance. "We turn up there," she directed.

Sam heaved the steering wheel to the left, and the car turned onto a hard-packed, gravel track that led into the little dale that was Liberia. Callie watched his face for any reaction. He took in the small frame houses, some whitewashed, some not, the gardens now stripped of their summer greenery, and the sparkling creek that meandered through the floor of the valley. He slowed as they came upon the church, and Callie watched as he examined it, the car idling loudly.

"It's lovely. You said this was settled by former slaves?" Sam asked as he peered out the window.

Before Callie could answer, the doors of the little wooden church opened, and a stream of people began to trickle out. They paused on the steps and gawked at the fancy automobile that idled in front of their house of worship. Several folks waved, but most just stood and stared.

"Aren't we a sight to behold?" Sam murmured.

One of the congregants raised a hand and shouted, "Mizz Callie!" He removed his hat and bounded down the steps to the car. "Mizz Callie, we was expectin' you. Granny'll be so happy you came."

"Zeke, how are you?" Callie exclaimed. "We didn't mean to interrupt church services. But it's after one o'clock."

"Oh, yes, ma'am." Zeke chuckled. He nodded toward the big man standing with authority in front of the double doors, thumbs hooked through his suspenders. "Well, Brother James preached today—and Brother James always has a lot to say."

He laughed easily and peered into the car. "Oh, Granny'll be fit to be tied. She told us you was comin'. She's cookin' a fried chicken Sunday dinner," Zeke said.

"Oh no, we couldn't impose," Callie began. "It's just that the other day I got a letter from Seeta asking me to come visit. It was dated days ago. I should have written. We can't disturb your Sunday dinner."

"She knew you'd be coming." Zeke shrugged. Behind him, curious people streamed down the steps and stood around admiring Sam's car. Delia soon appeared on the steps, carrying tiny Ezekiel Calvin, tightly bundled against the cold. The milling crowd parted, and she quickly made her way to her husband's side.

Zeke pointed to Callie. "Baby, look who it is. But she says they can't stay."

Delia frowned and said, "Mizz Callie, Granny told us you were comin' today. If she hears that we let you go, she'll tan both our hides. We headin' that way now." She leaned toward the car and displayed her infant son's chubby face. "See? Ain't Cal fine? Come to the house an' I'll let you hold him."

Callie beamed at the tiny brown face, snug in his swaddle. "Delia, he's perfect. And you look well." The crowd began to disperse, and Callie looked over at Sam. "May we stay?" she asked.

Sam nodded. "I have nowhere to be—and a homecooked meal sounds superb."

Zeke grinned and slapped the car door. "Alright. Drive on around the corner. You know where we live, Mizz Callie. Granny's at home with Delia's mama. We be there in a bit." He paused and peered through the window toward Sam. "Say, is this a '27 Touring Car? It's a beauty."

Sam sat up proudly. "You know motor cars! It is. Electric start. And a windshield wiper!" Sam exclaimed, jiggling the small wiper lever.

Zeke nodded. "All steel body, too. Yeah, one o' these days, I'd like to have me one," he sighed. "Alright. Y'all go on to the house. Granny will be happy to see you made it." He stood and shooed the car on down the road.

Sam motored down the street and soon pulled the car off of the dirt track and onto the shoulder in front of Seeta's house. Several chickens scurried out of the way of the shiny Ford. He hurried around to the passenger side and opened Callie's door. As she hopped out and adjusted her hat, she heard a voice call out, "You're here!"

The pair looked up toward the front porch. Seeta stood there supported by a middle-aged woman, both wearing colorful aprons over simple housedresses. Callie smiled, took Sam's arm, and climbed the steps.

"Hello, Miss Seeta. It's so nice to see you again," Callie said. "This is Dr. Sam Epstein. He just joined Dr. Davis's practice in Pickens."

Sam extended his hand. "How do you do, Miss Seeta?"

Seeta stepped back, surprised, but then regained her composure and shook Sam's hand warmly. "Well, I am jes' fine, Dr. Epstein. I was prayin' for a doctor to come up, but I didn't pray for one as handsome as you." She nodded toward her friend and said, "This here is Delia's mama, Mattie Alexander. She lives in Dacusville. We always eat Sunday dinners together."

Mattie smiled and nodded. "How y'all?"

Callie smiled in return. "It's so nice to meet you. But we shouldn't stay, Miss Seeta. We don't want to intrude on your family dinner. I should have written and asked about when to come up."

Seeta waved away Callie's words with her hand. "I knew you was comin' today. That's why we set extra chairs at the table, and Mattie cooked up two whole chickens." She chuckled. "And you brought me the doctor I prayed about. Y'all come in now. It's cold outside. Zeke and Delia be home any minute. They late." She shook her head. "Brother James musta preached today."

The women led them into the small front room. A cheery little Fraser fir stood in the corner. Its fragrance filled the space. It was covered with red and gold ornaments, popcorn strings, and tiny crocheted snowflakes. "Your tree is lovely, Miss Seeta," Callie said.

Seeta grinned. "Thank you. We like to put Cal in front of it and watch his little eyes go every which way at all the play-purties. Here, Doctor, set down your coats, and I'll get you and Mizz Beecham some coffee."

"Please, Miss Seeta. No need for formalities in front of Sam. And let me know how I can help. I'm not much of a cook, but I can set the table," she joked.

Sam took their coats and laid them aside then said, "And please, call me Sam. Thank you for welcoming us to Sunday dinner." He smiled, and his blue eyes crinkled. Callie was tickled to see Mattie shyly drop her gaze. Sam's eyes had that effect on women.

Seeta eyed the man and nodded. "You call me Granny—or Seeta."

Mattie spoke up. "If you can mash taters, Sam, we could use the muscle. Mizz Callie, I 'spect we just give you forks to lay out."

Sam began to unbutton his cuffs and push up his sleeves as they followed the women into the warm kitchen. "Oy. Ladies, the smell of fried chicken is making my mouth water. The meals at Sara Cane's have been weeks of vegetable casseroles. She means well. I'm her only boarder right now, and she has been patient with me in my attempt to keep kosher."

"Kosher—what's that?" Mattie asked.

"He tries to keep himself from eating anything cooked with lard," Callie said with a chuckle.

"How else you gonna fry chicken, Sam?" Mattie shrugged.

Sam sighed. "And that chicken smells like heaven on earth. I'll risk it."

"How did you know I would come today, Seeta?" Callie asked. "I don't have a car, and we only just this morning decided to make the trip."

Seeta patted Callie on the shoulder. "I just knew. I'm glad you brought Sam. Ain't been any doctors up this way I can remember. Callie, baby, you go on an' set the table. The silverware's in that drawer there," she directed.

Mattie steered Sam toward the large cast-iron pot full of boiled potatoes. She handed him a potato masher, and he set to his task immediately.

She scooped a large spoonful of butter from a crock and dropped it into the pot of potatoes. "So, you is a doctor, Sam? That's mighty fine."

Sam nodded. "Yes, ma'am." He paused. "You all up this way sure have a long way into town to see Dr. Davis. I guess his practice is the closest."

Seeta and Mattie exchanged glances. Seeta chuckled. "Sam, Dr. Davis don't see folks like us. Never has."

Sam looked from Seeta to Mattie and then to Callie, confused. "What do you mean?"

Mattie smiled at Sam's ignorance as she set a cup of steaming coffee down near Callie. "Dr. Davis don't treat coloreds, sugar."

"Unless we can find a way to the hospital way down in Six Mile," Seeta added. "They'll see coloreds—if we pay cash up front."

She steered herself around the table and sat heavily in one of the chairs. "Isn't that why y'all here?" she asked. "We thankful to the Lawd for bringing you. Folks here been without medical care for too long."

Sam plunged the masher into the pot of steaming potatoes and shook his head. "Dr. Davis is a decent man. He may not make house calls to many folks anymore, but he will see any patient who comes to the office."

Mattie snorted and quickly covered her mouth in embarrassment.

Callie sipped her coffee. "Sam, Dr. Davis has been here longer than I've been alive, and he's always been—selective—about who he would see on a house call. He'll see the mayor's family. The bank president, Grady Wilcox. He would probably never visit the likes of my neighbor, Silas Roberts. Even some white people don't get office appointments with Davis unless they pay upfront. That's probably why I've been able to make a living with my herbals. Poor people have no choice . . . My own mother didn't." She shrugged. "You see why I was so surprised when Mildred Davis showed up for treatment."

Seeta folded her arms across her chest. "Colored folks ain't allowed into his office. There used to be a sign near the back door of the building that said as much. I don't know if it's still there," she said.

Sam blanched. "I've never gone through the back door." He resumed his work, head down. "I'll have to check on his policy about house calls. But I assure you, I cannot imagine a doctor refusing to treat a patient who shows up in the office. Any patient. We take an oath."

Mattie cackled. "You ain't from around here, is you?"

Callie looked to Seeta. "Seeta, I would be happy to see y'all up here if folks want herbals. If I can find transportation. It's a long way—my backside can't take much of Subie, for sure."

Seeta patted Callie's arm but kept her gaze focused on Sam, who was furiously mashing potatoes. "Of *course* it would help us, baby girl. Maybe you and Dr. Sam could think on a plan? Before he turns those taters into soup?"

Sam turned and looked at his host. "I doubt I can help much, Seeta. I work in the office Monday through Friday and I'm on call on weekends."

Callie spoke up. "I was a nurse's aide during the war. What do folks here need?"

Seeta thought. "Most have minor ailments I used to have treatments for. We got stomach complaints and some vitamin deficiencies. I suspect Mrs. Merck has somethin' wrong with her nerves . . ."

Callie looked toward Sam for help, but he only stared into the pot of potatoes. She swallowed hard. "I'll come up and help. I can't promise I have everything folks need, but I'll try."

Seeta raised her eyes toward the ceiling. "Thank you, Jesus!"

— • —

The front door suddenly opened, and a gust of cold air blew into the warm room. Zeke and his little family hurried in. After more greetings and compliments on little Cal, the group sat down to eat dinner.

"Sam, would you say the blessin'?" Seeta asked.

Sam glanced at Callie nervously before bowing his head. "Blessed are you, Lord our God, Ruler of the universe, who brings forth bread from the Earth."

Unsure eyes opened slowly. Soon dishes were being passed, and the conversation began again. Fragrant fried chicken, creamed corn, mashed potatoes, and hot yeast rolls slathered in butter were piled in heaps on everyone's plates. The mood was cheerful and light. The baby lay nearby in his bassinet, swaddled in blankets. Delia looked the picture of health and cooed at her boy lovingly. Callie listened to the women gab about family, neighbors, and plans for Christmas, as Sam and Zeke discussed automobiles.

This must be what it's like to have a family, she mused.

After a while, Seeta passed the platter of fried chicken around a second time. Sam took the platter and helped himself to another leg. "Ladies, this is the best chicken I've ever had. I believe I'll make it another few weeks on boarding house casseroles after this delicious meal."

Seeta smiled. "Thank you, Sam."

Callie eyed Sam's plate. "Given up on kosher?"

Sam patted his stomach and grinned. "How can anyone find fault with Mattie's cooking? God will forgive me this once, I'm sure."

Seeta regarded her guests. "What's this *kosher*?"

Sam swallowed a mouthful of corn and dabbed his mouth with his napkin. "I'm Jewish. Keeping kosher is a Jewish dietary law that just went out the window with this delicious meal. I have no regrets."

Zeke slapped his hand on the table. "A Jew?" he gasped, with an air of incredulity. "Well, I'll be!"

Seeta looked at her grandson. "Mind yo' manners, Zeke."

Zeke dabbed his mouth with his napkin. "I thought that was a funny blessin' is all . . ."

Sam smiled. "It's called the *Hamotzi*. Jewish people say it before any meal including bread." He winked at Zeke and added, "We have another blessing for fruits and one for vegetables, too, but the *Hamotzi* usually covers it all."

Callie detected the flush of embarrassment crawling up Sam's neck and decided to change the subject. "Seeta, were you always a midwife?"

Seeta sipped her water before speaking. "I midwifed babies black and white since after the war. When I was young, well, I won't talk about that time. That's the dead time."

Callie felt her own face go crimson.

Sam leaned forward. "So, you've midwifed the past ten years?"

"No, darlin'. Not the war with them Germans. The big war—the war with the North," Seeta said proudly. "I delivered my first baby in 1878."

Sam's eyebrows went up. "You must have seen some amazing things. I'd love to hear your stories."

Callie put a hand on Sam's arm. "Sam, I'm not sure that childbirth stories are dinner conversation."

Sam reddened. "Oh, of course not. My apologies. I just can't imagine all that has changed in fifty years."

"Babies still come the same way," Seeta said with a smile.

Behind them, Delia had gotten up to soothe her fussing infant. Mattie stood at the sideboard and began to slice and plate thick wedges of apple pie.

"That's alright, Sam," Seeta said. She sat back in her chair and watched him finish the last of the chicken. "When I first came to Liberia, Mama Jane was all we had in this corner of the world. She wasn't my real mama, but she took me in. I was a young widow woman with two little boys . . . She taught me what she knew. Everyone that needed someone here called on Mama Jane. Mama Jane never lost a baby nor a mother. She delivered near two hundred babies in her time. Showed me how to make plant medicine. How to conjure. When she died some years later, I kep' bringin' babies into the world and treatin' folks with herbs and tinctures I'd make up," she said. "I bet I delivered two hundred babies in my time, too."

Mattie set pie plates in front of everyone, but no one moved to raise a fork.

Seeta's face fell. "But around 1900, the cotton mills came on, an' white men could get payin' jobs. They stopped trustin' a colored granny woman to tend their wives. The ones that could pay the new white doctor—they did. Even the ones who couldn't pay the white doctor would barter with him. The town doctor started tellin' folks that midwives and granny women was ignorant an' dirty."

"Dr. Davis?" Callie asked haltingly.

Seeta nodded. "Truth is, I never seen a doctor that knew more about deliverin' babies than a good midwife. But he kep' it up. An' so white folks stopped callin' on me."

Seeta pointed to Callie. "She was the last baby I birthed. 1901. Probably because her mama lived so far out in the sticks they might as well have lived in Liberia." She chuckled. "They paid me with a haunch of venison and fresh butter."

Seeta continued. "When Mr. Beecham died, her mama asked me to stay on and tend Callie so she could go back to work. My boys was—" She hesitated. "Was both grown by then. We got on fine. I grew her garden, made my plant medicines there, and watched over Callie. But some white folks in town didn't like me takin' care of her baby. I remember a few times rocks was thrown through Kizzy's windows. One evenin', someone set fire to an old dead tree in the front yard real near the house. Kizzy and I 'bout run ourselves ragged tryin' to tote water from the well so's it wouldn't burn down the house. We wasn't botherin' nobody way out there, but boy, they sent Kizzy an' me a message—an' I said, 'Message received!'" Seeta put her hand to her forehead in mock salute. "When Mr. and Mrs. Gilstrap from the mill got involved, I had to go. Mr. Gilstrap was the mill boss. He was also a leader in the Klan."

Zeke and Delia exchanged glances. "Granny, they don't need to hear that," Delia said softly. "Let's eat our pie."

Seeta glared at Delia over the rim of her spectacles. "Child, they should know. Folks got to know the truth. Anyway, after men in bedsheets showed up one night an' scared Kizzy half to death, she tol' me I wasn't needed any more." She toyed with her napkin. "They put the fear into her."

Callie paled. "I didn't know that. Mrs. Gilstrap—I stayed with her until I was maybe five or six? After that, I remember I was back with Mama, on my own after school. I had chores to do until she came home. She wouldn't let me get a job at the mill. Absolutely forbid it. She always came home dog-tired and coughing, with lint in her hair. She wanted better for me."

She shifted in her seat. "I don't remember Mr. Gilstrap very well. I was sixteen when Mama passed away, and he sent flowers and offered me her job as a spinner. I finished school, instead, and that made him angry. Anyhow, that was the last I heard of him. He died around the time we went to war, and I left. I surely didn't know the Klan was here then. Or that Mr. Gilstrap was involved." She thought for a moment. "I guess that when I saw Klan rally notices in the paper, I ignored what they stood for."

"They still here." Seeta directed her gaze toward Callie. "Girl, you wouldn't believe what some folks'll do with their hatred. I seen it firsthand. They's ugliness in the world. They's lots of beauty, too, but the ugliness has got the upper hand right now. Lots of folks is church-goin' on Sunday, but they'd as soon burn down our houses or shoot at us on Monday—an' you'd never believe who would join that nasty bunch."

Delia shook her head. "Granny, please."

Callie leaned forward in her seat. "It's alright, Delia. Who is so bent on harassing y'all? You keep to yourselves." She instantly reddened after hearing her own words. "I mean, not that they have *any* excuses for violence."

Seeta sighed. "Some people got to have someone else beneath 'em. Maybe it's human nature. After the war between the states, most black folks I remember stayed where they were an' sharecropped for white bosses. But when the boll weevil came on, the white farmers an' then the mill workers fell into hard times. People was either starvin' on land they didn't own or had left an' gone north. The ones that was still livin' here? We felt like we was lucky to be left alone. We have our own land an' grow most of our own food. Even so, they's many a time a white man'll still just come up here and stake out land an' then tell black folks it ain't theirs. Even though we been on this land for near fifty years, most ain't got papers on it, so white folks come an' take it away. Happens all the time."

"Can't the law help?" Sam asked.

Zeke snorted. "The sheriff comes up from time to time, checks things out, act like he doin' his job. But the very next day, a truck full of white men will come up the road to harass folks, to let it be known we got to keep in our place. That they didn't like us callin' the law. Joe Bibb 'round the corner tried to fence some acreage handed down from his own daddy. They cut all his fencin' and then burned his corn field. Killed his cows." He looked at his wife and added, "I been stopped on the road a time or two."

"Some white men don't like that Zeke has a payin' job," Seeta said. "I worry every time he goes to Dacusville."

Zeke leaned forward. "Sam, if you're a friend of Doc Davis, I guess we said too much."

Sam propped his elbows on the table and addressed Zeke. "I have a hard time believing Earl Davis is a Klan member, but you won't find me to be a friend of anyone in the Klan."

Zeke scowled. "The Klan don't like Jewish folks. No, sir." Delia elbowed her husband in the ribs, but he only shrugged. "That's a fact. Next to black folks, Jews is right down there. You have Klan after you before?"

"Oh yes. My family is in Atlanta," Sam began. "We had a pretty good life there when I was a small boy. My father was a surgeon and active in Jewish organizations. We went to Temple. I attended a Hebrew *shule*—a school. We lived in a nice neighborhood, and our neighbors knew we were Jewish . . . but people turned on us in an instant when something lit the flame."

He paused to take out a pack of Lucky Strikes. "No pun intended," he joked. He extended the pack to Zeke, who took a cigarette. Callie and the other women shook their heads. Sam produced a silver lighter and leaned to light Zeke's cigarette before lighting his own.

The men smoked silently for a while.

Finally, Zeke's eyes narrowed. "What happened?"

Callie watched a shadow cross over Sam's usually cheerful face. He looked around the table and continued his story. "My father had a Jewish friend named Leo Frank." He paused to see if the name meant anything to anyone. "They were in *B'nai B'rith* together." The table stared blankly at him. "Kind of like a club that does good deeds?" Heads nodded.

"He would occasionally come to our home for dinner. He was a young man, and my big sisters liked his visits—they found him quite handsome. I was a teenage boy. My interests were elsewhere."

"Anyway, in 1913, Mr. Frank was framed for the murder of a young girl at the factory he managed. It was quite the trial. It was in all the papers. People picketed at the courthouse and screamed 'Hang the Jew!' before the trial even got underway. Eventually, my father was called as a character witness, and he spent a few days being questioned. It troubled him greatly. He was under a lot of duress, and he was never the same after that. He was threatened and spit on as he left the courthouse each day. Patients started asking whether my father was really Jewish—and then canceling surgeries. Obscenities were screamed out of car windows whenever my sisters or mother walked down our street. It was as if neighbors discovered our Jewishness and were determined we'd pay for it. Christian folks we thought were our friends turned against us. And Mr. Frank was convicted, despite a lack of evidence. He was sentenced to death."

"Damn," Zeke muttered.

Sam blew out a thin column of smoke and continued. "But the governor intervened and said Leo Frank hadn't had a fair trial. He commuted Leo's sentence to life in prison. While he was serving time in Milledgeville, Georgia, a white supremacist mob busted him out of jail—and lynched him in an oak grove owned by the former sheriff."

Callie reached out and touched Sam's arm, but he didn't acknowledge her gesture. *I'm sorry. I shouldn't have brought you here.*

Zeke nodded his head. "Fear makes people do ugly things. I didn't know they'd lynch a white man."

"Well, he was a Jew," Sam shrugged. "After that, the Klan rose up and became quite popular. You know—the film *Birth of a Nation*, and all that. Atlanta is their Imperial City. They made it known that colored people, Jews—all immigrants actually—were not welcome. Still aren't. There are judges and men in city government who are proud Klansmen. They go to church, do charity work, support popular causes. They even formed an amateur baseball team and played in the Dixie League." He puffed on his cigarette. "I think one of their teams won the championship in '24."

Zeke inhaled until the cigarette tip glowed orange. He exhaled a stream of blue smoke. "So what'd y'all do?"

Sam shrugged. "My family stopped being Jewish for a while. No Temple. No *Shabbatt*. No Jewish clubs. Nothing. We tried to behave like the Christians all around us. We even put a Christmas tree in our front window for a few years. We were still harassed. Nasty letters showed up in our mailbox. Someone splashed red paint across our driveway and wrote 'Jesus killer' in the mess.

"My father's health deteriorated from the stress. He sold our house, and we moved to a different neighborhood," Sam said. "In time, he gradually won patients back, mainly because he was a fantastic surgeon. I enrolled at Emory University and spent four years there away from the worst of the racism. I thought about dental school, but Emory did not allow Jews to enroll. Still, I was lucky. I moved to New York City and went to medical school. I had Jewish friends who served in the war and came back to Atlanta to find the hate toward us even stronger than ever."

"What about New York?" Zeke asked, leaning forward. "Can a black man get a fair shake up there?"

Sam thought for a moment. "Maybe. But Seeta is right. It seems people always want to have someone else to look down on, don't they? Isn't that the vile thing about human nature? We always look for someone else to put below our own feet. In the city, there were always new immigrants, and some of them had to be the lowest of the low. For a while. Until the next group came. When I first got to New York, there were two million immigrants from other countries. Two million! I'd never seen as much poverty and disease as I saw in the tenements and slums there."

"Around here, we is the lowest of the low," Zeke muttered angrily.

Sam shook his head. "Zeke, I have to say—your home, this beautiful valley, compared to some of the Lower East Side slums I worked in, you live in a castle."

Zeke snorted. "So many folks are leavin' here for factory work an' jobs out west and up north. Sometimes, I think that me and Delia should pack up and move north, too. Like Uncle Marcus."

Callie watched Seeta's jaw clench at the mention of her long-gone son.

Sam stubbed out his cigarette on his plate. "Harlem is a neat place. I went to a lot of jazz shows there. Colored people and white people dancing in the same clubs. And colored people work at factories and shops, own restaurants and dance halls, and get better-paying jobs than down here. But if you're asking me whether they're treated equally up there? No. I'm sorry. They are not. Not even in New York City."

"Uncle Marcus got a good job up north, didn't he, Granny?" Zeke asked. "In Chicago?"

Callie's stomach wrenched. The day was spiraling out of control, and she didn't want to see Sam or her new friend, Seeta, slogging through any more bad memories.

Seeta nodded, eyes closed. "That was more than twenty-five years ago, Zeke."

Zeke seemed to ignore his grandmother's comment. "Yessir, sometimes I think about headin' up that way myself."

"Seeta, did your son write to you about the Red Summer?" Sam asked. "So many black people were killed. Whole neighborhoods burned down. The northern cities saw incredible violence. It was horrific. And after so many black men served our country during the war." He paused. "In Chicago, it started when a black boy swimming in Lake Michigan drifted into the white section. The crowd stoned him, and then he drowned."

Callie wanted to stand up, to thank Seeta for the meal, apologize, and run away. Instead, she heard Sam continue.

"But I think it actually started in the springtime in Georgia that year. 1919. I remember the headlines. In Jenkins County, two white policemen were killed in a scuffle near a colored church, and then a white mob burned down the church and lynched several men . . ." His voice trailed off.

"Sam," Callie murmured. "Please. We're guests."

Sam shifted in his chair. "Zeke, have you heard of the gifted Harlem poet named Langston Hughes? He writes about the black man's trials."

Zeke shook his head. "Ain't never heard of him."

"I'll lend you a book he wrote. There's a poem—"The Weary Blues"—about a black man standing on a corner, singing the blues." Sam sucked on his cigarette and exhaled slowly.

"I got the weary blues and I can't be satisfied.
Got the weary blues and can't be satisfied—
I ain't happy no more and I wish that I had died.
And far into the night he crooned that tune.
The stars went out and so did the moon.

The singer stopped playing and went to bed,
While the Weary Blues echoed through his head.
He slept like a rock or a man that's dead."

Zeke grinned. "I see as how that could apply to most anyone here in Liberia."

"And yet he was writing about people in Harlem," Sam said pointedly.

Zeke puffed on his cigarette one last time before putting it out on his plate. He exhaled a cloud of smoke and leaned toward Sam. "So you weren't worried about coming up here today?" He glanced at Callie. "Don't get me wrong. I was the happiest man in the world when Mizz Callie came up and saved my Delia. But she's a healer woman. You a real doctor. An' Jewish. Ain't you worried about Dr. Davis findin' out you was in a colored town?"

Sam smiled. "I wasn't—until you all told me he is in the Klan."

Callie felt a tightness in her chest, a regret that the talk of racism had brought the mood down so completely. Seeta began to hum, eyes still closed. Callie watched the woman and felt an old memory rise up from the haze of her past. She was maybe two or three years old. Toddling near a burbling creek on a late summer day, basket in hand. Seeta was with her, singing a song and watching over her as the little girl picked purple passionflowers. Callie stumbled and fell into the cold water. She remembered the basket upending, sending purple petals adrift like little boats, and the pain of skinned palms, a face full of cold water. Strong brown arms lifted her out of the cold creek, and held her close for warmth. A man's arms.

Mattie spoke up. "Well, I don't want to hear no more sad talk. It's almost Christmas, y'all. Sam, we is glad you here. Now, how did you end up workin' in Pickens?"

"I needed a job, Mattie. My mother remembered Dr. Davis and his wife from a medical conference where they'd met," Sam said. "She begged on my behalf, I won't lie." He chuckled nervously. "And I hoped that, here, no one would care that I'm Jewish."

Zeke looked at Sam with some humor. "Says the blue-eyed doctor. Least your skin don't give you away."

"Zeke!" Delia hissed, laying a hand on her husband's arm. "You is makin' this a awful Sunday dinner fo' Granny's guests."

Mattie stood to clear dishes. "That's enough of that. This is the Lawd's day, an' we all friends, ain't we?"

Seeta pointed a finger at Sam. "There's a powerful strong hate around here, an' one misstep is all it takes. You be careful now."

Sam smiled. "I will, Seeta."

Suddenly little Cal let out a wail, and the gloomy mood was broken. Delia lifted the crying infant, and there were soothing words from all around.

"Well, if y'all excuse me, I best feed this child and change his diaper." Delia nodded and left the room.

"We should go," Callie said, glancing out at the darkening sky. "We've taken up most of your afternoon." She stood and began to help clear plates.

Sam looked at Seeta. "I'm sorry. I had no call to bring you all that dark account of my past, especially during a family meal you so kindly invited us to join. Forgive me. The meal was delicious."

Seeta smiled. "I'm glad you came. You don't ever need an invite here. Don't worry 'bout the dishes, babies. Zeke got dishes on Sundays when me and Mattie cook." She looked at Callie as if to say something, but did not.

Callie placed a stack of plates on the kitchen counter. "I mean it, Seeta. I will find a way to help y'all out. When should I come back?"

Seeta smiled at Callie. "How about New Year's Day at the church? Can't think of a better time an' place to do the Lord's healin'."

— • —

The ride home was a quiet one. Sam seemed lost in thought. The early winter dark illuminated lamplit windows as the car turned onto Florence Avenue. Only when the car pulled up to the curb in front of Callie's house, did she dare speak.

"Thank you, Sam," Callie offered. "For the ride up there today. I had no idea it would bring up such terrible memories. I had no idea about your father . . ." There was no response.

She tried again. "I'd love to have you over for Christmas dinner. Silas Roberts is my only other guest."

Sam only nodded.

"I suppose that taking me to Liberia turned into a bigger day than you anticipated." She reached for the door handle. "If you want to join me up there on New Year's Day, let me know. They could really use your help."

Sam shook himself out of his distraction and opened his door. He hurried around to the passenger side, yanked the door open, and extended his hand.

When he didn't immediately release her hand, Callie asked hopefully, "Would you come in for a cup of coffee?"

He dropped her hand and shoved his own hands into his pockets. "I'm sorry I've been brooding. The conversation with Zeke makes me wonder. What am I doing here? Why *did* I think South Carolina would be an easy place to fit into?" He looked at Callie with sad eyes. "I know the answer. I assumed that bigots here would be focused on colored folks—and wouldn't know a Jewish name if they heard one. I was hoping to avoid being part of the problem. It didn't occur to me that I should be part of the solution."

"No one is harassing you, Sam." Callie tried to focus on Sam's features in the gathering dark. "Dr. Davis hired you. Mildred Davis and your patients think you hung the moon. So what—your last name is Epstein." She shrugged. "I think most folks here don't even know you're Jewish. It's fine."

"If I go back to Sara Cane's and stick a menorah in my window to celebrate Hanukkah or wear a yarmulke, will they be fine with it?" Sam asked. "If I make house calls in Liberia, will they be fine with it?"

Callie backed up. "Where is this coming from? Nothing has changed. Are you angry at me?"

"Maybe I am a little angry with you," Sam said. "I don't want to travel up to Liberia and treat people. I want to keep my head down. Fit in. Keep my job. Practice medicine, live a simple life, and just pretend the white world doesn't hate Jews. Because it does, Callie. Almost as much as it hates black people. And Poles and Italians and Irish . . . I may not be a Negro, but I know that I don't fit into what folks expect around here." He paused and shook his head. "I didn't know that Dr. Davis is a Klansman. Why would he hire a Jew?"

"Sam, stop. Even if it was as a favor, he hired you. You're doing well. He made a sound business decision."

Sam appeared not to hear her. "It is hard enough when patients think I am a Yankee." He shook his head.

Callie tried again. "You have to remember that the Civil War ended just sixty years ago. People don't forget the Yankee thing so easily. But they know you now. They know you're a southerner, and they like you. Being Jewish won't matter. You're here with Davis's blessing. I'm sure of it."

"You're naïve, Callie," he muttered.

She bristled. "I was wrong. Not naïve. I shouldn't have assumed you'd be happy to help me up there."

He ran his hand through his hair. "I have been given a chance. I could mess it up by going to treat people in Liberia—and the guilt from that will eat at me."

"Don't go, then," Callie said crisply. She opened her purse to retrieve her key. "No one is forcing your hand." She clicked the clasp of her purse closed and turned to walk up the sidewalk toward her front door. She saw George stand and stretch from his spot on the back of the sofa under the front window. She was suddenly eager to get inside to where her life was orderly and simple and quiet. "Good night," she called.

Behind her, she heard Sam's receding footsteps. The engine cranked and turned over. Soon the car was chugging loudly down the road.

Chapter Seven

A glorious orange sunset on Christmas Eve found Callie dressed in her burgundy wool suit, heels clicking down the sidewalk as she made her way to Hilltop Baptist Church's evening service. A steady stream of people approached the steepled brick building from different directions. She joined the queue and entered the warm and brightly lit sanctuary.

A surprised usher handed her a bulletin. "Good to see you here, Miss Beecham. Hope you'll join us again in the new year."

They think I'm a heathen. She smiled nervously and slipped into the last pew. As she tucked her purse at her feet, there was a tap on her shoulder. An older couple stood smugly and waited. Callie made her apologies and slid to the middle of the pew and out of the couple's regular seats.

The organ began to play "Holy, Holy, Holy," and the congregation rose as one to sing along. Callie fumbled for the hymnal and soon found the song on page one. As she sang, she scanned the crowd and noticed people she had known since birth. In such a small town, everyone knew everyone.

In the choir loft alone, she saw two old girlfriends, chums from grade school. Both were now married with several children apiece. She saw patients whom she had treated over the years, for everything from allergies to earaches to liver ailments. Grady Wilcox stood in the front row. She recognized him by his enormous girth and thunderous bass voice. Would he really deny her access to his bank? She had a stash of bills and coins hidden in her mattress and wanted to open an account somewhere.

Dr. and Mrs. Davis stood near him, heads bent together over their shared hymnal. Callie knew she should be grateful that Mildred Davis had chosen to seek her help. Despite her husband's dislike of Callie, Mildred had referred several new clients. Callie had been able to put a radio on layaway at the hardware store because of them. And the woman had been kind to invite Callie to Thanksgiving, despite how it turned out.

One pew over was Flora Price, owner of Flora's House of Beauty. *Why is it so hard for me to stop in and book an appointment?* Why did she feel unworthy of a good haircut? She kept to herself too much, she knew, and her reserved personality made it difficult for her to even bravely step out to church on Christmas Eve, much less be the center of someone's attention at a beauty parlor. She fingered the loose tendrils of dark hair that always managed to escape their pins. She'd been cutting her own thick hair for years, and it showed. Maybe 1929 was the year to be a little more daring. A little more courageous. A new look might help her win back Sam's affections. They had not spoken since their visit to Seeta's. She supposed he was in good hands at Sara Cane's for the holiday, but still wondered what abruptly changed his disposition. She was beyond sorry that she had tried to convince him to volunteer in Liberia.

The pastor came forward and began to read from Chapter Two in the Book of Luke. His voice boomed.

"And the angel said unto them Fear not: for, behold I bring you good tidings of great joy which shall be to all people. For unto you is born this day in the city of David a Saviour, which is Christ the Lord."

Good tidings, Callie mouthed silently. *To all people.* She found it hard to reconcile what Seeta had said about Dr. Davis and the Klan, seeing him here in church. True, she'd seen announcements in the local paper of Klan meetings and gatherings. Temperance rallies and picnics featuring Klan speakers. They were not at all secretive about their activity. Recently, the Klan had organized a Saturday series of lectures in a Greenville park. "*Everybody welcome!*" signs had said. "*Eats and Drinks Served on the Grounds!*"

Maybe they aren't the same branch as in Atlanta, she reassured herself. Maybe they were like the Masons. Maybe they were good people. They did seem to wave the cross around quite a bit.

A deacon stood and began to enumerate concerns and praise reports from the congregation. He asked that everyone consider a donation to bring clean water to a missionary's outpost in the heart of darkest Africa. Callie thought of Liberia, just up the road. No medical care, no electricity or running water or telephones. The nearest market was at the crossroads miles away. The people from Liberia were unwelcome at the doctor's office, the bank, the library, and Hilltop Baptist Church. When the deacon asked visitors to stand and be recognized, Callie shrank in her seat. Would Sam Epstein be welcome here? Would Seeta ever be invited to come and sit in this place and listen to the word of God? What if she brought poor, bedraggled Silas, with his tangled and stained beard and patched clothes? What would happen then?

The deacon asked everyone to turn to page 79 in their hymnals. The piano began the first strains of "O Come, All Ye Faithful" and the congregation sang as one.

The pastor rose and welcomed everyone again before beginning his sermon.

Callie tried to focus but found her mind wandering. Christmas as an eight-year-old meant only an orange, a new dress made of remnants from the mill, and maybe some drawing paper, if she was lucky. There were never invited guests to share Christmas dinner because there wasn't much to share. She and her mother were alone. She forced herself to think on the several years with the Gilstraps, years of relative plenty. Lottie Gilstrap made sure Callie had plenty of food. Plenty of clothing and toys. But the little girl ached for her own mother who could only visit on her day off. She'd never asked her mother about those years, but the feeling of being abandoned was still acute.

She suddenly remembered again being three years old, the basket of passionflowers hooked through her arm, not a care in the world. Again, she saw the basket topple and splash into the icy creek. Strong brown arms lifted her up, and a deep voice consoled her—a man's arms and a man's voice. He collected her petals and put them back into the basket with care. Who was he?

Of course, Seeta's late husband might have come to help out. Or one of her relatives. Some kind and gentle colored man had been there. She was sure of it. She'd have to ask Seeta.

Callie knew that several women in Mildred Davis's social circle employed Negro maids. Most white women of means did the same. Why would hiring Seeta to look after her baby have been any different for Kizzy Beecham? And what made the Gilstraps so upset they wanted Seeta gone? The Gilstraps lived on the other side of Pickens, far away from the tiny Beecham place near Pumpkintown. Why would Seeta have been chased away?

Callie blinked and tried to focus on the sermon. Her mind drifted to lonely Silas Roberts laid up on his sofa, and to Sam, probably spending the night reading alone by the fire, while the Christian world celebrated the most holy night of the year in church, with stockings hung by the fires at home.

Sam was right, of course. She had already heard talk from several of her regular clients about his being a Jewish man—and a Yankee at that. She had tried to set the Yankee story to rights, but the fact was he was Jewish. *Like Jesus*, she thought.

Where was Sam anyway? Was he in town? Was he with friends in Atlanta? What had happened to their budding friendship? She pictured his kind blue eyes and the shock of dark hair he was constantly pushing out of his eyes. His hair smelled of Brilliantine. The dark hair on the backs of his hands and his strong arms under thin shirt sleeves . . .

The congregation finally rose to sing "Angels from the Realms of Glory." Callie realized she hadn't listened to a single word of the sermon.

— • —

On Christmas morning, Callie tossed the quilts back eagerly and hopped out of bed. The sun streamed through the open curtains and played across her bare floor. She shivered and grabbed her bathrobe. Ever since she was a little girl expecting nothing more than a homemade dress and a chocolate bar from Santa, the magic and expectation of Christmas morning never faded.

She stood at the stove waiting on the coffee to boil, George winding around her legs and meowing for his breakfast. She expected Silas at three o'clock for Christmas dinner, and there was much to be done. She planned to serve ham and scalloped potatoes, his favorites, green beans, and corn pudding, with a chocolate cake for dessert. Same meal every year was what suited Silas Roberts, she knew. He would bring whiskey, and she was honestly looking forward to a bit of holiday cheer, despite what Sam Epstein had said about alcohol.

One year, she hoped to splurge on a standing rib roast, but they were incredibly expensive. All of her extra money went toward the new radio, which would be hers in just two more payments. She wondered what it would be like to celebrate Christmas in the Davis's home with its plush carpets, furniture polished to a sheen, and delicate bone china placed just so on the long dining room table. She remembered the beautiful arrangement of hothouse flowers displayed at Thanksgiving as the table centerpiece and knew that they must have cost Earl a pretty penny. She shook the thought out of her mind and grabbed her ceramic mug from the shelf.

Stooping to feed George, she heard the clink of bottles outside that told her the milkman left a quart of milk and the whipping cream she'd asked for special. The coffee pot began to gurgle, and Callie hurried to take it off of the stove. She poured the black coffee into her cup and watched the splash of cream turn the coffee a rich brown. *The color of Seeta's skin,* she thought.

There had been no word from Sam, and, most likely, he would not be celebrating anyway. The day in Liberia had apparently alarmed him greatly. She'd had no idea that he was worried about losing his job because he was Jewish. But his story of the lynched inmate Leo Frank was frightening, and it paralleled the fear that Zeke and his family probably faced every day. She had seen horrific photographs—black men swaying from tree limbs like low-hanging fruit, necks bent at impossible angles. A thing so wrong, and yet not a crime that was outlawed anywhere in the South. She shuddered.

— • —

Silas leaned back in his chair and sighed. "Callie, that was the best Christmas dinner I have ever eaten. I can't thank you enough for havin' me." He picked at some stray crumbs in his long beard.

Callie smiled. "I'm glad you came. I wasn't sure you'd be able to get up and around so soon after Dr. Epstein saw you. You were quite drunk, and you know that isn't good for you," she chided.

"Your medicine always works a cure on me. You know that. But I been drinkin' that apple cider vinegar and eating more vegetables like you said." Silas winked at Callie. "I thought I'd see that young feller here today, judgin' by what I heard at my place."

Callie reddened. "You old skunk. I wondered if you were awake or passed out cold." She stood and asked, "Coffee now?"

"Coffee sounds real fine, but first—I have a Christmas present for you." Silas's blue eyes were bright. "Step onto your front porch an' see what Santy Claus brung you."

Callie made to protest but Silas held up a hand. "I wanted to thank you for everything you do for me. Shoulda done it years ago. Now open the door."

Callie clapped her hands together excitedly and hurried to open the front door. There on the stoop stood a brand new Philco radio set, its beautiful walnut case polished to a high shine.

Callie could not help herself, and she squealed with delight. "Silas, oh my goodness! What have you done? I saw this one in the hardware store and could never have afforded it!"

"I know that." Silas beamed. "I went there yesterday, and he showed me the one you made the payments on in layaway, but this here's a better one. You got yourself a credit down there now. Help me bring it in and plug it up. We'll have ourselves some Christmas music. Sometimes, I can even get Bristol, Tennessee, on mine. The birthplace of country music!" He limped toward the door, and, together, they rolled the radio into Callie's front room.

"Thank you very much," Callie said. "This is the nicest thing anyone has ever done for me."

Silas plugged in the radio and twisted the dial. Faint voices came and went until they heard a crystal-clear tenor voice singing "Santa Claus That's Me."

"That there is Vernon Dalhart," Silas said. "I'm not a huge fan but at least it's a Christmas song."

Callie sat down and listened to the cheery little tune. She shook her head in wonder. "Silas, again, thank you so much—but it must have cost a fortune."

Silas waved away her concern with his large hand. "Naw... I ain't got nuthin' to spend my money on, so this made me real happy. You've done so much for me, the least I can do is bring a little joy into your own life."

Callie jumped up and kissed the old man heartily on his bristled cheek. "You're a dear. I have something for you, too." She crossed to the breakfront and opened one of the drawers. She pulled out a thin, wrapped package and handed it to Silas. "Merry Christmas."

Silas rattled the box against his ear. "Now what could this be? I ain't gotten a present since... well, since last Christmas when you gave me the fine scarf you knit." He tore open the wrapping paper and opened the box. "A wristwatch. Say, this is a handsome piece. Callie, you shouldn't spend money on an old codger like me."

"Nonsense. It's a dime store piece and you know it. But I was tired of you always asking me what time it is," she joked.

"Well, I like it. I surely do. Thank you," he said, strapping the watch to his wrist. "Now, how about some coffee, and we can sit a spell and listen to the radio?" He paused and then grinned. "That there is the Carter Family, an' boy, howdy, can they sing."

The two friends sat companionably and listened to Christmas songs, gospel tunes, and shows for several hours—until dusk fell and Callie found herself stifling a yawn.

"That's my cue to go," Silas nodded, checking his new watch. "It's past eight. I guess I overstayed, but it's nice to spend time with someone on Christmas. What a delightful meal. I get lonely at Christmas especially, an' you always have time for me." The man hoisted himself to his feet.

"I love having you over, Silas. Let me get your leftovers, and I'll walk you home. You're still a little unsteady, and the sidewalk is likely to be icy. That silly cane might be a liability," she said, glancing at the ubiquitous twisted laurel cane. She donned her coat and hat and grabbed the covered plate of leftovers. The two stepped out into the crisp night air. Stars winked in the sky and warm lights shone in windows up and down the street.

Callie held the old man's arm as they walked. "Tell me. Why do you use that cane? You know that the drug store sells nice straight canes with handles and rubber tips on the bottom, so you don't slip. I almost got you one of those."

Silas shook his head. "Well, I wouldn't trade this ol' cane for a million dollars. We had mountain laurel on our property when I was first married. My wife loved those trees. Every spring, those pale pink flowers bloomed, and she'd exclaim that the Garden of Eden musta been full of mountain laurels. She thought they was that pretty. When she died, I cut a sturdy branch from one of those trees and made this here cane."

"You still miss her," Callie murmured.

Silas nodded. "Yes, ma'am. I miss my wife and my boy, especially at Christmas. Maybe I'll go home and have a good cry."

Callie patted his hand. She had no words to offer.

"My turn to ask a question. Why did you want to go up to Liberia?" Silas asked. "That day with the young doctor? You asked him for a ride."

Callie hesitated but felt she could trust the man. "I have a friend up there. An old midwife I thought had died long ago. I found out that she was living still, and we paid her a visit. That's all."

Silas stopped in front of his house and stared at Callie in the deepening night. "A midwife? You don't mean Seeta Young now, do ya?"

Callie's mouth opened in surprise. "Y—yes."

He stroked his beard. "So, you remember Seeta? Well, I'll be danged. The Lord works in mysterious way, he does."

"No. I didn't remember her. Her grandson came to me one morning in October, needing a midwife. His wife was having troubles. Seeta sent him to fetch me. She is too old to do much anymore. I believe she's near ninety." Callie cocked her head. "You know Seeta?"

Silas chuckled. "Back in my day, lots of white folks knew Seeta. When I came to this area over thirty years ago, she birthed just about everyone's babies who didn't live in town."

"That's what she said!" Callie exclaimed. She helped at my own birth! She said she stayed on and helped take care of me for a while after my father died. I suppose she'd heard I'd become a healer of sorts. I about fell over. I mean, what a coincidence. There I was at the birth of her own grandchild."

"Is that what she said happened?" Silas asked. His face held a peculiar expression that Callie couldn't decipher.

Callie nodded. "Was she with your wife? When your son was born?"

Silas leaned over and spat on the ground. "I wished to God she had been," he said angrily. "I was too proud to let her."

Callie waited for him to continue.

"Had me a lumber company in Asheville, and it was doin' well. I was a confirmed bachelor—till I met my Rebecca at a concert in the park in the summer of '95. She was the most beautiful thing I'd ever seen. I was thirty-six an' uglier than a pig's backside. She was just twenty. Auburn hair and skin like peaches an' cream. Her family lived in the hills an' didn't have two cents to rub together. Why she fell for an ogre like me, I don't know. Probably my money, but I didn't care." He chuckled. "We married that same year. She was my world."

"I sold my house there, an' we came down here to live, while one of my timber stands near Caesar's Head was logged out. I looked for the chance to live a quiet life, away from all the folks who bowed and scraped to me because of my money. Folks here was good to us. Real kind. I had plans drawn up for a fine house for us. We stayed in a cabin up on the road to Caesar's Head while I worked on those plans. Rebecca was soon pregnant, an' I was king of the world. She wanted the local granny midwife to help her at birth. Seeta Young." He looked at Callie sadly. "But I overruled my wife. I was proud. I called the brand-new doctor in town at the time. Dr. Earl Davis." Silas swallowed hard.

Callie felt the evening chill working its way into her bones. "What happened?"

The man stared into the night sky. "My darling Rebecca died of childbed fever."

"Puerperal fever. . . . I'm so sorry," Callie said softly.

Silas nodded. "Dr. Davis had come from a patient with scarlet fever. He told me that hisself, when he rushed in that mornin'—although he later denied it—and I let him in. He went straight to her bedside. Didn't wash hands—nothin'. She was in so much pain by the time he got there, I jes' stepped aside. William was born soon after. She took ill that night an' died three days later."

"Did he come back when she got sick?" Callie asked incredulously.

"He dawdled, let me say that. I suspect he knew it was his fault. We didn't have a hospital then. I'd sent a rider for Davis, but by the time he came out to see her, she was too far gone, he said. There was nothing to be done, he said. It was awful to watch. So, I sent a message to Seeta Young to please come and help her. She showed up as soon as she got word, but Rebecca had passed." Silas sighed heavily. "So, Seeta cleaned her up and said prayers over her and helped me with baby William until Rebecca's parents could get down for a funeral."

Callie drew her coat around her shivering shoulders. "That's awful, Silas. I had no idea. I didn't know William in school . . ."

"Naw, you wouldn't have. I sent him to live with his grandparents. What was a bitter old cuss like me gonna do with a newborn? I went up there to see him every month. Sent money. When he was ten, I sent him to a fancy boarding school in Charleston, and summers, I'd go down to the coast and meet up with him. We had some good times on the coast. Then he went to the Citadel."

Silas stumbled, and Callie caught his elbow. "Never was a daddy prouder. When he got killed in the war . . ." Silas wiped his eyes with his free hand. "Well, I miss my boy somethin' fierce. It's an ache in my heart that won't never go away."

She patted the old man's hand. "I can't imagine . . . Tell you what, let's go inside, and we'll have a glass of your good stuff before I go home. I think we could both use a drink, and after all, it's Christmas."

Chapter Eight

Sam scanned the road ahead, looking for a filling station through the bug-spattered windshield. With its twenty-horsepower engine, the car purred like a kitten as it sped up the road at forty miles per hour. He was king of the road. He just needed gasoline. The joy of the open road thrilled him, but places to get fuel weren't as plentiful in the country as in Atlanta.

He was anxious to get back to South Carolina, which surprised him. The brief holiday with his mother and his sisters had done much to relieve his worries about their happiness. His sisters had their mother, the widow Margaret Epstein, well in hand. She loved the whirl and busyness of her social scene and seemed to have made peace with the past. His sisters didn't need him at home either. They had children, their charity work, and husbands.

The enumerable social gatherings where he ran into his ex-fiancée, Edith, and her new husband, quickly confirmed his decision to work far away from Atlanta. Edith was stunning, as always, draped in diamonds and mink. Her new husband, a successful surgeon in a major practice, seemed a nice enough fellow, if not put out at seeing his bride's ex-fiancé at every function. Sam felt a surge of relief that he had not married Edith. It surprised him. In fact, his thoughts had turned to Callie many times over the holidays.

The fast pace and the noise of the city suddenly annoyed him. He missed the owl that hooted outside his room in the boarding house deep in the night, and the twinkling stars he could see so clearly in the midnight sky. He missed the distinct southern drawl, slow as molasses, of so many of his patients, down-at-the-heel folks that Davis would not typically see. He even missed their payment in dimes and nickels and an occasional jar of pickled dilly beans or beets. He missed Callie.

He had discussed the Sunday dinner at Seeta's and the little settlement of Liberia with his mother. To his amazement, she seemed supportive of his helping the people there. "We can't let them win, Sam," she'd said knowingly.

He'd told her about Callie and explained his interest in learning about herbal medicine from her.

"You like this girl," his mother had said. "I can tell. Is she—educated?"

Sam had felt the heat crawl into his cheeks. "She was orphaned early. There was no chance of that. But she is smart—resourceful. Beautiful. Owns her own business. She is a very nice girl, Mother."

Margaret Epstein had sighed heavily. "You know there are any number of very nice Jewish girls here who would love to be seen with you, Sam. But if you find someone you care for, truly care for, it is the greatest comfort in life."

She gave her blessing, and Sam drove north that very morning, feeling better than he had in a long time. New Year's Day was two days away, and he had much to organize before he set out for his first day treating patients in Liberia.

There was the issue of medical supplies and medicines. He could not ask Dr. Davis for supplies—that was out of the question. He'd purchased medicines, syringes, a few boxes of bandages, swabs, and mercurochrome from the medical supply shop at Emory. Eventually, he would need to tell his employer about what he was doing. Maybe Earl Davis would be delighted and willing to help. But the odds were that he would be angry and berate Sam, if not sack him. Especially if what Seeta had said was true. The man was a segregationist. Still, armed with his mother's approval, Sam had summoned the courage to treat indigent patients in Liberia. On his own time. On his own dime.

There was the matter of Callie. She had invited him to Christmas dinner, and he'd not responded to the invitation, much less apologized for his rude behavior. How could he explain that he'd been afraid? Afraid to jump in where Callie had no fear. Afraid to appear weak where she seemed so strong. He'd been a cad. She was a beautiful and intelligent woman. Not frivolous. Not worldly. But, oh, so appealing. Her shape, her lips, her dark eyes, and her wild mane of long hair. He smiled and gave the car more gas.

A billboard on his right announced a Standard Oil filling station with ice-cold Coca-Colas ahead at the South Carolina border. He crossed into South Carolina and made a silent promise that he would make it right with Callie somehow.

— • —

Callie turned her head from right to left, admiring her pert new bob. "I like it, Flora!" she announced. "I didn't know a hairstyle could make me feel so happy." She fluffed her hair with her fingers.

"Your smile even looks brighter," Flora said. "Your eyes just shine. Oh, Callie, if I had your thick curls, I'd keep it this way. You look amazing. Your old style was dated. You look years younger with this French side-part bob. You could be a flapper in the pictures," she said with authority. "You have the bone structure of a Clara Bow."

Callie pulled a face and smirked. "I'm just plain me."

"Nonsense!" Flora said. "You're a beautiful woman. So—do you have big plans for New Year's Eve?"

Callie shook her head. "Sitting quietly by the fire listening to the radio."

"Pity. I'd heard that you had lunch a few weeks back with that handsome new doctor. He's a catch." Flora winked. "For a Yankee."

Callie felt her cheeks warm. "It turns out he isn't a Yankee. His family is from Atlanta."

Flora nodded. "But he is a Jew, right? A name like Epstein? Not that I care. But it is a surprise to have one in town. It's quite exotic."

Callie removed the drape and handed the woman a folded five-dollar bill. Flora glanced at it and shook her head. "That's way too much, dear."

Callie shook her head. "Flora, you made me look better than I have in years. Take it. Oh, and if you want that salve we talked about, come see me." She placed her hat jauntily atop her curls, waved, and left the shop quickly.

On Main Street that morning, traffic hummed along, pedestrians, wagons, and a few cars. Callie lifted her face to the warm sun, anxious to make 1929 a fresh start. The day was mild for the end of December. She carried her coat in her arms, her blue wool suit warm enough for the bright day. She scanned a list of supplies to purchase at the drug store.

Two of Mildred Davis's bridge club friends were stopping in later for appointments. Things were looking up. She would be able to get to

Liberia without Sam Epstein, thanks to Silas Roberts' stunning revelation that he owned a car. Sure enough, parked in his dilapidated garage he had shown her an old Model T Ford, ready to be of service. He taught her how to crank the engine, gave her a few driving lessons, and handed her the key. Silas told Callie it was hers to use any time she needed a car.

Suddenly, Callie saw a familiar automobile coming down the street in her direction and her heart jumped. She turned away and gazed intently into a store window as the car rolled by. When it passed, she was chagrined to see Sam, oblivious, at the wheel. Next to him sat proud Sara Cane, surely enraptured by his attention. *So much for that*, she thought. She stomped down the street, her good mood spiraling downward.

After the drug store and several other errands were accomplished, Callie found herself in front of the bank. She did still want to open a small checking account. Would it really cause a scene if she pushed through the doors and stood in line to speak to a teller? Surely, Mr. Wilcox had overreacted in embarrassment when confronted. Spying a long line at the teller windows, she sighed and continued down the block toward home.

When she turned onto Florence Street, she spotted Silas sitting on his front stoop in the sunshine. "Silas, good morning!"

The man leaned back against the steps and grinned. "This is one of them special warm days. Gonna make the daffodils come up too early, but it sure is nice."

Callie nodded. She turned her head coyly from side to side.

The old man squinted in the sunshine. "Girlie, what'd you go and do? You cut off your beautiful hair!"

Callie deflated a little bit. "That wasn't the reaction I was looking for. A new haircut for a new year."

Silas shrugged. "It's fine, I suppose. All you young folks go for short hair on women. But I'm an old man, an' I like long hair. You look like one o' them flappers."

"Well, when I roll my stockings and raise my hemline, you'll know you were right," she teased.

"You all ready for your big day tomorrow? I was thinkin' I might go with ya. I could help out a little." Silas looked at Callie hopefully.

Callie sighed. "That's a long day. You sure your legs can handle it?"

In response, Silas stuck out his spindly legs, and they danced a little jig in the air.

Callie laughed. "I can't very well say no. It's your car. And I am a bit nervous about driving it all the way there on my own. Would you really be alright sitting there all day while I see patients?"

Silas nodded and stroked his beard. "I've been sittin' here for nearly thirty years. It's about time I changed my locality."

— • —

As the clock approached three o'clock, Callie patted her hair and smoothed her apron nervously. A Mrs. John Walton was expected shortly, coming in for what Callie assumed would be women's complaints. Her previous appointment had been a Mrs. Sapp, Mildred's bridge partner, who had come in for just that reason. The shop was clean and orderly, scrubbed and polished, tinctures and syrups for purchase in even rows on shelves. The kettle was on, and George had been banished to the outside for the afternoon. The radio played jazz tunes.

A shiny blue Duesenberg pulled to the curb in front of Callie's house. The car was a showpiece, chrome polished to a high sheen. Callie watched in awe as a uniformed driver hopped out and ran around the car to open the door for his passenger. As the woman emerged, Callie ducked from view. The little bell over the door tinkled and in walked Anne Walton, right on time.

Mrs. Walton appeared much younger than Mildred Davis, perhaps even younger than Callie. She was striking. Her haute couture navy suit and matching cloche appeared to come straight out of *Vogue* magazine. Platinum-blonde hair was set in a perfect wave. A fox stole, complete with small glass eyes, was draped around her delicate shoulders. She carried an expensive leather briefcase. Callie had never seen a woman dressed so well in Pickens.

"Mrs. Walton?" she asked expectantly.

The woman coolly appraised Callie from head to toe with emerald eyes lined in kohl before answering. "Yes. Miss Beecham?"

Callie smiled feebly. "I am Callie Beecham. Please come in and sit down." She extended her hand toward the faded sofa and instantly saw the shabbiness of her own small front room. A peeling wallpaper seam suddenly appeared large and obvious. The front windows were dirty in the late afternoon light. She noticed a faded stain on the hem of her apron as she sat and placed one hand over it nervously.

The woman sat down and removed her kid gloves delicately, revealing a large diamond on her left ring finger. When she crossed her slim legs at the ankles, Callie couldn't help but notice silk stockings as sheer as a whisper. The scent of Chanel No. 5 perfumed the air. Callie wondered if she had been a sophisticated Paris flapper prior to marriage.

She looked the part.

"May I get you some tea? Coffee?" Callie asked.

Mrs. Walton smiled politely. "No, thank you." She tilted her head slightly. "You're younger than I'd imagined."

Callie inhaled and forged ahead. "And so are you. How can I help you today, Mrs. Walton?"

The young woman's cool demeanor wobbled a bit, but she regained her composure. "I–I am looking for something to help me." She paused. "I must ask you to keep everything said here confidential."

"Of course," Callie said. "I honor all the conversations with my clients with the utmost secrecy."

"I am unable to have children," the young woman said softly. She stared at her red lacquered nails, hands folded in her lap. "I am sick."

"I see." Callie leaned forward. "Mrs. Walton, there are many reasons why a woman might not be able to conceive—temporarily. There are also men who are unable to produce children."

Looking up at Callie with clear blue eyes, she said, "I am aware of that. My husband is not the problem. It is me. I have cancer. Uterine cancer."

"Oh." Callie exhaled a long breath. "Have you seen a doctor?"

A look of despair crossed the young woman's face. "I have seen several. They all tell me that surgery is the only option. And yet surgery will mean I can never have children of my own." She hesitated. "I do not think my marriage can survive that. My husband expects children."

Callie steepled her hands together under her chin in thought.

The woman reached into her large briefcase and pulled out a manila file and a black and white photograph. "I have an x-ray," she said. "And copies of blood tests if you need them."

Callie reached for the x-ray and held it up to the light. She had only seen x-rays when working for the Red Cross, crude and hastily taken pictures. This was a crisp image that showed the small gray shadow of a tumor. Clearly, Mrs. Walton had access to the finest medical care. She scanned the pages of extensive bloodwork for several minutes.

Finally, Callie handed the x-ray and paperwork back to Mrs. Walton and smiled. "Mrs. Walton, maybe we need to back up a bit. I may be able to help you. I will make some coffee and we can chat. I have no other appointments today, and I have many questions. Will that be alright?"

The woman's façade seemed to crack. "Anne. Please call me Anne." She checked her diamond watch. "I do have to get back to Greenville where we are staying—we have a late New Year's Eve dinner with friends.

But I can stay for an hour or so." The young woman—Anne—managed a shaky smile and seemed to relax a bit. "And yes, I would actually love a cup of coffee and a cigarette if you don't mind?" She reached into her bag and pulled out a silver cigarette case.

"Actually, Anne, I do mind. If I'm going to help you, the first thing I'll ask is for you to stop smoking." Callie was quite prepared for the woman to stand up and flounce from the room. Instead, she nodded and put the cigarette case back in her bag.

"Very well. I take my coffee with cream," Anne said, smiling. "And I just love your hair."

— • —

Callie stood with both hands gripping the edge of the kitchen counter, gathering her wits, while waiting for the coffee to percolate. What was she thinking? This young woman was clearly a very wealthy friend of Mildred's, able to afford the finest care, and yet she was sitting in Callie's front room, wanting an herbal cure for cancer. She heard a noise behind her and turned to see Anne enter the small kitchen, shoes in hand.

"May I help you?" she asked. She held up her fabulous shoes. "I didn't want to scuff your beautiful floors." She paused and listened to the song on the radio. "Oh, 'Black and Tan Fantasy!' I positively adore Duke Ellington!"

"Me too!" Callie smiled. She had to admit she liked Anne Walton. "Get two mugs off the shelf, there. I'm waiting for this ancient coffee pot to perc. It's slow, but it gets the job done. So tell me, where are you from? You don't live in Pickens County. I've lived here all my life and have never seen you, yet we look to be about the same age."

Anne crossed to the low shelf and grabbed two mugs. She turned and smiled. "You caught me. I am Mildred and Earl's niece. Aunt Mildred is my late mother's sister. John and I live in Charleston. He is a banker there."

"Is your Uncle Earl responsible for getting you top-notch bloodwork and an x-ray?" Callie asked.

"Yes," Anne sighed. "Well, Uncle's advice and John's money and connections. John moves in some powerful circles. Aunt Mildred told me to see you. But truth be told, Uncle Earl was adamant that I not waste my time with you, which made me want to see you all the more." She grinned and revealed a mouthful of pearly white teeth. "There must be a delicious story behind all that. I can't wait to hear it."

Callie smirked. "You'd have to ask him. Let's just leave it at that."

Anne set the mugs down in front of Callie. "Uncle Earl can be infuriating. Old-fashioned. But I saw what you did for Aunt Mildred's face, which was a small cancer, was it not? If there is anything you can do to make this go away, I'll gladly pay top dollar. John wants to start a family. He wants oodles of children. I'll even try a voodoo doll if you have one." She laughed nervously.

Callie could see that Anne was a young woman used to getting what she wanted. She opened her mouth to clarify, but Anne cut her off with an upheld palm. "I know. This is different. This is serious. But I read that a positive attitude goes a long way in healing. I shall have a positive attitude. And I will be healed. What else do you want to know?"

Callie poured coffee into two mugs and splashed a bit of cream into each before handing one to Anne. "Enjoy this cream. You won't get any more for a while on the new diet I'm prescribing. Let's go sit."

Anne nodded obediently and followed Callie to the sofa. Callie appraised the young woman quickly. Slim and healthy-looking. Her eyes were clear and not jaundiced. Complexion rosy. Gums pink. Teeth white.

She set down her cup and began. "I may ask personal questions, but they will help me understand how to treat your case. I can't promise anything—but there are some things we can do that should shrink a tumor." Callie leaned closer. "May I see your tongue?"

"M-my tongue?" Anne stammered. When Callie nodded, the woman stuck out her tongue.

Callie peered at the woman's tongue for some time and then spoke up. "Hmm. Tummy troubles?"

Anne nodded.

"Malabsorption. You're already quite slim, but your diet will need to change. You aren't digesting your food properly."

Anne grinned. "You can tell that by looking at my tongue?"

"Yes, I can. Now, here are some of the foods I want you to add. And some I want you to avoid," Callie said. She handed Anne a typed sheet of paper.

"Cook will have apoplexy," Anne joked after reading the instructions. "She makes an excellent veal parmesan."

"It's not easy, Anne," Callie chided. "I use medicinal plants in tinctures and teas, but the change in diet should be primary. And no smoking. Eat lightly cooked foods, raw or steamed vegetables, and just a small amount of fruit and dairy. A small amount of chicken or fish is allowed. No desserts. No alcohol. We're going to detoxify you."

Anne gasped. "But Uncle Earl gives me a prescription for whiskey twice a month. He says it helps tonify"—she paused and blushed—"female organs."

Callie pulled a face. "No. It doesn't. And my diet is a firm directive."

"Sounds painful," Anne said. "May I start tomorrow? How can I turn down *Moet & Chandon* at midnight on New Year's Eve? You understand."

"Divine," Callie sighed. "I'll grant you that. But to tackle something as serious as uterine cancer, you'll need to do everything I prescribe. And check in with a doctor regularly. Especially if you want to avoid surgery. I have questions for you to answer before I write up a treatment plan. Now, I have to ask—"

There was a shrill ring from the kitchen telephone. Callie paused and glanced that way. *It might be Sam.*

"Do you need to get that?" Anne asked.

Callie shook her head. "Is there any reason to think that your husband will not be on board with this plan? You have already said that Dr. Davis isn't."

Anne shrugged and drew her legs up under her casually, her stockinged toes peeking from below the hem of her skirt. "Callie, this is *my* body. My decision. I'm a modern woman. We're blasting into 1929 at midnight, for goodness sake! Let's get started."

When Anne Walton finally left late that afternoon, Callie believed she had found a new friend. Not only was Anne fun and easy to talk to, but she also heartily believed in what Callie could do for her. Callie locked the front door and sat down wearily on the sofa. She wished that she could call Sam for advice on Anne's case.

The strains of "I Wanna Be Loved By You" on the radio only served to drag Callie's mood down. It was New Year's Eve, after all. The telephone ring startled Callie and she jumped. She crossed the room quickly and lifted the receiver. "Hello?"

"Callie. It's me. Don't hang up!" Sam blurted. "Can you forgive me? I am sorry for the way I have behaved, and I have no excuse."

Callie pressed her lips together and waited.

"I was a terrible cad. I was angry with you for no reason. I left town for the holidays and didn't let you know. Please let me make it up to you. Would you please go out with me tonight? There is a little Italian restaurant in Greenville we could try."

There was no denying the remorseful tone in Sam's voice. Callie remembered the sight of him cruising through town with Sara Cane by his side and said curtly, "No, Sam. I'm not up for this."

"Well, we could do something else. You decide," Sam offered, too cheerfully.

"You don't understand. I can't do *this*. You ignored me after Thanksgiving because of something someone else told you about me. You didn't have the courtesy to respond to my Christmas dinner invitation. And here it is five o'clock on New Year's Eve and you ring me up to see if I am free? Well, I am not! I have plans. Call Sara Cane!" She hung up the telephone angrily. "The nerve!"

She grabbed her hat and pulled it down over her new bob, picked up her coat and purse, and stormed out of the house. In several long strides, she reached Silas's doorstep. She knocked on his door and waited.

The door opened, and Silas leaned against the door frame. He chuckled. "Changed your mind, did ya?"

Callie nodded sheepishly. "I did. If your invitation to see a picture show is still open, I accept."

Silas's eyes narrowed. "It is. But I'll make you drive. You need the practice, and I can't see so good after dark." He checked his watch. "I hope you like Charlie Chaplain. It's one called *The Circus*. Let me get my coat and lock up, and I'll meet you out back."

"Sounds perfect," Callie said.

She walked around the corner of Silas's small house, her pulse still banging away. "The nerve!" she muttered again.

Silas appeared behind her. "What's got your goat, Callie? It has to be that young Dr. Sam. I don't remember much these days, but I remember what a woman angry at a man looks like."

"Silas, that man makes me furious. But I don't want to talk about it. I want to enjoy the evening."

He shrugged and turned to Callie. "You got the key?"

Callie held out the small key. "He just called to ask me to dinner on New Year's Eve—at the last minute!"

Silas shook his head. "Didn't you want to see him?"

"I said I don't want to talk about it," Callie chided. "And that woman—Sara Cane—was sitting all snug and cozy next to him today on their ride through town. The nerve! She must be forty!"

She extended the key again and Silas held up his palms. "No, ma'am. I'm the passenger. You're the driver." He climbed into the car and sat down heavily. "Alright. Remember what I taught. Tell it to me as you do it."

Callie bit her lip in thought. She pointed down at the foot pedals. "High/low, reverse, and brake." Silas nodded.

"Key in the ignition to BATTERY," she said. She hopped into the driver's seat and put the key into the ignition. "Hand brake is set. Pull the choke . . ." She climbed back out and stood in front of the car, hands on hips. "Why should I accept his apology anyway?"

Silas cocked his head. "Don't you like this feller? Seems ya do."

"Let's not talk about it, Silas." She bent toward the crank. "I push the crank in. Prime the engine to get fuel up into the cylinders." After a few quarter-turns of the crank, she released the crank. "Primed."

She climbed back into the car with a heavy sigh. "I mean, the last thing I need is Sam Epstein in my life . . . I set the throttle and the choke. Spark lever up. Now I crank the engine?"

Silas nodded. "With what hand?"

Callie smiled. "Prime with the right. Crank with the left. Always with the left hand. Thumb underneath. So if it backfires, I don't break my arm."

"That's my girl." Silas smiled proudly.

Callie climbed out of the car again and proceeded to give the crank a solid turn. The engine turned over and hummed loudly. "If he really is sorry, he should apologize in person, right?" The engine came to life.

When she got back into the car, an exasperated Callie looked at Silas. "Right?"

"We're not talking about it, remember?" Silas barked over the engine noise. "Now, spark lever down a bit. Throttle up."

Callie nodded.

"And away we go." Silas smiled.

Chapter Nine

"Happy New Year, 1929," Callie murmured to George, who was curling and weaving around her legs. She opened the brand-new calendar to January and hung it on the wall next to the kitchen window. Outside, the morning was clear and bright. It would be a pretty day for her first trip to Liberia as a healer. Her medical bag was packed, and boxes of supplies and treatments were already loaded in the car. She switched on the radio and soon her feet were moving to a Louis Armstrong tune. She was surprised at how much the new Philco lifted her spirits. She could be connected to the world whenever she wanted to be. She was overcome with gratitude and vowed to return her neighbor's kindness somehow. Their trip to Liberia would be a good start. She'd make it a fun outing. She had packed peanut butter sandwiches, root beers, and apples and cookies for the trip.

Callie knew Silas was eager to meet Seeta again after so many years. She wondered if Seeta would remember him at all and if Seeta would even remember she was coming. The woman was near ninety. Would anyone show up to the church to be seen?

Silas has encouraged Callie to take the car home after their evening out so she could get an early start on the loading. Everything was packed and ready, waiting on Silas to come hobbling up the walk.

Callie sipped the last of her coffee and tried to keep her mind off of Sam. She assumed he had found another date last night, but hoped, instead, he'd gone to bed brooding over her refusal. "Serves him right," she huffed. And he hadn't once offered his own car for her trip to Liberia.

There was a knock on the door and the little bell tinkled. "Come on in, Silas," she called.

She stepped around the corner and stopped in her tracks. Sam stood in the doorway, hat in hand, looking sheepish and glum, but as handsome as ever. A red cashmere scarf was draped around his shoulders, probably a Christmas gift from an admirer. He seemed to notice her new haircut, and his blue eyes widened.

"What are you doing here?" she asked, her voice trembling.

"Callie, I knew you'd be going to Liberia. Please let me drive you," he said quietly. "It is the least I can do."

Callie looked past Sam and saw Silas through the window, limping up the sidewalk toward her door. "I don't need a ride from you at the last minute, Sam. My neighbor and I are going up there together."

Sam stepped forward tentatively. "Callie—"

"Sam Epstein, this isn't the time or the place. Silas and I are leaving now in his car. I have a full day up there, and we need to get going." Callie picked up the large bag on the floor.

"I am going, too," Sam announced. "I had to think it over, I'll admit. But it is the right thing to do. I'm a physician. I have my car loaded. Could I persuade you both to ride with me?"

Behind him, the door opened and Silas stepped inside. He stopped abruptly. His eyes went from Sam to Callie. "Can I assume that this young man is Dr. Epstein?"

Sam extended his hand. "Sam Epstein," he said.

Silas shook Sam's hand stiffly. "Silas Roberts. Thank you for your help before Christmas—when you came to see to my legs."

Sam smiled. "I just brought aspirin. Callie did the hard work of nursing you."

Silas studied Sam for a minute and then turned to Callie. "We ready to go? I got me a lap blanket because of the cold."

Callie nodded.

"Callie, I will see you at Soapstone Church then?" Sam asked dolefully.

"Oh, you goin' up there, too, Doc?" Silas asked.

"I am," Sam said. "I have room for all of us if you'd like to stretch out. Sara Cane even made me a thermos of hot chocolate to take along—in case we get chilled."

Callie turned to Silas. "Silas, your car is all packed."

Silas pointed toward Sam's car with a grin. "Is that a touring car, Doc? She's a beauty. Room enough for all of us and the baggage, you say?"

Callie glared at Silas. "Silas, *your* car is packed and ready to go. If Dr. Epstein is also going that way, we will just see him up there." With that, Callie shoved the bag into Silas's free hand and stormed out the door. Both men shrugged silently and followed.

— • —

Callie was nervous to crank the old Model T in front of Sam, but the car started right up. She climbed in and heard Sam start his own car parked behind them.

Silas chuckled. "You should've ridden with your young man. That's a fine touring car he's got. Much more comfortable. Electric start."

Callie bristled. "He is not my young man," she said. "And I like this car just fine." She slipped on a pair of driving gloves, put the car in gear, and set off for Liberia.

Silas shifted in his seat. "Callie, that man was the saddest sight I've seen in a month of Sundays. He clearly favors you. Don't waste your time tryin' to make him feel worse than he does. If you like him, forgive him."

Callie frowned and tried to concentrate on the road. It was true. Sam had apologized. And here he was, following her to Liberia. *Isn't that what I wanted?*

"Silas, I'm just not sure that he will stay around. Pickens is tiny. He's a young doctor with a whole life in Atlanta. He had a rich fiancée there. I'm a country girl with no money—running a small business out of my house. He comes from a large family with money. I have neither. And he's Jewish. He'll want a Jewish wife, you can be sure. A rich one."

Silas put his hand on Callie's arm affectionately. "Girl, me and my Rebecca was the same way. I had all the money, and she was a poor country girl. Oil and water. But she was my heart. My world."

Callie knew that Silas was right. She was holding a grudge because she was afraid, the same way that Sam had. And he had apologized. The pair rode in silence as Callie navigated the bumpy dirt road, made much worse by winter's snow and ice. But the fresh air and sunshine worked like a tonic on them both, lifting their Christmas melancholy. They chatted amiably about life in their small corner of the world all the way toward their destination.

When the car finally veered onto the gravel path that was the Liberia road, Callie acutely felt the knot in the pit of her stomach return. "Silas, this was a foolhardy idea, I think."

Silas gazed out at the magnificent face of Table Rock in front of him. "Fiddlesticks. Look at that view. I miss them mountains, Callie. This is God's country. Simply beautiful." He patted her arm. "An' this was a good idea. You're going to help lots more folks than the few back in town who come see you. An' with your young doctor here, too? Why, think of the good y'all can do today."

Callie craned her neck to check behind them. She saw Sam's car through the cloud of dust kicked up by their car. Suddenly, she wanted nothing more than to run into his arms the moment they arrived at the church and tell him he was forgiven.

As they entered the valley, she scanned the small homes and fields, looking for townsfolk. She searched for the now-familiar wooden spire that marked the church. She slowed the car and pulled off in front of the church. There wasn't a sound except the wind in the trees and a bit of birdsong. Not a soul was in sight anywhere near the grounds. The church doors were closed. She heard Sam's car pull up behind her. Without a word, Callie hopped out and began to unpack the car. She quietly handed Silas a box of tinctures and teas and headed toward the steps dejectedly. Behind her, Sam was quietly unloading his own car.

"It's mighty quiet," Silas said.

Callie was about to agree when the door opened and a booming voice cried, "Granny, they're here! We're so glad you made it." Zeke's wide smile instantly put Callie at ease. Seeta hobbled out from the doorway and smiled a greeting.

Callie felt a rush of relief. "Oh, Zeke, Seeta, I'm so happy to see you. I thought we would have more people here though."

Seeta grinned. "Baby girl, we moved everyone over to the new schoolhouse. Better light—since we ain't got electricity." Seeta pointed to a distant building. "An' Zeke got the woodstove goin' early so it's nice an' warm. Happy New Year!" She held onto her grandson with one arm and leaned on a cane with the other. "I see the Lawd brought Dr. Sam. I knew he'd change his mind. We had folks prayin' he'd come today."

"It's good to see you both again," Sam called out. "Zeke, why don't you help Seeta into my car, and we will head to the school?"

Zeke helped his grandmother down the rickety steps toward the car. She stopped in front of Callie and Silas. "Baby girl, who is this man? My eyes isn't what they once was."

Silas removed his hat and stepped toward Seeta. "I'm Silas—"

"Mr. Roberts," Seeta murmured. "Oh yes. It's been a long, long time."

How you been?" She extended a gnarled hand, and Silas shook it gently.

"I been fairly well, Miss Seeta. When Callie told me she knew you and was comin' up, why, I had to come along to see how I could help."

Seeta patted his pale hand with her brown one. "That's mighty fine, Mr. Roberts. Mighty fine. We both so old now, the best way we can help is to stay out the way." She chuckled. "How about we set together and talk a spell once these youngsters get started?"

Silas nodded and extended his arm. Together, he and Zeke soon had Seeta sitting up like a queen in Sam's car. Zeke happily climbed in the back. Sam started the car and motored slowly toward the new whitewashed school building, Callie and Silas close behind.

— • —

The schoolhouse was packed with people chatting, sitting side by side on the floor and in the ten small chairs awaiting students after the holidays. When Callie and Sam entered with Seeta close behind, everyone stood. Silas and Seeta were offered the two teachers' chairs on the small stage, while Zeke had everyone form an assembly line to quickly empty the cars of supplies.

The room was large and spacious. Sunlight streamed through the tall windows, and Callie found the space all-together perfect. She put on her apron and bobby-pinned wayward curls back from her face. Someone tapped her on the shoulder, and she turned to find Delia, little Cal strapped to her chest.

"I thought I could help you as long as the baby behaves," she smiled.

"Delia, how are you?" Callie asked.

"I'm fine. Hopin' Cal will start to sleep through the night." Delia sighed. "Colic is keepin' him up nights."

"Remind me to give you something for that. I'm sure he will sleep through, soon."

Delia nodded shyly. "Thank you."

Callie scanned the crowd. "And yes, I can sure use your help. Can you distribute these index cards to everyone here? They should fill them out with their name, age, and complaint. I have a box of pencils here somewhere." She rummaged in her bag and produced the small box. She paused and asked quietly, "Can you read?"

Delia nodded. "I can read and write. Most here can read a bit."

Callie smiled. "If a person can't write, can you take their notes? And send any serious cases directly to Dr. Epstein?"

Zeke had dragged a table toward the front of the room, and soon folks were lined up, waiting their turns to see Callie or Dr. Sam. Callie glanced at Sam furtively, admiring his form as he donned his crisp white medical coat.

The morning went by quickly. She treated an infected hangnail, stomach complaints, worms, a child with lice, several cases of rheumatism, and a man with a hacking cough. She handed out many copies of her typed paper titled *Diet for Fine Health*. Occasionally, Callie would look up and catch Sam looking her way with a smile. She'd quickly look away, cheeks flushed.

— • —

Around noon, Zeke loudly proclaimed a lunch break for "the doctors." He shooed the remaining patients outside and asked them to return at one o'clock.

Callie sat down in one of the small chairs and exhaled audibly. She watched from across the room as Sam pulled a book from his supply bag and handed it to Zeke. *It must be that Langston Hughes book. He's a good man.* She smiled.

Sam shook Zeke's hand and then turned and strode toward Callie. He sat down near her on the floor, cross-legged, and quietly looked over some notes. Delia's mother, Mattie, soon appeared from the back door with a large basket. She came toward them and set two plates of hoppin' john, squash, collards, and biscuits, along with a thermos of hot coffee, at their feet. "Ain't nothin' fried in lard. So you can do the kosher thing, Dr. Sam," she said sweetly.

Sam's eyes widened appreciatively. "Mattie, you're a dear. Thank you so much. Say, how many folks live up here in Liberia?"

Mattie thought for a moment. "They at fifty-eight right now, fifty-nine when I count my grandbaby." She grinned. "Now eat your lunch. I heard you didn't bring any lunch at all, and Mizz Callie only brought peanut butter sandwiches, so Delia and I decided to feed y'all right."

"Thank you, Mattie," Callie said, taking a plate.

"I may just live to see another day!" Sam said, eyeing the spread before him. He picked up a plate hungrily.

Mattie beamed. "Eat up. They comin' back in a bit." She waddled away toward Delia and Zeke.

Callie looked at Sam. "You know that hoppin' john is seasoned with ham."

Sam smiled at her. His blue eyes danced. "I know. And I see fatback floating in the collards. But I will eat every bite."

"I'm glad you came," she said.

— • —

The two ate in companionable silence for some time. Sam finally looked up from his lunch and smiled. "Fifty-nine souls in Liberia, and we've seen twenty-six this morning."

Callie stabbed a forkful of squash. "I'm tired. But in a good way. What have you seen today?"

Sam glanced at his notes. "Pellagra. Dyspepsia, possible stomach ulcer, an abscessed tooth, eye infection, rheumatism, high blood pressure. Oh, and one pleurisy."

"I have butterfly weed root—for the pleurisy. And a poke mixture that can be used in a decoction for the rheumatism," Callie offered.

"I really would like to take that crash course on medicinal plants," Sam said hopefully. "I saw one woman with a bunion. Her shoes were full of salt. What is that about?"

Callie nodded. "Oh, that's for protection from illness or accidents," she said matter-of-factly. "Dr. Davis keeps you so busy that I doubt you'd have the time to take even a crash course. For today, I'll leave some things with Seeta. She used to know all of this and was hopeful that another woman up here would step up and learn the old ways. She's so happy we're here."

"People today have tried to pay me." Sam dabbed his mouth with his napkin. "You know, back in the office, some people of means ignore their bills completely. For months."

"I could guess who they are," Callie said.

"How do Seeta and Silas know each other?" Sam tried to change the subject.

Callie gazed at her neighbor and her friend, their heads bent close together in quiet conversation. "She cared for his newborn son for a few days after his wife died of puerperal fever. Thirty years ago. There is more to the story, but I'll save that for another time. He didn't know Seeta was still alive and was anxious to see her."

Sam nodded. "What a coincidence. He looks better. His gout must not be bothering him as much."

"I've kept him busy, and that helps," Callie said. She turned to look down at Sam. "Something is bothering you. I can tell."

Sam put his plate down. "I told Earl Davis that I was coming up here today."

Callie took a bite of collards. "How did that go?"

Sam frowned. He remembered how Davis's eyes narrowed when he told him he planned to visit Liberia with Callie and see indigent patients—pro bono and on his own time. That he'd also like to try out some naturopathic remedies.

"It didn't go well. Even when I told him I had purchased meds out of my own pocket."

Callie put down her spoon. "Oh, Sam. I am sorry."

Sam shook his head. "He believes he owns me. He pays my salary, sets my schedule. Said I shouldn't have other patients outside of the practice. Especially colored folks. When I started, I did sign a contract—I cannot practice within fifteen miles of his office. I didn't think of this as practicing medicine. I thought of it as charity work. And technically, this is about sixteen miles from his office."

Sam stopped short of telling Callie about the rest of the conversation. He picked up a biscuit and bit into it. He chewed absentmindedly and thought back to the conversation in late December.

Davis had pushed back from his desk and spat, "Treatin' niggers? Sam, I didn't hire you to come up here to my town and spend time with that Beecham woman, treatin' folks who can't pay their bills and wouldn't even if they could. She put you up to this? You leave them alone. Remember, you're a Jewish boy yourself. Don't go upsettin' the apple cart. I need you here."

Sam looked at Callie. Was Davis threatening him? Or Callie? "Hopefully, he will come to realize that in no way will this compromise my work with him. We're doing good things here. And, Callie, you're a good nurse. You have quite a way with people."

"Thank you. But I should never have gotten you involved in this. Please don't let it cost you your job," Callie said softly. "You're busy enough during the week. You don't need to add to your worries. I never would have said a word had I known it would cause trouble."

Sam was quiet for a moment. "That's the thing. I went home to Atlanta at Christmas. I had a lot to think about, but I was miserable the whole time I was home. The noise. The traffic. The endless round of parties and social obligations. My mother lives for it. My sisters, too. My friends there have moved on. They have their own lives, wives, and children. Then I realized that I have come to appreciate this place. This corner of South Carolina." He waved a hand around him. "The people here. The clean air. The mountains outside our windows. And you. Mainly, I missed you."

Callie dabbed her mouth with her napkin and looked down at her plate. "Me? I'm the last person you missed. I saw you with Sara Cane in town yesterday."

Sam was confused. "Sara Cane? Oh no. She just wanted a ride into town. That's all. I have a car. I couldn't very well say no."

Callie shook her head and smiled. "You don't know women, then."

"I like you, Callie. I can't stop thinking about you." Sam leaned toward her and said, "I told my mother about you. The country girl who knows more about treating illness than I do. The brave girl who will do what she thinks is right at any cost. The most beautiful woman I have ever laid eyes on."

Callie rolled her eyes playfully. "And what did Mrs. Epstein say?"

Sam took a chance and reached for Callie's free hand. Their fingers intertwined comfortably. He continued. "She said you sound quite courageous."

Sam felt Callie relax her grip, and he reluctantly let go of her hand. "I am not courageous, Sam," she said. "I'm returning a kindness. And I enjoy it."

Sam ran his free hand through his hair and sighed heavily. "Callie, Seeta and Zeke were right. There are white people in the county who do not approve of anyone helping out up here. Davis and his ilk. What if it costs you clients? Clients you can ill afford to lose?"

"The people I see don't have too many options." She paused. "Although, I do have a new client, a rather wealthy young woman from Charleston with uterine cancer. Can you help me with her case?"

"Uterine cancer? She should consult a doctor," Sam warned.

"She has." Callie looked down at Sam. "She is Earl Davis's niece. She has seen several specialists and surgeons. I've looked at her x-ray and lab reports. The tumor is small, and she doesn't want to have surgery. She wants children. I think I can help."

Sam let out a low whistle. "Earl's niece? The plot just keeps getting thicker. I'd better stay away from that one. If she is Earl's kin, I shouldn't get involved. Neither should you."

Callie sighed. "Dr. Davis told her not to waste her time on me. But she is a grown woman."

Sam shook his head. "Neither of us is on Davis's good side right now. Still, he can't very well tell you which clients you may see, and he can't tell me how to spend my occasional day off. We're up here doing good work. Together." He looked at Callie. "And if you and I are together, well, then—everything will be fine. Are we—together?"

Callie leaned over and kissed Sam quickly on the cheek. "Be quiet and eat your squash," she whispered.

— • —

Across the long room, Seeta peered at the young couple over the rim of her spectacles. "They is a fine couple, ain't they?"

Silas licked crumbs from his fingers before answering. "Yep. They is indeed. She likes him a lot—I can tell. Callie has been good to me. I don't want to see her get hurt. These years since my William died have been hard, and she's the only person in town what's given me the time of day."

Seeta nodded. "Losing yo' babies is never easy, even when they is grown."

"We ain't supposed to outlive our children," Silas muttered.

Seeta nodded. "I lost two. An' a grandson, Willis." Her voice trailed off.

"Your Jacob was a fine man. I didn't know Willis. An' Marcus? Nah . . . He ain't dead," Silas said. "He's just gone away."

"May as well be dead," Seeta murmured. "If he be alive, why don't he write?"

She shook her head as if to clear his memory from her mind, folded her arms across her chest, and said, "When you wrote me that Callie's mama died an' Callie was goin' to Washington, DC, to help with the war effort, I thought I'd never hear a thing about her again. And then years later, you wrote she'd turned up back in Pickens, on yo' same street! I was so happy, but she shoulda stayed away."

"You never went into town to see her." He looked over at Callie and watched as she shared a bit of biscuit with Sam. "Not in all these years?"

"No. You know I couldn't. I jes' knew she was safe with you there and that had to be enough," Seeta said sadly. "As long as Dr. Davis is around, I need to stay away from town. From her. He ain't a man I want to tangle with again. An' I didn't want him botherin' her."

Silas dabbed his mouth and beard with his napkin and said, "He won't touch her as long as I'm alive. You know that. I'm sorry I didn't let you know more about her these past years. Nine years is a long time. I was so caught up in my own loneliness and grief after William died. Well, you understand."

"You didn't owe me nothin'."

Silas pointed a bony finger toward Callie and Sam. "I'm an old man now. Sometimes, I'm surprised I even wake up in the mornin's—but I won't go easy until I know that girl is cared for. Maybe he's the one to care for her."

"Maybe so."

"You gonna tell her?" Silas asked.

Seeta turned to glare at Silas, her brown eyes hard. "Nah. That would only bring pain. No, sir."

"I think she deserves to know."

"She don't need that pain," the old woman said.

Silas shook his head. "She deserves to know the truth. There are folks in town, like Davis, who might, one day, decide to mess with her. Especially if she keeps up with the new young doctor. Until they're all dead, she's not out of the woods. Hearing it from you is better than hearing it in town."

Seeta's eyes narrowed. "And what about that young man there? What's he likely to do if he finds out?"

"He's a good one," Silas said. "I think he could help her work through it. She's surely fond of him." Silas clicked his tongue. "Best she knows firsthand before someone else comes along and tells her."

Seeta shook her head sadly. "Ain't no reason to tell Callie I'm her grandmother."

— • —

Late that night, almost to dawn, Seeta lay in the dark, eyes wide open, letting the feel of things wash over her. The last hours before sunrise were when she best sensed *the thin place*—where the veil between this world and the next was fragile. Sometimes, she wondered if she herself was a thin place, a conduit between what was and what would be. The ghost of loved ones who had gone before her would sometimes visit in the early hours, their presences warm and comforting. In her younger years, dark entities also tried to come through. She learned not to fear them, for that was what they fed on. Best to swat them away like black flies.

She fumbled at the neck of her nightgown and found the charm that hung between her breasts by a leather cord. The tiny bag contained herbs, a lock of her hair, a toenail clipping, and a small twig from the sunny side of the oak tree in her yard. The bundle was tied shut with red string. She grasped it in one hand and began to pray.

These days, even if she perceived an evil spirit, she saw it once removed, set apart and in the distance, unable to hurt her or her loved ones. But this was different. Tonight, the energy was all around. There was *bad juju* in the air. A sizzling malevolent undercurrent. She sat up and listened in the dark. There was only the sound of rain beginning to fall on the old roof, pattering softly at first and getting heavier. She waited for direction.

Slowly, she sat up and groped for her glasses. She leaned hard against the bedside table and felt for her cane. Her tiny body could barely hoist itself, but the orange glow from outside her window spurred her strength. She hobbled the few paces to her window and cautiously pulled back the curtain. Wisps of fog rose from the warm ground, giving the land an eerie appearance. Straining to see down the road, Seeta watched in sadness as tongues of flame shot from the large windows of the new schoolhouse. It was already too late, she knew, and the rain would ensure it didn't spread. Several figures, neighbors who lived closer than she who would see the fire as evidence of some new aggression, ran toward the fire, buckets in hand. Seeta shook her head. She knew it was only evidence that nothing had changed. Nothing at all.

Chapter Ten

Callie sat at her kitchen table, George curled at her feet. In the background, the radio played quietly, her new and constant work companion. Outside, the overnight rain had softened to a cold drizzle. Early morning was cozy and warm in her little kitchen. It was still dark outside in the heart of winter, so she pulled a reading lamp close to better illuminate her writing. She studied the notes she had made about Anne Walton and referenced her formulary frequently, hoping to create the best blueprint for Anne's treatment. The woman was paying her generously. Sam would stop by after work, and over supper, they would decide next steps for the woman. Anne had called and said that she had only backslid once on smoking and had given her cook Callie's list of dietary requirements. The woman had balked but had dutifully gone shopping for the long list of herbs, vegetables, and strange new grains her employer's wife required.

Silas had become strangely silent after New Year's Day in Liberia. In fact, their drive home had been a quiet one, Silas lost deep in thought and Callie reviewing cases and treatments in her mind. She had checked on him twice that week, and both times found him lying on his sofa, listening to the radio, eyes closed. His gout seemed better, and he had no physical complaints, only a deep melancholy she couldn't shake out of him. Yesterday morning, she had taken him some ham biscuits, which he'd thanked her for half-heartedly before setting the platter down without taking a bite. She'd suspected he had another long night at the bottle and clucked her tongue disapprovingly.

Callie still wondered what had transpired between him and Seeta. Their conversation on New Year's Day had appeared so serious. She was scheduled to return to Liberia the following morning, a Saturday, to check on patients and see any new ones. Silas had not asked to go back. Sam also decided to stay in town, taking care not to aggravate his boss. Callie would do her best to treat minor cases and apprise Sam of patients who might need his medical care.

She paused and rubbed the small of her back, quick to seize up in someone used to being on the move constantly. The rain pattered on the roof, and George stretched once before returning to his curled-up position under the table. Callie had no appointments lined up and planned to spend the rainy day making decoctions and filling capsules. She leaned back in the chair and rubbed her eyes.

There was a loud thud against the front door that sent George skittering out of the kitchen for the safety of his hiding place under Callie's bed. She looked up, curious. It was too early for the paperboy, and the milkman came on Tuesday and Saturday. She stood up and pulled her bathrobe around her closely, then padded to the front door in her slippers and put an ear against the door. Nothing. She flipped the switch to turn on the front porch light before opening the door a crack.

A large, crumpled paper sack lay across the small mat on the step. As she lifted the sack, a piece of writing paper fluttered free. Callie picked it up with her thumb and forefinger. In the dim light of the single front porch bulb, she read the scribbled words.

Stop visiting them niggers or you will lose your white customers. And leave the Jew doctor alone. This is a warning.

Callie felt her blood chill. She glanced to the right and left, but the dark street was empty in the cold drizzle. She tucked the note into the pocket of her robe and noticed through the fog that Silas's front window was lit, which comforted her. She contemplated the crumpled brown bag at her feet, afraid of what she might find inside. Her curiosity got the better of her.

With trembling fingers, Callie bent to open the mouth of the bag. She let out an audible gasp and closed it quickly. She picked up the bag and held it away from her body, then hurried around to the backyard. The sky was beginning to lighten, and Callie could see the outline of the back fence. She closed her eyes and tossed the bag over the fence, waiting to hear the thud as the bag hit the alley ground behind her house. She would bury the contents later in the day if a stray dog didn't come along and take care of it.

The first songbird began its morning call, and Callie heard the rumble of a car going down Main Street. She could still feel her heart beating rapidly, slamming against her rib cage and took several deep breaths to calm herself. She walked quickly up the back steps and into the house.

Callie glanced at the wall clock, which read 7:10 a.m. She picked up the phone hesitantly. Silas would know what to do—if anything could be done. She didn't want to alarm Sam.

"Operator."

"Y-yes, please get me Silas Roberts. His number is 346," Callie replied.

Callie waited for only a moment before she heard a grumpy, "Hello. Silas Roberts."

"Silas, it's Callie. I'm sorry to bother you so early but something has happened. May I come over?"

"You alright, girl?" His tone shifted to one of concern.

"I am. But someone just left a nasty present on my front porch. I-I'm a little shaken up."

"Come on over. I'll wait out front." The line went dead, and Callie hurriedly dressed and threw on her coat. She hesitated only a moment before grabbing the scribbled note. She locked the door behind her and made her way down the sidewalk. The front porch light was on at Silas's house and the man was standing in its halo.

"My angel!" she called into the drizzle.

Silas scratched his unruly beard and harrumphed. "You got my curiosity up somethin' fierce. Come in for coffee."

Callie stepped into Silas's messy front room, relieved to have a friend who she could call at dawn when something was wrong. The fireplace was lit and the room was cozy, but like always, disheveled and filled with cigarette smoke.

Silas closed the door firmly and hung his own damp coat on the nail by the door. He limped ahead of her to his kitchen. "Have a seat and tell me what's what," he directed, taking her coat. He poured a cup of coffee and set the steaming brew down in front of Callie before taking a seat across from her.

Callie pulled the wrinkled paper from her coat and slid it across the table. Silas peered at the note for a long moment before laying it down. He sighed heavily.

"Should I be worried?" Callie asked. "It came with a paper bag—mutilated kittens inside. I didn't look too closely. It was sickening." She shuddered. "Do you think it was a prank?"

"No. No, I don't," Silas said slowly.

Callie cocked her head. "Someone doesn't want me visiting Liberia. Why on earth not?"

"You were helpin' folks that some here in town would rather you not help." Silas stared into his coffee cup.

Callie waited for more of an explanation but none was forthcoming.

"I gathered that," she said. "Do you think this is from a disgruntled patient or—someone else?"

Silas looked up. "There's a lot of people in this town who put on a good Sunday face but aren't exactly followin' the Golden Rule. Important people." He snorted. "Rather, people who think they are important."

"Maybe I should take the note to the sheriff's office," Callie suggested.

Silas ran a hand through his gray beard. "A sack full o' dead cats ain't exactly a threat you should call the law about. Nah. I can tell you that won't help you at all. Earl Davis knows you both were up there. He told Sam not to go. He knows that Sam favors you. He hates colored people, Callie. If I had to guess, I'd say he's worked up about it. He's a Klansman."

"Seeta told us that." Callie shook her head. "Silas, Earl Davis is a doctor. Pledged to treat sick people. Why would he get this worked up about me treating people in Liberia? Why not throw dead cats on Sam's doorstep? He's Jewish."

"I know what I'm talkin' about," Silas said. "This time you got a sack of dead cats from one of his goons. What's to come next time? There is a lot more to this story, an' I'm not the one who has to tell it."

Callie's eyebrows knit together. "What do you mean?"

"You goin' to Liberia again?" he asked.

Callie nodded. "Tomorrow." She crossed her arms defiantly.

"Maybe I'll ride up there with ya after all. You need to talk to Seeta."

— • —

Callie eased the car off of the main highway and onto the dirt road to Liberia. As soon as the old Ford crested the hill, she gasped. "Silas! Look! The new schoolhouse . . ." There in the low valley, the charred ruins of the newly erected building scarred the postcard-pretty view before them.

Silas let out a low whistle. "I'll be damned."

Callie put the car in gear and headed closer to the collapsed building. There was nothing salvageable that she could see.

The pair left the car and approached the site. Their shoes crunched across shards of broken glass and the scorched remains of a few precious textbooks.

A voice behind them startled Callie. "Y'all go on back to town now. Please!" a man called, coming toward them. He waved his hat in the air frantically. "See what your helpin' got us? Go on! Please!" He looked to be shooing away a stray dog. He twisted his hat in his hands and looked past them down the road back to town.

"I remember you," Callie said, attempting a smile. "I saw your wife when I was here last. Mr. Merck, right? How's she feeling?"

The man stopped in his tracks and nodded. "Better, ma'am. But they'll burn us out if you come back here. Go on now! Please. I ain't got nothin' but my house, and if they burn it, my wife and me got nowhere to go."

A sense of shame washed over her and she stepped back. "Silas, let's go."

Silas shook his head. "Hold on now. Mr. Merck, you know as well as I do that Miss Beecham did nothin' wrong. She came to help y'all at your neighbor's request. And you did nothing wrong in acceptin' treatment. Are you gonna let them bastards win?"

"How do I know ya'll didn't send them here?" Merck challenged.

"You have my word," Silas said, his steely blue eyes boring into the man.

Merck seemed to ponder Silas's pledge for a moment. "Mister, I ain't got no quarrel with you." He tipped his head toward the scattering of plain houses down the road. "My wife is crippled up and can't work. I feed us on huntin', the garden I tend, and a patch of corn behind my house."

He paused and looked at Callie. "I'm sorry, ma'am. There ain't many white people that come ridin' into Liberia lookin' to help us. But your comin' made someone mad. I gots to think about my wife."

Callie had been quietly studying the man's faded and patched, olive-drab trench coat. "Mr. Merck, you served in the war, didn't you?"

Merck's dark eyes narrowed. "Yes, ma'am. Private in the 118th Infantry." He touched the collar of his coat. "This O.D. coat is still the warmest thing I own. It brings back some painful memories, but I got through it. I did."

Silas reached out a hand. "Silas Roberts. It's an honor to meet you, soldier. My own son was in the 33rd. Shoulda known by your coat you was over there."

"Charles Merck." Merck shook his hand and asked, "What's your son's name?"

Silas lifted his chin proudly. "Captain William Roberts. He was pulled out at Ypres, Belgium, and sent into France on a secret mission. Turns out he was with the group who eventually took the Germans' Amiens gun. He died at Amiens—machine-gun fire."

Merck whistled. "He died a hero, sir. Amiens was the start of the Hundred Days campaign. Couldn't'a done it without those soldiers."

The men stopped speaking, lost in memory and regret.

Callie began cautiously. "Mr. Merck, I can't imagine what it was like for you to have fought for your country overseas only to come home to find nothing had changed here. I worked as a nurse's aide in Camp Service with the Red Cross. I saw how unfairly wounded colored soldiers were treated—even there. Let me do something. Please. I can't in good conscience leave sick people without treatment when I can help."

Merck seemed to consider her plea, but he finally shrugged. "No one is at the church waitin' on you today. Folks is scared. If you leave us be, we can build it back. Over time. But if you keep comin' up here, they gonna hurt us. I know Seeta Young asked you up here. But someone burned our school down."

He kicked at the charred debris at his feet. "The only reason we can figure is you and the doctor came here. Next, it'll be the church. Or houses shot up. Or someone strung up outside of town for driving too fast. Or too slow." His anger seemed to rekindle. "Nothin' you can do, except make it worse."

Callie nodded, chastened. "That's the last thing I want. I'd like to visit with Seeta if I may. Then we'll clear out." She reached into the bag slung over her shoulder and produced a small bottle. She extended it toward Merck. "This'll help your wife's neuropathy. She should take one dropperful daily. Write me when she needs more. That's all I have with me today."

Merck shook his head. "I got no money to pay you."

"No," Callie said. "It's a gift." She reached for his hand and closed his palm over the bottle. "We'll stop in and see Miss Seeta, but we won't stay long. Thank you for your honesty today, Mr. Merck."

The man nodded, and Callie and Silas returned to the car. Callie's cheeks burned, but she was unsure whether it was anger, shame, or regret that stung. "Silas," she muttered. "Why would someone burn down a school because we brought medicine?"

Silas was quiet. She glanced at the man as she got behind the wheel. He stared straight ahead, unwilling to meet her gaze. "What's going on in that head of yours?" She fumbled with the dash controls and then stepped out to crank the engine. It roared to life and she hopped back in the car. "You'd better tell me what's going on." She steered the car down the gravel street.

Silas just shrugged. "I'm an old man. What I think don't matter much. But it seems to me there's a fine line. Just so much the Klan will allow. A bit o' kindness here and there. But you crossed a line, girl. Dr. Davis invited Sam to come to Pickens County to treat white folks. It makes it look like the Klan is good people. But Sam wasn't supposed to do charity work with colored folks."

Callie's eyes narrowed. She didn't like Dr. Davis, but couldn't imagine him countenancing the burning of a school. She opened her mouth to speak but Silas cut her off.

"You've caught his eye—Dr. Sam. Maybe that's why Davis told him you were engaged. Not to make him jealous, like Sam thought, but to throw him off your tracks."

"But Mildred Davis invited me to her Thanksgiving dinner."

"So what? Mildred Davis is a formidable woman. I doubt Earl would uninvite someone his wife likes. You're lucky she likes you. Nah, he would work another way . . . Them cats in a bag, for instance."

"You think he did that?" Callie scoffed. "It won't stop me from coming up here."

"Then get ready for more threats. Not him direc'ly. One of his boys," Silas snapped. He softened immediately and said, "I'm sorry, Callie. Seeta needs to be honest with you about somethin' that may be important, an' I think now is the time."

The car came to a stop in front of Seeta's small home. A wisp of smoke curled from the chimney. There was movement behind the curtains, and they closed quickly.

Callie and Silas left the car and approached the house. Callie took Silas's elbow and helped him up the steps before knocking on the door softly. The door opened a bit and Delia peered out. "Mizz Callie. Can I help you?"

"Hello, Delia. Is Seeta here? We saw no one at the church," Callie said.

"Let em in, Delia," a voice called from inside.

Delia stood aside and opened the door, her head down. "Come in."

Callie and Silas entered the front room. Delia clutched her sweater tightly across her chest and stared at the floor. "Coffee?" she asked.

Callie shook her head. "No, thank you." She hesitated. "How is Cal?"

"Ezekiel's fine," Delia said, her eyes hard. She glanced toward the kitchen. "Granny's in there. I'm gonna take the baby out for some air." She turned and left the room.

A pang of sadness hit Callie hard. Delia had called the baby Ezekiel, not Cal. "Thank you, Delia," she called after her.

Seeta was at the sink drying dishes when Callie and Silas entered the kitchen. Her back was toward them, but Callie watched her lay down the dish towel and grip the edge of the sink. "Silas Roberts, you here to cause trouble?" she asked softly.

"Miss Seeta, it's time," Silas said. "We saw the schoolhouse."

Seeta turned slowly. Her eyes were rimmed red from crying. "Mr. Roberts, this ain't gonna help things. Not one bit."

Callie glanced from Silas to Seeta. "What's going on?"

Seeta hobbled to the small table and sat down wearily. "Sit down, girl." Callie sat down next to the old woman, and Silas took a chair across from her. "I'd take your coats but you probably ain't gonna stay," Seeta said. She reached for Callie's hand and squeezed it gently.

Callie looked down at her smooth, pale hand in Seeta's dark, wrinkled fingers and waited.

Seeta began. "I need to be honest with you about somethin' and it's hard, so just let me talk."

"You've got me worried," Callie tried to joke. The look exchanged between Seeta and Silas frightened her.

"Your mama, Kizzy, was a young thing. Real young when she married. Not even sixteen when she had you. I got there right as you was comin' into the world." Seeta glanced at Silas. The man had his eyes firmly fixed on Callie, his face wan and tired.

Seeta dabbed her eyes with her free hand and continued. "Callie, Mr. Beecham wasn't your father."

Callie pulled her hand away. "What do you mean?"

"Kizzy told me," Seeta said in a voice barely above a whisper.

Callie inhaled sharply. She sat still, trying to rein in her feelings. When she glanced toward Silas, he nodded a confirmation. She exhaled and asked, "My mother was with another man?"

"It happens," Seeta chuckled.

"This isn't funny," Callie snapped. She thought of her young mother, who eked out a hardscrabble existence as a spinner at the cotton mill.

Dead before she was forty. Kizzy'd never talked about her own parents, nothing at all, nor about her husband. Jim Beecham had been so much older. Maybe he'd married a pregnant Kizzy out of kindness. Maybe she'd been raped. Callie's thoughts began to race.

Seeta looked beseechingly toward Silas.

Silas began. "Callie, I already told you that Seeta had been a Godsend to me when my wife died. I told her that if she ever needed a favor, to call on me. An' then, in 1904, she did. She'd been livin' outside of town with your mama, carin' for you an' tendin' house while your mama worked in the mill. Lots of folks knew that. I jes' thought she was Kizzy Beecham's hired help."

He sheepishly pulled a small flask from his coat pocket. "I need a nip of liquid courage." Callie made to chastise him, but he held up a hand and added, "You may, too."

He unscrewed the cap and lifted the flask to his mouth. He swallowed the whiskey and closed his eyes. "Kizzy was a young widow with a baby girl. Poor as a church mouse. Times was hard. There was rumors around town about who the daddy was, but I didn't put stock in gossip. An' I had my own sorrows. Then, around the time you was three, Seeta sent me a letter. She'd been banished. Sent home at the—I'll call it the request—of the mill owner, Carl Gilstrap. Seeta wrote and told me the whole story. She asked me to look in on y'all from time to time. As a favor."

"So I was illegitimate?" Callie asked.

Silas leaned forward. "And enough folks knew to make it a problem for Kizzy. But we've started in the middle . . ."

"I see," Callie said. But she didn't see. "Mr. Gilstrap was my father?"

"Lawd, no!" Seeta spat.

"If my mother told you who my father really was, please tell me," Callie said.

Seeta shook her head. "Callie, when you came into this world, the first thing your mama asked me was if you was white—or black."

The ground under Callie's feet shifted. She had the sensation of falling.

"You was a pale enough baby to pass fo' white, but she tol' me you had a Negro father." In a rush, Seeta continued. "When I came back to check on her a week later, I found Kizzy was beat black an' blue around her face. She started cryin' an' began to tell me what happened. Mr. Beecham had done the math and didn't think you was his baby, so he slapped her around good. She'd begged and pleaded and told him of course he was the daddy an' he backed off."

Callie cocked her head. "I don't understand."

"When Kizzy was tellin' me the story, she let the young man's name slip out," Seeta said. "Marcus. Marcus Young."

Callie placed trembling fingers over her lips.

Seeta reached for Callie's other hand once more, but Callie shrank back. "Marcus was my boy's name. My son. When your mama said his name, I cried out. Couldn't help myself. I told her that Marcus was my boy."

Callie opened her mouth to speak when Seeta interrupted her. "Jim Beecham was away for a spell. It wasn't forced. Marcus and your mama fell fo' each other. Kizzy said the same. They was young—and stupid."

"He'd gone over there to reroof their barn. I remembered him spendin' all that time on that Beecham barn and never gettin' paid fo' his work..." Seeta looked at Silas for help, but he only nodded for her to continue. "I confronted him, and he told me true."

Silas extended the flask toward Callie. She pushed it away and waited dully for Seeta to continue.

"I told Marcus he had to go away. If Mr. Beecham suspected, I knew the truth would come out. They'd come lookin' fo' him. Hang him from a tree. It was only a matter of time. That's what happens." Seeta dabbed her red eyes with a handkerchief. "They'd throw a rope around his neck and jerk the life outta him. So he left. Went up north ten days after you was born."

"An' one day when you was a month or two old, Kizzy and Mr. Beecham had a big ol' fight. She was a fool—she tol' him flat out he wasn't the daddy. He'd suspected all along."

Callie reddened, thinking of her mother that way.

"He beat the snot out of Kizzy. Beat her up good. Threatened to kill you. Thank God, he died soon after," Seeta said softly. "Heart attack." She paused for some response from Callie, but Callie only stared at the table in a daze.

"That's when Kizzy asked me to come and watch you. She had to go back to work. I went an' kept you every day. An' folks left us alone until around the time you was three years old. Oh, sometimes, there'd be a bottle rocket tossed into the yard or a nasty letter... But Kizzy came home from the mill one night jes' fumin'. Mr. Gilstrap had called her into his office. He said things to your mama—he wanted things—that weren't fittin'."

Callie could barely hear Seeta's words over the rush of the blood in her ears. It was too much to take in, and she wasn't sure she wanted to hear anymore. "Did she—"

"No! But when she refused him, he got real angry," Seeta said. "Mr. Gilstrap had been in the Klan with Mr. Beecham. He knew Mr. Beecham's suspicions." Seeta looked to Silas for help. "Ain't that right?"

Silas nodded. "Lots of folks in town heard the rumor."

Seeta went on. "Mr. Gilstrap threatened to fire Kizzy and tell everybody that your father was colored. It would have ruined your life, even as a child. It would have taken the last shred of decency from your mother. So Kizzy took him up on the only other option he offered—he sent his wife to take you away. Tol' Kizzy that unless Lottie got to keep you, he'd tell everyone that Kizzy whored around with a black man, and that you was black."

"Why would my mother allow that?" Callie asked bitterly.

Silas shrugged. "She didn't have much choice, Callie. Either way, Lottie Gilstrap was bound to get you. To have a colored parent, it meant you'd be treated as colored. No matter how pale your skin was. You went to live with the Gilstraps, and the gossip died down. Your mama did that for you. Lottie was gonna raise you as her own. The Gilstraps never had their own children, so I suspect Lottie saw it as a chance to raise up a child. They kept you for a couple years in exchange for silence about the whole thing. It was blackmail—but your mama had to work. An' keep your secret safe."

Seeta spoke up. "Kizzy was so sad, but she let Mrs. Gilstrap take you. It was better fo' you, she thought. You was treated white. You ate better, was kept clean and dressed better, an' Kizzy kept her job. They allowed her to visit for a few hours here an' there."

Callie turned to Silas. "You knew about this?"

Silas held up his hands. "I was busy with my own life, a young widower an' a son without a mama. Then, like I said, Seeta wrote me in '04. She asked me to look in on you as a favor, but didn't tell me the whole truth. I'd heard the stories, and the way Seeta seemed to care about you made it easy to believe it was true. But when I went to your mama's to check on you, she told me that Mrs. Gilstrap was watching you out of the goodness of her heart and that it made it easier for her to work. I offered her money. She wouldn't accept a dime from me."

Callie nodded. "I remember being away from home. I remember when they took me from Mama. I had forgotten . . ."

Silas paused and shook his head. "Two years later, I ran into Kizzy in town. She broke down and told me the truth. About Marcus. She asked me for help getting you back. I went straight to Gilstrap. I told him I knew what was going on and would call down a storm of Greenville attorneys if he didn't return you to home. You was old enough to be in school by then. He told me that your father was a colored man. I told him that didn't matter. And if he so much as spoke a word of your parentage out loud in town, I would see him charged with kidnappin' and blackmail of an employee. And that I would speak to his wife about his lewd behavior toward Kizzy."

Despite all of the feelings and old memories swirling in Callie's mind, the words that poured out were simple, defiant ones. "I'm not a Negro. Look at me." She held pale hands up to her face as if to prove her point.

Seeta nodded. "You do favor Kizzy. But when you smile, I see my boy in your smile. I know that's not what you want to hear."

Callie stood slowly. She buttoned her coat and picked up her handbag. "Silas, let's go. This can't be true, and I've had enough."

Silas stood, pocketed the flask, and limped slowly after her. He turned to look at Seeta, but the woman had dropped her head into her hands.

Abruptly, Callie turned back toward the old woman. "So, you're my grandmother?"

Seeta looked up through teary eyes and nodded.

— • —

Callie tried hard to focus on the road through her own veil of tears. The car bumped along the rutted road and slammed into several potholes. Silas remained quiet until they reached the outskirts of town.

"I know you're angry, Callie. But please don't destroy my car," he tried.

She only threw the car into high gear.

"That's a lot to take in, and it's hard to believe. But it is true," Silas said wearily. "You needed to know the story before plowin' ahead with this plan to treat folks in Liberia," he said sharply.

"I'm supposed to believe I had a Negro father," Callie snapped.

"Seeta never wanted you to know. She kept outta your life for twenty-some years! But she's your grandmother, for God's sake!" Silas said. "She only wanted to keep you safe. Hell, I thought she'd died by now. But when you told me you'd been to Liberia, I knew. I jes' knew this was gonna happen. Blood will tell, girl."

Suddenly, the childhood memory of falling down near the creek took shape again in her mind, the upended basket of purple passionflowers rushing away in the current. The strong brown arms lifting her up and holding her tight. Wiping away her tears.

Callie slowed the car and turned onto the road toward town. "Silas, the Gilstraps are long dead." She swallowed hard. "Who else knows?"

"Davis and Grady Wilcox were young men in the Klan even then. Friends of Jim Beecham. Maybe even related. As I recall, there was a rally in the park once, and I saw Earl and Grady there in full costume. They was proud of their affiliation with the Klan, and Davis held some important office, as I recall. A wizard or a dragon? The whole organization should go to hell." Silas scratched his gray beard. "I managed to keep them quiet about you for this long. I have a little money in Grady's bank. If you keep away from Liberia, you won't rile anyone further."

Callie remembered the confrontation with Mr. Wilcox in the bank. "Grady Wilcox. I should have known. No wonder he was willing to let me rent from him at exorbitant rates, but balked when I went in to buy my house." She shifted in her seat. "I was so saintly and self-righteous, ready to charge up to Liberia and help colored folks. Now look. Their new schoolhouse has been burned down, and the thought of being half black has me in shambles. And Sam! Silas, what about Sam? If he finds out—"

Silas swatted the comment away with his hand. "Sam Epstein would care for you if you was blue, purple, or green. That boy is in love with you, Callie. I can see it when he looks at you. Back off from goin' to Liberia, and they'll simmer down. I won't let those men hurt you. You have my word."

"Silas, you're a dear, but how could you stop them from ruining my business?" Callie turned onto Florence Street and pulled into her neighbor's driveway. She guided the car into the old garage and turned off the engine. "And I've brought Sam into this. Sam is Jewish. Here only by the good graces of Dr. Davis." She leaned her head against the steering wheel. "So, what happens now?"

Silas exhaled heavily. "That, my girl, is up to you."

Chapter Eleven

The pine woods were dense and tangled with underbrush. Callie felt the sharp briars snag at her dungarees. She congratulated herself on wearing pants and boots this time. A chill breeze scented with pine whispered in the tall evergreens. It wasn't quite freezing, but it was winter still and close to dusk. She pulled her wool cap down low over reddened ears.

After Seeta's stunning revelation the week before, Callie had sunk into a depression. She had begged off from a date with Sam, claiming a cold. She had no appointments and no sales, which only threw her into a worse state of melancholy. She hadn't answered the phone or Silas's repeated knocks on her door. After three days of hiding, she decided to venture out. A walk in the quiet woods on a quest for rose hips and ginseng root would help get her mind off her troubles, she hoped. Just being outside made her feel a bit better.

The deer track through the woods was hard to follow that winter day, especially where the mountain laurel and dog hobble grew thick and low to the ground. A dusting of snow the night before had also worked to disguise the narrow path. The running pine that threaded its way across the floor of the forest made it difficult to keep to the trail that she usually followed with little trouble. She glanced behind her to be sure of the usual markers—the broken dogwood with the branches dragging the ground, the three sweet birch trees on one side of the path with the oak stump underneath. The small creek burbled as it tumbled downstream on her right. Satisfied with the way she was headed, she looked up, searching for the large white pine further up the hill, the one with the old eagle's nest in the crown.

She seemed to be going in the right direction, but the tree wasn't where it should be. The tree marked a spot she knew, a patch of ginseng root at its base. She had come in the early fall and harvested some, being careful to plop the berries back into the holes after taking the root. She wanted a bit more now, to make a tonic for Anne Walton. She spun around slowly, trying to get her bearings. The sun was low in the southwestern sky, and its filtered light was sinking fast. *Another day, then.* With a rising sense of dread, she hoisted her pack onto her shoulder reluctantly and decided to turn and head home.

A branch cracked behind her, and she stilled to listen. Something bigger than a deer was coming up the hill. The sound of footsteps crunching carelessly through the leaves raised the hairs on the back of Callie's neck. The murmur of men's voices sent her pulse racing. She stepped off the path and behind a large poplar, held her breath, and waited. After some time, two young white men appeared, shotguns slung over their shoulders. Behind them, stumbled a black man, mid-thirties maybe, shirtless, his hands tied behind his back. A rough rope around his neck was pulled taut, the other end in the hand of one of the white men. When the young man tripped, the rope would jerk and Callie heard the gurgle as the rope squeezed the man's windpipe.

Her stomach convulsed and she gasped before quickly covering her mouth. The white men were in conversation, but made no effort to hide their passing.

"Keep up, boy!" The first man turned and spat a fetid stream of tobacco juice on the ground, jerking the rope.

"Jeffrey, I ain't thinkin' this boy takes what he done serious enough," laughed the second man.

"He gonna take it serious soon enough when we meet up with Daddy an' the others on the ridge."

They crossed the very spot where she had just been standing and continued up the hill. Her heart banged in her chest. When they had been gone some minutes, she exhaled slowly and emerged from her hiding place. *They'll kill him if he doesn't freeze to death.* She did not recognize either of the white men, but easily guessed their intention.

What if they see me? Would they know she herself was half black? She had heard the stories—mulatto women were depicted as lustful, craven Jezebels. There were books and newspaper articles about mulatto women passing as white women, only to be discovered and beaten or raped for their deception by crowds of men. *But I can't just turn away.*

Her lips moved in silent prayer. Limbs shaking, she crept back onto the path, ashamed of her vulnerability, and afraid of its source. The men had moved up the hill quickly. She stepped through the woods with careful footfalls and a new awareness of her surroundings, her pulse rapid.

Slowly, she followed the sound of their voices up the hill, the terrain growing steeper as they climbed. She'd never been up this far. Twice, she slipped and fell on sharp rocks in her path. In the gathering darkness, she barked her shins against stumps. She heard the sound of the creek on her right still, splashing over stones on its hurry downhill.

From around the curve in the deer path, she glimpsed a clearing. She smelled the tang and yeasty odor of corn mash before she saw the still. Seeing the large metal container connected to several old barrels and piping froze the blood in her veins. Suddenly there was the snort of a horse's breath and then voices.

"What the hell you doin', Jeffrey? George?"

Callie crouched behind a rock and willed her breathing to slow.

Jeffrey stepped forward. "Daddy, this here nigger winked at Patty today, out front of the Burgess store. Lem Jones saw him do it. Saw him whistle at her, too. We found him at the crossroads." He paused. "I thought you was bringin' the others. We was gonna have us a show!" The young man grinned and looked around, as if expecting a crowd.

Callie watched as the older man on horseback dismounted and stood before the black man now kneeling on the damp ground, shivering uncontrollably in the chill. His pants were stained with his own urine.

"That so, boy?" demanded the man, a chew of tobacco lodged firmly in his cheek. He nudged the kneeling man's leg with the toe of his boot. "You made eyes at my daughter?"

"No, suh." The frightened man coughed. "I swear—no, suh!" The man coughed again and sat back, trying to take in enough air to speak. "Please, suh. I work at the Cateechee Mill—a night janitor. Ask Mr. Connor, the mill boss. I'm a good worker. I wasn't at Burgess Store today. I swear. I never bother no white woman, I swear to God."

The older man cursed under his breath. "Get the damn rope off o' his neck, George."

"Daddy, he's lyin'. Ain't we gonna punish him?" George cried.

The older man removed his hat and ran a hand through his gray hair. "Dammit, boys. Did you see Patty at the store? With your own eyes? You see this nigger at the store—with your own eyes?"

George and Jeffrey exchanged glances before shaking their heads sheepishly. George moved to take the rope from around the young man's neck. Callie cringed at the purple bruising and blood welling across his throat.

The older man jerked the black man to his feet roughly.

"Boy, what's your name?"

"D-Daniel. Daniel Cross, suh."

"Daniel, I'm gonna let you go. This time. But if you ever—"

"Daddy—" Jeffrey cut in.

"Shut the hell up, Jeffrey!" his father shouted. "Patty wasn't even at the store today, you idiots! Mama said she ain't left the house all day. An' you call for me to come up here this late?"

He turned back to the young black man. "Boy, if you ever cross a member of my family, we kill you. If you tell anyone what you saw here today, we put so many bullets in your body, they won't find no piece of meat bigger than a dime. Now git!"

With that, he pushed the man backward. Callie watched in horror as he stumbled, hands still tied behind his back, down the hill and out of sight. The older man leveled his shotgun in the general direction of the fleeing man and pulled the trigger. The percussive blast shook the forest, and Callie winced and covered her ears reflexively.

George and Jeffrey roared with laughter. The older man quickly turned on his sons. "If you pull that crap again, boys, I'll kill you myself. The last thing we need is to bring down the law, dammit! You brought that nigger all the way up here to the still? Damn, I musta raised the stupidest boys in the state." He spat hard, launching a glob of tobacco juice toward his sons. "Y'all git on down to home. Tell your mama to hold supper. I'll be there shortly." He mounted his horse, cursing under his breath.

Her heart banging in her chest, Callie tried not to move as the two young men shouldered their shotguns and headed down the path, near enough to catch the stench of their greasy, unwashed bodies.

For what seemed like an eternity, she watched orange streaks of sunset turn to red in the western sky. The man on horseback hadn't moved. The horse whinnied and snorted, anxious to move on, but his rider sat still in the saddle.

When the sun dropped below the ridgeline, twilight would fall quickly. Callie felt an electric current of panic coursing through her body, and cursed under her breath at her stupidity in following the men. Her bicycle was probably a mile away parked at the edge of the clearing by the road. And peddling back into town would take another thirty minutes.

The horse whinnied softly in the stillness. "I know you're here. Best show yourself now and let's be done with it," the man said. She heard him shift in his saddle.

Her pupils widened. She stepped from behind the rock and emerged into the clearing.

"A woman," the man said with some relief.

"I-I was hunting for ginseng," she apologized, her voice shaking from chill and dread. "Please. I won't say a thing. Your business is no concern of mine." She pulled her worn sweater tight across her chest.

The man snorted. But he sheathed his shotgun. "You live in town."

"Yessir. I sell herbal medicines. Tinctures. Teas. Things like that," Callie said.

"I know who you are," he said gruffly. "My wife has gone to town an' seen you. On Florence Street?" He paused. "You're up too high fer 'sang, girl."

Callie swallowed hard. "Probably so."

The man removed his hat and wiped his forehead with a handkerchief before replacing it. He glanced at his still and then regarded Callie with steel-blue eyes. "I 'spect you won't be up this way again. I 'spect you didn't see anything here to talk about."

"No, sir," Callie answered, keenly aware that the man knew where she lived.

He touched the brim of his hat. "Ma'am." He clicked his tongue, and the horse moved off slowly through thick dog hobble.

Callie exhaled a long breath. She leaned forward, the feeling of nausea strong, but nothing would come up. Stars began to wink overhead in the sapphire sky. Callie finally crept into the clearing and made her way, hands outstretched, downhill. Hearing no passing cars or trucks, she struck off tentatively along the creek, following the sound of the moving water now on her left. The creek would eventually branch, and one fork ran parallel to the road. Tree limbs slapped her face, and twice, she misstepped into the icy water. Soon, her boots were soaked, toes numb. The temperature began to drop in earnest and she shivered.

Eventually, the ground leveled out and Callie believed she was close to her familiar ginseng patch. The image of the white-hooded men in her dream came to mind. *It's that horrible nightmare. No.* The threatening note and the grocery sack of mutilated kittens on her porch was real. The burning of the school was real. Finding out she had a black father was real. And now this.

She paused to catch her breath and listen for the comforting sound of the burbling creek. In the quiet, she thought she heard the faint sound of a car engine coming down the road in her direction. The car backfired once as it came closer. She moved more quickly, her bearings now clear. Her bicycle was still parked right off of the road where the creek split. She whispered a silent prayer of thanks, and, after several minutes, finally emerged onto the shoulder of the road. Dim headlights greeted her, and the old Ford pulled over, engine chugging loudly.

Callie stepped into the road and waved her arms, grinning with relief. She jogged to the driver's side of the car and exclaimed, "How did you know where to find me?"

Silas scowled. "How'd you know it was me?"

"The backfire." She grinned. "I'd know that blessed sound anywhere. Oh, Silas, thank you so much for finding me. I'd never been lost in these woods before."

"Oh, now you'll talk to me! You're lucky I watched you peddle off a while back. I've been up and down these roads for hours. Get in, girl," he said gruffly.

"My bicycle is over there," she pointed. "Can I strap it to your roof?"

"You drivin'." Silas leaned over and fidgeted under the seat, pulling out a length of rope, then stepped out of the car, muttering under his breath.

They loaded the bike onto the roof of the old car and set off for home. Before long, an eerie fog settled over the road, swirling across the pavement like wisps of smoke. Callie operated the windshield wiper silently as Silas chastised her for her negligence in setting off so late.

"I've never gotten so turned around before," she explained. She shivered and tried to wiggle frozen toes. "I was lost."

Silas erupted. "There's several stills up in them woods. You coulda landed in a heap of trouble if you'd stumbled onto a still. You need to find a new place to look for 'sang. I can't keep you safe if you run off an' do fool things like this!"

Callie nodded, chastened.

"It's the God's honest truth—we don't know about most of what happens in these hills," Silas muttered. "Best to stay away."

Callie sighed and thought of the colored man's face. She'd never seen such fear. "Silas, I had a nightmare right after I met Seeta. I dreamed I was in the woods and Klansmen found me. One was a big man on horseback. The other men wore robes and hoods but didn't say a word. They'd killed my cat, and the big man threw George's body at my feet. He warned me to stop messing where I didn't belong. It was awful. And then the bag of dead kittens . . ." She shook her head.

Silas kept his eyes on the road and said nothing.

Callie needed to ask the question that haunted her, the one that would show how shallow, naïve, and high-and-mighty she was, despite her brave speeches to Seeta and Sam.

"Silas, do I look mulatto to you?" she asked, her cheeks flaming.

He did not laugh. "Callie, the color of your skin didn't change overnight. You look white. Brown-eyed and dark-haired—and white."

Callie couldn't help the feeling of relief that swept over her.

Silas stroked his scruffy beard. "But it doesn't change the truth. Jim Beecham wasn't your daddy." He shifted in his seat. "You're a mixed-race, girl. Anyone as old as me heard the rumors years ago an' probably just don't care anymore. Hell, if you go back far enough, there's a mix of black and white in a lot of folks around here. But you don't go puttin' yourself in situations that could be dangerous."

He patted Callie's shoulder. "You're a pretty gal, a good citizen mindin' your own business and doin' unto others. I know it's hard fo' you to hear, but if you look on the positive side, you jes' found a grandmother you didn't know you had."

"A grandmother . . ." She swallowed hard. "So you think the bag of kittens was a warning because I was helping folks in Liberia?" she asked hopefully. "And not because I'm half black?" She heard the scared little girl in her own voice.

Silas shook his head. "I can't lie to you. You might have riled them up a bit. As long as you stayed outta their way and behaved, they was willin' to extend Christian charity. Grady Wilcox did sell you a house right smack in downtown. But now you helpin' colored people and steppin' out with a Jewish doctor. You wander off your path, an' you'll find trouble, whether you're black or white. But it'll be worse if you're black."

Callie opened her mouth to speak, but Silas held up a hand. "The Klan likes to prop themselves up as good folks, fine Christians. They advertised a community picnic in a downtown park last weekend. Free sandwiches and lemonade. Had a church choir there. Signs were posted all over Main Street." He snorted. "You couldn't have missed 'em."

"I saw," Callie said dully.

"You can polish a brass piss pot but it's still a piss pot. 'Scuse my language," he said as she turned onto Main and headed for Florence Street. "And you've stirred the pot, so to speak." He grinned at his own pun. "Dr. Sam may be Jewish, but what a great way to show the community that they're welcoming to all sorts of folks—without actually welcoming *all* sorts of folks. They ain't Christian at all."

Callie's hands were numb from the cold. She rubbed them together briskly after pulling the car up to the curb in front of Silas's house. She glanced at her own house. She'd left no lights on, and her cozy nest appeared a bit foreboding in the thick fog. "Say what you mean, Silas," she snapped.

Silas put his hand on Callie's arm. "I ain't lettin' no one hurt you. I promise. But here's the ugly truth. Earl Davis will not countenance his token Jewish doctor takin' up with a mulatto girl."

— • —

Sam hung up the telephone and sat back in his desk chair. She was still not answering her telephone. He glanced at his watch. He was between appointments but without enough time to drive by Callie's house. She had claimed a cold and had put him off when he tried to reschedule their Saturday night date. He hoped nothing had happened to sour her on their budding relationship. He decided to stop at the florist's after work and drive by later with a dozen roses. It was worth a try. After all, she had kissed him on New Year's Day.

Since Liberia, Sam had tried to work especially hard for Dr. Davis. He'd seen several patients after hours and offered to help the nurse, Norma, with a new accounting system. He'd heard nothing more about his visit to treat Negroes and prayed that was the end of it.

The memory of Davis's fury when he announced his plan stayed with him. The man seethed with rage, and which part of Sam's plan actually made Davis the angriest was hard to decipher. The man hated black people, which chilled Sam to the marrow. As a Jew, Sam knew he was only one place removed from Negroes in the eyes of the Klan. Davis had made that painfully clear.

The man clearly didn't like Callie either. Sam sensed it at Mildred Davis's Thanksgiving dinner. While Mildred thought the world of her, Earl Davis did not. Mildred may have meant for the lie about Callie's engagement to make Sam jealous, but Earl clearly hoped it would discourage Sam from seeing Callie again. Surely, he didn't think her small business was in competition with his thriving practice. Callie barely eked out a living with her medicinal plants and postpartum care of indigent women.

There was a knock on Sam's office door, and Norma stuck her head in tentatively. "Nellie Woods just called to cancel her son's appointment. Bobby feels fine now." She smiled. "You're done for the day, Doctor. And a long day it was," she said, glancing at the wall clock. "It's almost supper time. Dr. Davis is long gone."

Sam smiled. "Very well, Norma. I think I'll head home soon. Unless you have questions about the books."

Norma shook her head. "Not tonight. If I leave now, I can get to the butcher shop before he closes. I want to try a new pork chop recipe I saw in *Good Housekeeping*."

Sam smiled. "You go on then. I'll lock up and be right behind you."

"Thank you, Dr. Epstein. Good night," Norma said and closed the office door. Sam sat for a moment and thought of Callie. He had been quite impressed with the way she treated patients at the Liberia schoolhouse. She had been professional, yet kind and gentle. Her treatments, however simple, seemed to work. His thoughts wandered, and he remembered that her hair smelled of lavender and her smile made his heart skip a beat. Their kiss, in front of Seeta and Silas, surprised and thrilled him and sent his senses into overdrive.

He hoped his gesture of flowers would be well received. Callie was a mercurial woman, he was finding out. He stood and removed his white coat and hung it on the back of the door. Shoving his arms into his suit jacket, he adjusted his tie, set his hat at an angle, and began to whistle a tune as he headed out the door.

— • —

Callie closed the front door, slid the lock in place , and sighed heavily. George came trotting from his hiding place under her bed and wound around her ankles, meowing for his supper. Callie flipped on the lights, removed her sodden boots and socks, and padded into the kitchen.

"George," Callie crooned. "Sweet boy, I've had quite the afternoon. Let me get you fed, and then I need a hot bath and some soup." Her head reeled with all that Silas had divulged. He was blunt, but she'd needed his honesty. She would break things off with Sam. If his career was at stake because of her, then she would do everything in her power to save it. Besides, she reasoned, if he found out who she was—what she was—then he would end it anyway. She would save him the trouble.

She opened a tin of cat food and stooped to spoon it into George's dish, then sat back on her heels and stroked his silky fur while he ate. The nightmare image of his lifeless body being tossed at her feet by a hooded Klansman passed through her mind and she shuddered.

Trying to set those worries aside, she turned her focus to her to-do list. Anne Walton would be coming in a week's time and there was no ginseng for one of Callie's preferred remedies. Still, she had a few things for Anne to try and her diet to discuss. Besides that, she welcomed the young woman's company. They had gotten along despite their contrasting backgrounds. It bothered Callie that her house appeared so shabby, but Anne didn't seem to notice. Her advance payment would tie Callie over for a while, too. She had noticed a worrying drop in patient visits after Christmas.

There was a knock on the front door, and she froze. George looked up from his bowl and then skittered toward the safety of Callie's bedroom. The grocery sack full of mutilated kittens flashed in her mind. The knock came a second time, and Callie stood up. *Have they come back?*

She nervously smoothed her wild hair, silently debating whether to telephone poor Silas yet again or answer the door. Only weeks before, she would have answered the door without hesitation. But now . . .

"This is ridiculous," Callie muttered, and crossed the room. "Who is it?"

"It's Sam."

She slid back the bolt and wrenched the door open.

Sam stood tall in the halo of porch light, a spray of long-stemmed roses clutched in his arms. His blue eyes scanned Callie from top to toe, twigs stuck in her curly bob, the knees of her dungarees caked in clay, and feet bare. "I came to see how you were feeling. You said you had a cold?"

Callie stiffened. "Sam," was all she offered.

"For you," he said, extending the fragrant bouquet. "According to the florist, red roses mean love and respect."

She took the flowers and held the bouquet to her nose, inhaling the heady fragrance. "And courage," she added.

"It looks like you've been out foraging," Sam tried. "I guess you're feeling better."

She looked down at her bare feet and dungarees. "My boots were soaked. I've only just come home."

Sam looked at Callie hopefully, but she did not invite him in. "I guess this is a bad time. Can we—can we reschedule our date?"

Callie's resolve nearly melted away when his eyes met hers. He reached out to remove a bit of debris from her hair, and his fingers brushed against her cheek. A jolt of electricity shot through to her core. It was too much.

"Sam, I don't think we should take this any further," she said abruptly, backing away.

His hand dropped to his side. "What happened? A little over a week ago, you kissed me. I'd like it if you'd do it again," he said sheepishly.

Callie felt her cheeks redden. "Sam, I–"

Sam jumped in. "If this is about me not being able to get up to Liberia again with you, I'm sorry. It's a busy time for me. Lots of patients with winter coughs. And I wanted to give Davis time to cool off. But next week looks better, and I'm not on call next weekend. I could go back."

"No, Sam." Callie shook her head quickly. "Don't go back. You're needed in town. Dr. Davis made that clear. You're busy here. People need you. I can handle anything up that way. I promise."

"What about us? You don't mean we shouldn't see each other. Do you?" He shoved his hands into his coat pockets. His soulful eyes pleaded with her. "Can I at least come in? You're letting the heat out, and you'll take sick standing in the doorway barefoot."

"That's an old wives' tale." Callie shivered and stepped out onto the porch, closing the door firmly behind her. She pulled her ratty sweater close and peered at her own bare toes. *Well, you sure look the part now. A no-account, skinny, wild-haired mulatto girl in dirty clothes and bare feet. Leave this rich white doctor alone. You don't deserve him.*

"Sam, please. Don't make this any harder than it has to be. We can be friends if you like, but—nothing more." At the sight of his misery, she faltered. "Good friends. Now, if you'll excuse me, I need some supper and a hot bath. Thank you for the roses. They're beautiful. You shouldn't have, but they're beautiful." Callie turned and stepped into her house. She slid the bolt across the closed door and turned off the porch lights.

She sank to the floor in despair. She pressed the roses hard to her face and inhaled their heavenly scent again. A hidden thorn pricked her cheek, and she began to cry. It wasn't until that moment she remembered it was her twenty-eighth birthday.

Chapter Twelve

Callie stood resolutely in front of the mill and watched the workers move in and out of the building as shifts changed. The day-shift workers streamed out tired and bedraggled, cotton lint dusting their overalls and in their hair like a fine frost. She blinked back tears at the memory of her own mother coming home in the same state, along with a cough that rattled her bones.

A chill wind blew, and Callie shoved her gloved hands into her coat pockets. Her dark eyes scanned the line of men and women queued up to punch timecards and head home after a long day. After a few minutes, Callie realized what was wrong. They were all white. She craned her neck looking for another entrance. When her eye caught sight of a young black man hurrying to the side of the building, she quickly followed him. Several black men were clustered at a narrow side door, where a white guard stood and nodded as each man went through the door.

Callie inhaled and exhaled a steadying breath. She waited until the guard was free and approached him. "Sir?"

The man was older, perhaps in his fifties. He looked up and his blue eyes scanned Callie from head to toe. He shook his head. "Ma'am, we ain't hirin' right now. An' this is the colored workers' entrance. You need to go 'round front an' look for the office if you need somethin'."

Callie smiled sweetly and backed down the steps. "Thank you. But I'm looking for one of your workers, a Mr. Daniel Cross? I believe he is a night janitor here? He did some work for—my husband—and I'm here to pay him. The office told me to come this way."

The guard sighed as if the ins and outs of the managerial staff in the front office were a mystery to him. "I just want to get home and have my supper." He leaned through the door and yelled, "Daniel! Get out here, boy!"

Callie's heart leaped when she saw the young man emerge, nervous as a rabbit, but clearly alive despite his horrible experience in the woods.

"That young woman," the guard said, stabbing a finger toward Callie. "See her and then get on back to work."

Cross removed his hat and came down the steps toward Callie. "Yes, ma'am?" he asked, and Callie's heart wanted to break for both the fear and the courage she saw in his large eyes. She noted the tell-tale signs of bruising and tissue damage barely concealed by the man's shirt collar.

"Mr. Cross," she began quietly, "You don't know me. But I saw what happened to you the other day in the woods, with those hooligan boys. I was out picking herbs."

Daniel waited silently.

"Mr. Cross, if you ever have need of a witness, of someone to come to your aid, my name is Callie Beecham. I live in Pickens. I'll attest on your behalf to what I saw them do. How they threatened you. And hurt you."

The young man glanced back at the guard slumped against the doorway and turned to Callie. "Please, ma'am. I don't know what you talkin' about," he whispered. "You must have me mistaken fo' someone else."

Callie sighed. "I told that guard I was here to pay you for work you did. I want to help you." She extended her gloved hand. "Thank you for your time."

As Daniel shook her hand, his eyes widened when he realized she had slipped a five-dollar bill into his palm. "Why you doin' this?"

"Thank you again, Mr. Cross," Callie said loudly. "My husband will call on you again. Your carpentry skills are exemplary." She turned and walked quickly away, tears burning in her eyes.

Chapter Thirteen

Something is wrong, she thought. Worry had dogged her all morning. She hadn't heard from Silas in days. She'd wanted to give the man some space after he'd chased over kingdom come looking for her. But this morning, something felt off. Wrong. A cold February rain thrummed on the roof and against the windows. After pacing the length of her kitchen for several minutes, she turned and headed for the coat closet. She pulled out her raincoat and umbrella, already saying prayers against what she dreaded finding.

Callie hurried down the sidewalk, up to Silas's front door, and knocked loudly. Where yesterday, she'd at least seen smoke curling from his small chimney, today was ominously different. The house appeared dark. Icy rain began to come down a little harder and she shivered.

"Silas, I'm coming in to check on you. I hope you're decent," she called. She knocked again and opened the unlocked front door.

The room was dark and cold. She groped for the electric light switch by the door and flipped it. The dim lightbulb overhead revealed the still shape lying under a patchwork quilt, the radio playing in the other room, Ethel Waters' "Sweet Georgia Brown." Silas's latest favorite song.

Callie knelt and shook his shoulder roughly. "Silas! Silas!" She turned him over to face her. There was no response. His once bright eyes were half-closed, and his face was mottled purple. She placed the back of her hand against his gray cheek and found it cold as ice. She felt for a carotid pulse, but there was none. "No. No. Silas, Silas. Please come back!" She patted his cheek several times forcefully. When there was no response, she dropped her head to his chest and listened. *Nothing.*

"Silas, don't leave me," she whispered. "You're all I have."

— • —

On another chilly morning in an unending rain, Callie gripped Sam's arm for support under the black umbrella and watched four employees of the Mountainview Funeral Home lower Silas Roberts' casket into the gaping earth. Days of rain had turned the ground into a boggy mire. Callie's shoes and stockings were caked in red clay. Sam's pants were soddened and mud-spattered.

He turned to look at her. She'd had no one else to call. After finding Silas dead, her first response was to telephone Sam, sobbing into the receiver. Callie had curled into a ball on the floor and gone into near shock.

Sam had come immediately and taken over. He made funeral arrangements, messaged Anne Walton that Callie wouldn't be able to keep their appointment as planned, and sat with her late into the night while she processed the loss of her friend.

There were no friends or family gathered to grieve the man's passing, no one to act as pall bearers. There were no comforting hymns. Callie had been unsure about what to do for Silas. Sam had arranged everything. Paid for everything. The eulogy was brief, based on the weather and what few facts Sam could give the funeral director. *Ashes to ashes, dust to dust . . .*

Silas Roberts was laid to rest next to his beloved wife and son in the soggy ground of the county cemetery. After a few words, Sam handed the funeral director several folded bills. The mortuary employees draped a tarp over the gaping hole and scattered like mice. The plot would be filled in when the steady rain ceased.

The grieving pair hurried silently toward Sam's car. There was nothing else to say. Callie had berated herself constantly for not catching Silas's deteriorating health. Sam assured her repeatedly that it wasn't her fault. The next-of-kin to contact was Silas's daughter-in-law, but Callie had no idea of the woman's name, much less how to find her. The small death notice in the newspaper might catch her eye, but what then?

Sam helped Callie into the car and jogged to the driver's side as the rain began to come down in sheets. He eased the car down the muddy lane and toward Callie's street. Occasionally, he flipped the windshield wiper lever back and forth, but the deluge made it practically useless. He squinted, trying to see through the windshield, and drove slowly, knowing that Callie would speak when she was ready.

He glanced away from the road for a moment to look at her. She sat stoically, staring straight ahead, her mouth set in the cupid's bow that he found so endearing. Her wet curls clung to her cheeks, her black wool cloche sodden and drooping. She was shivering. He still found her the most compelling woman he'd ever known, but she had shut him out. Completely.

"Callie, you're soaked through," Sam chided.

She turned to look at him and smiled wanly. "I plan to change and then go over to his house to tackle some chores. It was a mess. Can you stay for lunch first? I can put some soup on."

Sam glanced at her sheepishly. "I would love to, you know that. But I think I should go back to the boarding house and get out of this waterlogged suit before I see patients later."

"Of course. You'll catch your death otherwise. Drop me off. I'll be fine. I promise." She patted his hand. "You've done so much for me already. You're a good friend. Thank you. I'm sorry you have to drive all the way back to Sara Cane's in this rain."

Sam cleared his throat. "I hate to be crass and invite myself over later, but may I come by after work? Just to check on you?" He pulled the car up to the curb in front of Callie's house.

Callie sighed heavily. "I'm not a charity case, Sam. You don't have to check on me."

Chastened, Sam nodded. "I'm sorry. That didn't come out right. Let me take you to dinner—to celebrate Silas. It would be my pleasure, and it would be good for you to get out. Carunchio's in Greenville has excellent food. Maybe it will cheer us both up."

Callie turned toward him, her smile genuine this time. It made his heart skip a beat. "I don't want to be alone, so I would like that—very much."

— • —

When the rain finally let up after lunch, Callie hurried into town with her mind made up.

There was one dress shop in town, a simple brick storefront with a black awning, and a hand-painted pink and white shingle swinging overhead. *Mabel's Boutique.*

She pushed the heavy glass door open and entered the little shop. An elegantly dressed older woman appeared from the back and smiled a welcome. "May I help you, dear?"

Callie recognized the proprietress, Mabel Keith, right away but wasn't sure whether she should remind the woman that they'd met. Mrs. Keith had come to see her several years ago for digestive complaints.

"Yes, I'm looking for a new outfit. For a special dinner with a friend tonight?" Callie asked.

"Callie Beecham? It is you! I love what you've done with your hair," the woman exclaimed. "You look like Clara Bow in that lovely movie, *It*!"

Callie touched her new bob. "Thank you. I do like the cut, although it is a mess today after the rain. I've been—outside." She paused. "I can't believe you remembered me!"

Mrs. Keith put her hands on her hips. "You helped me through that rough patch in '25 when I was ill. You haven't been in here in well over two years, though. But I try to remember all the potential clients in town. And that's every woman I see." She laughed, putting Callie at ease. "So do you need a dinner dress or a suit?"

"I'm going to Carunchio's in Greenville," Callie said expectantly.

Mrs. Keith smiled and steepled her hands. "Fancy! I think a dress." The woman appraised Callie from head to toe and proclaimed, "I have just the thing." She flipped through the long rack of dresses and pulled out a fashionable midnight-blue beaded number, shorter than what Callie was used to, and quite stylish. "Knee-length silk crepe. Lovely flared skirt, of course. And look at that beading."

Callie was relieved that Mabel Keith didn't pry about the details of the dinner. "It's sleeveless," Callie said hesitantly. "In February? And the back plunges quite low."

"Yes, dear, so you can bare your arms and your lovely back. You're young. That's what evenings are for! We'll wrap you in a silk shawl and drape your decolletage in faux onyx beads. Unless you have a fur?"

Callie shook her head. "I don't own a fur." She wasn't sure she was ready for such a dress, but the thought of Sam painting the town with Atlanta debutants gave her the courage she lacked.

"I'll try it on." She took the slip of a dress and ducked behind the curtain. Moments later, she emerged.

Mrs. Keith smiled. "I knew it would fit you like a glove! It's lovely, Callie. You look amazing. That color against your pale skin... And I have a beautiful pair of silk pumps—pricy, but wait until you see them." Mrs. Keith hustled to the storeroom.

Callie blanched at the mention of her pale skin. She paused briefly to gather her courage once more. She was just going to dinner, she reasoned. Not marrying the man. Maybe Silas was wrong. Maybe no one knew except Silas and Seeta.

Her cash in hand from Anne Walton's payment would be enough to cover the outfit, and besides, it would pull her out of the gloom of losing Silas. Looking in the mirror, she shimmied a little, and the beading sparkled. She had never worn such a revealing dress before. The plunging back was quite the rage but made her blush just the same. Thin straps revealed her bare shoulders and arms. She tugged on the dress, hoping to drag it below her knees but to no avail.

Mabel returned with several shoe boxes piled high.

"I feel naked," Callie said.

"But you look divine!" Mabel beamed.

— • —

Callie hung the beautiful dress on the door of her bedroom and opened the shopping bag containing new shoes, a feathered headband and a silk shawl. She stood back to admire the ensemble, checked her watch, and realized she had only three hours until Sam arrived. She would have to set about the task of making herself into a glamorous woman.

The little bell over Callie's front door tinkled. With a start, she realized she hadn't taken the OPEN sign down nor locked the door. "Coming!" she called. *If I'm going to buy fancy dinner dresses, I need all the sales I can get.* She headed for the front room.

Callie stopped short and let out a small gasp.

"Well, if that's the reaction, I'll assume you didn't know our appointment was rescheduled for today. By your friend, Dr. Epstein?" Anne Walton smiled and looked at Callie playfully.

"What?" Callie fumbled for words. She remembered that Sam had called Anne to make her apologies the morning Silas died. He'd apparently forgotten to tell Callie the appointment had been rescheduled. "Anne! I'm awfully sorry. No, he forgot to tell me that. But do come in. Here, let me take your coat." She took the luxurious sable and draped it across the sofa carefully, taking note of Anne's Chanel tweed suit and heels. As usual, the young woman smelled divine and her platinum hair was perfectly coiffed, finger waves intact despite the morning rain.

"Men!" Anne sniffed. "Well, do you have time for me?"

Callie put a hand to her squirrel's nest of a hairdo and sighed. "Of course. Follow me. We'll be more comfy in the kitchen. I have a tea I want you to try anyway."

The women moved into the kitchen, Callie self-conscious of the messy space and the realization that she wasn't quite prepared to have an Anne Walton appointment without some warning.

"I'm sorry about your friend, Callie. Dr. Epstein told me you lost someone very dear." Anne began to work the fingers of her kid gloves off her manicured hands.

"Y-yes, I did," Callie said. "He was a dear old man, my neighbor." Callie spooned fragrant tea leaves into two tea balls and placed them in cups.

"If this isn't a good day to meet, I could come back another time," Anne offered.

"No! Not at all," Callie said. "I want to hear how the diet is going and give you the next steps for your treatment. There's more to this than vegetables and tinctures. It's just that I had no idea that Sam had rescheduled you for today. But I have my notes, and we can chat after this tea is ready."

"Sam? You mean Dr. Epstein? Aunt Mildred thinks he is the cat's meow. His voice *is* lovely over the telephone. You two are close?" Anne asked with more than a hint of curiosity. "His name sounds Jewish. How positively daring!"

Callie fumbled with a teaspoon and sent it clattering to the floor. She glanced at Anne and said, "Oh, no! Sam and I are friends. Just friends." She picked up the spoon and put it in the sink before retrieving another one from a drawer. The teapot began to whistle, and she tried to pour out without her nervous hands betraying her.

"Well, alright then," Anne murmured. "We won't talk about the divine Dr. Epstein. It's clearly making you as nervous as a rabbit."

Callie wheeled around. "Oh, Anne. I need your help. I really want to get down to the business of your appointment, which is extremely important. But—but Sam is taking me to dinner in Greenville in three hours. I bought a fabulous new dress. I think it's too ultra. And this hair?" she wailed. "The rain today ruined it, and I don't have time for finger waves to set. I forgot to buy stockings. And—"

Anne cut her off with a raised palm. "Callie. Enough said. Let's grab our tea and then show me the dress. I actually feel great on your diet of weeds and grass, and I am not in the mood to talk about my problems today anyway."

Callie motioned for Anne to follow her into the bedroom. The unmade bed, messy vanity, and general disarray didn't seem to bother

Anne in the least. Her eyes zoomed in on the beautiful dress hanging on the door.

"Callie, well done. This dress is heavenly. Silk crepe. Look at the beading. And the color will really pop against your white skin," Anne said, gently touching the fabric.

Callie felt her heart jump. The color of her skin was never something she had given any thought to, and now, every mention of it made her wobble. "It has a very low back," she apologized. "Not sure I'm up for that."

Anne swatted away the comment easily. "Callie, you should see some of the dinner dresses I own. I feel positively nude in a few of them. I know! You can borrow my sable tonight! To cover up in style." Her eyebrows rose. "Methinks this is not a dress for an evening out with a friend, my dear."

Callie blanched and shook her head. "Anne, I don't want to look like it's a date. And I won't borrow your sable. If something happened to it, I'd die. And Sam knows me well enough to know I wouldn't own a fur. No offense."

Anne shrugged. "None taken. Not everyone can pull off fur."

Callie was glad that Anne didn't seem easily miffed. "But can you help me figure out this hair? I stood out in the rain this morning at my friend's funeral." She ran her hand through her thick curls running to frizz.

Anne studied Callie's bob. "The cut is perfect. Tell you what! I am staying overnight at Aunt Mildred's. Let me send back for my curling tongs. Some silk stockings. And maybe some lacquer for those nails," she said with a scowl. "And I'll lend you a cocktail ring. Do you dig in the dirt every day?"

"Just about!" Callie laughed and felt her nerves calm. "Thank you, Anne."

Anne reached for Callie's hand. "I like you. You're real. I don't get much that's real in my life these days." She gave Callie's hand a squeeze and then turned for the door. "Let me tell Luther to run back and get what we need."

— • —

Callie sat glued to the chair while the hot curling iron shaped her hair into perfect Marcelled waves. Anne sat nearby, chattering on about life in Charleston, her trips abroad, and the hardships of the strict diet Callie prescribed. Callie could only watch in the mirror as Anne's maid,

Laura, expertly wielded the curling iron. The young woman's black hands combed and pulled and twisted each lock of hair, and soon Callie began to see the transformation.

"You look like Nancy Carroll in *Easy Come, Easy Go!*" exclaimed Anne. "I confess I am a bit jealous. Dark hair and eyes are all the rage now."

Callie bit her lip in amusement. "Nancy Carroll? I keep hearing I look like Clara Bow." She tried not to move her head. "Laura, you're very good with hair."

"Thank you, ma'am." Laura kept her eyes on her work, as if pulling and crimping Callie's hair was the most important task in her day. She did not speak unless spoken to, but Anne freely spoke her own mind in front of the young woman.

"My Laura is ever so good at hair. When I found her, I scooped her up as a maid. In a pinch one night, I had her do my hair and here we are. She's even gone to Paris with me a few times . . . You should have seen her getting on the ship to sail the first time. Her big eyes were like saucers. Weren't they, Laura?"

"Yes, ma'am," the woman answered dutifully.

Anne continued. "We stayed at the same hotel as Josephine Baker. Along the Champs Élysées. She was playing at *Folies Bergère*, and she danced topless and wore a skirt made of bananas! She was fabulous. When her makeup artist fell ill, Laura stepped in and did her makeup before one of her shows." She leaned closer. "Miss Baker doesn't really look colored, even in person." Anne continued her chatter. "So, tell me about Dr. Sam Epstein. Is he really Jewish? How exotic!"

"Sam is a friend. Nothing more. And yes, he is Jewish." Callie tried to change the subject. "Anne, I don't think I'll want the kohl around my eyes. I'm not a flapper." She gazed in the mirror. "I'm twenty-eight now."

Anne rolled her eyes. "Stop playing the old maid! You're only a few years older than I am. Nancy Carroll wears kohl and mascara. Honestly, Callie, I need to make you my pet project. We're going to get you out of Pickens. You're still young! You may not be flapper material, but you're not unattractive. Greenville has a few speakeasies that are in my husband's realm. Maybe we can double-date one evening. John loves a good bourbon. And I hear that Dr. Epstein lived in New York City. I bet he's a jazz fan. I love jazz. Harlem jazz really gets me going on the dance floor." She clapped her hands together. "We should go dancing!"

Callie couldn't imagine dancing with Sam. She hadn't danced in years. She watched Laura's eyes flicker briefly before she turned her focus to Callie's head once more. Callie was uncomfortable with the way Anne ignored Laura. *If Anne knew about me, she would never spend her time this way. A mulatto friend? Never.*

As Laura put down the hot iron, Anne leaned toward Callie and studied her protégé in the mirror. "Your hair looks amazing. I told you that Laura could work wonders. That's why I take her everywhere I go," Anne said.

Callie felt herself emboldened after an hour with the young maid. "Laura, I love it. Where did you learn to do hair?"

Laura's eyes grew wide, and she glanced at Anne before answering. "Mrs. Walton's last maid taught me before she left, ma'am," the woman said softly. She dropped her head and busied herself with Anne's makeup kit.

Anne groaned. "Laura's cousin—Fannie. She did good hair, but that girl was the worst! She positively was the worst. Lazy and dull. Horrible attitude. When she got pregnant, it was *Good riddance!*"

Laura quietly removed cosmetics from Anne's makeup bag.

Despite Callie's unease with the way Laura was treated, she had to admit that it was fun to have someone fix her up, and to have a friend to gossip with about a possible new beau.

But Sam could not be a new beau. The revelation that she was a mulatto would surely stop things in their tracks. She missed Silas terribly. He would have known what to say to Sam. Laura came at her with the stick of kohl, her eyes unreadable.

Callie tried not to blink. It was one dinner out. A chance to celebrate Silas Roberts' life with someone who knew how dear the old man was to her. That was all. After the kohl, Laura deftly flicked a coat of mascara onto Callie's long lashes.

Laura stepped back, and Anne leaned in to admire the girl's work. "Ravishing!" Anne pronounced. She reached into her purse and pulled out a tiny bottle of perfume. "Shalimar," she said with a grin She dabbed a bit behind each of Callie's ears and then playfully applied a drop to her own decolletage.

Callie peered at her reflection in the mirror. The transformation truly was amazing. Her dark eyes appeared large and well-defined after an application of kohl and two coats of mascara. Her perfectly Marcelled hair did, indeed, make her look like a movie star. Laura helped her slide the silky dress over her head and carefully buttoned the row of tiny faux onyx buttons at the small of her back. She draped the long string of onyx beads around Callie's neck and then placed the ebony feathered headband atop Callie's head. When Callie turned to see herself in the mirror, she gasped.

"That is not me. It is, but I mean, I never knew I could look like this. Oh, Anne! Laura! Thank you both so much. I haven't been this dressed up ever. The closest was a Red Cross party in DC after the war ended." She turned and watched the beads sparkle in the lamplight. "I can't tell you how much this means to me. I could cry."

"No waterworks! You'll mess your eyes." Anne handed Callie a handkerchief and glanced at her diamond watch. "Let's go sit and chat about me for thirty minutes. It will help your nerves. But I plan to come back tomorrow. You owe me a real appointment. I'm the one with cancer," she kidded.

Callie couldn't help herself. She hugged Anne tightly and then turned to Laura.

"Thank you, Laura. I'd like to pay you." Callie grabbed her purse.

"No, dear," Anne said sharply. "This is my gift. Now let's go have that chat. Laura, pack up my things and wait out in the car. Tell Luther we will leave in about half an hour."

"Yes, Mrs. Walton," Laura said demurely.

Chapter Fourteen

Callie paced anxiously until the glare of headlights from Sam's car signaled the approach of their date. She inhaled deeply and exhaled a long, slow breath. Why the knock on her front door made her jump she could only imagine. It wasn't like she was sixteen. Sam was a friend. Never to be more, she knew. *Just go and enjoy a good dinner.*

When Callie grabbed her new beaded clutch and opened the door, her resolve melted. Sam stood in the porch light's soft halo, wearing a trendy black double-breasted dinner jacket over a black vest, black tuxedo pants, and black bow tie slightly askew. His hair was slicked back, and as always, he ran his fingers through it nervously. Before she could say a word, she was gratified that Sam's blue eyes opened wide and he gasped audibly. "Oy . . . Callie, you look beautiful. Absolutely beautiful. That dress . . ." He nodded. "I approve."

Callie felt her face and neck blush crimson. "Thank you, Sam. I hope it's not too much for dinner."

Sam extended his gloved hand. "It's perfect. I'm a lucky man, indeed." He smiled as Callie took his arm.

I'll tell him we're through. But not tonight. This is a celebration of Silas's life. Not a date. As much as she wanted to focus on a lovely evening out, her anticipation was marred by the fact that she'd have to break it off. Firmly.

— • —

Sam steered the car into the valet parking lane and deftly handed the keys to the uniformed attendant. He watched as another attendant opened Callie's car door and helped her out of the car. In the revealing beaded dress and silk wrap, every man's eyes were on her. Sam couldn't believe his good fortune. As they entered the restaurant, the smiling coat-check girl approached and took Sam's coat and Callie's wrap. Callie was impossible to ignore, and the girl whispered a word of approval in her ear as the dress was revealed.

Sam's pulse jumped when Callie turned away, revealing the dress's plunging back. He noticed the way stray tendrils of dark hair fell toward the nape of her pale neck. His eyes traveled down her spine down to her lower back. And when she turned, her painted lips formed that perfect Cupid's bow that meant she was deep in thought.

He swallowed hard and ran his fingers through his hair. It was hard to reconcile this woman with the one who had answered the door only days ago in bare feet, with twigs in her messy hair, and mud-stained dungarees. Callie was a knock-out in this dress, but he had to admit that he wasn't sure which girl he actually preferred. They had hardly spoken on the drive to Greenville—just small talk about the weather, the car, and life in a little town. Sam's nerves were getting the best of him, and Callie seemed especially quiet. Whether she was downcast after Silas's funeral or had something else on her mind, it was hard to know. She had kissed him on New Year's Day and then tried to break off with him days later. Sam felt a bead of sweat trickle down his temple and quickly withdrew his handkerchief to wipe his brow before Callie turned around.

The maître d' seated the couple at a tiny corner table and poured water, then presented them with menus and backed away quietly.

"I'll never get used to fine dining without drinks," Sam tried. "A bottle of Chianti goes so well with Italian food. I'm not a fan of Prohibition."

Callie smiled and leaned in. "Me neither. We had some amazing mint juleps when I was living in Washington. That's one thing about Silas. He had quite the supplier. I don't know where he got his liquor, but he was mighty proud of it. He wasn't one for bathtub gin or moonshine if he could get the good stuff."

Sam was relieved to see her smile. "Well, we're not at a speakeasy." He shrugged apologetically. "We can toast Silas with water or tea, though." He lifted his water glass. "To Silas Roberts. A kind man. Your good friend."

Callie raised her glass as well, and they sipped their water. The waiter soon appeared and they placed their orders. A strolling violinist wandered by, playing "O Sole Mio." Callie gazed around the crowded room but seemed to avoid making eye contact with Sam.

He was grateful for the din of conversation and the music because their conversation was stilted and off. Callie barely said a word and seemed in a daze. His gut told him this wasn't about Silas. Not really. "So, tell me about Liberia. You went back. How were the patients?"

Callie's face, already sullen, became morose. "Sam, it's better if we never bring up that place and those people again." He could see the tiniest quiver in her lower lip and knew that she was hiding something bothersome.

The waiter appeared with a basket of fresh bread and a shallow dish of fragrant olive oil. Sam waited for him to leave before speaking. He leaned forward and put his hand on the table. "Hey. It's me. What happened up there? Callie, I know you say we're just friends. Well, alright then. I don't like it, but I accept it. But as a friend, if something happened, please tell me. Maybe I can help." He lowered his voice and added, "Whatever it is, I can take it. Did it cause a problem—my going there?"

Callie bit her lip. She looked at him sadly, shook her head, and dropped her gaze. "Sam. Don't make me talk about it. I can't bear it," she murmured. "It's not you. It's me."

Sam watched her pretty shoulders sag. His eyes darted around the busy restaurant. "Wait here," he said. "I'll be right back." He stood up and headed for the maître d's podium. He leaned close and spoke to the man for some time before shaking his hand and slipping several bills into the man's palm. He hurried back to the table and looked at Callie, his eyes bright.

"Change of plans. Come with me, beautiful." He extended his hand.

"Sam? What are you doing? We just ordered," Callie balked. She looked around at the other diners, but each table was engrossed in its own little world.

"Come on," he said again. "I promise I'm going to cheer you up."

Callie stood and followed Sam toward the front of the restaurant. The coat-check girl returned Sam's coat and Callie's wrap, as if leaving Carunchio's before the main course was the rule and not the exception.

The maître d' bowed graciously and said, "Come back again, Dr. Smith," before opening the door for the couple.

They stepped out into the street, and Sam burst into laughter.

"Sam, what are you doing? Why are we leaving? Who is Dr. Smith?" Callie asked. "And this dress cost a fortune!"

He stabbed a finger in her direction. "There! Those are the first honest words you've said to me all evening. I don't know what's really wrong, but it doesn't matter. I'm going to cheer you up, if only for one night. That dress deserves it. Come with me!" He grabbed her hand and led Callie down the street at a rapid pace, her heels clicking across the pavement.

— • —

They ducked down a dimly lit side street. Tall buildings loomed on either side, old office buildings and storefronts abandoned and in decay. Sam stopped in front of a brick building, its dilapidated steel door bent and rusted. The place looked about to fall down. Sam smiled slyly and said, "Watch this." He knocked three times, paused, and knocked twice more. He backed up and waited.

Suddenly, behind them, a boarded-up door across the alley creaked open and a man's husky voice called from the shadowy interior, "Who's there?"

Sam stepped forward. "We're here to see Michel," Sam said confidently.

Callie tilted her head and was about to speak, when the man answered, "Michel? Who's askin'?"

"A friend of Giuseppe's."

The door opened fully, and the young man stepped out into the alley. He wore evening clothes and carried a notepad. He glanced both ways. "Welcome to Michel's." The man stepped aside and motioned for Sam and Callie to enter the building.

Callie squeezed Sam's hand tightly as her eyes adjusted to the dim light of a single overhead bulb. The dark passageway crept down a long flight of stairs, turned abruptly right, and ended at another door—this one solid oak and ornately carved, with the name Michel's in raised gilt lettering carved into the wood. Sam pushed on the brass handle and opened the door into a smoke-filled room. People milled around drinking, laughing, and dancing to a small jazz band situated on a platform in the corner. Plush burgundy banquettes lined the walls, and small candlelit tables ringed the dance floor. A gleaming marble bar extended the length of the room near the back, where two snappily-dressed bartenders were hard at work with shakers and fancy stemware.

"Sam!" Callie exclaimed, her eyes dancing. "How did you find this place?"

"I'd heard Earl Davis mention a speakeasy near Carunchio's. So, I slipped the maître d' ten bucks and told him my date needed some cheering up." Sam winked. "You were just sitting there, so glum in that gorgeous dress." Sam reached for Callie's hand once more and led her to a table near the dance floor. "I wondered if he'd given me the right password, but here we are!"

Immediately, a dark-skinned waiter dressed in a white dinner jacket approached the table. "Good evening, sir. I'm Peter. What can Michel's make for you tonight?"

Callie noticed the variegated carnation in his lapel, red and white stripes. In the language of flowers, it meant regret for a love that cannot be shared. The symbolism threatened to topple her mood once again, but she dismissed it quickly.

Sam smiled. "Peter, this lovely lady needs a mint julep, and I'll have a bourbon on the rocks."

The man nodded and left the table. Callie felt her spirits lift as her eyes scanned the festive room. "Sam, thank you. This is fabulous."

The band struck up their rendition of Louis Armstrong's "Heebie Jeebies," and Sam stood. "May I have this dance, Miss Beecham?"

Callie balked. "I haven't danced in ten years, Sam. I don't know any of the current dances." Despite her words, she realized her toes were already tapping to the music. "Oh, who cares! Let's try it. I think I can remember how to foxtrot," she laughed. "But you may have to find a new partner for the Charleston—Dr. Smith!"

The pair moved onto the crowded dance floor and were caught up in the merriment of the room. Couples young and old danced through several popular songs, and Callie was soon swept up in the fun. She had never been to a speakeasy before and gradually felt her inhibitions melt away. She sang along to "Heebie Jeebies," and then "Bye Bye Blackbird" as Sam capably led her across the floor. She enjoyed the sensation of freedom, the live music, the touch of Sam's strong hand on her bare back, and the joy of being young and pretty. When the drum player began an extended solo before Jelly Roll Morton's "Blackbottom Stomp," the crowd erupted, and they picked up the pace. Sam swung Callie around, and they attempted the Charleston together, Callie laughing so hard at his antics that she felt a stitch in her side. The song finally ended with loud applause from the winded dancers.

A woman wearing a green sequined dress, skin like ebony, stepped to the microphone. She turned to cue the band, and the lights dimmed. The musicians started in on Gershwin's "Someone To Watch Over Me," and her rich voice was smooth honey to Callie's ears. Sam pulled Callie tight against his body as they danced. She felt a jolt of electricity to her core and leaned her head against his shoulder.

She felt his coarse cheek, warm against her ear. "There's a somebody I'm longing to see, I hope that she turns out to be someone to watch over me," he sang to her softly.

Callie felt such a sting of sadness that she pulled back and looked up at Sam. "I'm sorry. I must be tired. I think I could use that drink now," she said. Sam looked confused but led her back to the table.

The waiter had just left their cocktails, and as she sat down, Callie had to admire the artistry of her beverage. In its tall, frosted silver tumbler, the bourbon concoction was topped with sprigs of bright green mint; a striped green and white straw stabbed jauntily into the glass. Her first thought was of the invasive mint needing to be weeded from a plot in her herb garden, but she shook her head, banishing the thought.

Sam sipped his bourbon and closed his eyes. "Ah, I needed that," he said contentedly. "How is your julep?"

Callie gazed across the table at the handsome man, to whom only seconds before she might have surrendered her very soul. "Delicious. I think this is the nicest thing anyone has ever done for me. You're a good friend, Sam."

Sam frowned. "Ouch," he said playfully.

Callie was about to respond when there was a tap on her shoulder. "I thought I recognized that gorgeous dress!" said a familiar voice. She turned to see Anne standing behind her, an elegantly dressed older gentleman at her side. Callie gasped and stood. Sam rose slowly.

"Anne! What are you doing here?" Callie was incredulous. *Of course, Anne would find me.* The two women exchanged kisses on the cheek. Callie instantly fell in love with Anne's red sequined dress, with its long swinging fringe. The decolletage was quite low, revealing far more cleavage than Callie would ever dare. But on Anne, it was stunning.

"I could ask you the same question. I didn't know your dinner out included this disreputable place." Anne smiled easily and tossed her glossy platinum hair, her diamond-encrusted tiara glittering in the low light.

Callie reddened. "Sam thought I needed some cheering up." She tilted her head toward Sam. "Anne Walton, this is Dr. Sam Epstein. Sam, my friend, Anne. Or as I should call her, my fairy godmother. Anne helped put me together for our dinner tonight."

Callie knew that Sam had registered the woman's identity as her cancer patient, but wisely said only, "It's nice to meet you, Mrs. Walton."

Anne stared at Sam approvingly. "Well, hello, Dr. Epstein. This is my husband, John Walton."

John Walton merely glanced at Callie before turning to appraise Sam with hard blue eyes. She remembered that Anne had decided to see her despite her husband's objections and hoped he wasn't even now putting two and two together.

Sam extended his hand. "How do you do?"

The man nodded curtly and shook Sam's hand. "Epstein?" he said slowly. "I am not familiar with that name. Are you new to the club?"

It was Sam's turn to redden. "We're guests tonight," he said simply.

John's eyes narrowed, but he didn't pry.

Anne noticed the nearly full drinks on their table. "Come away, John. Let these two finish their cocktails." She reached for Callie's hand. "I'll be by tomorrow for a visit before we leave town. I can't wait to catch up, Callie dear." She winked slyly and hooked her arm in John's. "Enjoy Michel's, you two," she said.

John silently turned away with his wife. Sam helped Callie into her chair and took a long drink of bourbon. "That fellow seems a real hoot."

Callie sipped her mint julep. "I can't believe they're a couple. She's so young and fun-loving. He's so . . . dour. Thanks for not divulging that she's my client. Her husband clearly wasn't happy to meet me." She paused. "But I could use your help on the next steps in her treatment."

"I think his reaction has more to do with seeing a Jewish man in his white man's club." Sam smirked. "But if you want my help, that's a relief. It means I get to see you again." He grinned and pushed back the lock of dark hair that had fallen into his face. "You said that Anne is Mildred Davis's niece? John Walton's sour expression looked just like Earl's when I mentioned I was taking you out tonight. I would have pegged the husband as a blood relative."

Callie felt as if the wind had been knocked out of her. "Sam, no. Did you tell Dr. Davis that you were taking me out—on a date?"

Sam nodded and continued, oblivious to Callie's distress. "Yes, and the old goat seemed steaming mad. After the Liberia trip, I tried to lie low. I've worked several hours past dark most days the past two weeks. And I was back at the office the afternoon of Silas's funeral, for heaven's sake. I deserve a night off the clock. He doesn't own me. And I'd like to go back up there and help again. The people in Liberia need medical care."

"No!" Callie blurted. "You know he doesn't like me. Don't antagonize him." The room began to spin. She took a long drink of her cocktail. "I—I need some food."

"Of course." Sam signaled for the waiter. "Some finger sandwiches please?" he asked. Peter nodded and left the table.

Sam leaned forward. "Is that what's worrying you? That I might lose my job because I went to Liberia? Don't let old Davis bother you. He won't fire me. He knows how much I'm helping him. Why, I've brought in five new patients this month. Mildred has been singing my praises, and patients like the idea of natural treatment options for illnesses."

"Watch your step, Sam. Especially now that John Walton has seen us out together."

Sam frowned. "That sounds odd coming from you. Weren't you the defiant one? I thought that you had no problem with my being Jewish." He downed his drink and stared across the room, his eyes suddenly cold.

Callie leaned forward, stunned. "Says the man who called himself Dr. Smith just a while ago to a maître d'."

Sam opened his mouth to speak, but Callie interrupted him. "I'm sorry. I shouldn't have said that. It's me that Dr. Davis doesn't like. Me! He associates me with Liberia—and that's not a good thing for you." Callie hoped that Sam would make the connection she was going for. *We cannot be together.*

She reached across the table, but he withdrew his hand. "For all I know, Sam, Dr. Davis brags about you to everyone in town, but our relationship isn't one he is happy about."

Sam swirled the ice in his glass and didn't answer.

She turned her head toward the dance floor as the band reconvened on the small stage. They started in on a bluesy number that she didn't recognize.

"Sam, I said I was sorry. I'm sure that—"

"Davis said he didn't hire me to come up here and spend time on colored people who can't pay their bills. He said, 'Remember, you're just a Jewish boy yourself. I took a chance on you. Don't go upsetting the apple cart.'"

There it is. Before Callie could respond, the waiter reappeared with a small plate of finger sandwiches. The plate slipped and plopped onto the table. One of the small sandwiches fell onto the tablecloth. "Oh, I'm so sorry!" Peter said with horror. "How clumsy of me."

Callie hadn't noticed before, but the man wore white gloves. How difficult it must be to serve drinks and small plates in cotton gloves, she mused.

"That's alright, Peter." Callie smiled at the young man. She picked up the errant sandwich bite and popped it into her mouth. She knew the alcohol was having its way with her, but she didn't care.

"May I bring you another round of drinks?" he asked nervously.

Callie chewed the mouthful of food and swallowed thoroughly. Sam seemed a million miles away. She answered wryly, "Sure. Why not? I'm celebrating my birthday." The waiter nodded and hurried away.

Sam broke out of his stupor. "Callie, it's your birthday?"

"Was. January twenty-third. The night you came by with roses," Callie said sheepishly.

"Damn. You must think me an utter heel. I had no idea!" Sam exclaimed. "Can we start again?"

Callie softened, the bourbon lifting her mood. "I didn't think that at all. You've had a lot on your mind, too. But you know what? I do need a night of fun. I am sad about Silas, and my business is not doing so well, and—well, other things. Thank you for this. Let's dance." She stood up and grabbed Sam's hand as the band shifted into an upbeat Bessie Smith number. Soon, the floor was crowded with dancers.

Callie leaned into Sam and felt him respond by tightening his arm around her back. He smiled, and his blue eyes crinkled in the way that purely curled Callie's toes. As they circled the tightly packed dance floor, Callie threw her head back and laughed. From the corner of her eye, she saw the Waltons seated at a nearby table, Anne staring into her cocktail glass sullenly, while John glared at Callie and Sam with thinly veiled disgust.

— • —

A thick fog blanketed the narrow road back to town, rising and swirling, ghostlike. Sam kept his eyes on the road and crept along. Callie tried to stay awake and alert, but it was long past midnight, and the four mint juleps were proving too much for her. Her queasy gut and pounding head testified to the useless day she would have ahead unless she remembered to take a hangover remedy before crashing onto her bed.

"I had a wonderful time tonight. Be sure to drink a lot of water before you go to sleep," she murmured sleepily. "We're drunk."

"Yes, ma'am. And what else does the herbalist recommend?" Sam asked.

Callie smiled in the darkness. "The best hangover cure I know involves oranges—and I'm fresh out. So I'll drink water, take some wild ginger and peppermint, and a tablespoon of honey."

"Honey?" Sam asked.

"It speeds alcohol oxidation. Gets the toxins out faster." Callie felt her eyelids growing impossibly heavy. "Mind if I nap?"

Sam nodded. "Of course not. It's after two in the morning, sleepy head. We should be back to town in forty minutes or so."

— • —

Sam reached a hand out tentatively to stroke Callie's warm cheek. She was already fast asleep. The initially doubtful evening had been a rousing success. Callie had loosened up and forgotten whatever weighed so heavily. She had pressed herself close to his body when he held her on the dance floor. She'd kissed his cheek at one point, long and lingering. He struggled to keep his composure the more she let down her guard, the bourbon surely responsible for both of their giddy moods.

I'm crazy for this girl, he thought. He wondered if she would travel to Atlanta with him to meet his family. Callie was proud, wary of folks with money, and poor as a church mouse. Although he knew his mother was no Grant Park snob, the widow Epstein did expect her son to marry well. He had the family name to carry on, and eventually, the expected path of a private practice, and a lovely, rich Atlanta Jewess for a wife.

The anemic headlights barely pierced the thick fog, and he braked in front of a looming pothole in the road. The car bounced hard, and Callie woke with a start.

"I'm sorry," Sam said. "This fog is the devil. I can barely see the road."

Callie suddenly sat up tall. "Sam! Oh my God. Look!"

Sam peered into the distance and saw the shadowy figures Callie was pointing toward. As if from a nightmare, Sam watched as four white-robed men emerged onto the road from the shoulder. They wore pointed hoods over their heads, comical uneven eye holes cut into the fabric. One man's robe featured a purple cross stitched onto the chest. Two carried signs nailed to boards. One man waved his flashlight and then aimed it straight at Sam's oncoming car.

Sam slowed the car to an idle and leaned out the window. "What seems to be the problem?" he asked. He gripped the steering wheel tightly to keep his hands from trembling.

The figure with the purple cross on his robe neared the car and aimed the flashlight into Sam's face.

Sam held up a hand. "Hey, cut the light, please," he snapped.

The man pointed the flashlight at the ground and approached the car. "Who are you an' what're you doin' out this late?" the man growled.

Sam lifted his chin. "I could ask you gentlemen the same questions."

"We lookin' fer troublemakers. We was settin' out signs for a rally tomorrow. Someone tore down our first signs. You seen any niggers walkin' down this road?" The peaked hood bobbed as the man spoke.

"I detest that word," Sam said gruffly. "And no, we haven't. But this isn't a Sundown town, is it?" Sam asked.

"Naw, but it should be. Vandalism and tom-foolery at night is because we got drunken niggers runnin' around all night," the man griped.

"You have no business stopping cars this late. You're lucky I saw you standing in the road in all this fog. I could have hit you. Now, let us pass so I can see the young lady home." Sam prayed the man would not hear the panic in his voice. His eyes were drawn to the small, even stitches around the appliqued cross. Surely, the man's wife had taken her time with the work.

The man eyed Sam warily and then peered at Callie for a minute. "You best get on then," he grumbled. "Spread the word about the rally tomorrow night. God-fearin' decent folk are invited. Up ahead near the service station at the crossroads. You'll see the tent. Now git this pretty gal home."

Sam nodded and turned to put the car in gear when the man added, "And y'all can sleep well tonight, knowin' we're out here on patrol," then raised a fist and declared, "The watcher never wearies."

Sam revved the engine and the car sped forward. He didn't realize that he was holding his breath until he let out a deep sigh. He flexed his fingers, cramped from gripping the steering wheel so hard, and shook his head. "Damn them," he said gruffly. "Damn them to hell. You know, if he'd smelled the bourbon on my breath through that dirty sheet, it might have been a whole different outcome."

He glanced over at Callie. She had slumped against the car door, her hands over her face. She was shaking and crying softly.

— • —

Sam pulled the car up to the curb in front of Callie's house. He tried to make out her tear-stained face by the glow of the streetlamp. "Callie, it's alright. You're safe. Let me see you inside."

Callie hugged the silk shawl around her shoulders and grabbed her clutch as Sam came around to her door. She stepped out into the chilly night and hurried toward her front door. Fumbling for her key, she finally handed it to Sam, who opened the door and flipped on a light before Callie would enter.

"Thank you for a lovely evening. Would you like some coffee?" she asked.

Sam smiled. "I would love to come in, but it's nearly three a.m. Those Klansmen sobered me up, so I should get going. I have an early day."

Callie briskly rubbed her bare upper arms. "I suppose you're right." She shifted from one aching foot to the other. "Sam, I'm afraid."

Without waiting for an invitation, Sam enfolded her in his arms. She leaned into the hug, weary and frightened. *I can't do this alone,* she thought.

"They were a scary bunch, to be sure. We probably should aim to be back earlier in the evening the next time we go dancing," he quipped. "The watcher never wearies."

She pulled away. "Stop it. That's not funny! You know they would have done something else if they'd known!" She paused. "Known that you're Jewish, I mean."

"I'm only making light of it because it was so frightening."

"You were brave," Callie said with admiration.

Sam snorted. "I was scared stiff. We were right outside Dacusville when they stopped us. If I had said we were from Pickens and given my real name, we might have had problems."

"Seeta said Zeke had been harassed on the same road," Callie said softly.

"Let's not let those men ruin what was a great night. May I call you tomorrow—to compare hangovers?" His blue eyes crinkled as he grinned down at her.

Callie felt the familiar zing of electricity in her gut. "I'll be here." She hoped that Sam would take her in his arms and kiss her properly, slow and deep. But she prayed he wouldn't, because she wouldn't be able to resist him any longer if he did. She stepped back. "Good night, Sam."

Sam nodded and shoved his hands into his coat pockets. "Good night, Callie. Lock up after I go."

Chapter Fifteen

Callie tossed and turned in the last hour before dawn. She had slept so little, the quick cup of ginger tea ineffective in dealing with her pounding head. The images of the hooded Klansmen had seared themselves into her brain. She knew that her fate could have been a different one, had the men known that she was a mulatto girl out late with a Jewish man.

George hopped up on her bed and nestled himself under her arm. "You're lucky you're a cat," she muttered. As soon as the words left her mouth, she pictured the grocery sack of mutilated kittens, decapitated, still warm. The bile rose in her throat and her gut clenched. She threw back the covers and hurried to the bathroom, barely in time, as her stomach rebelled against the meager supper combined with too much alcohol.

For some time, Callie lay spent, draped across the edge of the toilet. *The watcher never wearies.* How could she possibly hope to keep her secret from Sam? Davis must surely have told John Walton the tidbit about the new physician in his office—a Jew. And Davis's objection to both Mildred and Anne seeing Callie for medical treatment was a fact. Both women had said as much. Would he one day tell them why he objected?

She recalled Silas's final words to her. "I ain't lettin' no one hurt you. But here's the ugly truth. Earl Davis will not countenance his token Jewish doctor takin' up with a mulatto girl."

She reached for a towel and wiped her mouth before slowly struggling to stand. Once vertical, she realized she did feel a bit less nauseous, less wobbly, as she shuffled to the kitchen. The wall clock read six o'clock, and Callie could already see the dim outline of trees outside her kitchen window. George appeared, winding between Callie's legs, meowing for his breakfast. Anne would be coming for her appointment at two o'clock.

Callie thought for a minute and made her decision. She looked down at the cat. "George, after I drink a gallon of coffee and feed you, I have an errand to run. I need some answers. Hold down the fort."

An hour later, she was dressed and on the road to Liberia, her black leather bag tucked securely at her feet. She'd wrapped a paisley scarf around her Marcelled hair, hoping to preserve Laura's masterpiece as long as possible. She had seen Silas's coat stashed on the seat when she'd gotten in the car. She'd hurriedly removed her own shabby coat and slid into his oversized, moth-eaten black duster. It smelled of him, of tobacco and wood smoke. She rolled back the cuffs a bit and smiled. It seemed like a hug from the old man himself.

The early morning was cold and clear, but the air carried hints of spring to come. She inhaled deeply and took in the fragrance of new grass, rising sap, and hidden waterfalls. Being outside always did much to lift her mood, and today was no exception. It also helped to settle her queasy stomach.

The old car backfired once as she picked up speed. *Silas, I miss you.* She glanced in the rearview mirror. There was no traffic, just a lone truck far behind her. Her plan was simple. She would go directly to Seeta's to ask about ginseng patches the old woman might know of near the Oolenoy River or Table Rock. Callie would never go back into the woods near her old patch again.

Callie horsed the steering wheel hard to make the left turn onto narrow Road 288. Silas's old car was nothing compared to Sam's sleek and modern Ford, but she was terribly grateful to have use of it. At some point, Callie knew that Silas's daughter-in-law would get wind of his death. She'd take the house and the beat-up old car. Probably sell them for next to nothing.

She glanced in the rearview mirror again and noticed the lone truck had also made the turn. Callie watched it get closer in the mirror. The throttle was switched down—as fast as the car would go. In her prior trips to Liberia, she'd never had anyone behind her once she was this far along. In another mile or so, Callie would turn off the pavement onto the gravel Liberia road. She wouldn't stay long, just a quick visit, so as not to attract attention. She wanted ginseng for Anne—and some answers—nothing more.

Callie's pulse quickened as the truck came even closer. She steered the car to the road shoulder, despite a steep bank right off the road, leading down to the shallow, green Oolenoy River. She reached her left arm out and waved for the truck to pass her.

In a split second, Callie felt her neck whip back as the truck rammed into the back of Silas's car. She gripped the steering wheel hard as the vehicle careened off the shoulder and down the grassy bank. The front of the car plunged into the waist-deep river, drenching Callie in icy water before the engine sputtered and died. She screamed and looked up toward the road, in time to see the truck accelerate and continue east.

Icy water began to puddle at her feet. She grabbed her black bag from the flooded floorboard and tried the door handle with cold fingers, but it was jammed and would not open. The bottom of Silas's coat was soaking wet and heavy. She grabbed her own coat from the seat. An adrenaline surge allowed her to swing her legs up over the door frame one at a time and ease out of the car, feet first, into the moving water. She held tightly to her dry coat in one hand and her supply bag in the other as she scrambled up the slippery bank, her feet quickly going numb.

She tore off the wet coat and pushed her shivering arms into her own dry one. Her teeth chattered, and she knew she must get warm soon or risk hypothermia. The turn-off onto the Liberia road was about half a mile away, and then there was another mile or so to any houses.

She peered down the road in both directions but saw no other traffic. Biting her lip to keep from sobbing, she jogged toward the turn-off, certain now that she had, indeed, enraged the wrong people. *The watcher never wearies.*

Bone-weary, she limped down the hard-packed gravel road, the welcome sight of Soapstone Church ahead of her. She didn't see a soul outside, so she continued toward Seeta's house. She climbed the several steps with leaden feet and knocked on the door loudly.

"Seeta? Delia? It's me. Callie. I—I was driving Silas's car. I've been in an accident," she called through the door, trying valiantly not to cry. She heard movement behind the door and it opened wide.

"Good Lawd, come in! I just got Ezekiel down to nap," Seeta said quietly, without hiding the surprise in her eyes. "Are you alright?" She took in Callie's appearance. "Never mind." She motioned for her to come inside before closing and locking the door securely.

"Callie, you soakin' wet. An' freezin' at that. Come in the kitchen. We dry yo' things by the woodstove. I'll make tea." Seeta bustled around, cane in one hand, as Callie pulled off wet shoes, stockings, and finally, her dress. She stood shivering in her slip, covered her breasts, and looked around nervously.

"You ain't got to worry. Zeke is at work all day. Delia, too. The baby'll sleep awhile if we quiet." Seeta moved toward a shelf and brought back a blanket. "Here. Wrap this around you. You're as pale as a ghost." She draped the thin blanket around Callie's shoulders as the tea kettle began to whistle. She poured two cups of steaming tea and set one in front of Callie, slid the other across the table, and then sat down wearily. "What happened?"

Callie cupped the warm mug in her hands and lifted it to her lips. She took a sip and it burned her mouth, but she didn't care. The heat from the mug began to relax her stiff fingers and the blanket warmed her shaking arms.

"Seeta," she began. "Someone ran me off the road just now. I was in Silas's car, and a truck came up behind me and rammed the car into the river, right before the turn-off."

"Did they stop to help?" Seeta whispered.

"They kept going. They just kept going." Callie wanted to cry, but the tears wouldn't flow.

"Did you see faces?"

"No. There were two men wearing caps. I-I don't know who they were," Callie said. "But I had another awful thing happen a while back. Someone threw a bag of dead kittens on my porch, along with a threatening note about coming to Liberia." She set down the warm mug. "Silas told me straight out. I've angered the wrong people."

Seeta nodded. "I've been prayin' for you since you came last. What I told you wasn't easy to hear, I know. It changed everything in your world. Everything. I surely didn't expect you to come back."

"I need ginseng for a patient," Callie began sheepishly.

Seeta pulled a face and shook her head. "That don't sound at all like the truth. I'm sure you have a plot somewhere you dig from. What's the real reason you come out here?"

Callie sighed. "I had a patch of ginseng in the woods north of town and—almost ran into moonshiners the last time I went." She decided not to worry Seeta anymore. "But truthfully, I wanted to see you."

Seeta sipped her tea. "Moonshiners is trouble. You best stay away from those woods if moonshiners have moved in."

"Silas came looking for me and saved the day," Callie said.

Seeta grinned. "He's a good man. He always has your back. I'd be a heap more worried about you down there if he wasn't around to keep tabs on you."

Callie's smile faded and tears began to pool in her eyes. "Oh, Seeta, you didn't hear? Silas died a few days ago. I thought you'd have seen his obituary in the paper—or something. I should have written you. His funeral was only yesterday."

Seeta closed her eyes. "I had a feelin' someone good left this world last week. Someone older in they years . . . I woke up a few nights after your birthday and jes' felt it. I must be losin' my touch because I sure couldn't sense who it was, but I shoulda known. He was a good man. He watched over you like I asked him to. All these years."

"I miss him very much," Callie said. "Wait. You know my birthday."

Callie felt a dam burst in her soul. "Oh, Seeta," she whispered, and reached for the old woman's hand.

Seeta lifted the pale hand to her own lips. She kissed Callie's hand and said, "Well, you gone have to wait fo' Zeke to get home tonight before someone who knows cars can get Silas's automobile outta the Oolenoy. An' then someone gotta get you back home. No one up this way has a telephone, or we'd call Dr. Sam." She leaned back and smiled contentedly. "I suppose we'll have all day to catch up."

Callie nodded. She was stranded for the time being. A rising dread tried to set in, but she willed herself to stop worrying. There was nothing she could do. She was stuck until Zeke got home. No matter that Anne Walton would show up for an appointment at two o'clock and find the door locked. That would surely doom their friendship, and probably their working relationship. She wanted so much to help Anne through her illness. The woman would think she'd been forgotten—again. But a chance to talk to her grandmother, a grandmother she'd never dreamed of finding, and to learn about her life, was priceless.

"We have some time, then. I want to hear everything," Callie said. "Start from the beginning."

Seeta squeezed Callie's hand. "Your daddy was a good man."

Callie jumped in. "I have this vague memory of a man—a black man—scooping me up after I fell into a creek, when I was maybe three," Callie said. "I dropped a basket of flowers. I remember I cried because the petals were floating away. Was that him?"

"No, baby," Seeta sighed. "That was my brother, Ben. Half-brother, really. He was fathered by a white man, one of my mama's owners. I didn't know I had a brother 'til I got a letter from a Ben Burgiss, all the way in Canada, about thirty years ago. He didn't know about me either until an old white doctor he knew wrote an' told him about me. Seems the doctor's conscience got the best of him on his deathbed."

"How did he find you?" Callie asked.

"Ben put advertisements in colored newspapers an' tracked me down. It's what people did after the war. Mamas tryin' to find children. Husbands tryin' to find wives." Seeta paused. "Ben said the doctor wrote that I was born in 1840 to his mama, a slave named Ona. Down in Pendleton. Said my mama had lost two baby girls already. When I was born, I was too early. Real puny an' hardly breathin'."

"What happened?" Callie's eyes grew wide.

"The white missus tol' Ona she was takin' me to the doctor. But she just wanted to get rid of me," Seeta murmured. "Missus herself had a baby due soon after an' didn't want Ona occupied with her own sickly baby. She tol' the doctor to get rid of me. But that doctor saved my life. He took me to a white family down in the middle of the state, friends o' his who had a slave woman already nursin' a baby."

"Didn't Ona wonder what happened to you?" Callie asked, incredulous. "Did she think you died?"

"She was a slave, Callie girl," Seeta said sharply. "Slave mamas and their babies were separated all the time. What could she do? I knew the woman who raised me wasn't my mama. She tol' me so. It weren't a surprise."

Callie saw the pain in Seeta's eyes. "How did Ben end up in Canada?"

"He escaped at the beginning of the war," Seeta said, dabbing at her eyes with the back of her hand. "With the help of that mistress's grown daughter, a good woman named Polly Burgiss. She got my mama, Ona, to freedom later, too."

Callie swallowed hard. "So this Ben Burgiss is my great uncle?"

Seeta nodded. "He came all the way to South Carolina on a train to meet me when you was about three," Seeta said, smiling. "We had a grand visit. He met my family. I wanted him to meet his niece, so I took him out to Kizzy's to meet you."

Seeta chuckled. "He was surprised you was so white-lookin'. Ben was half white, too, but he was the color of weak coffee. We took a walk by the creek while your mama was at work. It was summer and the wildflowers was bloomin'. We talked about Mama an' Marcus, an' the sorry ways of this world. You was runnin' ahead with your basket, lookin' for those passionflowers. You tripped and fell in the creek. You set to screamin' an' Ben scooped you up. He hugged you tight an' kissed your skint knee. Then he splashed into the water an' gathered up all the flowers. Every one." She smiled at the old memory, so sweet still.

"He didn't come back after that?"

Seeta sighed. "No. He only came the once. Ben didn't like comin' back down south—that don't ever leave a black man. I could see it in his eyes. 'The Klan's everywhere,' he said. An' he had a big family of his own up in Canada. A good business. He tol' me not to expect Marcus to come home. It was too dangerous. But he said he'd look for him."

"Canada," Callie murmured.

Seeta continued as if she hadn't heard. "He had the prettiest speech. Like a fine white man. Oh, he said he still had people call him names, and he couldn't talk to white women on the street, but he didn't have to step off a sidewalk when white people was passin' by. He could go into any store. Buy an' sell. I was happy for him. So, we got family in Canada, an' his boys are out west." She removed her glasses and wiped the lenses with the corner of her apron. "He did go to Chicago, to see if he could find Marcus. But he didn't find him." She sighed. "Ben's wife wrote a few years ago to say he'd died."

"Why didn't my mother go with Marcus up north?" Callie asked.

Seeta snorted. "You ain't that ignorant. Where do you think a black man and a white woman can be together? Not even in Michigan."

Callie swallowed hard, the idea of a real father of any color difficult to comprehend. "Did Marcus write?"

"Once," Seeta said. "I never heard from him after that. It was as much to protect us as to protect himself. That's what I have to believe. I like to think he's alive and livin' a good life somewhere. Happy. Maybe with a wife an' kids of his own. Maybe grandkids. Leastwise that's the way I like to think of him," Seeta said. "It hurts to think of him any other way."

"Do you have a picture of him?" Callie asked.

Seeta stood. "I do."

The baby let out a loud wail. "I'll get him," Callie offered. She stepped into the tiny bedroom and leaned over the crib, regarding her cousin's child. Ezekiel squirmed until his brown eyes found Callie's. He smiled a toothless grin and gurgled with glee. Callie hoisted him into her arms and stood, crooning softly to him. "Hello, little man. I'm your aunt—or your cousin. Something like that."

Seeta came into the room and put an arm around Callie. "You look good with a baby on your hip."

"That's the last thing I need." Callie chuckled. "But he sure is cute."

"Might as well change his diaper, and then you can feed him." Seeta pointed to the stack of folded cotton squares on the bedside table. "You know how to change a diaper?"

Callie bounced Ezekiel and kissed the top of his fuzzy head before laying him on the bed and grabbing a fresh diaper. "Seeta, I changed grown men's diapers when I worked for the Red Cross. Ezekiel will be easy." She swiftly removed the wet diaper and pinned a fresh one in place.

"Hand me the wet one. I'll add it to the bucket for washin'." Seeta took the diaper and shuffled out of the room.

Callie swaddled the baby again and carried him into the kitchen, where Seeta stood stirring powdered milk into water on the stove, for the bottle. "Isn't he a bit much for you all day? Caring for a baby must be exhausting."

"You don't say!" Seeta snorted sarcastically.

"What about Mattie?"

"She's a maid for folks in Dacusville. I can do it for now. I'm still tickin'," Seeta said. She tilted her head toward a framed photograph she'd placed on the table. "That's Marcus."

Callie carried Ezekiel to the table and sat down. He began to fuss when Seeta handed Callie the bottle.

"Test it on your arm," Seeta directed.

Callie tipped the bottle and felt drops of the warm liquid fall on her skin. "Just right." She gave the bottle to Ezekiel who took to the nipple eagerly. "Now, let me see my father."

Seeta held up the framed photo for Callie to see. "This was the one picture he sent. It was taken outside the buildin' where he lived in Chicago."

It was an image of a young black man in a dark suit and tie sitting proudly on the concrete steps of what looked to be a shabby brownstone apartment building. He sat forward with his elbows on his knees, long and lanky legs, a wide smile, and a Derby set at a jaunty angle.

"He's handsome," Callie murmured.

Seeta nodded, her own glistening eyes on the photo. Callie could see that it still hurt Seeta tremendously to know her boy was gone forever. "I don't want to bring any more pain to this house, Seeta. Will Zeke and Delia be angry that I am here? Delia was ice cold to me after the school burned down." A slow realization made Callie gasp. "Oh. Zeke and Delia don't know that Marcus is my father, do they? That I'm Zeke's—cousin."

"No, they don't. That wasn't my secret to tell," Seeta said. "If you decide you're ready for them to know, that's up to you." She picked up the photo.

Callie couldn't help the panic rising again. "What do I do? About the car?"

"Zeke's a mechanic," Seeta said calmly, clutching the frame close to her chest. "He'll get that car workin' and back to town fo' you. I wouldn't go tellin' the police. It won't help anything. If I was you, I'd jes' let it be. They know you here."

— • —

Ezekiel slept again after his mid-day bottle, so the women had lots of time to talk. They stepped outside to Seeta's garden, where a smattering of herbs grew along with the family's vegetables. Seeta cut grass for her chickens and gave Callie some of her most precious saved heirloom seeds. Callie promised to return the kindness.

Callie watched with wide eyes when Seeta grabbed a forked willow branch propped against the house and said, "Follow me." The old woman hobbled toward the far edge of the property. She held the forked ends of the branch in her fists and began to walk the large yard.

"Are you a water witch?" Callie asked. "My mother was, too."

"I taught your mama," Seeta said proudly. "I cut this dousin' rod from a east-pointin' branch under a full moon. It hasn't failed me yet. The well I share with Mr. Lewis is about tapped out. Figured it's time to find a new one." She continued to walk back and forth across the rear of her property.

After twenty minutes, Callie was stunned to see the branch begin to bob, and as Seeta slowed down, it finally pulled straight toward the ground.

"It jumped down. We here," Seeta announced. "Callie, take a stone or somethin' and mark it. The men gonna dig here when they come."

Callie quickly found a large rock and laid it where Seeta's willow branch pointed. "That's amazing. How deep will they have to dig to find water?"

"Mama Jane always said measure how far we is from the place we started. That's how deep we need to dig." Seeta shook her head. "But diggin' ain't my job. My job is just to find water." She smiled and turned back toward the house. "Now, time for more tea."

Inside, Callie related stories of working in the Red Cross, and of seeing the way the wounded white soldiers were treated compared to the returning Negro soldiers. "Granny, it broke the nurses' hearts. Those boys had fought and bled for our country, same as the white boys, but we were instructed by the matron to save the best supplies, the best food, for the white boys."

She told Seeta about the worrisome drop in her business after Thanksgiving, divulged her feelings about Sam, and her fear that he would abandon her if he knew her paternity. She related the frightful run-in with the Klansmen on the Greenville Highway only the night before. She lamented the loss of dear Silas, the only father-figure she'd known.

Afternoon shadows lengthened, and Callie lit Seeta's three precious oil lamps against the winter dark. She sat with the baby on her lap, watching Seeta stir a pot of vegetable soup. She felt at peace for the first time in months. Baby Ezekiel leaned against Callie, mouthing a rattle, and cooing contentedly. "Granny? Would you tell me about your childhood as a slave?" Callie asked.

"I don't talk about that. That's the dead time," Seeta said sharply as she stirred the soup.

Callie stumbled with her words. "C-can I ask—how you met my grandfather?"

Seeta tapped the wooden spoon on the pot and laid it aside. "I met John Young when I was workin' as a washerwoman after the war. Down near Orangeburg, where I was a slave. John had the kindest smile, an' every time he saw me, he'd call me Sweeta. Not Seeta." She chuckled. "Sweeta. He liked to tease." She grinned at Callie. "I loved that man."

"How did y'all end up here?" Callie asked.

Seeta hobbled toward the table and sat down. Her smile evaporated. "John sharecropped the Owens farm outside of town. About a hundred acres of cotton and corn. I did laundry for Mrs. Owens. We got married in '69. Had us a shack on the edge of the farm. It wasn't nothin' but a old slave cabin, an' we knew it, but we was blessed to have it to ourselves. We was free! Our first boy, Jacob, was born in 1870. John was so sick of tendin' cotton. He had big plans for savin' to buy some land. Sharecroppin' wasn't but one step up from bein' slaves, but it kept us from starvin'. An' there was white folks all around us havin' to do the same." She reached down to stroke little Ezekiel's soft cheek.

"So how did you end up in Liberia?" Callie tried again.

Seeta frowned. Her thoughts seemed to drift elsewhere, but then she looked at Callie. "We was doin' alright, I s'pose. I lost two babies after Jacob. Two little girls. Just like my mama, Ona. I didn't have no one to help me at my times. Both babies died bein' born. One born puny, before her date. The other had the cord 'round her neck. I named them April and August because that was the months they was born in. When Marcus finally came along in '78, John an' me was fully 'spectin' him to be born dead like the girls. I was thirty-eight! But Marcus—your daddy—he was healthy an' strong. Praise the Lawd."

Seeta clasped her hands together tightly in her lap and continued. "It weren't but a month after I had him that Mr. Owens showed up one day. John an' Jacob was in the fields. I was nursin' the baby. Mr. Owens jes' walked into my house. I looked up an' there he was." She shook her head. "I thought he came with laundry. But that wasn't it . . ."

Callie felt a wave of nausea seize her. She lifted Ezekiel and placed him on a quilt on the floor and set a rattle in from of him. She returned to the table and sat down. "Granny, you don't have to go on."

Seeta reached for Callie's hand. "Nah. You should know. I ain't never told anyone else. When your granddaddy came home an' found me, I was a mess. You know a woman ain't healed enough at four weeks."

She looked at Callie with such sorrow. "I never seen John so angry. Like it was his fault. He tol' me to get ready because the next mornin' we was headed north to where we could be free of cotton and workin' land that wasn't ours. He'd heard about Liberia. John said we'd walk if we had to. He went off to see Mr. Owens, angry as a rattlesnake. I begged him not to. Said it wouldn't come to no good. But he didn't listen to me. Said he'd worked hard for Mr. Owens for ten years an' thought that meant somethin'. It didn't mean a damn thing. Such a mule-headed man . . . That night, he said his piece to Mr. Owens an' came home. He thought it was done with. Tol' Mr. Owens don't ever step foot near me again. But I knew it wouldn't be done with. I knew it in my gut. Not no way a black man can have the last word, can defend his own wife. Not no way . . ."

Seeta lowered her voice. "They came fo' him after midnight. They dragged John outside. Jacob was screamin' and the baby was screamin'. I was in shock. They dragged yo' grandfather across the yard and stripped him naked. Tied him by his arms to a long cord wrapped around the saddle on a horse. Slapped the horse an' sent him down the gravel road. That damn horse dragged him clear down the road a mile an' across the cleared corn fields, with that sharp stubble . . . then through the creek an' down the road again. Those men followed on they own horses, carryin' torches, eggin' that horse on. When the horse would stop, they egg it on some more. The flesh musta ripped from his body in shreds."

Seeta sat up and wiped her tear-stained cheeks. Callie had never seen such rage in the woman's eyes. "Thing is, they did it to scare me, too.

They sent that horse in a wide circle around our shack. It was such pure hate. I heard they voices, an' John screamin' fo' mercy, and saw them torches of fire ... Round an' round our shack. All the way till dawn. I could see it all. Hear John screamin' fo' mercy. An' knew that I wouldn't never get my man home alive."

Callie sat still, stunned into silence.

Seeta glanced at Ezekiel playing contentedly on the rug. "They left him hangin' in a tree outside our place. An' that mornin' before the sun came up full, I left. I took the boys an' ran down the road to the white preacher's house. I tol' Jacob not to look back, but he did. He saw his daddy hangin' there. He let out such a scream. I wished I could scrub it from his little head. He weren't never a happy child after that." Her eyes filled with tears.

Seeta squeezed her granddaughter's hand. "I didn't know if the white preacher was a good man or one of the men who had lynched John, but I was desperate. Turns out, thank God, he was a good man. He fed me an' Jacob, put me an' my boys in his wagon, and drove us all the way to Columbia. Put me in care of another white preacher there who could he'p. Can't remember his name, but he tried to give me a train ticket to Atlanta. I refused. Said I wanted to get to the freedom settlement called Liberia, where my husband wanted us to be. The man took us as far as Greenville, an' we hitched a wagon ride and walked the rest." Seeta leaned back in her chair, spent.

Callie ran a shaking hand through her hair. "I've heard stories all my life about the terrible things white people have done to black people. I'm embarrassed to say that this is the first time I ever really listened. I'm so ashamed."

Seeta shrugged off Callie's comment. She stood wearily and returned to the stove. She stirred the soup pot and began to hum softly.

Callie glanced at the baby, who had fallen asleep face down on the soft quilt, his little bottom hoisted high. His gentle rhythmic breaths were a hard juxtaposition against the tale Seeta had related.

"How can you look at me—half white—and think of me kindly? How can you look at any white person and think of him kindly after all that?" she asked.

Seeta pointed the wooden spoon at her granddaughter. "You naïve if you believe only white people can do bad things." Seeta snorted. "Blue-eyed monsters ain't the only monsters in this world. Believe me, black folks is jes' as capable of hate as white folks. What good would it do—bein' filled with hate? Isn't that jes' what's wrong with Dr. Davis? He's consumed with hate. Remember, it was a white doctor who saved me at birth. An' two white preachers who saved me an' my boys. An' Silas who watched over you."

Seeta turned to gaze at her sleeping great-grandson. "When this baby boy is grown, God willin', that kind of hate will be gone."

Callie wished she had that kind of faith. "From your lips to God's ears, Granny. This world is so messed up. I don't know if we'll ever see the end of hatred because of the color of someone's skin. How do you stay strong?"

Seeta regarded her granddaughter with tender eyes. "I see glimpses of kindness every now an' then. Back when we first came to Liberia, it was a young white man gave us a ride in his wagon to about two miles from here, where he had to turn off. It was on toward evenin', and I was bone-tired. In shock, after what happened to my John. Jacob could hardly walk no more, and Marcus was jes' like a limp sack of potatoes in my arms. The man gave me a flask of water and some apples an' wished us well. We got out of the wagon. All I saw ahead of us was hills and mountains in the distance. I'd never seen such. It looked like we was headed uphill the whole way. Jacob started cryin' and then Marcus started cryin'. I had to be strong. We was so close . . . I knew we didn't want to be caught on the road after dark. I asked the man, 'Where we head to? My boys is so tired. So scared.' The man pointed to the sun lowerin' in that orange sky and said, 'Keep climbin'. You almost there. Godspeed.' Then his wagon pulled away."

Seeta closed her eyes. "So, we started to climb toward the sun. I tol' Jacob that when we caught up to it, we'd be celebratin' our new life, safe in Liberia. We'd be free. That's what we did. We kept climbin' to the sun. An' that's what we still got to do, baby. Keep climbin' to the sun. Like those passionflower vines you like so much. Get up every mornin' and keep climbin' to the sun."

— • —

The play of car headlights across the kitchen ceiling quieted the women instantly. A car slowly motored toward Seeta's house in the gathering dusk. "Is that Zeke and Delia?" Callie asked hopefully.

"No, baby," Seeta said quietly. She reached for Ezekiel, who had started to fuss. She held her great-grandson tightly. "Zeke an' Delia git dropped off by Bob Johnson, a white man who has a place up the valley. They ride in his truck bed an' then walk from the main road. He ain't never brought them to the house before—and that sure ain't his truck."

Callie peered through the sheer window curtain, waiting for her eyes to adjust. She gasped.

"Who is it?" Seeta asked in a whisper.

Callie let the curtain fall back into place. She smiled broadly. "It's Sam!"

She hurried to the front door and pulled it open before Sam could knock.

"Thank God!" Sam barked. "What in hell happened to you?"

Callie impulsively threw her arms around Sam's neck. "How did you know where I was?" she cried, relief written across her face.

Sam pushed Callie away gently. He ran his hand through his brown hair, exasperated. "Your friend, Anne Walton, came to the office. She was worried because you two had an appointment. She went to your house, and you weren't there. She wondered if I knew where you might be and insisted I go find you. Dr. Davis was not amused, but he didn't cross his niece." He looked from Callie to Seeta. "I could swear I saw Silas's car in the river. What on earth—"

"I—I came up to get ginseng from Seeta and—" Callie paused and glanced at her grandmother standing behind her with Ezekiel on her hip. "I accidently drove Silas's car into the river."

Sam's jaw dropped. "You did what? Are you alright?"

"Yes, yes, I'm fine. I was cold and wet and pretty shaken up, but I'm fine now." Callie glanced at Seeta, and her heart lurched. "Let me get my bag and coat. Seeta said that Zeke'll be able to get the car out of the river tomorrow."

Sam nodded, still standing awkwardly in the doorway. "How are you, Seeta?"

Seeta lifted her chin. "I'm fine, Dr. Sam. Come in and close the door. Don't want this baby to catch cold."

Sam nodded and stepped inside, closing the door behind him. "You look well."

"Can't complain," Seeta said. "How is the town doctorin' goin'?"

Sam shook his head. "Busy. I can't complain, either. At some point, I'll get back up this way to see to folks again." He paused. "I saw the new schoolhouse. It burned down? What happened?"

Callie reappeared, rapidly tying her scarf under her chin. "I'm ready, Sam." Her pleading eyes stared at Seeta's face. "I'm sure Seeta would like me out of her way."

Seeta gazed at her granddaughter with such a despondent expression that Callie had to look away.

"Oh, Dr. Sam, who knows? Probably that ol' wood stove caught fire," Seeta said.

"Well, that's a shame," Sam said. "Glad it wasn't anything more frightening. Did Callie tell you that we had a run-in with some Klansmen last night coming back from Greenville?"

Seeta nodded. "Lawd knows they everywhere."

"They scared me, that's for sure. If they'd known a Jew was out with one of their Southern belles, I might not be here now," Sam joked. "But seriously, tell everyone up here to stay off the highway to Greenville after dark for a while. They're holding a rally soon. No sense looking for trouble."

Callie caught Seeta's smile at Sam's naivety.

"I will. Thank you, Sam." Ezekiel began to cry, and Seeta hoisted the baby to her other hip. "Well, Zeke an' Delia be home soon. I best get supper on the table."

"Did you get your ginseng?" Sam asked Callie.

"She got what she came for," Seeta said quickly.

Callie left Sam's side and rushed to give Seeta and Ezekiel a brief hug. "Thank you," she whispered in the woman's ear. "I'll be back soon." She pecked Ezekiel on the top of his head and turned abruptly for the door.

"Good night, Seeta," Sam called. He followed Callie out the door and down the front steps. The night was cold and clear. Early stars winked overhead in a sapphire sky as Sam opened the car door for Callie. She sat down wearily, praying the ride home would be a quiet one. She had much to think on and didn't need Sam's questions. Questions she was not prepared to answer.

Sam started the car and eased down the rutted dirt road. The headlights briefly shone on the charred rubble of the school. He made the turn onto the narrow two-lane road and slowed when the same dim headlights caught the fender of Silas's car poking out of the muddy Oolenoy on his left.

— • —

When the car finally turned onto the road into Pickens some minutes later, Sam's hurt voice cut the silence. "Callie, I think it's time you let me in on what's really going on."

Callie pulled the collar of her coat up around her ears. "What do you mean?"

"You kissed me one day, and completely shunned me the next," Sam said. "You wouldn't let me into your house the night I stopped by with roses but called me first when you found Silas dead. We had a wonderful night out—but then, some hooligans tried to intimidate me on our drive home, and I got the feeling again that you don't want to be seen with me."

Callie craned her neck to look at a car approach from behind. "Just take me home, Sam."

Sam's frustration mounted. "You don't want *me* going up to Seeta's anymore, but there *you* were on an errand so important that you missed an appointment with the only paying client you've had in a while. And then I had to come bail you out."

"That isn't what happened at all. And I didn't ask for you to come save me," Callie murmured. "But thank you."

"You seemed happy enough to see me." Sam pushed his dark hair off his forehead. "Callie, you know I'm crazy about you."

He remembered the way Callie had cowered in the car when the Klansmen appeared. *That's it. She doesn't want to be seen with a Jew.* Sam eased the car onto the road shoulder. The car behind them passed and continued down the road. He cut the engine and turned to her. "It's the Jewish thing, isn't it? You were so quiet last night after we ran into Anne Walton at Michel's. And—those men who stopped us. I could see how it scared you."

She stared out the window and wouldn't look at him. "You're right," she mumbled. "I'm having trouble coming to terms with that. You being Jewish, I mean. It makes me ashamed but it's true. So, you never need to see me again. My behavior is despicable."

Callie finally turned to him. "You and I can't be—what you want. Please stop phoning me," she said softly.

Sam tried to reach for her hand, but she yanked it away.

He wanted to believe that she had the same feelings for him that he had for her, but it was obvious now that something had changed. "Very well. The last thing I want is to hurt you."

Callie sighed. "I'm incredibly tired. And I miss Silas more than I thought I would. I just need to be alone."

Sam started the car and continued down the road. He gazed through the windscreen at the warm glow of lamps lit against the dark in people's homes. *People who have not a care in the world.* He turned onto Florence Street, pulled up to Callie's house, and cut the engine. As she fumbled for the door latch, Sam opened his door and hurried around to help her out.

She hesitantly took his offered hand, clutching her coat and her bag to her chest.

Sam followed her up the sidewalk. He took the key from her hand, unlocked the door, and pushed it open, feeling for the light switch on the wall. He flipped the light on and heard George's loud meow of greeting. The cat wrapped around Callie's legs a few times before slipping outside into the dark.

Callie turned to close the door, but Sam's hand on the doorknob stopped her.

"Callie," Sam said softly. "Please."

"Go ahead," she said, slowly unwinding the scarf from her dark hair. "It's been a horrid day. Go ahead and say what else you have to say and then we're done." She would not look at him.

I love you. I'll protect you. I would do anything for you. Sam cleared his throat. "Can we still be friends?" He searched her brown eyes for the affection he had seen there so recently.

Callie dropped her eyes and his heart lurched. "I don't think so," she said wearily.

He nodded and shoved his hands in his pockets. "All right then. Good night. Lock up."

Callie closed the door gently. Sam listened for the sound of the deadbolt sliding across the door. He walked slowly to his car, then turned and watched her through the front window.

Callie smiled and waved at him through the large window, then stooped to set down her bag, as if dropping the weight of the world. When she stood, the smile was gone.

Chapter Sixteen

Callie bolted upright at the sound of shattering glass in the front room. Her heart thudded in her chest, and she sat still for a moment, listening in the dark. The bright moon cast shadows across the floor, and she waited, frozen in place. There was the sound of a car slowly motoring away, and only when it faded, did she dare swing her feet out of bed. She uttered a quick prayer of desperation and stood.

She grabbed the poker near the bedroom fireplace and tiptoed toward the dark kitchen and the telephone on the far wall. In the moonlight, she could see into the front room. The cold night air poured into her home through the jagged glass, raising goosebumps on her skin. The curtains billowed, ghostlike, on either side of the window. She realized she'd been holding her breath and exhaled audibly before a gasping inhalation.

The clock on the wall pointed to 3:30. Callie crossed the kitchen quickly and reached for the telephone receiver. "Operator," the disembodied woman's voice said too cheerfully for so late at night.

"Jenny? Get me Deputy Donaldson. It's Callie Beecham." Callie tried to keep her voice from shaking. "Someone just threw something through my front window. Shattered the glass. Who would do such a thing?"

"Oh, bless your heart!" Jenny sighed. "Young kids actin' the fool, I bet. I'd put you through, honey, but there's no one there until morning. I could ring his house. I don't think Minnie will like me waking up her husband in the middle of the night for a window, but I can ring him up if you want."

In a town of one thousand people, Callie knew the woman was right. Everyone knew everyone. Jenny would have the story all over town by noon anyway. And what if the deputy knew about her and decided to look the other way?

Callie tried to calm her trembling nerves with a deep breath. "You're right, Jenny. I'll call the office in the morning. It was probably kids. I heard a car drive away but saw nothing. They're gone now—and it is just a window." Saying the words gave Callie some hope of their veracity.

"I'm glad you aren't hurt. All right then. Good night, honey." Jenny's sing-song voice was hard to take at noon, much less in the middle of the night.

Callie flipped a switch and light illuminated the kitchen. She padded into the dark front room and gasped. In the eerie glow of the dying fireplace embers, she saw jagged shards of glass sprayed across the wood floor, on the examination table, and the sofa. Callie wanted to scream, but instead donned her muddy boots and headed toward the window, crunching across broken glass to close the curtains against the chill. She poked at the fire and then added kindling and a log from the hearth basket. The fire began to crackle and flicker. Shivering, she grabbed a quilt that lay across a chair, shook out the broken glass, and hung it over the curtain rod to help hold in some warmth.

In the kitchen, she turned on the radio and spun the dial in an attempt to find an on-air signal. When she found a station, she grabbed the broom and dustpan and set to work cleaning up the mess, the strains of Duke Ellington drifting through the small house. *I won't cry. I won't cry.*

Something caught her eye, and Callie turned toward the sofa. She crouched down and retrieved a rock about the size of her fist. A piece of paper was wrapped around it with twine. The sight made her pulse race and she unwound the twine with trembling fingers. She unfolded the paper carefully, and read the typed, misspelled words.

Go live with your colored family. You an't welcome were white people live. Go quitly and we won't come back. If you stay, everone will know you a nigger and you will be burned out. No coloreds living downtown.

Callie folded the paper and tucked it in her bathrobe. She stood and leaned against the wall, tears welling in her eyes. From the kitchen, Jimmie Rogers began to croon "T for Texas." Callie's demeanor shattered like the window, and she slid down the wall, defeated, her body wracked with sobs. She missed Silas so much, and she knew that Sam's good intentions would soon fall by the wayside. She was colored. Folks in town knew it. And the powers that be wanted her out. Now.

The Fire Spell. Her mother's spell for protection. Callie hurried to her bedroom. She pulled open a drawer in the maple breakfront that had been her mother's pride—a furniture piece bought and paid for with mill earnings. She rummaged under a stack of underthings until she found what she was looking for. She crouched in front of her bedroom fireplace and snipped a piece of paper into a triangle. She poured a small handful of dried herbs into the center of the paper and then folded it tightly. After saying a small prayer, she tossed the packet into the fire, closed her eyes, and sat quietly until the packet was consumed by flames. *There.*

From the kitchen, Jimmie Rogers strummed his guitar and yodeled,

'Druther drink muddy water,
Sleep in a holler log
Sleep in a holler log
Than to be in Atlanta
Treated like a dirty dog.

— • —

Golden morning sunlight streamed into the bedroom window. Callie shivered and pulled the quilts up around her shoulders tightly. As she came to consciousness, the nightmare revealed itself to be true. The little house was ice cold, the fires only smoldering in both fireplaces.

The radio was still on in the kitchen, a soothing voice in the early hours.

She'd made her decision. She would close the shop immediately and list the house for sale before she could get any more threats. She had no cash to speak of, but the small house should sell quickly. She'd go to Seeta's—until she could figure out her next steps. She would not see Sam again. If she wanted to keep him safe, she'd have to stay far away from the man.

She would need a few days to make it all happen. First, she would call someone about repairing the window. Then she would go to Silas's house and tidy it up. The house had been in such a mess when she'd found Silas dead. She would set it to rights, get the car repaired, and have it ready for the daughter-in-law to show up. She owed him that much. Then she would move. She tossed back the quilts and put her feet in her slippers.

After brewing a pot of coffee, she steeled herself with a steaming mug and stepped outside to survey the extent of the damage. The morning sun warmed her face as she stared at the empty window frame.

"What happened to your window?" called her neighbor, Mrs. Gibson, from across the narrow street. The woman stood on her own front porch, milk bottle and newspaper clutched in her hands. "You gotta get that fixed," she said accusingly.

"Hello, Mrs. Gibson," Callie said. The woman had never been very friendly. "Yes, I'll get a handyman out here right away. It's quite cold inside my house, as you can imagine. Someone certainly had their way with my window last night. Did you see anyone suspicious?"

"Well, we ain't up all night like you. You have people comin' and goin' at all hours. It's no surprise—Harold and me wondered when somethin' like this would happen. It's a neighborhood, not a store on Main Street."

Callie stumbled for words. "I–I'm sorry. I didn't realize my clients were bothersome."

Mrs. Gibson grew emboldened at Callie's apology. "Clients? Seems like a campground for hoboes half the time. You got cars an' people out front at all hours. A few months back, I saw a colored man with mules tied up outside your house at daybreak. Don't know what that was all about, but I saw it. Almost called the sheriff. We're church-goin' folks just tryin' to live a quiet life." She shook her finger in Callie's direction. "But I saw you leave with that man when I stepped out to get my milk. What in tarnation?"

Callie blanched at the verbal assault. "He needed medical care for his wife."

"He can go to a charity hospital in Six Mile that takes coloreds. That's what it's for. Shouldn't be loiterin' around here. We can't have that, for Christ's sake. There's children on our street!"

The woman paused as if reconsidering her bilious words after the announcement of her Christian piety. "Least you keep your yard nice, Miss Beecham. That old hermit"—she pointed at Silas's house—"has the messiest yard on our street. He hardly ever rakes his leaves. Harold's asked him many times. Them bashful oaks finally dropped leaves an' it's ugly. We're tryin' to raise standards is all. I've seen you over there at his place helpin' him out. Can you tell him to keep his yard cleaned up?"

Callie bit her lip to keep from calling the woman something nasty but couldn't let the comment go. "Mr. Roberts passed away recently, so I doubt he's able to comply with your husband's request to rake the damn leaves," Callie said sharply. "And no one on our street even sent condolences. No one."

The woman mumbled and stepped back inside her home, slamming the door behind her.

Callie shook her head at the woman's audacity and turned to go inside, when she realized that George had not shown himself that morning. She wondered if he'd been scared away by the shattering of the window. "George!" she called. "Here, kitty. George!"

She headed through the gate into her backyard. "George! Kitty!" She noticed that the scraggly raised beds looked especially neglected and made a mental note to clean them out. It was almost time to plant again. Some prized perennials would need to be dug up and divided. Her beloved passionflower vines would need to be trimmed back to the ground, their climb over the fence halted by winter's assault. She glanced at the pecan tree in the far corner of her yard and stopped in her tracks.

At first, her eyes did not trust what they saw. She dropped her mug, and it shattered on the ground. She covered her mouth with a trembling hand. "No. No. No. No." There was George's limp body hanging by a rope tied tightly around his throat. The orange body swayed from a low branch, his swollen tongue protruding from his pale mouth.

"George!" she cried. "My sweet boy. What have they done to you, my precious boy . . ." Despite her shaking hands, she hurried to untie the noose from around his broken neck. She laid him gently on the ground, buried her face in his cold fur, and sobbed until there were no tears left.

— • —

Dark clouds had replaced the earlier sunshine, and cold rain would soon make the day even more melancholy. Callie returned the shovel in its spot in the shed. There wasn't anything else they could truly take from her. Someone had seen poor George at the front door, managed to catch him, and then do such a horrible deed. It was proof that the window was no accident. Running the car into the river was no accident. She swallowed hard, to hold back more tears. What else could they take?

Nestled in his blanket, in a shallow grave under the pecan tree, lay the only thing left of Callie's old life. She closed the shed door and sighed. The house would feel incredibly empty without George. But then, the house would not be hers for much longer. What had Seeta said about Klan threats? *Message received.*

From the front yard, Callie heard the sound of hammer and nail, and said a quick prayer of thanks that a handyman had come out right away to replace the shattered window. It would cost her the last bit of

Anne Walton's initial payment. Callie winced at the thought of how she had let the woman down and wasted most of the money on a dress she'd never wear again.

Stop this. Figure something out. Callie stepped through the gate and went around to check on the repairman's progress in the front yard. "How's the window coming along?"

The man nodded, two nails clamped between his lips. He removed one and hammered it into place. He removed the second one and paused. "You're lucky I had this old one in my shop from a remodel I did. These big plate-glass ones are prone to shatter. You sure you don't want me to price you a set of new smaller double-hungs in the same space?"

"No, thank you, Mr. Smith." Callie shook her head. "If it costs more than the one you're putting in, it's too much."

"Suit yourself." Smith shrugged. "Say, you should let the sheriff's office know. Single woman living alone an' all . . ." He pounded in the final nail and stood back to admire his work as raindrops began to patter. "Probably kids acting up, but you never know these days."

Callie was already forming the words to tell the man she wouldn't be doing that when a strong compulsion to do the very thing struck her. "You're right, Mr. Smith. I should have called them before you began the repairs. They need to know someone did this."

"They sure do," the man agreed. "Go see Deputy Donaldson. He should patrol the area for a few nights and look for troublemakers. It's his job, and it'll give him something to do besides sit outside the filling station." He looked up at the leaden skies. "You were smart to telephone me early, with this rain coming. And it's gonna be cold again tonight. The weather can't decide if it's spring or still winter."

Callie's aplomb went up another notch. "Thank you, Mr. Smith. Have you—have you heard of any other trouble like this in town? I'm trying to run my business from home—remedies for people who would like natural methods for healing. I hate to think someone targeted me on purpose."

The man shrugged. "Nope. I'm not one for tonics and such, but I can't see why someone would break a window over that." He paused. "Unless it was Doc Davis, worried you're taking away customers." He laughed at his own joke.

Callie pasted a smile on her lips. "No. I surely wouldn't want to take business away from the good doctor."

Smith nodded his head. "All right then, you got a new window. Well, an old window. I'll bill you for my time only." He tipped his hat and quickly headed for his truck as the rain came down in earnest.

"Thank you again, Mr. Smith," Callie called. She turned to go inside but not before she noticed Mrs. Gibson at her own front window. The woman quickly yanked her curtains closed when she saw Callie's stare. Callie felt her confidence draining away as she turned to go inside.

The jangle of the telephone sent her into the kitchen. She picked up the receiver cautiously. "Callie Beecham."

"Well, well. I was beginning to think you were trying to get rid of me."

"Anne!" Callie smiled into the telephone. "I am so sorry. I had an accident on the road yesterday. Ran the car into a river. Thank you so much for sending Sam to find me."

"I knew you wouldn't stand me up on purpose. Are you alright then?" Anne sounded genuinely concerned.

"Yes. Just a little shaken up."

"I can imagine," Anne purred into Callie's ear. "May I stop by later this week? We'll be leaving for a trip abroad next week, and I'd really like to get my marching orders. The diet is well in hand, and I feel great." Anne lowered her voice. "And my monthly friend is back. So, thank you!"

"Anne, that's wonderful! That's a very good sign," Callie said, elated at Anne's news. "How's four o'clock Friday?"

"Perfect. I will see you then." Anne hung up. Callie stood with the receiver to her ear, wondering what might happen if Anne mentioned the appointment to her Aunt Mildred. Was Mildred Davis still a fan? For a brief moment, Callie entertained the thought of staying put, weathering whatever Davis and his cronies could dish out.

But her home had been vandalized. Her cat was dead. Silas's car was in the river. And she knew enough to know that she could have easily been hurt or killed in the car's plunge down the steep riverbank. *It's too much*, she thought. *I'm waiting for the next kick. They mean to break me—or kill me.*

She inhaled and then exhaled a weary sigh before collecting her hat and raincoat. There were two errands to run. She grabbed her handbag and counted out the spare change in her coin purse.

— • —

Callie hurried the few blocks to the sheriff's office and jail. It was a large brick building, turreted and crenelated like a small castle, strangely out of place, ostentatious to Callie's mind. She straightened her cloche nervously and smoothed her dress before pushing the glass door open. A small bell tinkled overhead.

"Help you, ma'am?" A plump receptionist sat, arms-crossed, behind a large and remarkably tidy wooden desk, which made Callie wonder if the only crime lately in Pickens had been the ones directed against her.

"Yes. I would like to report vandalism and harassment," Callie began bravely. "Is Reggie in? Deputy Donaldson?"

The woman shrugged. "The deputy is out on a leave of absence. He broke his leg last week. The sheriff is in. Would you like to speak with him?"

Callie swallowed hard. "The sheriff? Yes. I would. My name is Callie Beecham."

The woman stood and inclined her head toward the hallway. She led Callie down the hall lined with wanted posters, black and white photographs of hardened criminals, gangsters, bootleggers, and such. She knocked at a closed door. "Sheriff?"

"Come in, Clara."

The woman opened the door and a cloud of acrid cigar smoke assaulted Callie's nostrils.

"A woman here has a complaint. A Callie Beecham? You got time to see her?"

"Show her in." The sheriff cleared his throat and stood. "Yes, ma'am? I'm Sheriff Woods. How can I he'p you?" He pointed to a chair.

Callie walked into the office, a simple, windowless room thick with smoke. Indeed, the sheriff's cigar sat smoldering in the ashtray. Callie had never met the sheriff before. He was a middle-aged man, stocky and balding. Callie was relieved to see a wall of framed accolades behind his desk, hoping that it meant he was one of the good ones.

Callie sat down. "Thank you for your time. I was expecting Deputy Donaldson. I knew Reggie in school," she said. "I wasn't expecting you'd be here."

The man opened a drawer and pulled out a clipboard. "It's your lucky day," he quipped. "You here to file a complaint?"

Callie summoned her courage. "Yessir. Sheriff, I'm not sure how to begin . . . but someone has been harassing me. And vandalized my house."

— • —

Callie's shoes clicked furiously up the hill toward the hardware store.

It was a mistake. I shouldn't have gone to the sheriff. What was I thinking? The man had dismissed every one of her complaints out of hand: the threatening notes, the sack of kittens, George's death, the rock through the window.

The sheriff had sucked on his cigar with narrowed eyes, as if everything Callie reported was an exaggeration or even a lie. "Have you seen anyone suspicious?" he'd asked.

She had tried to explain, when he cut in. "Kids will be kids. No need to get all hysterical," he'd chastised.

Callie had balked, afraid. He had scribbled the scantest of notes on the page, nodded quietly, and told her he'd look into it.

She felt a creeping tendril of fear begin in the pit of her stomach before winding into her chest, a heavy pressure that climbed up into her throat and threatened her breath. Was there no one on her side?

Miller's Hardware was busy with customers, despite the rain. Callie loved the old store, with its smell of chicken feed, lumber, and turpentine. She had visited many times since moving into her home—for nails and glue, paint, and hand tools. The owner, Clark Miller, had always seemed overly nosey about the home improvement projects she seemed so willing to tackle without the expertise of a husband.

She nodded and made small talk with several customers before heading toward the stack of printed signs. *Open. Closed. To Let. Help Wanted.* She rifled through them until she found the one she wanted. *For Sale.*

She placed the sign on the counter and began to count out pennies.

"Whatcha sellin', Miss Beecham?" Mr. Miller asked, too loudly for Callie's comfort.

She glanced around quickly, but no one seemed to have heard the man. "I'm cleaning out for a yard sale," she said simply, sliding three cents across the counter.

The man nodded, his curiosity sated for the time being.

— • —

The doorbell tinkled, and Callie's thoughts shifted back to Anne's visit. She checked her wristwatch and wondered why Anne would show up two hours early. Her heels clicked across the floor and stopped short when she saw the tall, angular man standing in her front room, a Chesterfield clamped in the corner of his mouth.

Her pulse raced, and she clutched her hands together tightly to steady her nerves. "Dr. Davis." She pasted a smile on her face and regarded the man.

"Callie Beecham," he said, his eyes wandering across her neatly organized shelves. "This is a fine little place you have here. A fine little place." His gaze traveled from the shelves to her trembling hands.

"What can I do for you?" she asked.

"I was passin' by and saw you've put the house up for sale." He removed the cigarette and pointed it in her direction. "That's good. That's real good." He blew a plume of smoke toward her. His eyes stared, snake-like, hard slits in his long face.

Callie wished she were expecting a client, a repairman, anyone. "I don't see why that's any of your concern."

"You stirred up some trouble for yourself," Davis said.

Callie's gut clenched. "I know you've never liked my line of work. But my business has never been a threat to yours."

He feigned surprise. "Oh, darlin' is that what has you all a-tremble? That you might be takin' business away from me? No . . . You don't need to worry over that. You'll have no business here when I'm done with you. I hear you practicin' midwifery without a license from the state. My niece, Anne, will not be comin' back to see you. You're not a doctor, Callie. You ain't even a nurse." He spat the words from his mouth.

Callie straightened. "Anne has an appointment Friday."

Davis frowned. "Not anymore. I'll set her up with one of the finest surgeons in the country, down in Palm Beach. You touch a hair on her head, and I'll have you arrested for practicin' medicine without a license."

Stunned, the words tumbled from Callie's mouth. "She wants me to help her. She wants to avoid surgery."

"Why would John Walton waste money on you and your nigger voodoo? He saw you draped all over Dr. Epstein at a speakeasy in Greenville, and he let me know all about it." He shook his head and puffed on his cigarette. "A mulatto girl and a Jew? Michel's used to be a fine place. Too bad they're lettin' in the trash now." Davis snorted.

Of course. There would be repercussions after being seen in public with Sam. "Don't use that word in this house," she said sharply.

"Nigger? Or mulatto?" Davis chuckled. "I told Mildred that she is not to put a foot in here again. It looks bad when the doctor's wife is steppin' out for—colored—remedies an' such."

"Get out of my house," Callie said.

"What's that? Your house?" he asked, a hand cupped to his ear dramatically. "No. No. Here's how it's gonna go, Callie." He flicked ash onto the floor and continued. "You done the smart thing. You already put the sign up in your yard. I'm simply here to buy the house."

He looked around the room and nodded. "I'll pay what you bought it for from my friend, Mr. Wilcox. You move out and go away." He crushed the cigarette on Callie's exam table and then brushed more ash to the floor.

Callie had no words.

"You can go live with your nigger cousins, your aunties, and what-not in that colored town," he said sarcastically. "They'll take you in."

"Leave my grandmother alone!" Callie cried, fists clenched.

Davis's eyes narrowed. "Your grandmother? Ah, so that old witch *is* still alive . . ."

"If you go near her, I'll call the sheriff," Callie warned.

"Don't threaten me. You don't know who you're dealin' with," Davis snapped. He took a step toward her.

Callie whirled around and headed for the telephone. "I'm calling the sheriff's office!"

"No, you won't," Davis called out. "What would you say?" He snickered. "Sheriff Woods didn't take your complaint seriously. I'm the town doctor, after all. He just called me to warn me of the crazy lady who thinks I'm out to get her."

Callie suddenly realized her predicament. What could she say? There was a *For Sale* sign in front of her house. She had opened the door to one of the prominent citizens in town who wanted to buy the place. She swallowed hard.

Davis continued. "No one will want you living here once they know you're colored. It's just the way of things, Callie. Oh, people say they're fair and want everyone to get along, but tell 'em a colored gal is livin' on their street, and well, all bets are off. Property values, you know."

Callie thought of her neighbor, Mrs. Gibson. She opened her mouth to speak, but Davis held up a hand and continued. "Your mama was a whore. You follow in her footsteps, am I right? John Walton told me how you were pressed up against the young doctor. Sam Epstein has no idea about you. Yet. You got that hot, colored blood. That mulatto blood." He smirked. "I'll let him know."

Callie pulled her sweater close around her shaking body.

"You need to leave town," Davis said. "I don't want to see any more of you."

His eyes traveled down the length of Callie's body. The man took a step toward her, and Callie backed up, trembling.

"Stay away from me."

"Don't get your panties in a bunch, Callie. I'm not here for that." He grinned. "Do what I say, and I'll keep your dirty secret—and I'll let Dr. Epstein keep his job. Do you know how hard it could be for him if folks hear he is steppin' out with a colored woman? Sam is a good doctor. Folks seem to like him an' he's takin' a load off my shoulders. Don't ruin his career before it even gets started."

His smile faded. "It's by my good graces that he's here at all. Bein' a Jew is one strike against him already. If patients hear he has a taste for mulatto girls, you think he'll last long? It's nothin' to me. I can get a new doctor here like that." He snapped his thin fingers. "Give the boy a chance to make a go of his career. To find a fine, white, Christian woman to marry and give him children. Maybe dilute the Jew part," he said with a chuckle.

Callie froze in her tracks, defeated. "Why do you hate me so much?"

Davis's face clouded. He pulled a fat envelope from his coat pocket. "Jim Beecham was my great-uncle. Your mama whored around with a nigger an' ended up with a nigger baby. 'Bout tore up Uncle Jim. He loved your white-trash mama for some reason, and she broke his heart. Made a laughingstock of him. And the way he died was real suspicious. That old black witch probably poisoned him. Every time I see you, I'm reminded of that." He dropped the envelope on her kitchen table with a thud. "So, here's payment for the house. Give me the deed. Go away. Leave Sam Epstein alone."

"You're a vile human being," Callie said. "Silas was right about you."

"Go away. Leave Sam Epstein alone," Davis repeated calmly.

"You can't blackmail me."

The man's face darkened. "Of course I can. Silas Roberts ain't here anymore." He pulled another cigarette from the pack in his jacket and struck a match to light it. He drew on the cigarette and then exhaled blue smoke through his nose. He held the cigarette aloft and looked at Callie with hard eyes.

"Girl, I'm not playin'. Leave Sam alone and get out of town. Or you'll be burned out. You think I won't? An' I'll send my boys up to that colored town and burn your granny out, too."

"We were only trying to offer care to people who aren't allowed in your office," Callie tried. "Let Sam be. He's a good doctor. A good man."

"Dr. Epstein knows he's on thin ice with me. Now, do you have the deed?" he asked impatiently. "I have patients to see."

Callie's heart sank. She nodded.

"Good. Good." Davis nodded. "I knew you'd see the right solution

Go get it, darlin'."

Callie walked to her bedroom and rummaged in a drawer nervously. She half expected the man to follow her into her bedroom. When she returned with the folded document, she extended it at arm's length, willing her hand to remain steady despite her frayed nerves.

Davis took it and drew a fountain pen from his pocket. "Sign it over to me. An' date it."

Callie took the pen and scribbled near the bottom of the deed.

"There's a good gal." Davis blew on the ink to dry her signature, then folded the deed and tucked it into his jacket. "You learn quick. I wouldn't want to send one of my boys out tonight with another sack of dead cats or to break that new window—a window that I now own." Another heartless chuckle.

He tipped his hat and turned to go. "After all, it's a school night. My boys gotta get up early." As he reached for the doorknob, he said, "I'll grant you a few days. You collect your things and be out by the end of the week. I'll be a help an' take down the *For Sale* sign in your yard."

With that, he walked out the front door. The little bell tinkled cheerfully as the door closed behind him.

— • —

Evening fell, damp and mild. Seeta listened to the spring peepers croak a riotous song outside her windows, their early homage to spring always a delight. Her granddaughter lay curled up on her threadbare sofa, a crumpled handkerchief clutched in one hand. She watched Callie dab her swollen eyes and sniffle. Zeke paced the floor, and the old pine floors creaked and groaned in response. Delia stood in the hallway, half-hidden, bouncing Ezekiel on her hip, while Seeta rocked in her chair, slowly winding a ball of blue yarn by the light of the oil lamp.

She waited patiently to see how this would unfold, hoping against hope for the outcome she wanted. *Time with Callie.* She watched her granddaughter agonize over the horrific turn her life had taken. The pain in Seeta's heart was wrenching, and it seemed that years spent on her knees in prayer hadn't helped at all.

"Granny, I've spent the past few days just frozen, unsure of what to do," Callie sniffed. "I didn't know who to call to move my furniture. My things. But Dr. Davis scared me bad, and the sheriff was no help. So, when Zeke showed up with Silas's car this morning, I told him everything. We put as much as we could carry into Silas's house for now with a note for the daughter-in-law to contact me." She looked at Seeta. "I just need a few days here. I have the money he gave me for the house. I'll find a room somewhere. And I'll hold on to Silas's car as long as I can . . ." Her voice trailed away.

Zeke faced Seeta, arms folded across his broad chest. "Granny, you should have tol' me the day you sent me down to fetch her fo' Delia. You should have tol' me I was fetchin' my own cousin. A white cousin! Look how this has all gone to hell. That man'll come after you now that he knows you're alive."

"According to white people in town, I'm your colored cousin," Callie said wryly.

Zeke ignored her. "Granny, she don't even look black!" he accused. "You sure she's Uncle Marcus's daughter?"

"Zeke, watch your mouth. That's enough sass. She can stay here as long as she wants," Seeta snapped. "She's family."

"We in it now," Zeke said, shaking his head. "A white woman stayin' up here. We sure in it now. The sheriff'll be along soon. Mark my words."

"He won't come on my account. He's on Dr. Davis's side," Callie said.

Seeta's chair stopped its rhythmic movement. "You two stop bickerin'," she scolded, exasperated. She put down her yarn. "Lawd, you two even argue like family. Callie, stay here as long as you need."

She thought back to the day of Callie's birth, and the frightened expression on the young mother's face when the baby was born. "Is she white?" Kizzy had asked fearfully. She remembered the look on her own son's face several days later, when he took her hand in his as they sat on the porch. The last day Seeta had seen her son. "I have to go away for good, Mama," he'd said. "I don't have no choice. They'll kill me."

Zeke snorted and brought Seeta back to the present. "Granny, we don't have room for her here. We barely have room for the four of us!"

"Watch yo' manners, boy. I got the sofa. She can sleep on that." Seeta eyed Zeke over her glasses.

Delia stepped fully into the room, still jostling the baby on her hip. "Granny, I know you love bein' with Calvin, but I think he's gettin' to be too much for you."

Seeta smiled at Delia and nodded. "He's a good baby, but I ain't a spring chicken, it's true."

"Zeke, what if we go live with Mama?" Delia asked tentatively. "She has a spare room. She'll take us. The baby is too much for your granny now he's crawlin' around. Mama and my aunties can watch him. An' it'd be closer to work for both of us. If Callie's here with Granny, we can go. Can't we?"

Callie sat up straight. "I'd be happy to do that! It would give me a chance to get to know Seeta—Granny. I can do chores and cook. Chop wood. Plant the garden," she said eagerly. "I can't go back."

Seeta regarded the beloved faces around the room. Callie and Delia looked hopeful. Zeke looked worried, as always.

Zeke sat down next to her and reached for her hand. "Granny, you sure Callie ain't gone bring stuff down on you?" Zeke's gaze went from his grandmother to his wife to his cousin, before resting on Seeta's wrinkled face once more. "They already burned the school."

Seeta patted her grandson's hand. "Zeke, you've taken care of me all your life. Now you got a family of your own to tend. A wife an' a baby. You go live with Mattie, if she'll have you. Think how much easier it'll be for your family. But grandson, as much as you don't like it, the fact is—Callie is my grandchild, too. She's blood. Your uncle Marcus's daughter." Saying it out loud suddenly thrilled Seeta's heart—it was true. Having Callie back in her life was a little like having Marcus here.

Callie stood up. "Zeke, I can take care of Granny."

Zeke sighed. "Alright, we give it a try. Maybe I can pick up a few more hours at work if I ain't havin' to hitch a ride or take a mule ten miles to town."

"Well then," Delia began, her voice upbeat. "I s'pose me and Zeke have some packin' to do. I best get Calvin down for the night, and then we can make a plan." She turned and left the room.

Seeta resumed her rocking, a smile on her lips. She steadily wound the blue yarn around the ball in her lap. For the first time in a long time, her heart was full.

Chapter Seventeen

Seeta's bantam rooster woke Callie early every morning with his loud crowing. She opened her eyes and turned over in the sagging bed, the same bed where Delia had given birth last fall. She turned her face toward the cracked window. A silver fog hung heavy outside of Seeta's house and obscured the first light of an April dawn.

Zeke and Delia had been gone for a month, and Callie was still getting used to her new and isolated world. She studied the framed photograph of Marcus Young on her bedside table, taken outside a brownstone in Chicago, dated 1903. The photographer's shadow stretched across the bottom of the photo, a woman's silhouette. He was sitting on the steps, cigarette in hand, a hat pulled low over his brow at a rakish angle. He was handsome, with a friendly face and a big smile. He looked to be tall, with elbows resting on his lanky legs. His skin was brown, like coffee with a splash of cream.

Callie sighed and stretched. Despite the downward turn in her circumstances, she found that she slept better in her grandmother's house than she had ever slept in town. There were no streetlights, no automobiles rumbling through town, no jangling telephone, just quiet. Her days were physically hard, and she fell into bed good-tired and ready for sleep. Sometimes, an owl hooted in a nearby tree, and coyotes howled in the distance, but to her, they were lullabies. She'd gaze out her small window at the night sky where she saw so clearly the constellations that she read about in Seeta's *Farmer's Almanac*, and as she gazed at the twinkling stars of Leo or Gemini, she always drifted to sleep.

She stared at the water stain on the plaster and lath ceiling, which was really mostly lath now. *The stain resembles a map of Africa,* she thought. *And here I am in Liberia.* The small hand on the clock near her bed pointed to seven. She pulled the quilt over her head, closed her eyes, and dozed, remembering the warmth of Sam's kisses. Was Sam looking for her? She wondered briefly if he missed her the way she missed him. She tossed back the covers and sat bolt upright. *That will not help anything. Forget him.*

She wrapped herself in her frayed robe and padded to the kitchen to stoke the wood stove and boil water. While she waited for the water to heat, she looked around the tiny kitchen. There was no gas stove, no electricity, no telephone, no milkman with his cold glass bottles of fresh cream, no newspaper, and worst of all, no indoor toilet. The privy at the back of the lot felt a million miles away when nature called. An old-fashioned chamber pot, oil lamps, and cooking on a wood stove were hard adjustments. She could have kicked herself for not removing the electric washing machine from her house before ceding it to Davis. It would have cut her work load tremendously. But then, there was no electricity here to make it work. Seeta had just an old washboard and tub for washing sheets and her threadbare cotton housedresses, which she told Callie were to be laundered on Mondays. Callie had wisely decided to store her better clothing away and stick to cotton dresses and aprons herself. It made Mondays easier.

She rose early each day, anxious to show her grandmother that she was equal to the task Zeke had reluctantly released to her. She split wood if needed, stoked the woodstove, heated water for cooking and washing up, and made tea for them both. She cooked Seeta a simple breakfast of grits or eggs, and then tidied up. After she had Seeta comfortably settled in her rocker by the front room fire, she'd kiss her grandmother on the top of her gray head and venture outside to feed the chickens, collect eggs, and tend the garden plot. Only then was she free to wander the woods beyond, looking for medicinal plants. Today would be no different.

Callie found herself humming while she waited for the kettle to boil. The precious radio and her Victrola were stashed at Silas's house, and she sorely missed having music, shows, and news features at her fingertips. She had procrastinated about making a run back to town and to Silas's house to get more of her belongings. She and Zeke had loaded the car with Callie's clothing, some books, bedding, and towels. But everything else was still at Silas's house. She knew she'd have to retrieve her belongings before the daughter-in-law showed up.

But what if someone saw her coming and tried to run her off the road again? What if Dr. Davis saw her on Florence Street? Worse, what if he really did rent her house to Sam, and Sam saw her? He must know by now. Surely, Dr. Davis told him what she was and why she'd gone away.

The kettle whistled and Callie roused from her daydreaming. She removed the cast-iron kettle from the hot eye and poured water through the tea strainers in two mugs. She missed coffee so much, but until she found the courage to go to town, there would be only tea. She carried one mug into Seeta's room, where the woman was awake and reading her worn Bible by the dim light of an oil lamp. The room was small, with only a single bed, a small dresser with a framed watercolor over it, and the lamp to read by.

"Good morning, Granny," Callie said, with a kiss to the old woman's cheek. She placed the mug on the nightstand. "Grits are on the stove. Can I help you to the front room before I go outside?"

Seeta shook her head. "I'm feelin' kinda puny today. I may jes' stay in bed an' read."

"What chapter are you reading from this morning?" Callie asked.

Seeta beamed at her granddaughter. "I'm in Hebrews 13 today. Be content with such things as ye have: for he hath said I will never leave thee, nor forsake thee. So that we may boldly say, The Lord is my helper and I shall not fear what man shall do unto me."

"Ouch," Callie grinned. "I'm not feeling very content. Or fearless."

"No sin in missin' what you had to give up. Or bein' afraid after what they done to you. But it ain't permanent. Trust Him. He got good plans for you—a bright future. The Lawd's gonna use this mess." Seeta nodded. "You got to lift your eyes to the hills, from whence cometh thy help."

Callie smirked. Eager to change the direction of the conversation, she pointed to the watercolor painting on the wall. "Speaking of hills, who painted that watercolor of Table Rock? It's beautiful."

"Your father." Seeta beamed. "Marcus painted that when he was about twenty years old. He was very good."

"I'll say." The grays and blues of the mountain range were stunning, and the artist had captured the weathered granite face of the mountain perfectly. Callie's gaze moved back to her grandmother. "You miss him very much."

"I do. I expect he's in heaven with his brother and his father. I wanted to believe he was alive for the longest while. But after a time, it was easier to believe he passed on." Seeta shifted in the bed. "It ain't fo' us to worry on. God is in control. *He that keepeth thee will not slumber,*" she said with a jut of her chin and a wag of her finger.

Callie remembered the Klansman's words. "The watcher never wearies," she muttered with a roll of her eyes.

"Well now, that's real pretty," Seeta said.

Callie hadn't realized that she'd said the words out loud. "No. No, Granny." She folded her arms over her chest. "It's something that horrid Klansman said when he stopped Sam's car on our trip back from Greenville. It's not pretty. It's vile. Scary."

Seeta regarded her young granddaughter with what Callie took to be sympathy. "Callie girl, if you give words that kind of power, them men win. But if you take 'em the way *I* heard 'em, it's a whole different meanin'. You think about that. Now go on so I can get back to my quiet time with the Lawd." Seeta dropped her gaze to the worn pages she had been studying.

Admonished, Callie left the room and stepped outside into a fragrant April morning. The vegetable plot in the side yard was an oblong quarter acre past Seeta's house, fenced in with chicken wire against rabbits and squirrels. In the far corner, stood a compost pile, even now steaming in the early sun. This morning, she would plant the seedlings she'd started in her grandmother's kitchen weeks ago. The emerald-green shoots would be lined up in rows, soil warmed by the spring sun. Straight rows of peas, broccoli, carrots, lettuce, spinach, and chard would lead the charge toward summer.

She carefully handled the first tray of seedlings. The sun had burned off the morning damp, and she lifted her face to its warmth. In the distance, the granite face of Table Rock loomed. She inhaled the moist air, the breath of spring filling her lungs. *What a beautiful place.* Callie had always reveled in the feel of the freshly turned soil between her fingers, the heady scent of the humus. She crouched in the soil, happy to have Seeta's kneeling board to keep her dungarees dry.

She was eager to begin a new garden, a place where she could grow her medicinal herbs. Seeta had given her directions to a ginseng patch and drawn a map of a woodland trail behind the house where there was witch hazel, elderberry, Indian cucumber, sweet birch, and yellow root. The yard was already dotted with dandelions and chickweed. It would be a good start. She ached for her old yard, her established plants, and trees. *Who is tending them now?*

As she brushed a stray lock of hair from her cheek, she noticed a woman coming down the dirt road, head down, a pocketbook clutched under her arm. Callie hadn't seen many folks. When word had gotten out that Callie was in Liberia and staying with Seeta, people were leery. She knew that they couldn't fathom why the white woman they'd blamed for the school fire was now staying at Seeta Young's. Several times, when Callie had answered a knock on the front door, a neighbor would be standing there, hands on hips, ready to launch a verbal assault on Seeta for allowing Callie back. Surprised when Callie herself was at the door, they usually demurred, made excuses, and backed away, afraid to speak their minds.

Callie turned her focus back to a delicate broccoli seedling. She gently pried it from the eggshell that had been its home and nestled the seedling in the soil, before patting the earth around it. She smiled and recited the age-old planting song Kizzy had taught her as a child.

"Some for the birds and some for I,
Some for the beetle and some for the fly.
Some to rot and some to grow,
Lord, bless these seeds I now do sow."

She glanced up and realized the woman had left the road and was coming up the small rise into Seeta's backyard. Toward the garden.

Eyes narrowed against the bright sunshine, Callie stood and tossed down her trowel. "Good morning," she called hopefully, wiping dirt from her hands. The tiny woman came toward Callie, with a furtive glance back toward the road. She was dressed in Sunday clothes, a tweed suit, and scuffed high-heeled pumps that made it difficult to navigate the bumpy yard. Clearly, the woman had dressed for this visit.

"You plantin' broccoli too late," the woman said accusingly. "Like as to fail."

Callie nodded. "I guess I'm taking a chance with broccoli and lettuce."

"Yep. Your beans an' squash should be goin' in." The woman shrugged. "I'm Mary Talbot. I hope I ain't disturbin'. You saw me a few months back. At the schoolhouse?" The woman adjusted her straw hat.

Callie had seen so many people the day that she and Sam had come to Liberia. Her old life. But she did remember the small woman with a large voice. The woman was all of four and a half feet tall. "Mrs. Talbot. You're the schoolteacher here. Didn't I give you a liver tonic?"

Mary nodded. "Yes, ma'am."

"Of course I remember you. How are you feeling?" Callie asked, aware that she might be in for a tongue-lashing over the destroyed schoolhouse.

"I'm much better. That tonic made me feel like a new woman. I ain't been so seized up lately." She patted her stomach proudly.

Callie hadn't realized how much she missed her clients and her work. She noticed the woman shift the purse in her arms and glance toward the road again. "Mrs. Talbot, would you like to come inside, where we can talk?"

The woman's dark eyes lit up. "Yes, ma'am. My husband don't know I come up here an'—" She faltered.

"I understand. If you're alright with Seeta being inside, follow me."

Mary nodded, and Callie led the woman up the back steps and into Seeta's kitchen.

"You done for the mornin', Callie girl?" Seeta called from the bedroom.

"No, Granny. I have someone here for a tonic," Callie said. "We won't disturb you."

"Howdy, Sister Seeta. It's me—Mary Talbot," Mary called out. "I hope you feelin' alright. We missed you at church the past few Sundays."

"I'm jes' feelin' punk these days, Sister Mary," Seeta called weakly.

"Well, let me know if I can help you out," Mary called again. She shook her head and looked at Callie. "You is kind to stay with her."

Callie motioned for Mary to sit at the small table. The woman pulled out a chair and sat obediently.

Callie sat across from Mary. "Would you like more of the tonic? I believe I have some on hand. Mind you, I don't have much of anything here right now, but *that* I do have. And I can certainly make up some things."

Mary leaned forward. "I *would* like another bottle, ma'am, and I can pay you. But that ain't why I came today," she said quietly.

Callie waited for Mary to continue.

"You see, my husband, Mr. Talbot, he has—he has the piles, ma'am, real bad. He can't sit down. An' I don't know how to get rid of 'em. He's sore an' itchin' somethin' terrible, an' when I saw you was stayin' here with Sister Seeta, well, I thought I'd come see if you have somethin' to help him." She looked at Callie expectantly.

Callie brightened. "Hemorrhoids?" she asked. "As a matter of fact, I do have a few bags of a dried tea for that very thing." She stood and rummaged in one of the crates stacked in Seeta's kitchen. After a few minutes, she found what she was looking for. "Ah! Here they are." She placed two neatly labeled paper sacks on the table in front of Mary, sat down. and pointed to the label. "You'll make a decoction."

"What is that?" Mary asked.

"Sort of a slurry." Callie demonstrated a stirring motion with her hands. "An ounce of herbs to a pint of water. Let it simmer gently, uncovered, for about an hour on the stove. He'll take one-half cup of strained tea two or three times a day. No more than that. This is quite strong. And he should avoid sitting on his backside for a few days. Eat more vegetables. Less meat."

Mary nodded. "A ounce of herbs to a pint of water. Let it simmer gently, uncovered, for about a hour. He takes one-half cup of tea two or three times a day. No more than that." She thought for a moment. "An' more vegetables. Less meat." She looked at Callie hopefully.

Callie smiled. "Exactly."

Mary nodded. "Now what do I owe you today?"

Callie shook her head. "Oh, no charge."

"That's nonsense. I didn't come here for charity," Mary huffed. She pulled a coin purse from her pocketbook.

"Very well, Mrs. Talbot. The price on the bag is forty cents. So eighty cents. I'll throw in the bottle of digestive tonic at no charge. It's my last one until I can brew a new batch. I'm so relieved that someone came to see me, I can't tell you!" Callie retrieved a small brown bottle from one of the crates. She felt a rush of satisfaction when the woman slid eight dimes across the table. Callie pocketed the change quickly.

"Thank you, ma'am." Mary Talbot stood and stuffed the bags and bottle into her purse. "Please don't go tellin' anyone I was here."

"I understand. It means a lot that the schoolteacher would come see me," Callie said.

"Well, lotta folks here do think the schoolhouse was burned down because of you," Mary Talbot began. "But what I see is you been here a month and nothin' bad has happened. Seems to me, white people didn't like their new town doctor come up here to help, is what I think. It wasn't you. You ain't a doctor. No offense." She shrugged. "We had buildings burned out before. We will again. It's too bad that havin' a doctor come up here made white folks mad. But don't let it stop the good you is doin' in the world. Your medicines work real fine. Like Seeta's—before she quit makin' tonics."

Callie led Mary to the back door. "Where are the children meeting for school now?"

"Back at the church. The Benson family moved away, so we down to seven children. It'll be fine. Unless they burn down the church. Then God himself will deal with 'em." Mary Talbot looked up at Callie. "Thank you fo' the medicines." She lowered her voice. "We know why you stayin' here," she whispered.

"Oh?" Callie asked.

The woman tilted her head toward Seeta's room. "I don't see it. You bein' mixed. But it's real good of you—takin' care of your granny." She winked slyly at Callie and let herself out the back door.

Callie stood still, stunned. *They'll let me stay.*

Chapter Eighteen

Callie steered the old car onto Greenville's Main Street and eased into an angled parking space in front of Leachman's Pharmacy. She was relieved that she didn't have to depend on the bus from Pickens anymore and said a silent prayer of thanks for Silas's old Ford, none the worse for wear after its bath in the Oolenoy River. Zeke was a good mechanic, and Callie had to admit that the engine sounded better than ever. She pulled up to the curb, grabbed her purse, and hopped out of the car.

The day was beautiful, warm, and sunny. The balmy April weather had her in a good mood. It was nice to get out of Liberia and pretend that things were normal. She had come all the way to Greenville for her errands, despite Seeta's rolled eyes. Callie knew no one in Greenville and no one knew her. It was a safe place for her to shop, she reasoned. She'd visited the beauty parlor, bought a new blouse at a small boutique, and gotten groceries. No one seemed the least put out in serving her, and she began to feel like her old self, not someone hiding a deep secret.

But for the first time, she really noticed the signs. *No Coloreds. Whites Only. Coloreds Use Back Door. Colored Water Fountain.* She was ashamed that she'd never given them a single thought. The long banner draped across the narrow street proclaimed, *White Christian Citizens Rally in the Park: Ball Games & Eats & Drinks!*

Her final stop was the druggist for aspirin powder and other supplies she could keep on hand for patients. She had seen a trickle of folks since Mary Talbot's visit. People seemed to warm to her when they saw that no harm had come to Liberia since she moved to the settlement. And there were so many needs. She had seen several minor complaints and one quite serious case of pellagra. She'd advised the man to go immediately to the county hospital, and had typed up and distributed a handout on avoiding the dread disease of Vitamin B3 deficiency.

It seemed that she was back in business. Somewhat. Of course, most folks paid what only they could, which was far less than Callie had been paid in town. She had accepted a few jars of preserves, eggs, some firewood, hand-knitted socks, and even a can of lard in trade. If she wanted to make ends meet without dipping more deeply into the house money, she knew she would need a wider client base.

Glancing at her reflection in the glass storefront, she felt right smart. Her hair was freshly bobbed and waved. She adjusted her navy-blue hat and smoothed her new pink silk blouse, a splurge to be sure. But it perked her up considerably.

She pulled open the heavy glass door. A tinkling bell reminded her of her own doorbell on Florence Street with a twinge of regret. The place smelled of Merthiolate and rubbing alcohol. A large soft-drink chest stood in one corner near the door. In the back, a white-coated druggist worked behind an elevated counter. Callie pulled her list from her purse.

"May I help you, ma'am?" The balding clerk barely looked up from his newspaper.

"Yes, I need aspirin powder, swabs, some Band-aids, and rubbing alcohol. That sort of thing." She smiled sweetly.

He nodded. "Yes, ma'am. On the far wall there. First Aid section." He pointed to shelves near the front window and then resumed his reading.

Thank God. Callie exhaled, relieved that her appearance didn't alarm him. The small *We Serve Whites Only!* sign in the front window had unsettled her. How had she gone her entire life not seeing these affronts for what they were?

She perused the shelf of first-aid supplies and gathered what she needed. She presented her items for payment as the clerk stepped up to the counter.

"That be it for you, ma'am?" he asked. One dollar and ten cents."

Callie heard the little bell on the door tinkle as she counted out her payment.

"No! You boys get outta here," the clerk snapped.

Callie turned to see two young black boys standing in the open door.

"Suh, can we buy two Coke-Colas, please? We got money, suh," the older boy said.

"You go get your Coke-Cola somewhere else. Didn't you read the sign?" He stabbed his finger toward the front window.

The boys backed out the door, dejected.

The clerk muttered under his breath and began to put Callie's items in a paper sack.

Callie watched the boys leave. "I'll take two Coca-Colas," she said brightly. She removed a dime from her purse and slapped it on the counter.

The man scowled, grumbling all the way to the drink cooler and back. He set the icy bottles on the counter.

"Thank you. Can you please open them?" she asked.

The man shook his head and grudgingly pried the tops off of both bottles. "If we encourage them, they'll keep coming back, you know!" he grumbled.

"Oh, I certainly hope so!" Callie offered the man her sweetest smile. She picked up the bag and the Cokes and headed toward the shop door. When she stepped outside, she scanned the street for the little boys. They were walking down the sidewalk, heads low.

"Boys!" Callie called, picking up her pace. "Coca-Cola boys!" Several white people stared at her as she hurried to meet up with the boys, who had stopped, wide-eyed.

The older boy grabbed the younger boy's arm and yanked him off the sidewalk into the gutter. Callie handed the two Cokes to the younger boy. "Here you are. Enjoy!" She smiled as the boy took the cold bottles tentatively.

The older boy stared at the bounty, mouth agape. "Thank you, ma'am. We got money. We can pay ya," he said, digging in his pocket.

Callie held up her free hand. "No. This is a gift. Someday, y'all do the same for someone else."

The boys grinned at each other and thanked Callie again before heading off down the street.

She turned and walked back to the car, feeling quite pleased with herself. She stashed her bag in the passenger seat and hurried around to get into the driver's side. As she adjusted her hat, her eye caught an attractive couple strolling in her direction. In a split second, she recognized Sam. Her heart dropped into her gut. The platinum blonde hanging on his arm was the gorgeous young flapper who had gushed over him in the diner the day they'd met for lunch. The mayor's daughter. The girl gripped Sam's arm tightly with manicured nails, as if he might escape should she let go. Callie glanced at her own bare nails, rough and stained from digging in clay.

Their faces were turned toward each other, and the girl said something that made Sam throw back his dark head with laughter. Callie dropped her gaze and waited for them to pass. They ducked into a tiny restaurant a few doors past the druggist. He looked so happy. *He never looked that way with me,* she thought.

Callie gulped and started the car quickly. As tears began to sting her eyes, she backed out of the parking space and headed for home. *Well. That's that. I do love him, but I can't have him. What did I expect? He's moved on.* She let the tears fall as she motored out of downtown Greenville. She wanted nothing more than to throw herself in bed and cry for days.

Near the edge of town, she wiped her tears and pulled into the filling station to buy gasoline. Strains of music caught her ear, and she turned to see a small brass band parading around the field across the street, toward a large circus tent decorated with red, white, and blue flags and bunting. A small crowd of people milled about under the tent.

"You want a fill-up, miss?" The elderly attendant rose from a bench in front of the store and approached the car.

"Yes, please," Callie said. "Say, what's going on across the road?"

The man looked up from the gasoline pump. "They holdin' a spring festival. I might go on over there myself later. The flyer says there's free eats and drinks. Dancin' and famous speakers. It'll really get ramped up tonight." He replaced the gasoline nozzle, pulled a pale blue paper from his shirt pocket, and handed it to Callie. "There ya go, ma'am. That'll be one dollar an' fifteen cents."

"Thank you." Callie fumbled with some coins and gave the attendant what she owed. She looked down at the flyer in her lap, her heart thudding in her chest.

The Knights of the Ku Klux Klan of the Upstate
Invite you, your family, and friends to attend their
White Christian Citizens Rally in the Park
Berea crossroads at Bowen's field
April 15 1 pm to midnight, rain or shine
Eats & Drinks, Guest Speakers, Dancing, and Music
Meet us at the sign of the fiery Cross.
Join and fight for Race and Nation.

Below the words was a photograph of a robed and hooded figure, arms outstretched, the outline of a dark cross surrounding him.

Callie swallowed hard. She glanced across the street again, where children ran and played, a few couples moved lazily around the dance floor, and the smoke from grilling hotdogs wafted into the air. It all looked so innocent, so benign. How many times had she passed by similar events and thought nothing of them?

Propped against one wall of the tent was a large wooden cross, rather innocuous in the bright sunshine. Comforting even. But tonight, it would be draped in kerosene-soaked rags, and set ablaze, a warning to anyone not pure white. She put the old car in gear and motored slowly across the street.

— • —

"I'm home, Granny," Callie called. Seeta heard the thump of the shopping bags on the table. Her granddaughter said, "I swear, some days, it is colder inside this house than out. Today is one of those days. We should sit on the porch. Give Brother James something to talk about."

Seeta liked hearing Callie's chatter, but she was so tired today. And she'd been in the middle of a good dream. She and her John strolled arm in arm down some country lane on a breezy afternoon, buzzing bees and pink mountain laurel blooms proclaiming spring had arrived. John bent to kiss her cheek.

Callie stepped into Seeta's darkened bedroom. "Granny?" she barked.

Seeta opened her eyes.

"This room is ice cold." Callie frowned and glanced at her watch. "And it's nearly three o'clock." She crossed the room and pried open a reluctant window. A warm breeze drifted across Seeta's face.

"I'm eighty-eight years old. I can nap when I want," Seeta said. "Stop naggin' at me. What you so cross about today?"

Callie shook her head and stepped out of the bedroom. Seeta heard the girl mutter, open the front door and windows, and only then begin to loudly put away groceries.

Seeta's eyes were heavy. She pulled the quilts up around her shoulders and tried to find the dream again. Suddenly Callie reappeared in the doorway, and Seeta knew she would take up the same argument.

"Granny, I want to buy us a new place. The envelope is stashed in my room, cash money."

Seeta snorted. "How many times you gonna ask me?"

"I'll make us some tea, and we can talk about it," Callie said.

Seeta listened to the rattle of dishes, and soon the tea kettle whistled its shrill call.

Callie maneuvered the tea tray into Seeta's bedroom. "Here we are," she said, carefully setting the tray on Seeta's bureau. Seeta sat up and folded the quilt back. She watched Callie cross the room and open the curtains wide, dispelling some of the gloom in the tiny space. Callie poured a cup of tea and handed it to Seeta.

Seeta noticed Callie's bleary eyes. "What's wrong with you? Did somethin' happen in town?"

"I'm fine."

"Hmm," Seeta said. "Somethin' has you agitated."

Callie ignored Seeta's comment. "Let's find a new house. Maybe over toward Greenville where I could see clients of either color." Callie sipped her tea and glanced at the open window. "Are you cold? I put another log on the fire and stoked the stove."

Seeta held the steaming cup close and nodded. "Old bones. I stay cold." She sipped her tea. "What happened in Greenville?"

Callie looked at Seeta sadly. "I saw Sam—walking down the sidewalk with a beautiful woman years younger than me. Her hair was perfect. Her dress was beautiful. Her figure was far better than mine—and he looked so happy," Callie said. "I cried the whole way home."

Seeta ached for her granddaughter. "Oh, baby. I'm sorry. You should go tell him what happened with Dr. Davis. I could see in his eyes how much he cares for you. An' I saw the way he kissed you—right there in the schoolhouse. You never gave him a chance to decide on his own what he wanted to do. I think he's in love with you, girl."

Callie shrugged, trying to hold back a fresh round of tears. "Granny, he must know where I am. He found me here once. He hasn't come looking for me. It's been two months. And we can't be together anyway. You yourself said that about Mama and Marcus. Not in this world . . ."

Seeta regarded her pale granddaughter, dark curls wild after her trip her trip to Greenville, brown eyes red from crying. She ached knowing the pain Callie was feeling and wished she'd never told her the truth. It hurt so much to see both of her grandchildren struggle, Zeke trying to make ends meet and support his new little family in a white man's world, and Callie trying to negotiate which side of the great color divide she would be able to build a life on.

Callie leaned against the door frame. "I stopped at a Klan rally. On my way home."

Seeta put a wrinkled hand over her heart. "Callie," was all she managed.

"I wanted to see what it was like." Callie shrugged. "There was a good crowd. A band. Normal people dancing and children eating free sandwiches and drinking lemonade. I wonder if any of them were there because they support the cause. The speaker was droning on about the Women's Christian Temperance Union."

"For it or against it?" Seeta asked wryly.

"For it," Callie smiled. "I didn't stay long. I suppose things aren't as friendly after dark. That's when the robes and hoods come out." Her smile evaporated. "And the flaming crosses."

"Grown men hidin' under bedsheets," Seeta snapped.

Callie sighed. After some time, she whispered, "Granny, who will want me?"

Seeta felt a great sadness well up in her own heart. She swallowed it down with all her might. "Trust the Lawd, an' don't rely on your own understandin'. He got good things in store for you, girl. But his timin' ain't ours. You wait an' see."

Callie stood quietly for a minute. Finally, she squared her sagging shoulders. "Anyway, that's that. I want to buy us a house. I have money set aside. We should be able to get something decent. Something that isn't in such disrepair. You'd be near to family, and I would be able to see more clients. Will you at least think about it?"

Seeta sipped her tea and then set the cup down on the nightstand. "Callie, I ain't movin'. I ain't takin' all the money you have."

Callie's face fell. "But we could be near Zeke and Delia. You could maybe have electric lights and running water . . ." Her voice trailed away.

Seeta held up a hand to stop Callie. "I don't need those things. An' you ain't stayin' with me forever. You got to go on to someplace where you can meet new friends, maybe start up a business again, or go to nursin' school, like Silas said. I never intended you to stay here permanently. I'm closin' in on ninety years old. Now that you know I'm your granny, I got all I need." She closed her tired eyes.

Before Callie could say another word, Seeta continued, "You fit to bust all cooped up here with a ol' lady. It's the spring fever. Start all over somewhere new—away from folks who hate you jes' because of the color of yo' daddy's skin."

Callie reached for her grandmother's hand. "I can't leave you."

Seeta's eyes opened. "You gonna have to go. Because Doc Davis is gonna make your life here miserable."

"He hates me because of Mama. He thinks you poisoned Jim Beecham." Callie screwed up her face. "Granny, did—did you poison him?"

Seeta wasn't about to explain herself. She gazed at her granddaughter without blinking. "That man 'bout killed your mama."

"That doesn't answer my question," Callie said.

Seeta snorted. "When Kizzy admitted the truth about you, he knocked her into the wall so hard she passed out. He tried to kill you, a newborn. When she woke up, she saw that he'd set you in a trough of cold water, deep enough that if you'd squirmed the wrong way an' turned over, you'd have drowned. He set you right next to her, to look like she drowned you. Thank God he didn't just do the deed hisself. She came to an' found you screamin' your head off, little arms and legs ice cold and turnin' blue. It was February!"

Callie waited for Seeta to continue.

"If he hadn't died, you and your mama would have."

"What did you do?" Callie asked, her expression more curious than shocked.

Seeta knew she could tell her granddaughter that Mr. Beecham hadn't suffered a natural heart attack or a stroke. She thought of the many plants that could be used in toxic amounts to stop a heartbeat or seize up a respiratory system. She recalled the abundant Jimsonweed she could have scavenged near the roadside. She could have dried several entire plants, root and all, before chopping it into bits and pouring it in an empty lard tin—saving it for a need. She might have instructed Kizzy to take the whole tin and mix it in her husband's boiled collards.

Instead, Seeta looked up at Callie defiantly. "I do anything to protect my babies. That's all you need to know."

Callie regarded Seeta. "I won't ever ask again, Granny. I don't question your motives. Not after all you've been through. But you'll be safer away from here, too. Dr. Davis could come for you. He didn't know that you were still alive. But he does now. And Silas isn't here."

"Shoot. I got no fear of Earl Davis. He gonna kill a old lady?" Seeta shook her tiny fist in the air. "The Lawd's watched over me for near ninety years. An' I know the Fire Spell."

"The Fire Spell? My mama taught me that one," Callie said. "I used it after they shattered my window."

"An' I taught it to her before I moved back to Liberia—for her protection." Seeta nodded and added, "It ain't never failed me yet."

Callie sighed. "If you won't move, I won't either. Not yet. I'll see to some repairs around here. I have the money for that."

Seeta smiled at her granddaughter and sipped her tea smugly, the battle won. "If that'll make you happy, go right ahead."

Chapter Nineteen

The man stepped out onto the back porch and came down the steps toward Callie. She stood up and stretched, taking a break from assembling tepee-like towers made from sticks and grapevine. The young bean plants would quickly climb up the towers, their tendrils twisting and coiling, hungry for the sun.

"Mizz Beecham?" he called, wiping his brow. "I finished plasterin' the ceilin' in the kitchen and the bedrooms. An' I fixed the front porch step that was loose. Mizz Seeta's asleep in the front room. My hammerin' didn't seem to wake her."

"She sleeps all day now. A freight train wouldn't wake her." Callie swiped her dirty hands across her dungarees. "Thank you, Mr. Louis. We sure appreciate your coming over. Those ceilings were a mess."

Ben Louis nodded and scratched his grizzled chin. "They was. I'm sorry it took so long to come over. I been puttin' in my corn, and it took me a while with all the rain we been havin'. I was happy to get some work though. Odd jobs lately have been few and far between." He inclined his head toward the house. "But your roof is sound. Zeke did a good job on it. You won't have no rain comin' in."

"Thank you again. And you'll come back next week to dig the new well?" She dug into her pocket and pulled out a wad of dollar bills.

"Yes, ma'am. Seeta and me been sharin' wells since 1900. She finds the water an' me an' my boys dig."

"I think this is payment for today, then." She handed Ben the cash and motioned for him to follow her. "Can I get you a cool drink before you go? I have some Coca-Colas hidden under the house where it's chilly."

His eyes widened. "Well, now. I wouldn't turn down a cold drink!"

Callie crouched down near the back steps. She reached under the house and pulled out a washtub filled with soda bottles. She grabbed two and shoved the tub back into the dark.

"Seeta hadn't ever had a Coke until last month," Callie said. "You should have seen her face when she tried it." She laughed and set a bottle into the bottle opener screwed into the porch railing. She popped off the cap and handed the man the drink. She repeated the process and drank a long draft from her own bottle.

Ben drank half the bottle in one gulp and then wiped his mouth with his sleeve. "Now that hits the spot on a warm day, for sure. It's too hot for May." Thunder rumbled far to the west. He paused and shifted the bottle to his other hand. "Mizz Beecham, can I ask you somethin'?"

"Depends what it is," Callie said. She already knew what the man wanted to know. It was what everyone was curious about—from white-haired Brother James who lived near the church and sat on his porch watching her every move, with a scowl on his face, to the little girl named Carolina, with her neat cornrows and gap-toothed smile, who came to the edge of the garden on Saturdays and loitered there, barefooted, waiting for Callie to come outside and give her a penny candy. From the woman who needed help for menstrual pain to the young man with persistent diarrhea. Each time, she had demurred and given the same answer to anyone bold enough to ask. *I'm here to help my friend, Seeta.*

"You been here a while. It's almost onto June," he said as he swatted a carpenter bee, then added casually, "Some folks say Mizz Seeta is kin to you. I ain't one to go messin' in others' business, you hear, but people are wonderin'."

Callie found herself smiling. The man didn't look at her. He gazed up at the darkening sky as if he were studying cloud formations. She had decided early on that she didn't want to do anything to anger the citizens of Liberia, but after Mary Talbot, it seemed harmless enough. She wanted to admit the truth to this gentleman. *Besides, it's a beautiful day. I feel good, and it'd be funny to see the man fall over when I tell him.*

"She's my grandmother," Callie said.

Ben's eyes grew as round as saucers. "That's what my wife said! I didn't believe her," he exclaimed. "You jes' don't look it. Black, I mean. You as white as can be!"

"My mother was white" Callie said easily. Before he could ask the next question, she offered the answer. "Seeta's son, Marcus, was my father. Zeke is my cousin. You can tell everyone to stop wondering. And beyond that, you'd have to ask Seeta. It's her business." She finished her Coke and set the bottle on the steps. "Now I better get back to the bean trellises before that storm comes. Those pole beans have probably grown six inches while we chatted. Thanks again, Mr. Louis."

"I heard they kicked you out your own home. How long you figure to stay?"

Callie considered his question. "I'll stay as long as she needs me."

"Where you gonna land? Bein' mulatto?"

"Mr. Louis, don't you start in," she chided. "It's bad enough that my family is asking the same question. I'll be fine."

Ben nodded, his curiosity sated. He set down his empty bottle. "Well, I be back on Monday with my boys to start that well." He turned and headed toward his house across the dirt track.

Callie watched him go and then returned to the garden. She crouched in the soil, winding lengths of grapevine around the trellises she was constructing. In the distance, she heard a car engine, and twisted around to see who would be coming into Liberia by automobile. The shiny new car motored up toward Seeta's house and stopped out front, sending up a cloud of red dust. As soon as she saw the door of the gunmetal blue Model A open, her heart jumped into her throat.

The tall, thin man emerged from the car. He smoothed his rumpled seersucker jacket and adjusted his straw fedora, before lighting a cigarette and gazing up at Seeta's house. She smelled the Chesterfield on the breeze. Callie knew that from a distance, he might not recognize her, in her dusty dungarees and wide straw hat that shaded her face. The garden was so near Ben's house that it would be easy to pretend she wasn't involved. She could turn away and continue to build bean trellises. But . . . Seeta.

Callie stood and removed her hat. She wiped her brow with her sleeve and replaced her hat, then strode toward the man, anger rising. "What do you want, Earl?" she shouted, coming toward the man quickly.

Davis turned. He seemed genuinely surprised to see her. "Callie Beecham, as I live and breathe. So, you did take my advice and come live with your kinfolk." He blew a stream of blue smoke toward her. "You look right at home."

"You have no business here," Callie barked. "You're trespassing, and I'll call the sheriff."

"You kiddin' me? There ain't any telephone lines up this way. I came to see for myself—that my old friend Seeta is still alive and kickin'."

Callie wished she really had a telephone. Or a knife. Even the garden spade she'd dropped into the dirt. How could she stop this man from hurting her grandmother?

The man puffed on the cigarette, then exhaled and tossed it onto the ground. He moved toward the front of the house.

"Get out of here!" Callie yelled. She moved past Davis and jumped up onto the front porch. She stood in front of the door and spread her arms wide.

Davis ascended the steps and leaned over Callie. "Open the door. I don't want to do anything ugly, but I will talk to that woman."

"Just a minute here!" barked a man's voice. Davis stepped back, surprised. Callie saw Ben Louis standing in the yard, a shotgun aimed right at the doctor. "I suggest you do what the young lady said and step off her property." He cocked the gun. "I ain't one to miss."

"Well, well . . . you coloreds are bound and determined to cause trouble," Earl muttered, hands on his hips. "I just wanted to come and visit Seeta, and look at the reception I get. You think I won't be back with friends next time? How dare you point a gun at me, nigger?"

"You don't scare me, you piece o' white trash," Louis growled. "Now git!"

Callie heard the door behind her open. She turned to see Seeta standing there, an old .45 caliber pistol in her outstretched hands. "Granny!" she gasped.

"Move outta the way, Callie. I expect Mr. Louis an' I need a clear shot if this poor excuse for a man won't git off my porch," Seeta said. She leveled the gun at Davis's stomach. "Gut shot. It might not kill you outright, but it's a start. An' it'll hurt. I guess my neighbor's shotgun will have to finish the job."

Davis raised his palms and stepped down the three wooden steps to solid ground. He scowled and shoved his hands in his pants pockets. "So, you're still with us, Seeta. My, how I hoped you'd passed on to your eternal reward by now. I may send my boys up to pay a visit."

Callie felt a flush of fresh anger. "You try that, and I will see you arrested. You're trespassing, making threats. If you lay a hand on anyone here, you'll regret it."

"Y'all need some help?"

Callie glanced away from Davis and was stunned to see Charles Merck stride into the yard, a hunting rifle slung over his broad shoulder.

"Thank you, Brother Charles, but this man is leavin' now," Seeta said calmly.

"Don't know that I've ever been treated so poorly by a bunch of niggers." Davis leaned and spat into the dirt. "Y'all gonna pay for this."

A shot rang out, and Callie instinctively clapped her hands over her ears at the percussive blast. A loud hiss came from the rear tire of Davis's Ford. Several chickens took flight and flapped toward their roost.

Seeta lowered the pistol. "Now you only got three good tires an' a spare, Earl. You fix that flat now and drive off, or I'll shoot out the others. You got three guns on you. Don't matter what hand is fixin' to pull the trigger—they all black."

Thunder cracked overhead. Davis spat a string of expletives and scurried to his car. Ben Louis and Charles Merck trained their guns on the man while he hurried to replace the destroyed tire with the spare.

Callie turned to Seeta, who was trembling. "Granny, let me have the pistol. Come inside," she murmured. Seeta nodded and handed the pistol to her granddaughter gingerly. Callie held it at arm's length and turned to follow Seeta into the house.

Seeta sank to a chair and closed her eyes.

"This is my fault. I let him know you're alive." Callie placed the gun on the floor and sat across from Seeta.

Seeta shook her head. "He's a hateful man. But he's too puny to do anything more than threaten me. He may send some men out to harass me, but he'll have the whole of Liberia fightin' back. This happens all the time, Callie."

"Granny, he'll come back. We need to find somewhere far enough that he won't come after you. Or send a bunch of thugs to burn all of Liberia down. Think of the others who live here. Maybe I should go back to the sheriff."

Seeta sighed. "That won't come to no good. What you gonna tell him? That Dr. Davis came to Liberia an' I shot out his tire? What'll that do? The sheriff don't come out an' investigate when a white man threatens us," she scoffed. "The last time we had real trouble up here, you know what he said? "If anyone tries to break into your homes, shoot 'em, throw 'em outside, and I'll pick 'em up in the morning.""

— • —

Callie woke to the sound of rain pattering on the roof and the dull realization that she had put off removing her stored things from Silas's house for far too long. Summer was just around the corner. Blackberry blossoms and honeysuckle dotted the roadsides and fields, and the nights were filled with the sound of croaking spring peepers.

For all she knew, Silas's daughter-in-law had already shown up and tossed Callie's furniture and belongings into the street. It had been months since she left her own house in haste, anxious to get away from Davis and his threats. And still, he had followed her to Liberia with a hate so strong that he would do harm to an old lady.

But now she had Seeta's promise. They would move away. As soon as she had Silas's house in order, she would use Davis's blood money to find someplace near Zeke, and they'd go.

While Callie hated the fact that her beloved radio, washer, and lamps were worthless without electricity, she could sell them or hold on to them, hoping for a house with electricity. She could retrieve her gramophone and records, and give Seeta a taste of the jazz she herself loved so much. She would check her post office box, sure that there were overdue bills. Her prized breakfront, handed down from her mother, would have to stay. There was no way she could bring it. No way to even hoist the thing out the door without help.

On this dreary day, Callie tied a bandana over her hair, donned a raincoat, and loaded the car with the cleaning supplies she remembered that Silas didn't have—vinegar and lemons, a broom and dustpan, a mop and a bucket.

"You sure you'll be alright, Granny?"

Seeta nodded. "I got the Lawd with me. An' that old Colt .45. An' Brother Ben is gonna check in."

Callie kissed Seeta on the cheek and headed out. She'd crossed her fingers and prayed that her trip would be uneventful. Now, in a steady rain, she steered the old car onto Florence Street for the first time since February. The trees had leafed out, emerald-green canopies on both sides of the road. Silas's house looked the same, but the grass appeared freshly mowed. *Someone has been here*, she realized with alarm. She hadn't really considered that someone might have taken over the house and was living in Silas's place.

Callie had hoped to pull the car into the old garage behind the house and then hide away while she cleaned and sorted. She hadn't even wanted to look further down the street to her own house. She couldn't bear it, she knew. But as the car idled, she realized she'd have to go to the front door, knock, and take it from there. At the very least, she would meet the new occupants.

She pulled up to the curb and cut the engine. "Here goes nothing," she murmured and hopped out of the car, key in hand. She took a deep breath and exhaled, before running up the sidewalk, her raincoat scant protection from the wet. She knocked on the door tentatively. There was no answer. She tried again and got the same result. With some trepidation, she tried the house key and was surprised that it fit the lock. *Surely, a new owner would have changed the lock?*

She opened the door cautiously and called out, "Yoo hoo? Hello?" The interior was dim, but Callie saw plainly that nothing had been touched since the day of Silas's death. Full ashtrays, blankets cast aside on the couch, and the musty smell of a closed house told her that no one had come. Even her note was there, shoved under an ash tray. Everything was exactly as it had been in January when she found him dead. While she was relieved to be alone, she ached for Silas amidst his belongings, his scent.

But the daughter-in-law hadn't shown up. No one had. She would have to go see the deputy about the house. Someone would need to find Silas's only family. But she would set it to rights as best she could first. Clearly, a neighbor had been kind enough—or worried enough about appearances—to keep the yard trimmed, for which she was grateful.

Callie pushed open the curtains to get some light into the dark room. She hadn't expected the electricity to work and was surprised when she hit the switch without thinking. The overhead bulb glowed. *How can this be?*

The revelation made her smile, and she clicked on the old man's radio. A jazz tune she'd known years before set her toes to tapping, and she went to work with vigor, scrubbing floors, airing bedding, sorting books into neat rows on the shelf. She plugged in the electric washer and washed the dirty clothes she'd collected. She cleaned the fireplace and wiped up old spills in the kitchen.

When Louis Armstrong's lilting "West End Blues" came on, she faltered. The song made her melancholy—missing both Silas and Sam. The memory of dancing in Sam's strong arms at the speakeasy made her weak in the knees, but she resolved to let the pain have its way once and for all. He was with someone else, someone young and white and blonde, acceptable to the powers that be. Both the house and her aching soul would get a good and final scouring this day. She wiped away a single tear and focused on scrubbing the worn kitchen linoleum.

She opened several boxes of her medicinals and arranged the concoctions on the breakfront shelves for counting. It helped her to see what was left in her stock and reminded her of what she needed to restock in Liberia. By late afternoon, the house had been thoroughly cleaned and her aching soul seemed finally at peace. The old breakfront and her other furniture would have to wait for another trip, but everything else was loaded into the old Ford. She penned a fresh note asking whoever bought the place to contact her through her post office box before disposing of anything.

Callie peered out of Silas's newly washed front windows, grateful to see the rain had finally let up. She picked up the laundry basket full of Silas's clean clothes and hoisted it to her hip. The old clothing could be distributed to men in Liberia. As she turned to go, she spied the gnarled mountain laurel cane that Silas had relied on everywhere he went. Callie smiled, picked it up, and balanced it across the laundry basket. She left the house, locked the heavy oak door with the spare key, and headed to the car.

A shiny beige Model A pulled up to the curb in front of her, thoughtlessly splashing through a large puddle. Callie jumped back, indignant. The oblivious driver stepped out and doffed his hat. His suit was impeccably tailored and his hair oiled to a shine. For a brief moment, Callie wondered if he was some gangster's goon, hired by Dr. Davis to intimidate her.

"Morning, ma'am. I'm looking for a woman who used to live on this street," the man said. "Perhaps a neighbor of yours?"

Callie slid the laurel cane from atop the laundry basket and gripped it firmly. "And you are?"

He stepped forward and extended his hand. "I'm Steven Cutler, from Cutler, Williams, and White in Greenville. May I have a moment of your time?" He handed her his business card. "I saw you come out of Mr. Roberts' house. I'm hoping you can help me."

Callie tightened her grip on the laurel cane. "I was cleaning up at his place." She gestured toward the laundry basket. "I tidied up in case his daughter-in-law comes to town. I didn't want her to see the house in shambles."

"Do you know Callie Beecham? I had her address as down this same street, but she moved out months ago. I haven't been able to locate her. She moved away without a forwarding address, and I have important business with her." The man seemed overly curious. "And she hasn't answered my letters."

Callie glanced around her but saw no one who could help her when the man made his move.

The man glanced at the cane and grinned. "Ah, Mr. Roberts' cane. I always wondered why he used such a twisted piece of wood as a cane. He was a character." He looked up at Callie. "I was his attorney, ma'am. Are you Miss Beecham?"

Callie felt her pulse slow, and she released her death grip on the cane. She smiled and said, "It's mountain laurel. It grows that way. His wife loved mountain laurel. He had it as long as I knew him. I used to chastise him about its safety on bumpy sidewalks, but he never listened." She laid the cane across the laundry basket. "I'm Miss Beecham," she admitted.

The man grinned as if he'd just won a sweepstakes. "Miss Beecham, do you know how hard it has been to find you? I was about ready to hire a Pinkerton. And here I am doing my weekly drive-by, and you walk right out of his house!"

He noticed her full hands. "May I help you?" He extended his hands toward the basket.

"Thank you, Mr. Cutler," Callie said. She handed him the heavy basket and opened the car door. "Silas was a dear friend. I'm anxious to know if you've wrapped up his affairs."

He set the basket in the seat and turned to her. "I'm trying to do that very thing. He was one of a kind," Cutler said. "May we go inside for a moment and speak?"

"Y-yes, I suppose." She smoothed her dirty apron. "I must apologize for looking like a scullery maid."

"It was real good of you to take the trouble to clean up. Silas said you were a kind lady. I myself didn't step foot inside. Probably should have . . ." The attorney chuckled and followed her up the steps. She produced the key once more and they entered the front room.

"It was a mess," Callie confided. "Won't you have a seat? I can make us some coffee." She removed the dingy apron and swiped nervously at her hair, removing the bandana.

Mr. Cutler gazed at the orderly breakfront shelves lined with labeled blue bottles, packaged herbs and soaps, scented potpourris, and jars of tea. "Say, these have your name on them. It looks like a general store. Are you a druggist?"

Callie smiled. "I had a business selling medicinal herbs and tinctures. I saw clients with minor ills. I hope it's alright—I had left some things here when I moved. These are supplies I don't have room to take with me just yet. I wanted to see what I had left, so I unpacked everything and set it out. I plan to move again soon, and I'll take everything then."

She measured coffee into Silas's coffee pot and made a mental note to take the remaining coffee with her. "I should have come back months ago. But it doesn't look like his daughter-in-law has been here yet," she said over her shoulder.

"Fascinating," Cutler said, peering at the labels. "My kids all have earaches and coughs this time of year. Allergies, I suppose . . . You have anything for that, Miss Beecham? My wife says she hates to bother the doctor with minor complaints."

Surprised at his interest, Callie nodded. "I do. After I get the coffee going, I'll show you what might work. How old are your children?"

"Twelve, ten, seven, four, and the little one is three months." He hooked his thumbs in his suspenders. "Mrs. Cutler would be calling the doctor every other day if she worried over every sniffle and sore throat."

"Goodness! That's quite a household," Callie said, with a twinge of jealousy. The coffee pot was soon percolating noisily.

"Let me see, Mr. Cutler." She scanned the shelves and soon found what she was looking for. She pulled down a pint bottle and handed it to him. "Dose the older children a tablespoon of this syrup three times a day when they're symptomatic. It should do the trick nicely." She picked up a small paper sack. "Tell your wife that this tea will help with the coughs. And a warm vegetable broth and soupy grains will also help to loosen phlegm." She paused. "Are you a smoker?"

"Yes, I am," the man answered.

"Try blowing tobacco smoke into their ears the next time one of your children has an earache."

"That works?"

"Old folk remedies usually have some basis in science. I don't know why that one works, I'll admit." Callie smiled.

Suitably impressed, Cutler reached in his pocket. "I'll take two of each, please. How much do I owe you?"

"The tea is thirty cents a bag. The syrup is fifty cents. So, one dollar sixty." Callie placed the merchandise on the table, and Mr. Cutler handed her two dollar bills in exchange. It was the first income she'd seen in weeks.

"Keep the change. You should charge more," Cutler said. "In Greenville, I'd pay twice that at the druggist."

"Thank you." Callie felt a surge of pride. "Now, I guess we can have that cup of coffee, and you can tell me why you're looking for me."

When the two were comfortably seated at the kitchen table with their steaming cups, Mr. Cutler began. "I'm sorry that you were left with Silas's funeral arrangements. You'll be reimbursed."

"No. A friend saw to everything," Callie said simply. "I wish I could have done more."

"Mr. Roberts was something of an enigma, Miss Beecham. I don't know if you knew his background?"

"He came down from Asheville. His wife died in childbirth, and then his only son died in the war. I saw the heartache it caused him until his dying day," Callie responded. "He didn't leave his house much."

"So you did know the man. He was a man of means—despite outward appearances," Cutler said.

"Silas told me he made money in lumber. He was very generous to me. He let me use his car. In fact, he bought me a brand-new radio for Christmas." Callie smiled at the thought. "He hasn't worked since I've known him. He wore the same threadbare clothes for years. His health was poor these last months." She sipped her coffee. "Were you able to locate his daughter-in-law?"

Cutler put down his cup. "Miss Beecham, Silas has been my client for a long time. After his son died, the daughter-in-law was able to collect William's military pension and life insurance, so we know she was taken care of financially. No need to fret about her. But she never contacted Silas after her husband's funeral. Not once in ten years. In fact, he came to my office in the fall and took her out of his will completely."

Callie remembered her conversation with Silas in the post office before Christmas. "Oh, he did mention that to me. I'd forgotten."

"He didn't know it, but she remarried," Cutler said. He pulled a thin folder from his briefcase and slid it across the table. "Miss Beecham, hold on to your hat. He left everything to you."

For a moment, Callie wasn't sure she'd heard correctly. "What?" she asked, her voice quivering. "His house?"

"Silas left *everything* to you," Cutler said with emphasis. "His house. His money. A place down on the coast. Everything. He owned a few stocks and bonds. He has money at the local savings and loan. That account has close to $60,000 cash in it. Mr. Roberts was a wealthy man."

Callie put down her cup with shaking hands, aghast. "No. You can't be serious. The man wouldn't buy himself new pants."

Cutler smiled. "I am, indeed. See for yourself. He was most concerned for your future."

Callie opened the folder and pulled out Silas's Last Will and Testament. She scanned the document and smiled. "That old coot," she said affectionately. Her heart began to beat wildly in her chest.

Cutler shook his head. "As I said, the man was an enigma. Don't know why he didn't put more of that money into the stock market. Invest it, I said! Anyway, the good news is the inheritance will not have to go through probate. It's yours now."

"What? How?" Callie stammered.

"Silas put your name on everything last fall. You jointly own the securities, the savings account, with the right of survivorship. He had me add your name to the land and house deeds. The land on the coast has a small cottage on it. It may be quite valuable. Should you wish to sell it, I can help you. I have a house down that way myself." He pulled a set of house keys from his vest pocket. "Keys to the Lowcountry cottage. As for this house, you already have the key. Do with it what you will. It is yours, free and clear."

Callie shook her head. "Are you sure?"

Cutler smiled. "I am. Mr. Roberts was very concerned that if he should pass away, you'd be financially protected—immediately. When I couldn't locate you, I felt as if I was derelict in my duties. At least we could keep the lights on and the grass cut."

"You did that?" Callie gasped. "Thank you."

Cutler leaned back in his chair. "Congratulations, Miss Beecham. You're a wealthy woman." He pulled a fat envelope from his vest pocket. "Here is the savings passbook with your name on it. He also left $200 cash and said to have a little fun with it. And he left a letter."

Cutler downed the rest of his coffee and stood to leave. "That concludes my business, for now, ma'am. Thank you for the syrup and the tea. I hope they do the trick." He smiled, tipped his hat, and opened the front door to leave.

"If you have any questions, my telephone number is on my card. I would appreciate your continued business if there is anything you need. He had me on retainer. I'd like to think I could be of assistance to you, too. Lots of mouths to feed." He winked. "Good day, Miss Beecham!"

Callie sat numbly, trying to take in what had just happened. She was a rich woman—instantly. Dear old Silas had given her the last gift he had to give. Her mind began to reel with possibilities. She could run away and reinvent herself. Go far away where no one knew who she was. She didn't have to worry about paying the bills, making ends meet, any of it. Just the thought of walking into the bank and withdrawing all that money—for she did plan to withdraw it—made her giddy with plans.

Her heart lurched. Seeta would be well cared for with such a large inheritance. She grabbed the envelopes and slid them into her purse. She let herself out the door and didn't even bother to glance at her old house as she started the car and sped toward Liberia.

— • —

That night, Callie sat with Seeta on the worn sofa and showed her the will. In the dim light of the oil lamps, it was difficult to read, but Seeta deciphered it after some minutes. The logs crackled in the small fireplace and threw shadows on the walls.

Seeta patted her granddaughter's face. "Well, I'll be. I'm happy fo' you, baby girl. This means you won't want fo' nothin' in this world."

Callie grasped Seeta's hand. "Granny, *we* won't want for anything. I want to do something wonderful for you. We could take a trip. Maybe we could go up north and look for my father. Or travel someplace warm so you don't have to sit wrapped up in quilts all the time. There is some land Silas left down at the coast. Near Charleston. With a cottage."

Seeta pulled the quilts around her bony shoulders. "Naw. But there is one thing I think *you* should do."

"And what is that?"

"Go away from here."

Callie pulled back and looked at her grandmother. "What?"

"Go away. You got a good head on yo' shoulders. Sell Silas's house. Your business won't be right again in town. Even with all that money. You still mixed, an' Dr. Davis won't let you be."

Callie cursed under her breath. "It's 1929, and we're in a lather over the color of someone's skin. My skin!" She stuck out a pale arm in protest.

"But you pass—you one of the lucky ones who pass," Seeta exclaimed. "Take advantage of it, Callie!"

"I can't leave you, Granny." Callie slumped against the worn sofa.

Seeta was quiet for a moment. "If I'm what's stoppin' you from goin' away, well, then, I jes' fold up and go home to Jesus right now. I want you to do this. For me. The world'll treat you a whole lot better if they think you white. It's jes' the way of things now. Stayin' here keeps you stuck, Callie. You worse than black—you mixed, honey."

The pain of Seeta's comment stung her. She was not white. Not anymore. Black people saw her as a white woman and white people saw her as black. "Where will I go?"

Seeta answered easily. "Silas left a cottage down the coast? Go there."

Callie tried to picture herself living in a Lowcountry shack in some humid swamp.

"I'm a mountain girl. The thought of tropical humidity and

mosquitoes the size of horse flies doesn't appeal."

"Jes' go and see. Get away from here for a while. It'll do you good," Seeta said.

Callie sat up. "Maybe I will. But first—I want to buy a place for y'all. Some place where Zeke and Delia and you can live without worrying over Earl Davis, with running water and lights. Space for a big garden. A yard for Cal to play. I can't go away unless you're safe. Unless I know you're cared for. Only then would I consider it."

Seeta harrumphed. "Ain't no place around here like that for black folks."

Callie kissed Seeta on the cheek. "Maybe not in Liberia. But you'll see. I will find you a special place. Closer to where Zeke works. I'll ask Mr. Cutler to help me."

Seeta nodded. "If the family can all be together again, well, maybe it is time for me to leave Liberia."

— • —

Callie sat up late, reading and rereading the letter from Silas. The sagging mattress pulled her toward the dip in the middle of the bed, despite her best efforts to stay near the flickering lamp on the nightstand. She hoisted herself nearer the lamp once more and squinted at the spidery handwriting.

Dear Callie,

I had planned to talk to you at Christmas about all this, but I just didn't have the words. I'm going to tuck this note in my papers with my lawyer and you'll get it soon enough. I have left all my worldly goods to you in my will. I have no family, and you're the closest thing I've had to a daughter. I don't like to get sentimental, so enough of that.

She closed her eyes for a moment and smiled. *The dear man.* Then continued reading.

There are no restrictions on what you do with the money. I hope you will think of nursing school. I have one request, though. Spend some time at my place on James Island before you think of selling it. It was special to me and my William. I think it could be special to you, too.

Love,

Silas Roberts

Callie clutched the note to her chest, a lump in her throat.

— • —

The next Sunday dawned hot and humid. Callie had asked the family to come to Seeta's for Sunday dinner. She had promised a ham dinner with all the fixings—and a big surprise.

The ham and potato salad had been consumed, the snap beans, slaw, and buttery biscuits polished off. The family sat outside in the back yard, savoring both the late afternoon shade and Delia's chocolate cake. Baby Calvin was sprawled out on a quilt, following birds and butterflies with his liquid brown eyes. Callie lay next to him, wholly at peace. The baby laughed and cooed when his Auntie Callie blew raspberries on his tummy. Her heart melted at his smile. She wondered whether she would ever have children of her own. She was nearly thirty. It was a passing thought—nothing would take down her mood today, she vowed. She turned on her side to watch Zeke reread the letter for the third time.

He smacked the letter with his hands. "So, this is for real? Silas left you everything?"

"Yep. I'm rich," she said with a casual shrug. "I'm going to buy you a big house, Zeke, where Calvin can have his own room. Granny, too. A whole wing! With a nurse, if she wants. And running water and lights. And a radio!" She smiled and watched a puffy cloud change shape as it drifted by.

Mattie chuckled. "Shoot. I'll take care of Seeta an' Calvin if I can move in, too. You don't need no nurse."

"Of course, Mattie," Callie said. "You're family."

Zeke shook his head. "Granny, electric lights and water at the tap. Think of it."

Seeta pouted. "Mattie an' I is tough. We don't need that new-fangled stuff y'all clamor for."

"Speak for yo'self, Seeta!" Mattie huffed. "Hot water baths an' lights an' heat from a gas furnace? A telephone! Lawd, have mercy." She clapped her hands together.

Zeke shook his head. "Does the lawyer know you got a black daddy?" he asked bluntly.

Callie propped herself up on an elbow. "I don't think so. I need to tell him. In case things go badly, he should know what we're up against."

"Don't tell him nothin'," Zeke said. "He might take away the whole deal."

"If Silas liked him, I have to trust that it will work out. After all, he knew." She sighed. "Anyway, the accounts are in my name now. Free to withdraw. And Mr. Cutler has been most helpful in giving me advice.

He's going with me to pull money out of the bank."

Zeke let out a low whistle. "So, you gonna go to James Island and see the house?"

Callie sat up and hoisted the baby onto her lap. "Once I get you all safely moved, I'll go. Silas asked me to spend some time there before getting rid of it. Of course, I'll sell it eventually."

She nuzzled Calvin's soft little neck and added, "But first things first. I can't wait to see Grady Wilcox's face when I take all that money out of his bank."

— • —

Callie gripped the steering wheel tightly. Despite Zeke's admonition, she was determined to set things straight with Steven Cutler. Her gut had roiled all morning at the thought of the man's reaction, but her conscience wouldn't let her proceed until they'd cleared the air. She had taken two doses of her own nerve tonic and was relieved that her pulse wasn't racing at top speed anymore. Her mind still spun in circles, trying to plan for the probability that Cutler would renounce everything he'd told her. Maybe even stop the will from being carried out. She still had most of the proceeds from the forced sale of her own home. That would see them through for a while, she hoped.

The car backfired once, and Callie nearly jumped out of her skin. She exhaled a calming breath and turned onto Cleveland Avenue. In the light of day, Callie was surprised to see that the white brick law office of Cutler, Williams & White sat squarely across the street from Carunchio's restaurant. She rolled her eyes toward heaven. *Are you kidding me?*

She pulled into a parking space and cut the engine. She straightened the seams in her stockings, adjusted her hat, and glanced down at her dress, green silk with a shower of printed daisies across the background. It was far from new, but she cut a fine figure in it. After a quick prayer, she hopped out of the car and made her way into the building.

The lobby was lovely and cool, with plush oriental carpets underfoot and exotic potted palms flanking the receptionist's desk.

"May I help you?" the young receptionist asked. Her Marcelled platinum bob reminded Callie of Anne Walton's hair, and for a moment, Callie wondered what had become of her chic, young friend.

"I am here to see Mr. Cutler. I have an appointment." Callie clutched her purse tightly.

"Yes. Miss Beecham, is it? He is expecting you. Follow me." The woman led Callie down a hallway and stopped at a closed door. She knocked tentatively.

"Come in," the familiar voice called.

The woman peered inside. "Miss Beecham is here, sir."

"Oh, good. Come in, Miss Beecham. Come in." Cutler came around from his desk and extended his hand. "I'm glad you were able to get in touch with me. You don't have a telephone, you said."

Callie shook his hand, and he motioned for her to sit. "I was able to use a telephone in town," she said simply. The office was sumptuously decorated. His mahogany desk, framed art, overstuffed chintz chairs, and the spray of hothouse flowers on the long credenza behind his desk spoke volumes about Cutler's status and success as a lawyer. *This won't go well,* she fretted.

"Please have a seat," the man said.

"Thank you, Mr. Cutler." She swallowed hard. "I do hope I'm not wasting your time. I have to tell you something, and I'm not sure how this will go." She removed her gloves and laid them in her lap.

"That sounds ominous." Cutler returned to his desk. "Say! My wife said that syrup worked wonders on the kids' coughs. And when the baby threatened to pick up another earache, I blew cigarette smoke right in his ear. Several times. It worked!" He grinned.

"I'm glad," Callie said, mustering a smile. "I can make up some more if need be." She shifted nervously in the overstuffed chair. "I'm so happy that you could meet with me. I'm not sure how to begin . . ."

"This does seem serious," Cutler said. "You're not firing me already, are you?"

"Well, you may fire *me*," Callie said lamely. "You see, Silas was aware of something about my past. In fact, he knew it long before I did . . . But it may have some bearing on our relationship and the idea of giving me his money."

"Ah. I think I know where you're headed, Miss Beecham." Cutler stood and came around the desk. He closed the office door quietly and returned to his chair. "Go on."

"No. You can't possibly. You see . . . I–I'm . . ." Callie stammered in a voice barely above a whisper. "My father was a Negro man. I didn't know until very recently. That's why I've been staying in Liberia. There were some people in Pickens who didn't like the fact that I was living downtown and—"

"I did know that," Mr. Cutler interrupted. "Silas told me that you are a mulatto. That's why he was so worried about you and your welfare." He gazed at Callie intently. "I must say—I don't see it."

Callie felt a rush of blood to her face. She dropped her eyes to her lap, still uneasy with people studying her for signs that she was bi-racial. Words would not come, so she sat still and waited for Cutler to continue his assessment.

The man crossed his arms and finally spoke. "It caused me some concern, I won't lie," he said. "I have never dealt with colored clientele. But Silas was one of my favorite clients, and one of my wealthiest. When he explained the situation—what you meant to him, the way you are being harassed by the Klan . . . He felt that it was partly his fault."

"How could it have been his fault?" Callie asked.

Cutler leaned forward. "Big fish in a tiny pond, right, Miss Beecham. That's what Klansmen are. Silas told me that he'd had run-ins with them long ago. He said the local doctor and the bank president are two of the Klan bigwigs in the area. They knew that he watched out for you. He put a lot of money in Mr. Wilcox's bank. Sort of insurance. Sent people to your little herbal business. Made it difficult for them to threaten you. He was worried that when he died, things might escalate. Is that accurate?"

"Yes," Callie said sadly. "That's why you couldn't locate me. Why I moved away. The harassment. Someone killed my cat—hung it from a tree. Threw a sack of mutilated kittens in my yard. Ran the car I was driving off the road into the Oolenoy River. Shattered my front window with a rock. Finally, the doctor in Pickens came to my house. He all but confessed to being behind all of it. He blackmailed me and threatened to tell everyone about my father. He made me sign over my house to him and told me to leave town. He did pay me—but it wasn't voluntary." She didn't mention Earl's appearance in Liberia.

"Hmm," Cutler began to scribble on a note pad. "That's grounds enough for legal action."

"No. Please. I don't want to do anything else to antagonize them. I went to the county sheriff, and it made everything worse." She thought of Sam and added, "They might take it out on my friends." Callie began to gather her belongings. "Is the will null and void then?" She stood.

Cutler pointed to the chair. "Miss Beecham, sit down, please. Let me finish."

Callie sat slowly, feeling like a child about to be lectured for bad behavior.

"I don't care what color your parents were," Cutler began. "The will is to be carried out. It is your money. And I am pleased to act as your attorney."

Callie felt such a wave of relief that tears welled in her eyes, and she bit her lip to keep from crying. "Thank you," she whispered.

Cutler reddened at the show of emotion. "Now, now. Don't go to blubbering. Truth be told, with five children to feed, I'm happy to have a wealthy client like you to help cover the bills." He winked and added, "My wife is fond of our lifestyle, so I wouldn't care if your parents were purple and green."

He reached in his pocket and handed her his handkerchief. "Silas told me about your grandmother, and how she came to help him when his wife died. About Dr. Davis and the man's negligence the night William was born. He said the doctor never gave him the time of day after that and wouldn't make a house call when he was too sick to get to the office."

Cutler leaned back in his chair. " He told me he couldn't believe it when you showed up living on his street after the war. You didn't know anything about his relationship with your mother—or grandmother— and yet you helped him with his yard, cleaned his house on occasion, nursed him when he was sick . No wonder he thought of you as a daughter."

Cutler smiled at her and picked up a pen. "Now, we can move past that and discuss how you'd like to proceed? I am at your service."

Callie swallowed nervously. "I do have an immediate need. Can you— can you hire protection for my family? Let me just say that I would like to be sure bad people don't bother the Youngs anymore."

"Miss Beecham, don't you worry about a thing. I have contacts with the Pinkertons. I will take care of it." Cutler scribbled some notes, then turned and reached for the crystal vase of flowers on the credenza. "These are for you. To congratulate you on your inheritance and welcome you as my client." He placed the beautiful arrangement on the desk in front of Callie.

"Thank you, Mr. Cutler. They're lovely!" She grinned and pulled a manila folder from her purse. "Now, I do also have several investments to ask you about."

— • —

Sam backed the car out of the parking space and eased down Greenville's busy Main Street. Long overdue at the barber shop, he'd decided to head into the city to get a trim and run some errands out of the Pickens County public eye. He purchased several new shirts and ties before his rumbling stomach sent him in search of lunch somewhere. He'd tried the little café down the block when he'd taken the beautiful and shapely Mary Kay Sweeney to lunch, but it was full of Furman

University men and Greenville Women's College coeds seeking each other out. Mary Kay had seemed all too pleased to be on the arm of the good doctor, but he soon understood that he was only there to make some hulking senior oaf jealous.

He turned onto Cleveland Street and scanned the buildings. When he spied Carunchio's "Open for Lunch" sign flashing, he braked and pulled into an empty spot. *Why not?* he thought. *What better way to put the ache behind me?*

He glanced at the cloudy skies overhead, which threatened an afternoon thunderstorm. The day was warm, and he'd dropped the top, so he worked to unroll and raise the canvas before heading into the restaurant. As he raised the frame, movement across the narrow street caught his eye.

Callie. His heart lurched. It was her. He watched as she approached Silas's old car. In her green flowered dress and matching hat, she was lovely. He was close enough to see that she was smiling. She had her arms full—folders, her purse, and a huge vase of flowers. She was attempting to open the car door while balancing the load.

Without thinking, Sam jogged across the busy street. "Callie!" he called excitedly. When she turned to see who had called her name, her face fell. The pretty smile evaporated, and instead, Sam saw the mask descend. His gut clenched. Whether it was fear or disgust or anger, he wasn't sure, but it was aimed at him. That part he knew. She had moved away from Florence Street and not given him a forwarding address.

He stepped up onto the curb and extended his hands, suddenly shy. "Oy. Callie. May I help you?" He exhaled and tried to slow his banging heart.

He could tell that she'd rather be anywhere than standing so near him, but her arms were full and his were empty. "Sam," she said. "Sure. Thanks."

When he accepted the vase of flowers, their fingers touched. Despite her gloves, he felt a jolt of electricity shoot up his arm. *God, I miss her.*

She fumbled with the key and pulled open the car door. After placing her purse and folders in the car, she reached for the flowers. He looked at her lowered eyes, willing her to look up at him, but she only retrieved the vase and set it behind the seat in a cardboard box.

"Beautiful flowers," he said feebly. He stared up at the sign above the building that read Cutler, Williams & White. *An attorney?*

"Yes, aren't they?" Callie said. She draped an old blanket around the colorful arrangement to keep it steady and then stood. Her pale throat glistened with perspiration.

"You moved away," Sam said softly. *I don't want to scare you away, but I don't want this encounter to end. I miss you. Why are you here? Where do you live? Who gives you flowers now?*

She finally looked up at him from under dark lashes. "Yes."

"Are you living in Greenville?" He shoved his shaking hands into his pants pockets, hoping to appear calm and easy. "I went by your house and it was vacant. Your number was disconnected."

"Yes," she said simply.

"If there is anything you need—"

"I'm fine, Sam. Really."

"Care to join me for lunch?" he tried. "Carunchio's is right there."

Callie's eyes darted around in an attempt to avoid his gaze. "I don't think so." She glanced at her wristwatch.

Well, that's that, then. It's over and done. "It was so good to see you again." Sam mustered a smile. "You look wonderful."

"Take good care of yourself, Sam." Callie smiled then, a real smile, and Sam thought he saw tears in her brown eyes before she turned away. She got into Silas's old car, started the engine, and backed out of the parking space. She waved once and motored down the busy street.

Sam closed his eyes and dropped his head. He stood like that for some time before getting back in his own car. He jammed the car into reverse and headed toward Pickens, his appetite gone.

Chapter Twenty

The next day, Callie pulled the car into a parking space in front of Mabel Keith's shop and cut the engine. *This is a test,* she thought. *Am I still welcome here? The latest gossip all over town? Or no big deal?* She glanced around furtively before adjusting her hat. She stepped out of the car, pushed the door open, and walked bravely into the small store.

There was Mabel at the register, checking out Edna Batson's merchandise. Edna had worked with Callie once on the Armistice Day parade committee.

"Callie Beecham!" the proprietress called. "I will be with you in a moment, dear."

Edna turned. "Why Callie, I haven't seen you since the Armistice parade we worked on years ago. How are you, dear? I heard you moved out of town."

Callie felt her jitters abate somewhat at the women's welcome. She watched as Mabel handed the woman her change. "I'm just fine, Edna. I hope those boys are doing well. Bennie must be fifteen now?"

Mrs. Batson beamed. "He is sixteen. Charlie just turned ten. Time flies."

"Yes, it does," Callie agreed. "Good to see you."

"Thank you, Edna. Come again," Mabel said.

Edna nodded cordially as she passed Callie and left the shop.

"How was the winter dinner date?" Mabel asked, sweeping around from behind the counter. "Are you perhaps a summer bride?"

Callie grimaced. "You remembered? That was months ago! The dress was a success, Mabel. Sadly, the relationship was not." She thought of her brief encounter with Sam the day before in Greenville, and how she had cried the entire drive home. He looked so bereft, so miserable. She almost leaped into his arms when he came running across the street—before she remembered that she was doing this for him, in part.

"That's too bad." Mabel winked. "I was hoping you were back for your trousseau."

"No trousseau any time soon." Callie sighed. "However, I do need a smart suit. Maybe two. And some dresses. I'm headed to Charleston for a little trip. Can you help me?"

Mabel studied her for longer than Callie found comfortable, before she finally clapped her hands together. "A trip to Charleston! Callie, you're such fun!" She motioned for Callie to follow her to a rack of beautifully tailored summer dresses and suits. She rifled through the rack and pulled out several lovely designs. "I know your size. Try these on, and I'll keep pulling while you dress. And, dear, may I say that I'm sorry you moved away." She leaned in and murmured, "We're not all as backward as it may appear."

Callie felt the heat bloom in her cheeks. "Thank you," she mustered.

Mabel smiled and began to pull suits and dresses from several racks. Callie ended up with several boxes that Mabel's stock boy piled high in the back of the old car.

She changed into one of the new dresses, a drop-waist pleated number in sapphire-blue silk. A beautifully tailored, summer-weight blue-silk coat with a satin collar and a matching cloche completed the look. She stood by the car and glanced up and down the street nervously, a hand to her forehead in the bright sunshine.

He'd agreed to meet here at two, and it was fifteen past, she fretted. She waited a few more moments before the sleek Model A finally pulled into the parking space adjacent to Silas's old car. Callie smiled and called, "Mr. Cutler!"

Cutler stepped out of the car, tipped his hat, and appraised Callie's appearance. "Miss Beecham, that outfit is divine. I must say, you look lovely. A picture of feminine pulchritude." He regarded Silas's old car. "Agghh," he groaned. "You haven't traded in this rust bucket yet?"

Callie laughed. "It's going to my cousin today. He's a mechanic. I am picking up my new Ford later this afternoon in Greenville. A burgundy Touring Car."

The man nodded approvingly.

She opened her purse and produced a sprig of basil, which she inhaled deeply. "All right. I'm prepared for battle. Carrying a bit of basil brings wealth to the bearer." She grinned mischievously. "It also keeps goats away from one's property, so we're covered."

Cutler laughed. "You will never cease to amaze me. I shall buy packets of basil seeds on my way home today."

Callie glanced up at the imposing building. "Mr. Cutler, I'm looking forward to this."

"As am I," he said conspiratorially. "Silas told me all about this old goon."

"You will see that my grandmother's family is safe while I'm away?" Callie asked.

Cutler smiled. "Yes, ma'am. The Pinkertons will be on duty until you decide you don't need them. You should really stay down there longer than a few days, though. The Lowcountry is spectacular, Callie. The change of scenery will do you good."

"I'm only going down there because Silas wanted me to. I have no reason to keep a house on the other side of the state," Callie said dismissively. "That's wasteful."

Cutler winced. "Ouch. I won't let that offend me," he joked. "My wife loves Charleston. And let me take a moment to thank you again for retaining me as your attorney. I appreciate the confidence you've placed in me."

"You're worth your weight in gold. I'm glad that you can oversee things here while I am gone." Callie tipped her head toward the end of the block. "Then, shall we?"

He extended his arm cordially. "Yes, Miss Beecham. Let's get you your money."

— • —

Steven Cutler pushed through the imposing doors of the Mountain Ridge Savings and Loan and held the door for Callie. They entered the lobby, with its scent of paper money, copper pennies, and ink.

Mrs. Ames approached the pair and stared at them, wide-eyed, over her bifocals. "Hello, Miss Beecham. I wasn't aware that you had business here anymore. How may I help you?"

Callie tried to still her shaking hands. "I'm here to make a withdrawal."

The woman tilted her head, confused. "I'm sorry. Do you have an account with us?"

Callie withdrew the leather passbook from her handbag. "I do."

"Oh, I see." The woman seemed perplexed. "Step into the line, and Bessie or Mary will take care of you."

"We need to see Mr. Wilcox," Mr. Cutler said curtly.

Mrs. Ames regarded them both warily. "I'm sorry. He's busy at the moment."

"Busy?" asked Mr. Cutler. He lowered his voice. "Hmm. My client is here to make a rather large withdrawal. I am not sure that Bessie or Mary will be able to authorize this withdrawal. My client, in fact, wishes to close her substantial account."

Mrs. Ames glanced past Cutler and waited for Mr. Wilcox's almost imperceptible nod.

"Very well. Follow me." The woman led them toward the glass office. Behind his desk, Grady Wilcox struggled to hoist his enormous frame. His seersucker suit was rumpled and too tight across his girth, while Steven Cutler cut a dashing figure in his custom-made gray Savile Row suit. Wilcox ignored Callie and extended his hand toward Mr. Cutler. "Grady Wilcox."

"Steven Cutler, Cutler, Williams & White in Greenville." He shook the bank president's hand. "You already know my client, Miss Beecham."

Wilcox attempted to feign surprise. "Oh, yes. Yes. Your client? Mizz Beecham? I didn't recognize the little lady. Please, have a seat."

Callie sat in the same chair she had been in nearly nine months earlier. She glanced at her legs in the sheerest of silk stockings and kid-leather pumps, crossed her legs at the ankles, and settled herself, waiting patiently for Mr. Cutler to speak.

"Miss Beecham, the passbook please?" Mr. Cutler smiled.

She handed him the small leather book.

Cutler began. "Mr. Wilcox, the lady here wishes to close this account. Because of its value, we knew this to be a serious matter you'd want to keep private." He slid the passbook across the desk toward Mr. Wilcox. "We'd like to do a wire transfer. If that isn't an option, we will take it in cash."

Wilcox looked smug. "I don't believe Mizz Beecham has an account with us." Curious, he picked up the passbook with one hand and grabbed his reading glasses with the other. He settled the glasses on the bridge of his nose and opened the book. He squinted at it for a minute with his small blue eyes. *Like a pink pig.* His face grew beet red. Callie watched with some trepidation as the man pulled a handkerchief from his pocket and dabbed at his moist brow.

He finally leaned forward and addressed the attorney. "Mr. Cutler, just what is the meaning of this?" he muttered. "This account belonged to Silas Roberts."

Mr. Cutler simply smiled. "It did. But he had it changed to a joint account with the right of survivorship last year. After Mr. Roberts' untimely death, the account became solely Miss Beecham's. I have the will and the bank forms, signed by your bank attorney, a Mr. Jones. Miss Beecham would now like to close the account. We will be depositing the funds elsewhere." He slid a file of papers across the table. "Into American Bank in Greenville. You'll see the routing information in these documents."

Wilcox glanced at the lobby and the milling customers. He leaned forward and stabbed a fat finger toward Callie. "This—girl—does not have an account here," he hissed. "What kind of fraud are you trying to pull?"

Cutler calmly pulled another sheaf of documents from his briefcase and presented them to Wilcox. "As you can see, the bank documents show that Miss Beecham was added as a signee to this account in November 1928 by Mr. Roberts. Joint owner with right of survivorship. All signed and documented by your senior bank staff . . . and you." He pulled out another document. "And here is the copy of the late Mr. Roberts' will, in which he specifies the account should go directly to co-owner Callie Beecham should he pass away. No other heirs. Our only question is whether we need to call the Federal Reserve to assist us? I do have the telephone number for the director of the Charlotte branch, if need be. Jack Pierce is a friend of mine. A great guy. Helluva golfer."

Callie was dumbfounded by Cutler's adept handling of the situation. She silently applauded her new attorney and wondered how much this little showdown would cost her. *Never mind. This is so worth it.* She shifted in her seat, and the movement was enough to distract Wilcox's beady eyes.

"You little—" the bank president muttered, glaring at her. "How dare you march in here and ask me for $60,000. It's not yo' money." He turned to Cutler. "Do you know about her?" he hissed. "She is—"

"Ah, Mr. Wilcox," Cutler interrupted, holding up a manicured hand. "Let's not make this ugly." He twisted around to observe the busy lobby. "A young lady wants to close her account. Do you really want to involve other customers?" He shrugged. "Banks are shaky institutions these days. I would think you'd like to keep this quiet. Very quiet. Unless you don't have the cash on hand? Now that would be a problem . . ."

Wilcox murmured curses under his breath. He stood with some

effort. "Mrs. Ames," he called brusquely.

The secretary hurried into the office. "Yes, Mr. Wilcox?"

He shoved the passbook and the wire transfer form toward her with a shaking hand. "Handle this account closure as quietly as possible."

The woman opened the small ledger and gasped. "Close it, sir?" She glanced from her boss to Callie, confused. "All of it?" she whispered.

Wilcox glanced past Mrs. Ames toward the busy lobby. "Yes, dammit. Do a wire transfer quickly. I want these folks out of my bank as soon as possible," Wilcox fumed.

"We will stay to receive confirmation the wire went through. The president of American Bank urged me to be sure it is sent immediately. He will send telegram confirmation when it has been received. And my client would like $2,000 in cash—to cover incidentals," Cutler directed. "In fives, tens, and twenties."

Mrs. Ames nodded and quickly left the office.

Cutler sat quietly, examining documents in his lap. He looked up once, and gave Callie a reassuring wink.

Wilcox paced behind his desk, red-faced, for several minutes before Mrs. Ames returned with a parcel in her hands.

"She will need to see it counted," Cutler said patiently, before Mrs. Ames could speak.

"The bills are banded," the woman protested.

"She will need to see it counted," he repeated.

"Very well. Follow me to the back, ma'am," she said quietly. Callie stood and followed the woman hesitantly through the bank.

Mrs. Ames led her to a small room and began to unwrap the stacks of cash. She placed the crisp bills into the bill counter, and as each batch set was reached, Mrs. Ames set a wood block between the batches. "This will take a while," Mrs. Ames said apologetically.

Callie watched in awe as her money was counted.

Mrs. Ames shook her head. "You're a lucky woman, Miss Beecham."

"I know," Callie said, suddenly giddy with happiness.

— • —

The next night, Callie sat on the floor in the front room of Seeta's old house, filling the last few boxes in the low light of an oil lamp. Her last night in Liberia. The windows were thrown open to the sultry air, and crickets thrummed outside. Underneath the windows, Seeta's tea roses scented the small breeze. She inhaled the scent and made a mental note to ask their name.

Her gut had rumbled all afternoon, nerves threatening to get the best of her. She sipped peppermint tea and tried to think of her future. She had enough money in the Greenville branch of American Bank to live on for quite some time. Possibly a lifetime.

Cutler had seemed nonplussed about Wilcox's anger. The man's rage was palpable. She halfway expected Wilcox to burst a blood vessel in his beet-red face, but Cutler had remained quite calm. Cheerful even. As they'd walked out of Wilcox's office, her wonderful attorney offered to take her to the diner for pie and coffee to celebrate her sudden wealth, but she had begged off. She couldn't get away from town quickly enough, afraid of repercussions when word got out. And it surely would—Wilcox would see to that. Without Silas's money in his bank, he had no reason to keep her story quiet.

At Cutler's urging, she would take an informal alias, of sorts, and become Carrie Smith. If Dr. Davis or Wilcox tried to track her down, it would be more difficult. She sipped her tea and tried to ignore the memory of Grady Wilcox's fury.

Seeta and the rest of the family were safe, now miles away in their new home on the west side of Greenville. It was an old farmhouse with five bedrooms, but with electricity, plenty of acreage for gardening, running water, a telephone, and close proximity to town.

At first, Callie had been frustrated in her search—Seeta and Zeke had no desire to move anywhere near a white neighborhood. And wouldn't have been allowed to, anyway. To find a home with modern conveniences, and yet still in the colored part of town was extremely difficult. A needle in a haystack, Mr. Cutler had warned.

Callie had not relented. Seeta's family had been especially good to her, and she wanted a nice place where they could feel safe. Mr. Cutler's real estate connections had come through in the end. On the western edge of Greenville County, the house was the former home of a black doctor and his family who had recently moved north.

When they saw the house for the first time, Zeke and Delia had run through the rooms, as excited as children. Calvin's nursery was soon painted a cheerful yellow, and Callie had arranged for new furniture to be placed in every room. The few neighbors nearby were black, which sealed the deal for Zeke and Delia. Zeke already had a lead on a mechanic's job at a nearby garage.

Zeke had moved Seeta over that morning, and Callie planned to follow the next day with the last boxes—Seeta's dishes, some odds and ends, and the handful of rosebushes that Seeta wanted to transplant.

Seeta decided to gift her home to the residents of Liberia, for use as a schoolhouse. As there were only seven children left in the community, the house would do nicely for that purpose. Mary Talbot had been elated to have it, and Callie's promise of new textbooks arriving in two weeks' time made the tiny woman squeal with delight.

After hugs and well wishes from her neighbors, Seeta and Zeke had motored off in Silas's old car, the residents of Liberia waving goodbye to their friend of fifty-plus years.

Callie closed the last box and stifled a yawn with her hand. Thoughts of Sam Epstein rolled around in her mind, and she paused to say a silent goodbye. If he did not already know, he would certainly hear soon enough. He would move on, relieved to have avoided an embarrassing breakup with a woman he hadn't known was black. But it still hurt. Their little fling had been just that, a fling. *A romance that never even had a chance to flourish or fail on its own*, she mused. But she suddenly knew that she had loved him.

She rolled her pallet out on the uneven pine floor and contemplated sleep. Tomorrow would be a big day. She rifled in her purse and found the envelope she was looking for. She removed the letter from Silas and held it close to the lamp. She scanned it repeatedly, delighting in the words that had changed her future. She refolded it and laid it aside. Her good luck talisman.

Silas, I don't know why you were so good to me, but I won't let you down. She fluffed the flat pillow as much as was possible and turned down the lamp, closed her eyes, and was asleep in minutes.

— • —

A dull thud on the front porch awakened her. Scrambling to get her bearings, Callie sat up and waited for her eyes to adjust in the moonless night. She looked toward the front door. She knew that the sound could have been anything—a raccoon, a stray dog, or something worse. But the smell of kerosene through the open windows told her otherwise. Did someone know she was alone in the house? She waited.

There was a scuffle, a groan, as if someone had tripped or lost his balance, and then quiet. *I knew someone would try*, she thought. *I can't wait to be gone from here.*

She listened intently and heard voices arguing in the distance. She recognized the sound of boots on the front porch. There was the play of a flashlight across the walls and ceiling. She heard a bucket of liquid slosh across the porch floor. And another. Finally, there was a quiet knock on the door.

"Miss Beecham?" a voice called. "Are you alright?"

Callie turned up the lamp and stood. "Who is it?"

"It's Detective Wilkerson, ma'am."

She crossed the room and opened the door. She held the lamp high, and the detective spoke up.

"Best to quit the oil lamp, ma'am. The boy tried to torch the house with kerosene. I washed it down with water, but you never know."

Callie quickly turned down the lamp and set it on the table. Wilkerson handed her his flashlight. She aimed it toward his car parked across the street and could just make out another detective standing guard at the vehicle.

The man smiled and switched on a second flashlight. "You were right. One of Davis's goons. This is the second time we caught someone up here sneaking around. My colleague cold-cocked the boy pretty hard, and he's down for the count. He left a car down the road at the turnoff. There were papers in it belonging to Earl Davis. We'll get a confession from this fellow when he wakes up. He'll spend some time in the county jail. Trust me—Davis will not bother you or your family again. We will be sure his cronies get our message as well. You sure you're alright?"

"I'm fine, Detective. I'm just glad you were here," Callie said. "The sheriff didn't seem too fond of me. Are you sure jail is a good idea?"

"Mr. Cutler told us what happened. Sheriff Woods is a law-abiding man. He may not have believed your story then, but we have evidence now." He inclined his head toward the car.

Callie stifled a yawn. "Mr. Cutler said he was sending me the Pinkertons, and he surely delivered. Thank you very much. What time is it?"

"Near four a.m., ma'am. We aren't going anywhere until you dismiss us. I'll clean your porch off if that won't disturb you."

"Thank you. How about you two come in for coffee and breakfast at six then? I may get a few more hours of sleep until then. I have a long day ahead."

Wilkerson smiled. "Thank you, Miss Beecham. We can't turn that down." He pulled a business card from his suit pocket and handed it to Callie. "We'll be outside. You have the office telephone number, but if you ever have an emergency, this is my private telephone number."

She took the card and shined the flashlight on it. She laughed in spite of herself. The card featured a large eye, and the slogan, "We Never Sleep."

Chapter Twenty-One

The sultry atmosphere and the heat shimmering in waves over the expanse of pavement made Callie miserable. Her skin glistened with sweat, and her new silk dress had wilted in the thick humidity. Stockings seemed altogether unbearable and felt like a fur coat on her legs, so she had rolled them all the way down to her ankles before stripping them off completely at her last stop. She tossed her hat on the seat and peeled off her gloves. *Too hot*, she thought.

Across the flat middle of the state, on a straight road headed southeast, Callie had lots of time to think about all that had happened. She tried to redirect her focus on the possibilities ahead and not the bad things behind her. This little trip could be a much-needed vacation.

Mr. Cutler had assured Callie that her family would be safe in their new home. After her experience with the Pinkertons, she didn't doubt it. When she had fed the two detectives breakfast that morning, they had given her more details about Klan activity in the area than even Silas had known. Klansmen were rumored to be responsible for two lynchings that year alone and had firebombed a small store owned by a black couple at a crossroads near Salem. Their crime was that they had dared charge white children for penny candy when they'd asked for it for free.

She dabbed her damp brow with her handkerchief. When the red clay and tall oaks of the Upstate turned to bleached soils and scrub pine, Callie began to notice fields spread with cotton. In some areas, she saw people, black and white, bent over rakes and hoes, sharecroppers tending their acreage. At times, they stood straight to stretch aching backs and to watch the shiny new car glide by.

The new car purred like a kitten and had given her no trouble on the drive. The long and straight highway lulled her into a sleepy daze several times, and she flicked her left wrist with her right fingers to stay awake. When her mind wandered to Sam, which it frequently did, she did the same. By the time she entered Charleston County, her wrist was sore, but her mind was clear. A new life beckoned, and the hope for what lay ahead was enough to think about.

Callie had written directions and a map to Silas's property on the Stono River. Mr. Cutler had even hired the former caretaker and his wife to ready the house for her visit. They apparently lived just down the road from Silas's place and had opened and aired the house and trimmed the overgrown expanse of jungle threatening the property.

Now that she was only an hour away, her nerves threatened to get the best of her. How long would she need to stay to be true to Silas's request? What if the cabin wasn't fit to stay in? What if it had no indoor plumbing? What would she do afterward? And she knew no one in the Lowcountry since Anne Walton had been banished from her life. It would be a lonely stay. *Stop it, Callie. You've been alone all your adult life. You can do this. It's just a look-see,* a phrase her mama had used whenever she was heading out to check a new patch of woods for medicinals.

Callie approached her first rickety wooden bridge and marveled at the change in scenery as she neared the coast. The land had flattened out, and the eastern horizon was bright and open. Now the terrain was white-hot sand and scrub, cypress knees and black swamp. The car crept over the swinging bridge. Soon, she inhaled the salt scent of the ocean on the breeze, earthy and damp. The smell sent her back to weekend trips to the Chesapeake Bay when she'd worked for the Red Cross. The tide was out, revealing grassy pools, oyster beds, and barnacled piers. A blue heron lifted skyward with a wriggling fish in its beak.

Palmettos hugged the roadside. Callie saw several black women sitting companionably in the shade of a grove of live oaks on her right, weaving beautiful sweetgrass baskets. A hand-lettered sign propped in the sandy soil advertised their wares.

Callie yearned to stop and chat with the women, but the shadows were lengthening, and she wanted to get to the property before dusk. The ocean breeze ruffled her hair and finally cooled her damp skin. Under her arms, half-moons of sweat stained her dress, despite new dress shields.

She wiped the perspiration from her upper lip and peered at her map. Ahead, the sign identified a river—this one the winding Stono. She was almost there. She drove slowly over the bridge and saw another sign proclaiming James Island. The paved road turned to crushed oyster shells and gravel before Callie found the turnoff she was looking for.

The car snaked through dense vegetation on either side, palmettos, and myrtles—and colorful oleander she knew enough to avoid. Birds called from the foliage, and the breeze carried the scent of the ocean. *I like this*, she thought. It was overgrown and isolated. A perfect place to hide for a while.

Suddenly, the road twisted left, and the vegetation fell away. In front of Callie sat a white clapboard house well off the ground on stilted legs, with a bright-blue front door that looked to be freshly painted. But it was what was behind the house that made Callie gasp. The view opened up on the river and the wetlands beyond, with a dock out into the water, tall marsh grass waving in the breeze, egrets feeding in the shallows, and a glowing orange sunset over it all. *It surely rivals the Blue Ridge Mountains in its beauty*, she thought.

Callie pulled the car up the drive to the cottage and cut the engine. As she stepped out, she heard a woman's voice call her name.

"Miss Smith? That you?"

She turned and saw a heavyset black woman coming down the steps. She felt a twinge of guilt at using a phony name. "Hello," she said. "Yes, I'm Miss Smith."

"I was hopin' you would get here before dark," the woman said with a bright smile. Her ebony hair was streaked with gray and done up in an array of braids that spilled down her shoulders, colorful beads woven throughout. "That turnoff is hard to find at nighttime." She waved toward the house proudly. "Welcome!"

Callie followed the woman's gaze and looked again up at the house. It looked to be only slightly larger than her house on Florence Street. On its raised legs, it appeared safe from storm surges and floods. It was neat and clean, with potted pink geraniums on the wide front porch. A cheerful bed of orange daylilies ran along the foundation.

"I'm Betty Pinckney. Mr. Cutler hired me an' my husband to clean the place up for you. He had us stock your pantry for your visit, too."

Callie felt her emotions threaten to overwhelm her. The place was already more than she'd hoped for. "Thank you," she managed.

"Let me help with your bags an' you can go in. I'll show you what's what." Despite her age and heft, the woman grabbed two suitcases easily, added a hatbox to her load, and climbed up the wooden steps.

"There's lights and runnin' water, too. You're lucky. On the other side of the road where we are, there ain't services. But when the white folks from up north started to build on James Island, they ran the pipes right down to this property. Mr. Cutler wanted this place plugged in."

"You worked for Silas Roberts?" Callie asked hopefully, following the woman up the steps.

"My husband did," Betty said over her shoulder. "Before I met him. Now he works for Mr. Cutler, over at his house on the Battery. He told us you was coming down for a visit before sellin' it."

Callie noticed that the front porch ceiling was freshly painted pale blue. She'd seen many houses back in the Upstate with the same color porch ceiling—to keep the *haints* away. And the bugs.

Betty opened the door and allowed Callie in first. The room was cool and cheerful. White ship-lapped walls were lined with framed paintings of the ocean, the shore, and boats at sea. A faded blue sofa and two wooden rockers sat near a fireplace, and a ceiling fan rotated slowly overhead.

Callie caught the aroma of frying fish coming from the cheery yellow kitchen beyond the living room. When her stomach growled, she remembered she hadn't eaten since breakfast with the Pinkertons. "That smells delicious—whatever it is."

Betty beamed. "I fried up some snapper and hushpuppies for you, Miss Smith."

Callie smiled and dropped a bag on the floor wearily. "Call me—Carrie." She'd almost stumbled.

Betty grinned. "Well, alright then. You've had a long trip—Carrie. Why don't you go freshen up in the bathroom down the hall, and then I'll show you around."

"Thank you," Callie said, relieved to know there was indoor plumbing. She regarded Betty for a moment. "Could you join me for supper? I have so many questions, and I'd love a good chat."

Betty's eyes registered her surprise, but she nodded. "My husband is workin' off-island . . . so, yes, ma'am. I can do that."

—— • ——

Callie leaned back in her chair and patted her lips with her napkin. "Betty, that was the most delicious meal I've had in ages. You'll have to teach me how to make those hushpuppies."

Betty beamed and sipped her sweet tea. "Aw, nothin' to it. I get your dessert in a minute. I made a key lime pie."

Callie groaned. "I'm not sure I have room for dessert. I ate seven hushpuppies."

"You so thin. I come over and cook for you whenever you want, to fatten you up."

"I won't be here long enough to get fattened up," Callie said, folding her napkin and setting it on the table. "I plan to stay just a few days, and then I'll let Mr. Cutler sell it. I have no family or friends down here."

"Well, that's a shame. Someone will prob'ly tear it down and build a fancy mansion in its place," Betty said wistfully.

"Have you lived here long?" Callie asked.

Betty nodded. "All my life. My parents lived here, and my grandparents before them. On the rice plantation."

"A rice plantation?" Callie asked. "I've heard of cotton plantations. I hadn't thought about rice."

Betty leaned forward. "Lawd, old Mr. Pinckney had over two hundred Gullah slaves on his place on this island," she said matter-of-factly. "It was called Four Winds. My granny was a house slave when she was young. Granddaddy was a driver. Second only to the overseer."

Callie cocked her head. "Gullah?"

"The Gullah people came from Sierra Leone, on the west coast of Africa. We rice people," she said. "A proud people. We losin' what we remember, though. Our traditions an' songs. Our roots an' recipes. Most Gullah have left the islands and moved away for jobs. Ain't got a choice."

Callie wondered whether Seeta knew where her own people were from, the way Betty did. "Are there any remnants of the place?" Callie asked.

Betty shrugged. "Not the big house. It burned down. But in the mornin' when it's light, go walk down the road east. You'll see wooden houses on stilts way down at the end of the road, right on the river. It looks out to Charleston Harbor itself. There's a Gullah settlement there, *Cumbaya*. Some families been on that land for sixty years. It's what's left of Four Winds' slave quarters. Mr. Pinckney gave that settlement to the black folks he trusted—the slaves who didn't run off when the war ended. The rest was bought up by northerners after the war. The big house burned in '99, and the hurricane the next year finished the job."

Suddenly uncomfortable with the talk of slavery and plantations, Callie changed the subject. "Is that where you live?" Callie asked. "By the river?"

Betty shook her head. "No. We got a little place near the bridge you came over, back a ways. Too much fightin' over that river property. White folks want it cleared for fancy new homes lookin' toward Charleston. It shrinks every time there's a storm, an' when one of the folks can't pay their taxes." Her expression clouded. "It'll all be gone to rich white folks soon."

Callie reddened, but Betty didn't seem to notice her distress.

Thunder rolled outside. "What does your husband do now?" Callie asked hesitantly. A trickle of sweat slid down between her shoulder blades. She fanned herself with one of the cardboard Vincent's Funeral Home fans on the table.

"He's a handyman—tends Mr. Cutler's gardens, things like that, at the house on the Battery. Oh, wait until you see Charleston." She shook her head. "There's some money there . . ."

She let out a low whistle. "In fact, there ain't a prettier town anywhere. When my husband takes our skiff across the marsh to town, he says he has the prettiest ride to work of any man."

Callie smiled at the woman's affection for the Lowcountry, but when she pictured the hazy blue wall of the undulating Blue Ridge Mountains, she wanted to disagree.

"I'd love to know why Silas Roberts built this place. Do you know? It's so far away from the Upstate. And so hot. We were neighbors—friends—up in Pickens, but Silas never mentioned this place." She fanned herself furiously.

Betty looked at her for a long while. Callie sensed that she wanted to consider her words before she spoke. *Maybe they parted on bad terms*, Callie thought. *Silas was a bit of a curmudgeon.*

"My husband said Mr. Roberts built this place when his boy was just a minnow. Called it Turtle Island. My husband got hired on to watch things, and he lived over the garage out back. When the Roberts came down, they kept to themselves and didn't go off property much. They had fruit trees and a big garden. The marsh is right outside this door, so they ate off the land and the water. They were here every year when the boy's school was out. Out on their boat fishing or crabbin' from the pier. They spent lots of time here—until the war."

"Mr. Roberts' son died in the war," Callie said softly.

Betty shook her head. "That's when Mr. Roberts stopped coming down." She stood and began to clear dishes. "After a while, my husband was a little uneasy livin' here without the owner around, so he quit caretakin' here an' found work in Charleston." She carried the plates and cutlery to the kitchen. "Been a handyman the last ten years."

Callie grabbed the glasses and followed Betty. "Is there still a garden?"

Betty laughed, as dishes clattered in the sink. "It ain't a garden no more. It's a jumble of blackberry vines, poison ivy, and weeds. Probably some snakes thrown in for good measure. You want me to get the dishes done before I go?" Betty asked.

"No. Thanks though," Callie said. "Why is the place called Turtle Island?"

Betty shrugged as if the answer was obvious. "Like a turtle's back when it's in the water. The boy, William, named it." She spread her hands in a wide arc. "This property kinda sits up on a hill with water around it. Everywhere else is flat as a pancake."

Callie smiled and felt herself relax. "I love the idea of this little world surrounded by water." *This beautiful place feels safe. I'm far away from anyone who can hurt me. Maybe this is why Silas thought I should come visit.* She tried to stifle a yawn.

"I saw that. I done overstayed," Betty said. Another roll of thunder rattled the dishes in the sink. "And there's a storm rollin' in. I give it thirty minutes before the rain."

"I'm sorry," Callie offered. "But it's been a long day. Can I give you a lift home?"

"No, I need to walk off some o' that food," Betty laughed. "It ain't far."

"The meal was great. In fact, please take the pie. Just leave me a slice. I've never had key lime pie, but I am stuffed now."

"You'll get no argument from me!" Betty exclaimed. "My husband'll be home in a hour or so an' this will be a nice surprise." She sliced a thick wedge of pie and left it on the table for Callie, before picking up the pie plate. "I think you should stay a while."

Callie smiled. "I might stay a little longer. Maybe work on clearing that old garden."

Betty seemed happy with the prospect. "I say give this place a month an' you won't want to leave."

Callie followed her to the front door, already making plans in her mind. Betty opened the door and they stepped outside. Frogs and crickets sang loudly in the summer twilight. The humidity was thick like a blanket.

"We just down the road if you need something. Good night, now," Betty said as she headed down the stairs.

"Good night," Callie called after her.

"Don't go out back after dark, Carrie! They's gators come up outta the marsh," Betty shouted. "Good night!" The woman was quickly swallowed by the dark.

"Alligators?" Callie murmured as she turned and closed the door. She removed her shoes and padded into the kitchen to wash the dishes. Callie made short work of the plates and cutlery, then picked up the lemony yellow wedge of key lime pie, with its fluffy meringue topping. She'd never had key lime pie. She cut a small piece and popped it into her mouth. *Lord above. Now I know I'm in heaven.*

She wandered into the living room, carrying her plate of pie, and began to study the oil paintings and watercolors hung around the space. She squinted in the dim lamplight and studied a magnificent watercolor of a beach, where a man and a child bent in search of shells. She looked for the painter's name. *May* was scratched into the paint. On every seascape and painting of shells and seabirds. The same person had painted every one. Whoever May was, she was incredibly talented.

She stepped out on the small back porch with her plate and immediately felt the weight of a Lowcountry summer. She sat down in a rocker and listened to the sounds of the marsh. Mosquitos hummed in her ears, and something scurried past her feet. As her eyes adjusted to the darkness, she watched twenty pairs of unblinking red eyes stare back at her from a distance.

"You don't scare me, gators!" she called into the night. She was beyond relieved to know that she meant it.

— • —

Callie pressed the receiver to her ear and waited for someone to pick up the telephone. After three rings, a man's voice answered gruffly. "Hello?"

"Zeke! It's me, Callie." She smiled. "I'm calling to tell you I got here safely. How are things there?"

"You the first person to call us on this darned thing," Zeke groused. "You know we don't know anyone else with a telephone. You wasting money. Ain't this a long-distance call?"

"I wanted Granny to have it if she needs something."

Zeke's tone softened. "Well, Granny's right here, and she's anxious to talk to ya."

Callie heard the shuffle of the receiver changing hands. "Callie, is that really you in there?"

She smiled at the sound of Seeta's voice. "Hello, Granny. Yes, it's me. All the way from James Island. I wanted you to know that I got here safely."

Seeta sighed. "What a miracle. Imagine, me talkin' to you so far away. Oh, it must cost so much money."

"Don't fret, Granny. Are you alright? No trouble so far?"

"We all fine. Little Cal misses you. He crawls around to every nook and cranny looking for his auntie," Seeta said. "Do you like it there?"

"I do. I'll take pictures with my new camera and bring them home to share. I may stay more than a few days. Is that alright with you—if I take some time to see what's what? It's a beautiful place, right on a marsh."

Callie sensed Seeta smiling into the telephone.

"Callie girl, you stay as long as you can. Silas musta gave you the place for a reason. Don't go sellin' it until you figure out what the reason was."

"You're a wise woman. All right. I'll stay a week or so and get the lay of the land. It's really beautiful. Very hot, though."

"A little heat never hurt no one. An' we fine here," Seeta said. "One neighbor came over with a red velvet cake to welcome us. The pastor of the church down the road came over to set a spell with me yesterday. I like him. I think I'll move my membership. It's not like I'm goin' back to Liberia for church, is it?"

Callie heard the sting of sadness in Seeta's voice. "Granny, Earl Davis could have hurt you. Now, you're outside of his little kingdom and you're safe. Silas gave us all a great gift."

"Oh, he surely did," Seeta murmured. "I love you, Callie girl."

"I love you, too, Granny. I'll be back soon."

— • —

One week stretched into two. Callie rested. She drove to the beach each morning and watched the waves lap at the shore hungrily as gulls and terns wheeled in an azure sky. She gathered shells and bits of smooth beach glass on long walks and added them to the brimming jars scattered around the house. Afternoons, she dozed on the back porch in the weathered Adirondack chair, a book in her hands. Evenings, she sat on the front steps and gazed at the fireflies flitting across the yard and the starry skies overhead, constellations drifting across a black dome.

At the peak of summer's dog days, Callie woke to find that her good mood had evaporated. She was lonely. Untethered. Despite the pull of the verdant Lowcountry, she missed home. Her business. She missed Sam. Seeta. Her one friend, Anne Walton, had been sent away. And Silas was dead. *Maybe it's time to go home. But where is home?*

She sat up, determined not to feel sorry for herself. She could go back at any time. Silas had given her a great gift, one she fully intended to enjoy. It was a Sunday—wasn't it? Days with nothing to do warped her sense of time.

She put her feet on the floor and felt for her slippers with her toes. She would spend the day tackling the blackberry brambles climbing the clothesline. Maybe throw a line into the marsh and see what bites.

She padded to the kitchen to make coffee. The summer day was already oppressive and thick. Dawn came early on the coast, and she watched the sun brighten the edge of the marsh to the east as the coffee burbled in the pot.

She opened the ice box and paused to let the cold air soothe her face. Callie had quickly realized that there was no early morning cool here in the summer on James Island. The days started warm and sultry and only got warmer. Afternoon thunderstorms only ramped up the humidity to unbearable levels outside. Callie had given up on keeping the mildew off the wide exterior planks of the house.

But it was incredibly beautiful. Watching life awaken on the marsh through the kitchen window hadn't gotten old. *How different this is from morning back at home.* She noticed a single heron poking along the shore, occasionally stabbing his sharp beak into the mud.

She downed her coffee and scurried to select an appropriate outfit to work in the yard. She'd already been poked by sand spurs, bitten by sandflies, and run into a wicked patch of poison ivy. After donning her dungarees and a chambray shirt, she grabbed a wide-brimmed straw hat and headed outside.

The thick air hit hard, and she said a quick prayer of thanks for the large pitcher of tea waiting in the ice box. Grasshoppers droned incessantly. A lone seagull wheeled overhead. At least there was an onshore breeze. It whipped past Callie and swirled through the sheets on the clothesline.

Callie scanned the backyard, hands on hips. The entire property was about three acres, wider than it was deep. Wappoo Creek was straight ahead about fifty yards. Morning sunlight glinted across the estuary, and tall marsh grasses swayed rhythmically with the incoming tide. From what Callie had seen on her map, the winding creek connected the Ashley River with the Stono River. A weathered wooden pier stepped out into the creek, its warped and splintered gray boards beckoning to deeper water. *Another time*, she smiled.

Beyond the clothesline on the left, there was a whitewashed garage with what appeared to be a room or attic space overhead, and a small poultry barn and yard. The idea of chickens and eggs appealed to her—should she decide to stay. Past the poultry yard stood the remains of the old outhouse. Callie found herself sending up another Sunday prayer, relieved that her time with outhouses was over for good.

To her right, palmetto scrub and wax myrtle thickets obscured the distant view of the Gullah settlement Betty had mentioned. Turtle Island was peaceful. Serene. Different from home, but wonderful nonetheless. In the distance, a small motorboat puttered across the estuary, sending a gentle and rhythmic wake into the marsh grass.

The overgrown garden was set behind a dilapidated wooden fence on the right side of the property. The space was truly a mess. Weeds and brambles three feet high covered the ground, and a few pine saplings even grew boldly through the mess. Callie sighed, not sure she was ready to tackle the task. Perhaps a new owner would whip it into shape.

Yet, her gaze lingered on the garden. *I could make a new life here. I could reinvent myself.*

Callie sighed and strode to the garage, yanked the door open, and peered into the dark. The only light came through cracks in the roof. The earthy smell of wood and decay was mixed with motor oil and turpentine. As her eyes adjusted, she was surprised to find an assortment of yard tools in the musty room. Rakes, a hoe, shovels, a scythe, and a rotary mower were lined up against one wall. A small skiff, complete with ancient outboard motor, was pushed up against the other wall. Fishing rods and tackle were shelved nearby, but two poles lay across the bow of the boat as if waiting for their owners to return at any time. It was as if Silas had left everything ready for her new life here.

She lowered the garage door, turned, and walked to the house.

Chapter Twenty-Two

Sam pushed himself back from his desk and glanced out the office window. He had no more patients that afternoon, a rare occurrence any weekday. He'd already let Nora go home for the day. Earl Davis was at a conference in Charlotte. There was always paperwork to review, patient files and medical journals to read. But outside, the early afternoon was a siren song, bright and clear, without the usual thick July humidity and oppressive heat.

He stood and quickly removed his white coat, grabbed his hat and keys, and walked out the front door, whistling a tune. He locked the door and took the steps to the small parking area two at a time. A small breeze rustled the leaves in the trees. *A good day for a hike in the hills.* When he reached his car, he stopped and looked back at the office.

He couldn't believe he hadn't given the matter anymore thought in over six months. He shoved his hands in his pockets and walked quickly toward the back of the building. As he rounded the corner, he was not surprised to see what Seeta had spoken of. A small wooden sign, hand-lettered, hung by a nail next to the back door.

NO COLOREDS TREATED HERE.

There was no need for such a sign out front. No black person would dare go to the front door. It was known across the South that, if you were black, you always went to the back door, drank from the rusty water cooler, avoided the local soda fountain, and sat in the filthy theatre balcony.

His jaw clenched. He pulled the sign from the wall and broke it over his knee in one quick move, before tossing the two pieces into the grass.

He hurried toward the front of the building, hopped into his car, and sped north toward the hazy line of blue mountains in the distance.

— • —

Sam turned onto Liberia Road and slowed as he passed Soapstone Church. As he approached Seeta's house, it was soon obvious that the house was empty. The porch chairs were no longer there, there was no wash on the line, the yard was weedy and unkempt, empty of Seeta's ubiquitous chickens. *Did Seeta pass away?* he wondered.

He eased out of the car, stood, and stretched. He gazed to the north, where the swell of low mountains rose like an undulating wall across his view. The majestic granite face of Table Rock loomed close in the clear air.

"You lookin' for Callie?" a voice called from behind him.

Sam turned to see an older man come from the yard next door.

"Yes, I guess I am," Sam said, confused. "Or Seeta Young? The house looks empty."

The man stuck out his hand and grinned. "Ben Lewis. I remember you from that doctorin' session New Year's Day. I figured you was lookin' for Callie."

Sam shook the man's hand. "I'm Sam Epstein. So—Callie was here recently? I actually came to see Seeta . . . but Callie has been here?" Sam asked.

Ben Lewis shook his head. "They moved away, a month or so ago. The whole family. Over to Greenville. Callie bought them a new place over there. Seeta gave the house here for a school in the fall. Gave me her chickens."

Sam's confusion must have registered. "You didn't know they left?" Ben asked.

"Uh, no . . ." Sam muttered. He thought back to his brief encounter with Callie in Greenville in the spring. "Well, maybe . . ." He shook his head sadly.

"Son, are you alright?" Ben asked.

Sam exhaled and ran his hand through his hair. "I wanted to tell Seeta that I would come back and see patients again. I should have come before now. If you all need help."

Ben grinned, exposing a mouthful of white teeth. "Doc, you kiddin' me now. After they burned the schoolhouse down? Naw, we ain't gone try that again. Thank you kindly though. We muddle through somehow."

Sam felt the full weight of his guilt. And shame. He had been afraid. Callie hadn't been afraid, but he had. And he had never even given any thought to the fire's origin. The trip to help sick people in Liberia was the cause of the fire—of course it was. And now she had moved Seeta's family away.

"Mr. Lewis, I'm very sorry. I had no idea." Sam gazed out at the charred ruins of the schoolhouse down the road, still very much a part of the landscape, as if the community was afraid to dare clean up the mess.

"Well, I'm sorry, too. Callie is a fine young lady. A good healer. We all got used to havin' her here with Seeta. But after Dr. Davis showed up last month and threatened them both, we figured they'd leave," Ben offered. "I don't have a forwarding address, son."

"Threatened them?" Sam asked. "Why would Earl threaten them?"

Lewis's friendly face closed up immediately. "No idea. You best go now."

Sam mustered a smile. "I'm sorry. Sorry I bothered you." He doffed his hat and quickly got into his car, cranked the engine, and sped down the dusty road.

— • —

The sun was low in the sky by the time Sam steered the car back toward the office. He was hungry for some supper, but he needed some kind of proof—something in Davis's possession that might shed light on what happened. He pulled into the empty parking area and hurried toward the front entrance. He unlocked the heavy door and flipped on the light before heading to Davis's closed office. Surprisingly, the door was not locked, and Sam entered the small room. Davis's white coat hung on a hook behind the door, his desk neat as a pin. Framed photos lined the far wall. Earl Davis shaking hands with the mayor. Davis arm in arm with Mildred at an Elks Club dance. Standing next to the president of the local chamber of commerce.

Sam's heart thudded in his chest. There had to be an explanation. Something that would explain Ben Lewis's words. Davis's actions. He crossed to the tall gray file cabinet filled with old patient records. One by one, he opened each drawer. On each file, the name of a patient was penned across the tab. Everything looked to be in order.

He turned to Davis's desk and switched on the lamp. He pulled open one desk drawer after another, rifling through files, looking for anything that might link Davis to Callie or Seeta Young. He crouched to open the lowest drawer.

A silver pistol lay on top of some papers. He carefully picked up the pistol and laid it aside. Underneath it lay hastily scribbled receipts made out to so-called delivery men Sam had seen come and go in the office, usually delivering jugs of "medicinal" whiskey. There were several old flyers from area Klan rallies. He picked up one last item, his pulse banging in his temples.

"What the hell are you doing in my office?"

Sam looked up to see Earl Davis standing in the doorway.

"I asked you a question, Sam," Earl growled, a cigarette dangling between his lips.

"You took Callie's house?" Sam gasped. "This deed—there is no way she'd sign her home over to you willingly. What did you do, Earl?"

Davis strode across the room and snatched the paper from Sam's hands. He grabbed the pistol lying on the desk and pointed it toward Sam. "You're fired. I want you to get the hell out of my business!"

"Put the damn gun down!" Sam slapped the office keys onto the desk with his hand. "I quit! What did you do, Earl? You burned down their school? Was it because I went up to Liberia with her? Because she befriended the people up there? Tried to help Seeta Young?"

"Befriended—" Earl stopped mid-sentence. "You stupid Jew-boy. She's colored! You're too stupid to even see it. Seeta Young is her granny. That girl overstepped, and things had to be taken care of. Now get out of my office before I call the sheriff," he growled. "Breaking and entering, Sam. That's what this is. Get out!"

Sam's mind spun with questions. "What do you mean, Callie is colored? Did you chase them away?"

"I don't owe you explanations, son." He cocked the pistol. "Don't think I won't use it."

Sam knew he was out of options. "I'll be watching you, Earl." He pointed his finger at the man. "The medical board will be very interested in all of this. You'll lose your license."

"For buying a house that was for sale? For defending my property?" Earl chuckled. "Just try it, boy. Just you try it."

Sam turned and left the room, slammed the front door behind him, and hastily got into his car. There was nothing he could do. Not a damned thing.

Chapter Twenty-Three

The imposing brick building was easy for Callie to find. The Medical College of South Carolina Administrative Offices loomed tall on a block of otherwise squat and nondescript buildings which Callie supposed housed all manner of classrooms and laboratories. She pulled the car into a vacant spot and set about putting herself back together after the long ride into Charleston. Her watch read 8:45. Perfect.

She'd seen the notice in the newspaper and made an appointment in a fit of hubris. Now, her nerves threatened to get the best of her.

She inhaled and exhaled a slow breath. She stepped out of her car and onto one of the many Charleston streets paved in old cobblestones and shaded by large live oak trees dripping with Spanish moss.

In minutes, she would meet the head of the nursing program and state her case. She smoothed her dress and checked the seams of her stockings. She was thankful for the stylish new hat, because her unruly hair refused to cooperate in the thick Lowcountry humidity. It stuck out in all directions, kinks and curls. She had run a dab of pomade through the thick bob that morning, but it wouldn't be tamed.

Between her nerves and the oppressive heat, Callie was a wreck. The idea of a new life here was so appealing, but underneath was the fear—the fear that someone would be able to tell that she was only half-white. The Lowcountry sun had given her skin a golden tan, despite her efforts to cover up whenever outside.

And she was uneducated. She'd be exposed—again. The fear

embarrassed her, and yet it was as real as any other emotion she felt. Callie clutched her new briefcase and headed up the stone steps. The full weight of what she hoped to undertake hit her hard. She sucked in a huge breath and exhaled loudly. She heaved the heavy door open and entered the tranquil lobby.

A young brunette woman looked up from her desk and smiled. "May I help you?"

Callie returned the smile. "I'm Callie Beecham. I'm here to see Mrs. Perkins."

The young woman's eyes widened. "Oh! You're the one," she said loudly. She lowered her voice. "Dean Perkins told me that a new applicant was coming in for an interview. The current gals started weeks ago, and things are just now settling down. Hard to believe we're already interviewing for 1930."

"Thank you," Callie said, her anxiety mounting. "Wait. Classes have already started this term? It's July. I hoped to apply for this fall. I saw the notice in the paper just the other day." Her hopes plummeted.

"The nursing program is fifteen months. The new cohort began in May." The receptionist shrugged. "But cheer up. Half the battle is getting to Mrs. P. If she's willing to talk to you, it's a good sign." She extended her hand. "I'm Mary Steele. Secretary to the dean. It's nice to meet you."

Callie extended her hand dully.

"Follow me. Dean Perkins is expecting you," Mary said.

Callie followed Mary down a hallway studded with potted palms and closed doors every few yards. She knocked on the one open door. "Dean Perkins, Miss Beecham's here to see you."

A distinguished-looking older woman with beautifully coiffed silver hair rose from behind a large desk. She wore a crisp white uniform, and a nurse's cap was perched on the top of her head. She looked at Callie over the top of her spectacles.

"Miss Beecham. Do come in. Welcome to Charleston." She extended a hand toward a chair across from the desk. "Thank you, Mary. You may close the door."

Callie found herself intrigued by the dean's accent. She pronounced Charleston as *Chahleston* and door as *doah*. It was distinctly Lowcountry, soft and smooth, an accent she'd only heard in Camp Service, where she'd met a recuperating captain from Mount Pleasant. "Thank you. I'm so glad to be here."

"Did you find your way in without too much of a problem? You're living on James Island, I see," Perkins said. "All settled in there?" *Thayah.*

"I think so. I had never been down here before, and the whole experience has been exciting. Charleston is beautiful. I plan to go out walking today after our meeting. I wore sensible shoes," she said, apologizing in a way for the low-heeled oxfords she had on.

"That's smart. Our cobblestone streets are pretty to look at but the devil on one's feet and ankles." She shuffled papers on her desk. "Let's get down to cases, Miss Beecham. You're in a unique situation—I'll be blunt. To be admitted to the Medical College of South Carolina's nursing program, our manifesto says you must be a girl of impeccable breeding and character."

Callie's stomach flipped. She struggled to focus on Dean Perkin's words despite the thud of her pulse in her ears. *How would she know?*

The woman leaned forward. "You are twenty-eight years old. You're hardly a girl."

Callie didn't know whether to laugh or cry. "Yes, ma'am."

"Candidates are generally between eighteen and twenty-one. You are much older than we usually see." Mrs. Perkins turned a page without looking up. "But you do have over ten years of work experience in the medical field and that speaks for you. Married?"

Callie shook her head. "No, ma'am."

"Hmm."

Callie gripped her hands together tightly and tried to remain calm. She studied the part in the woman's silver hair and waited.

"You worked in Camp Service in DC during the war. I'm doing the math... You must have been very young." Mrs. Perkins removed her glasses and looked at Callie with open blue eyes.

Too old. Too young. Callie nodded, wishing she could get up and flee from this inquisition. "I was a nurse's aide. But yes, I did have to lie about my age to be accepted." Callie dropped her own eyes and picked at a stitch on her glove. "I wanted to be of service."

"That was hard service, Miss Beecham," said Mrs. Perkins. "Some of those boys came back in pieces, limbs missing, lungs destroyed by gas. You girls had to tend serious wounds."

"We couldn't imagine what they went through," Callie said. "All we could do was try to offer respite and healing. But we *were* good at our jobs."

"The worst wounds were mental." Mrs. Perkins leaned forward in her chair. "The shell shock. I served on the Western Front. Did you see it? Shell shock?"

"I did. Some of the older nurses called it the Soldier's Heart—from the Civil War." Callie nodded sympathetically. "The Western Front—that must have been unimaginable." Her mind flashed back to Camp Service and a Private Morrison from Tennessee. He'd been maybe nineteen, his cheek still downy. Near the end of the fighting, he had suffered a concussion and a shattered leg, and been in her ward for weeks. He was due to go home in just days, the concussion healing and the leg gone. Quiet and sullen, he was open to accepting a cigarette or a book when she happened by.

But what Callie remembered was the night she'd been working third shift with Bess Chapman. They were just girls, sitting in a corner, quietly rolling bandages by lamplight and listening to the snores of the recuperating men in their ward. When Private Morrison began to moan, she stood, ready to offer comfort, a soothing word after a nightmare. But when piercing screams rose from his throat, she balked. He sobbed and called out "Mama! Mama!" in the most pitiful voice, and she'd backed into the corner. Bess had rushed forward and crouched at his bedside, stroking his brow with her steady hand. Callie had only dropped her head and cried.

"I should have done more . . ." Callie murmured.

Mrs. Perkins softened. "I apologize. I see that I've reminded you of something you'd rather not remember." She leaned back. "You know, Miss Beecham, the class of young ladies who have just started were children during the war. Three told me that they lost their fathers—as soldiers. But not a one remembers the war firsthand." She sighed. "Time is marching on."

"I'm glad that time is marching on," Callie said abruptly. "It was horrific. So many boys in my generation are—gone. Yes, I realize that I am older than you'd like. But that only means I bring more to the job than a girl fresh from grade school."

She crossed her legs impatiently, waiting for the ax to fall on her dream. Because she was twenty-eight years old. Not because she was mixed race.

The dean steepled her hands in front of her. "Why do you want to be a licensed nurse?"

"I would have gone to nursing school after the war, but I had no money. And then I contracted Spanish flu, like half of the women I worked with. So, I went home." Emboldened, Callie added, "Dean Perkins, I believe that I *am* a nurse. Have been for many years."

The dean waited for Callie to continue.

Callie cleared her throat. "I've been caring for people in my county for years—but more and more, I see that I need that piece of paper. I wanted additional training to make the lives of patients better. I spent the past ten years building a small business. I made and sold medicinal treatments, herbal therapies for patients." She thought of Sam's interest in her work. "Naturopathic cures, if you will. Most of the patients I saw could not afford the town doctor. Or were not allowed to see him. Plant medicines work."

"Were you able to gather any medical references? A local doctor, maybe? Patients?" Perkins asked.

"No. I left rather quickly. Many of my clients could neither read nor write well enough to offer a written recommendation anyway. But I can reel off fifty names—folks I made well from my treatments. I also visited mothers post-partum, and helped with lactation, as well as physical and emotional support."

"Midwives are to be licensed, Miss Beecham," Perkins warned. "And the new American Medical Association frowns upon . . . homeopathic medicine. All of that herb mumbo-jumbo."

Callie bristled. She knew that she was in dangerous territory. She lifted her chin. She thought of Delia and continued. "My services with new mothers were strictly post-partum, in an extremely rural area. Where I am from, many new mothers have home deliveries—without professional help. The doctor will not come to them. I had some nurse's training during the war and was able to help them. They delivered on their own. It's one of the reasons I want to go to nursing school. Many people in our county can't afford doctors or aren't allowed into their offices without payment first, if they're allowed to be seen at all. And now the old healers, the old medicines, are being outlawed. But herbal medicines are effective treatments that, in some cases, go back hundreds of years. You can read about their efficacy in several journals. If you give me an ailment, I can recommend a plant-based therapy for it. Why, deep in the mountains, that's all they have!"

Dean Perkins dropped her gaze to Callie's file without a word.

"And the town doctor? He and I did not get along." Callie crossed her arms defiantly.

Dean Perkins seemed humored by that revelation. She chuckled. "Trust me, Miss Beecham. Your local doctor will not be the last physician you don't get along with as a nurse."

Callie leaned forward. "I recently inherited some money which allows me to apply to school. Just give me a chance. Please?"

"My, you're quite bold. Are you planning to stay permanently? When

I called your one reference, Mr. Cutler, he was surprised to hear it." The woman looked at Callie with arched brows. "It's a fifteen-month program, and I would hate to offer you a position, only to see you abandon it on a whim."

"If I get into your program, I will stay." She paused. "I can pay for the whole thing up front. I'd like to begin this term. With the cohort that began a few weeks back. I didn't know that they'd already started. I can catch up."

Callie watched as the dean flipped through Callie's application. Finally, she pressed a button on her desk before quietly resuming the study of Callie's file.

I've blown it. An electric fan oscillated in the corner and blew a small breeze her way every few seconds, of little help in the suddenly stuffy room. Callie felt a trickle of sweat slide down her back and prayed it wouldn't be noticeable when she stood and turned away, rejected.

There was a perfunctory knock on the door and an auburn-haired young woman in a white uniform and nurse's cap stuck her head in casually. "Dean Perkins? You buzzed me?" She nodded toward Callie.

Dean Perkins looked up. "Yes, Nurse Kelley. This is Callie Beecham. Our newest student. She'll be joining the cohort already in progress. I will explain it to the Board at our next meeting. But she has a great deal of experience and should slip right in."

Nurse Kelley smiled. "Hello, Miss Beecham."

The dean turned to Callie. "You seem to be an ideal candidate, Miss Beecham. A passion for healing is most critical in the success of our students. I see that in you. You're older than the seventeen young women we currently have in the cohort—but I never liked that rule about age limits. You are already in the healing profession. You'll be an asset in our free clinic. We require that our student nurses work in the clinic ten hours per week. You're not wet behind the ears, not likely to leave and take up motherhood abruptly . . . and you want to treat the underserved." She peered into the file and added, "You have an excellent reference in Steven Cutler. Welcome to The Medical College of South Carolina's licensed practical nursing program." She stood.

"You're letting me in?" Callie asked, in awe of the ever-growing list of Steven Cutler's favors. Her gaze went from Dean Perkins to Nurse Kelley and back to the dean.

The woman smiled. "Yes, Miss Beecham. Go with Nurse Kelley now, and she will give you a quick orientation and your textbooks. She'll schedule your required entrance examination and give you other materials to study. You'll hit the ground running after lunch today. I believe an anatomy class is at one o'clock, and you're weeks behind. But I expect great things from you if you'll devote the time."

"Thank you, Dean! Oh, thank you!" Callie thought of Seeta and her family, safe in a home she'd paid for. Turtle Island was lovely and quiet. She had no family here. No business to maintain. No friends to see. She had nothing but time.

Chapter Twenty-Four

Callie pushed back from the kitchen table, stood, and stretched. Textbooks and legal pads were strewn across the table, after hours spent studying for a test the next morning. After several weeks in the nursing program, she'd realized that she was ahead of the group when it came to knowing the material. But she had also discovered that the younger girls kept to themselves and looked at her as an oddity. She was a spinster, older than them by a decade, an unwanted partner when it was time for labs and extracurricular activities. She hated that this bothered her so much—a grown woman used to being alone. She propped her chin in her hand and gazed toward the window. The marsh glittered in the late afternoon sunlight, beckoning. She stood, stretched, and stepped out the back door.

The overgrown garden was on her mind, she had to admit. It was late September now, and at home, she would have been harvesting the last of the summer crops, cursing the zucchini and yellow squash overrunning their beds. Her orange passionflower fruits would be ripe on the vine, and ruby cardinal flowers and yellow crownbeard might still be in bloom. It was high season for making liver tonics with herbs like dandelion root and sassafras, and the preparation of healing nerve tonics using lady's slipper and lobelia. *What will grow here?* she wondered.

As she stepped across the sandy yard, careful to avoid the heinous sandspur patches she'd encountered on her first morning in the Lowcountry, she decided that the only way to dispel her gloom was to do *something* with the garden. She opened the garage door and stood, eyes adjusting to the dim light. Finally, she picked up the scythe. As she turned, she saw a dark figure blocking the doorway.

"Oh!" she cried out.

"Miss Smith? Didn't mean to scare you. I'm Betty's husband," a voice called out. "We're on our way to church, but I left some fresh snapper in a bucket on your porch. Betty said you'd like some to fry up." The man put up his hands in surrender. "Best be careful in here. Likely to be black widows and snakes. When I lived here, I came out once and found a big old copperhead stretched across the doorway like he owned the place."

Callie pressed a hand to her pounding chest, embarrassed at her reaction. *It's not a snake I'm afraid of.*

The man backed out of the doorway, hat in hand. Callie emerged into the sunshine and let her eyes adjust. He stared down at Callie with large brown eyes, whites tinged yellow. His liver, Callie diagnosed.

He was tall, dressed in Sunday clothes—a rumpled mis-matched suit and striped tie. His head was bald, save a thick fringe of gray hair around his ears. He stared at her curiously, as if waiting for something from her. Finally, he nodded toward the back steps. "The—the fish is just there."

"Thank you, Mr. Pinckney. I'm sorry—you startled me," Callie said, her heart still pounding.

The man stared at her for a moment. He pointed to the back steps again.

Callie nodded. "I'd forgotten I'd asked Betty about fish. I hope you didn't go to any trouble."

The man shrugged. "No trouble, ma'am. I was out early and they was bitin'." He paused and regarded the weapon in her hand. "Looks like you're ready to tackle the garden. I don't think that scythe will do the trick. There's a tiller in the shed and maybe the disc harrow is there somewhere . . .."

Callie looked down at the tool in her hands. "I don't know the going rate on clearing a garden, but this one is a fine mess."

"You should let someone else get in that shed and shoo out the varmints before you go diggin' around." He shifted from one foot to the other. "I can clear the garden for you. I could use the work."

"Really? That would be wonderful. Twenty dollars?"

"I'll take it," the man said quickly. "I can come by tomorrow if that suits."

Callie smiled. "Deal. Thank you so much. I'll be in nursing classes all day, but I'll be home around five."

"Nursing classes? Well, I'll be." The man pulled an envelope from his coat pocket. "Oh, you had some mail. The mailman only comes out here once a week, on Thursdays, so this has been sittin' a few days." He handed Callie the envelope.

"Thank you." Callie grabbed the envelope and read the return address. From Zeke. *What if something has happened?* She tore open the flap and lifted out the letter, written hastily in blue ink on lined paper.

Dear Callie,

I'm writing to let you know that Sam is no longer with Dr. Davis. I worked on a car for a man last week who lives in Pickens. He said Dr. Sam left the practice and moved away. I thought you should know. You can come back without worrying that you'll see him.

Granny naps most days in the backyard in her new lawn chair. Delia lost her job with Mrs. Barker but hopes to find work again as a maid in Greenville. Mattie takes care of Cal, who is crawling everywhere now. When I get a little more work, I sure would like to pay our light and water bill. We cut that telephone. We're beholden to you with the house. I want to handle the rest of my family's bills.

The garden is good and Mattie and Delia have put up enough vegetables to keep us in corn, dilly beans, cukes, and stewed tomatoes for a year. We should be fine as long as I keep my job.

Granny asked when you'll be coming home. I know she wants to hear from you.

Zeke

The man cleared his throat. "Everything alright?"

"I'm sorry. A letter from home. I was worried it was bad news." She shook her head to clear the picture of Sam from her mind. "So, you can help me here? I thought you worked full-time for Mr. Cutler."

"It's part-time at best. I'd like to get back to full-time caretakin' somewhere, but those jobs are hard to find." He placed his hat on his head, shoved his hands in his pockets, and regarded Callie quietly a moment. He looked as if he wanted to say something else but changed his mind.

"So, you'll tackle the garden?" she asked.

He glanced back toward the road. "I'll be here tomorrow first thing. Have a good day, Miss—Smith." The man turned and limped toward the front of the house.

"Thank you for bringing the fish, Mr. Pinckney! And the mail! See you tomorrow!" Callie called. The man had already disappeared. She glanced down at the envelope in her hand addressed to Callie Beecham, clear as day. *Damn.*

— • —

Callie stood, books and white nursing smock clutched in her arms, watching the small tractor move across the one-acre garden. Visions of orderly rows of herbs and vegetables danced in her imagination. She'd passed a Feed and Seed store on her way into Charleston and hoped to make a trip there soon. Silas's old tractor pulled the harrow behind it. It sliced through weedy thatch and loosened the long-compacted ground. She could hardly wait to plant something—despite the late summer heat and humidity. The sun beat down hard, but an onshore breeze brushed across her cheeks and cooled her damp skin. Back in the Upstate, leaves would be changing and cool nights would be the rule by now.

The tractor moved across the final strip of tangled vegetation. The sandy ground behind it was tumbled and turned. "Mighty fine!" the man called. "Lots of organic matter in this soil. That's years of fish waste. I threw every part of the fish in here—what didn't get eaten—for nearly twenty years. And even ten years of weeds won't stand a chance with this harrow."

The rumbling engine sputtered to a stop at the edge of the garden. The unusable mess was now a freshly turned field, with soil richer in humus than Callie had imagined. Pinckney had worked wonders already. He hopped off the tractor and limped toward her with a wide grin, chambray shirt drenched, his face and neck glistening with sweat. "Whew! It's hotter than a fox in a forest fire." He pulled out a stained handkerchief and wiped his face and neck.

"It looks like a garden again!" Callie called. "Thank you. I'm sorry I wasn't here to sort things out in the shed."

"Not a problem. I found what I needed. Everything was right where I left it the last day I worked here, Miss Smith. Just needed some elbow grease."

He had not mentioned the envelope addressed to Callie Beecham. It stumped her. Wouldn't he assume it had been misdelivered? He had watched quietly as she opened it and read the correspondence clearly meant for her.

"Can I write you a check?" she asked, squinting in the sunshine.

"Any chance you have cash, ma'am? It'd be hard for me to cash a check anywhere," he said sheepishly. He blotted his glistening brow with his handkerchief.

"Oh, of course," she said, cheeks red. "I'm sorry. I have some cash inside." She glanced toward the house. "Care for a glass of iced tea?"

"That sounds like an invitation I can't turn down," he said. He followed Callie to the back steps and stopped when she stepped up into the slightly cooler kitchen.

She dumped her schoolbooks on the table and looked back. "You coming?" she called.

"Inside, ma'am?" he asked.

"Of course." Callie opened the ice box. She retrieved a pitcher and a tray of ice cubes. She set the frosty pitcher on the counter and noticed that the man was still standing tentatively by the back door, hat in hand. "Please. Come inside and sit."

The man nodded and walked into the kitchen.

"Twenty dollars and a glass of sweet tea are the least I can do," Callie said. "The garden looks great. I can hardly wait to start planting." She opened her purse and retrieved her wallet, before sliding four five-dollar bills across the table.

The man removed his hat and sat down at the table. He pocketed the money quickly and accepted the tea with a gracious nod. He lifted the glass to his lips and drank deeply. "Thank you, ma'am. For the work and the tea."

She leaned back in her chair and gazed around the room contentedly. "Silas asked me not to sell the place until I'd stayed here a while. He thought I might like it. He was right."

"The Lowcountry is a fine place," the man said. He drank the rest of his tea quickly and set the glass down.

Callie nodded and poured more tea into his empty glass. "During the war, I was a nurse's aide. I met a man from Mount Peasant. He sang the Lowcountry's praises."

"A nurse," he said. "That's a fine thing."

"Just an aide," Callie clarified. "But that's why I'm in nursing school now. I'm hoping that a nursing license will get me a job somewhere." Callie couldn't imagine why she was telling her life story to this hired man.

The man only smiled.

Callie sipped her tea. Pinckney certainly wasn't a conversationalist. Betty had that area covered. She leaned back. "Silas never mentioned Turtle Island."

Pinckney nodded his head.

Callie sighed. "Well, the garden looks good. I can get to work planting some perennials this weekend."

"There's a hurricane out in the Atlantic. Apt to be a rainy weekend," Pinckney warned.

"How do you know?" she challenged, before realizing how patronizing she sounded. She wondered if the man had a sixth sense. Or rheumatism that flared up when barometric pressure dropped, like Seeta.

He lifted his chin. "Mrs. Cutler gives me her old newspapers and catalogs when she's done with them. She thinks the help uses them in the privy she has out back for her workers, but we take the current ones home to read. Betty and I especially enjoy the *Charlotte Observer*. The weather forecast yesterday mentioned a hurricane in the Atlantic. I hope it stays offshore. Those Gullah stilt houses are barely hanging on as it is. Once they're gone, those folks'll have nothing, and this whole island will be sold away."

"A hurricane. I don't want to see that," Callie said, gazing at the tablecloth to avoid his eyes.

"Nope. You sure don't." Pinckney stood and replaced his hat. "Well, thank you for the tea and the work—Miss Smith." He nodded and turned to leave by the back door. He seemed almost eager to go.

Chapter Twenty-Five

Callie pulled a crisp sheet from the line and held it to her face, inhaling both October sunshine and the lavender spray she spritzed on the wash. The humidity of summer had finally given way and Callie was delighted with this Lowcountry autumn. The skies were clear and bright. A cool breeze blew continually.

She dropped the sheet into the basket. Her thoughts turned to home. And Sam. She'd dreaded going home for fear of running into him somewhere, and now the threat was gone. He was gone, probably back to Atlanta. She knew she should go home for the holidays, but her schedule was packed. She'd had no idea how much time she would spend with her nose buried in textbooks. Between studying, labs, and classes, there wasn't time to waste on trips home.

And she had a thriving garden. Elderberry, comfrey, vervain, and rosemary stood in emerald clusters outside her door. A few pots of calendula stood near the porch, ready to be planted. And two short-lived perennials, motherwort and her beloved purple passionflower, were already growing near the fence.

The breeze off the marsh ruffled the laundry still on the line and brought in the smell of pluff mud and a running tide. Smells that used to repel her, she now inhaled eagerly. Home. Was this place becoming her home? Was she reinventing herself down here in the Lowcountry? The house was hers. No one knew her history or her race. She would be a nurse. Maybe she would join a practice in Mount Pleasant or down in

Beaufort one day. Callie unpinned several pillowcases and turned to gaze out at the marsh.

Twilight was coming earlier as another year rounded toward a close. A movement caught her eye. The graceful blue heron swooped down and stood at the edge of the marsh. He stepped daintily through the waving grasses, paused, and stabbed his bill into the water. He stood up with a wriggling fish in his mouth. In the distance, a lone fisherman stood up in his skiff to pull in a crab trap.

She folded the pillowcases and placed them in the laundry basket. She eyed the long and rickety pier that stretched into the marsh and headed toward it, carefully watching for sand spurs as usual. She stepped onto the pier and walked out across the dark water. Hundreds of tiny fiddler crabs skittered underneath, claws clicking. She walked out to the end, where the river breeze met her with a kiss on the cheek. From here, she could see the wide river to the east and the setting sun in a bank of clouds to the west.

She scanned the darkening southeast. The cluster of marsh houses appeared in the shimmering distance, like shore birds on skinny legs, there on the spit of land on the river. There were nine or ten shacks on stilts, some with oil lamps burning, chimneys smoking. They appeared little more than lean-tos, but Betty had been right. The view out onto the wide Ashley River beyond was amazing. The electric lights of Charleston glimmered across the water in the gathering dark. *No wonder rich white folks want the black owners removed*, she thought.

Callie sighed. She did miss her grandmother—really, she did. She had written in July and given her the good news about nursing school. Written in September and told her that she was too busy to get home before the holidays. She knew that any time away would mean a bigger workload when she returned to school. Exams would be here before she knew it, and she could not let Dean Perkins down. Thanksgiving was not a great time to be away either, and the clinic was so busy that the student nurses were in a frenzy. Maybe Christmas. *Besides, Seeta has her real family with her*, Callie thought, with a twinge of guilt.

— • —

Tires crunched over crushed oyster shells as Callie steered the car slowly down the road to Turtle Island. The clear skies and fresh ocean breeze had done nothing to boost her mood on the drive home. The entire campus was in a panic, and she was anxious to hear from Steven Cutler about her own finances. The stock market crash days before had left everyone in a state of panic. Several women in her cohort had immediately left school, and her as-yet-unreturned telephone call to Cutler weighed heavy. Suppose her own funds had evaporated?

She began to tick off her assets. Seeta's house was paid for, thank God. And Silas's house on Florence Street had sold quickly. Money in the bank there. Turtle Island was hers free and clear. She had money in a local checking account. But long term, things no longer seemed as rosy as they had in June.

She slowed and turned onto the narrow lane toward the house. As she pulled into the circular driveway, Betty opened the screened door. "Yoo hoo, Carrie. Mr. Cutler's on the telephone," she called.

Callie slammed the car door and hurried up the steps. "Thank you, Betty!" She unclipped an earring and put the receiver to her ear. "Steven," she said breathlessly. "I was beginning to worry."

"I haven't leaped from a tall building yet," he quipped. "I can't find a tall enough building in Greenville to see the job done thoroughly."

"Is it that bad?" Callie asked.

"Very bad, I'm afraid. Some brokers have lost everything. But you have land, cash, two houses, treasury bonds that should hold their own and a few stocks that might make it. Your bank in Greenville seems sound enough. They've closed the doors for a few days to sort things out, but when I spoke to the bank president, he seemed cautiously optimistic. Thank God, much of your equity is in cash and not the stock market."

"Things have to rebound," Callie said hopefully.

"It might be a few weeks. Or a few months," Cutler offered. "I'll keep an eye on your accounts. How are things down there? My wife and kids are at the house in Charleston now. She said folks are in a panic."

"They are. So many men have dropped out of medical school classes already."

Cutler chuckled. "Their daddies were probably heavily invested in the markets."

"Everyone is scared," Callie said. "You should probably stop the Pinkertons. I'll check with my cousin, Zeke, but I think they're safe now. No harassment from that nasty Dr. Davis. Detectives on retainer seem an unnecessary luxury at this point, don't you think?"

Cutler sighed. "Keep them on. Desperate times and all that..." Then he added cheerfully, "Besides, Allen Pinkerton was a Unionist—a staunch abolitionist. If the old man was still alive, he'd probably take your family on as clients for free."

Callie frowned into the telephone. "I'll keep them, on your advice."

Cutler cleared his throat. "I'm sorry. That was coarse."

Callie checked her wristwatch. "I should hang up. This is long distance."

"Many people could be out of work by the time this is over. We're the lucky ones, Callie."

"I know, Steven. I've been given a great gift. I just don't want to waste Silas's money. I will graduate next year with my nursing certification. I'll be able to make a living. The world will always need nurses. Will you and your family be alright?" Callie asked.

"As long as I have clients who pay their bills, we will eat. It may not be shrimp cocktail," he joked. "But we won't starve. The world will always need attorneys. Thank you for keeping me on."

"Thank you for keeping *me*," Callie said. "I know full well how this might have gone if you were not an honorable man. Not every attorney would have honored Silas's wishes with, you know, someone like me." She glanced toward the kitchen, where Betty stood peeling apples.

"Study hard," Cutler said gruffly. "And let me know what I can do to help my favorite client."

Callie chuckled. "I will. Thanks, Steven." She hung up the receiver.

— • —

December 15, 1929

Dear Granny,

I was sorry that Zeke cut the telephone service. I miss hearing your voice.

I have some bad news. I will not be able to get back to Greenville to see you for Christmas. I have been asked to cover the clinic over the holidays, and I felt that I should take the duty since it is unpaid, and many women in the program must take on paid work over the break. I will try to come and see you in the new year. I am sending a package your way, with presents for all. Take care and Merry Christmas.

Love, Callie

Chapter Twenty-Six

The days of rainy weather were oppressive. Callie hurried across the slick cobblestones in yet another summer shower, her low-heeled sensible shoes dodging traffic and mud puddles on Calhoun Street. She stepped into the lobby and stripped off the wet raincoat. She hung it on the coat rack and turned to the young woman seated at the lobby desk.

"I'm going to float away on a raft soon if this rain keeps up," Mary said, looking past Callie at the gray day outside. "I had higher hopes for 1930."

Callie smiled. "I may join you on that raft, Mary. What a wet summer it's been."

Mary eyed Callie's feet. "You've got your own boats with those shoes," she joked.

Callie shrugged. "I know they're ugly, but what with the rain and labs in different buildings this afternoon, they're fine. And comfortable. I brought some adorable pumps and a new dress for the party tonight." Callie smoothed her hair. "Don't make me more nervous than I already am about meeting your brother on a blind date. He must wonder why I'm not married by now at twenty-nine."

Mary waved her hand in dismissal. "You are positively ancient, it's true. But how could Jimmy not like you? You're cute, smart. A little on the bookish side . . ." she teased. "But a great catch for any man."

"The last blind date you set me up with was that accountant who couldn't get past the idea that I wanted to continue nursing if I got married," Callie said. "And he was twenty-two."

Mary sighed and propped her chin in a manicured hand. "You know, I've dated six medical students in the past year. I'm blonde and beautiful—but brains and money I don't have. And I'm already twenty-three!"

Callie was used to her friend's dismal moods. She smiled and said, "Maybe you need to look beyond these ivy-covered walls, Mary. Find a handsome young man *not* affiliated with medical school. The men still here are too busy to look up from their microscopes. Besides, you're young and you have a good job. Times are hard. I passed three homeless men begging on the sidewalk just now. In the rain. Be thankful."

"Still . . ." Mary sighed. A streak of lightning lit up the sky outside the lobby windows and Mary flinched.

"Things will turn around for you," Callie said hopefully. She glanced down at her mud-spattered stockings and soaked shoes. "Now, I don't want to mess up the dean's rugs, but the professor said I was wanted right away? I had to leave class."

"Which class?"

"One of Nurse Collier's antiquated lectures." Callie rolled her eyes and whispered, "I was glad to leave. What's going on?"

Mary frowned. "I am such a dunce. You had a message from home. A telegram, I'm afraid. We may have to postpone our double date."

"Blast!" Callie blanched. "A telegram? Why didn't you tell me right away?"

Mary stood, wringing her hands. "I shouldn't have said anything at all, Callie. I'm sorry. Follow me. Dean Perkins said to bring you back as soon as you got here." The young woman led Callie down the brightly lit hall. She stopped in front of a closed office door and knocked. "Miss Beecham to see you, Dean Perkins."

"Come in."

Callie swallowed hard and walked into the dean's office. "Dean Perkins, you called for me?" She smoothed her white smock to give her shaking hands something to do.

The woman stood. "Callie, I'm sorry to have summoned you across campus in this weather. Sit down."

"Is something wrong? Mary mentioned a telegram." Callie remained standing.

Mrs. Perkins snorted. "That girl needs to keep her mouth closed," she murmured. "Yes, I have a telegram marked *Urgent*." She slid the envelope across the desk. "You may open it here if you like."

Callie nodded and picked up the envelope. She opened it and pulled out the thin paper, Western Union emblazoned across the top in bold print.

PICKENS SC 846A, JUNE 19, 1930
TO CALLIE BEECHAM CHARLESTON SC
GRANNY IS SICK AND IS ASKING FOR YOU. PLEASE COME.
ZEKE YOUNG

Callie dropped her head. "My grandmother is sick."

Perkins frowned. "Oh, I am sorry."

"She's quite old. And I haven't been home since I came down a year ago," Callie said. The guilt began to enfold her, seeping into her marrow.

"Of course you'll go home to see her," Perkins said.

Callie lifted her head. "Yes, I'd like to go home. But I can be back in a few days." She looked at the dean expectantly. "We have clinics. And an exam."

Lightning flashed outside the large office window. Callie flinched when the loud crack of thunder came only seconds later.

"Callie," Dean Perkins began, leaning back in her chair, unphased. "Take some time. This is your grandmother."

Too many ghosts up there. I don't want to go back. Callie started to interject, but the dean held up her hand.

"You have exemplary grades. Your skills are exceptional. Your dedication is admirable. Exams can be postponed, and August graduation is a formality." Dean Perkins frowned. "I understand your not wanting to miss the end—but this is your grandmother."

"I don't want to do anything to jeopardize becoming a nurse."

Dr. Perkins smiled. "And you haven't, my dear. You'll have your license. Haven't you already accepted a position with the new clinic on Calhoun Street?"

"I begin September first," Callie said proudly.

Dean Perkins leaned forward. "Well done. So go home. Stay a while. Your grandmother needs you. You'd regret it if you didn't. We will schedule your exams when you return."

"Yes, ma'am. Thank you." Callie stood. She could put it off no longer. It had been a year. She was going home.

— • —

Although it was only late afternoon, the heavy rain and low sky were dark and quite foreboding. Tears streamed down Callie's face as she drove home, wracked with guilt. Seeta was sick. In her grandmother's May letter, she had asked again if Callie would come home for a visit. The letter lay on Callie's bedside table, unanswered.

With classes and so much work at the clinic, she had always believed a trip home was a waste. She couldn't afford to fall behind. *It's not that, and you know it.* The thought pierced the veneer of grief and hit her hard. *You don't want to go back to being colored.*

In Charleston, no one knew. She was a white woman. A white woman who could go into any store or restaurant, any theatre or church. A white woman with a few friends, the law on her side, and the promise of becoming a nurse. She was hiding in plain sight. And the guilt was eating her up.

Thunder rumbled. She leaned forward, peering intently at the road through a veil of tears and heavy rain. The small windshield wiper oscillated frantically but barely cleared a small triangle for Callie to see through. Standing water covered the road in several places, and twice Callie slammed on the brakes when the water appeared too deep to cross. She wiped her eyes with the back of her hand. *How could I have been so heartless? I should have gone home before now.*

As she turned onto the narrow bridge to James Island, she breathed a sigh of relief mixed with sadness. *It's just a visit home.* She would come back to Charleston and continue her life as a white woman. She asked a quick prayer of forgiveness for the very thought, but the weight removed from her shoulders could not be denied.

Lightning flashed and illuminated a man limping down the side of the road, carrying a broken umbrella partially collapsed but held high over his head. His trousers were soaked below the knees. She pulled her car onto the shoulder and opened her door a bit, attempting to assuage her guilt with a good deed.

"Get in, Mr. Pinckney!" she called. "This storm is horrible. I'll give you a ride."

The man lowered the umbrella, hurried to the passenger side of the car, and opened the door. "You sure? I'm wet through—" A loud crack of thunder cut off the rest of his words.

"It's fine. Get in!" Callie shouted.

The man slid into the seat and slammed the door. He reeked of wet wool and perspiration. "Thank you, Miss Carrie."

"This storm is awful. I couldn't let you walk," Callie said. "How are you? I haven't seen you in ages."

"You're very kind, ma'am. I've been limping through the rain for fifteen minutes. Lost my hat a ways back." Beads of water glinted off his head like diamonds. "This old leg has only one speed."

Callie saw that he wore a chambray collared shirt. A purple striped tied was knotted at his throat. His pants were dappled with paint in various colors.

"Our turn-off is right over the bridge." He pointed straight ahead. "About a mile on the right."

Callie nodded and peered into the distance. "We're lucky the road is still above water. Charleston was practically flooded. I remember the first time I saw Turtle Island, and I wondered why on earth Silas Roberts built a house on stilts." She chuckled. "Now I know. The houses near the bridge always look ready to go under, even when there's just a shower."

The man wiped his bald head with his handkerchief and sighed wearily.

Callie remembered Pinckney to be a quiet man, so she focused on the road ahead instead of trying to make conversation.

He eventually looked her way. "You have any chores you need done? I sure need the work."

Callie shook her head. "I'm sorry. I'm leaving town tomorrow. My granny is sick. I'm going home to see her."

The man's expression clouded, and he turned away. "I'm sorry about that. Real sorry."

"She's around ninety. And I haven't been home since I first came down here . . ." Callie shifted uneasily in her seat. "So, what has you out in this weather? And in a tie! Betty said you haven't been working at the Cutlers as much."

"Mrs. Cutler cut back the help's hours. Times are hard for everyone, and I think she had to cut somewhere to make up for the new nanny she hired. She's expectin' a baby in a few weeks."

Callie shook her head. "Is that baby number six?"

"It's a litter," he laughed. "So, I've been working odd jobs elsewhere. Today, though, I had a real job interview." He pointed to his drenched clothing. "Unfortunately, the ride home dropped me off well before the bridge. It's quite the walk in a thunderstorm."

"I'll say. I thought you looked dressed up. Did you get the job?" Callie asked, wondering what kind of job the man could have interviewed for, dressed as he was. *Callie, don't be a snob.*

"No," he sighed. "I applied to be the caretaker of Mr. and Mrs. Patterson's winter home on John's Island. Mrs. Patterson seemed real pleased with me. I'm a hard worker. No one can prune a topiary better.

But Mr. Patterson took one look at me over his newspaper and told me they're holdin' out for a white caretaker."

Callie thought for a minute. "I have an idea. Would you consider coming back here as caretaker? Betty already works for me, but if Mrs. Cutler has cut hours . . ."

Pinckney's face fairly lit up. "Well now, that would be fine. I need the work, and I'll do a good job for you."

"I haven't even named a salary. I surely don't need topiaries." She grinned.

"What'd you have in mind?" he asked.

Callie did some quick calculations and blurted, "$80 a month? For keeping the outside trimmed and neat. Work in the garden? Handyman things inside as needed?"

"I'll take it. Thank you, Miss Carrie. I need the money, and I like to stay busy." He smiled.

"Would you mind coming to my house real quick to look at the bathroom faucet? It has a drip that I cannot seem to fix," she said.

"Give me a lift back home after that if it's still rainin'?" he countered.

Callie smiled. "I'll happily give you a lift—and a hot cup of coffee."

"That'll do nicely."

Callie relaxed. "When I come back from visiting my grandmother in a few days, we can iron out details of the caretaking job. I have ideas for plantings around the property . . . maybe expand the garden, clear out the side yard. And what is the name of those heavenly tea roses by the garage? Betty said you planted them. They remind me so much of home. I think they are the same roses my Granny had back in Lib—back home."

The man's smile faded, and he peered out at the rain. "I don't remember, ma'am. I'm sorry."

Callie wondered what she'd said to offend the man. In moments, they were in front of her house. She cut the headlights and grabbed her purse and the heavy canvas bag of schoolbooks. Pinckney hurried around to Callie's side of the car and extended his arms. "Let me help you."

The rain had slacked off to a drizzle. Frogs croaked a riotous song from the flooded marsh. Callie gave Pinckney the heavy bag of textbooks and led him up the steps into the house. "Betty's here. What would I do without your wife?"

Inside, lamps were lit against the weather and a fire crackled in the fireplace. Despite the chill damp outside, the house was snug and dry.

"Lord, Miss Carrie, that was some storm," Betty called from the kitchen. "You home early."

Callie removed her wet slicker and hung it on the coat rack. "I got a telegram. My grandmother is sick. I'll be heading up there tomorrow for a few days." She smiled at Mr. Pinckney. "I brought a neighbor out of the storm with me."

Betty ambled into the living room, curious, and grinned at her husband, hands on her hips. "Well, mercy me! How did your interview with Mrs. Patterson go?"

Pinckney removed his soaked coat and said, "Not good. And her driver left me off well before the bridge."

Betty slapped a dishtowel against her thigh in disgust.

"All is well, Betty. Miss Carrie offered me a caretakin' job," he said.

Betty gasped. "Really? Thank you, Jesus!" she exclaimed.

"And he's kind enough to come in and check that leaking tub faucet. I promised him a cup of coffee for his trouble," Callie said.

"I go get it. I got your laundry off the line before the rain started, Miss Carrie. Soup is simmerin' on the stove for your dinner."

"Thank you, Betty." Callie took the man's wet coat and hung it on the coat rack. "After she gets your coffee, we can look at the faucet. Have a seat."

The man gazed around the room, as if seeing an old friend after a long absence. He tilted his head. "You sure? I'm pretty wet."

Callie dismissed his worry with a wave of her hand. "Sit, please. So how did you get the job here the first time?" she asked.

Pinckney seemed to measure his words. "Mr. Roberts took me on as caretaker when he was building the place. Stayed in the room over the garage and took care of the house and the yard until the war."

Betty returned with a mug of coffee and set it on an end table. She patted her husband's shoulder and waddled back into the kitchen.

"Silas and I were neighbors," Callie said. "On the same street in Pickens. I helped him out when his health began to fail." She thought for a minute and added, "I didn't even know he had a house down here. He never spoke of it. I think any memories surrounding William were just too painful for him."

"I'm sure you're right," Pinckney confirmed. He stared intently at the painting over the fireplace. The painting of the man and young boy searching for seashells had become a favorite of hers. Behind who she thought was surely a father and son, the surf foamed and frothed. Seagulls wheeled overhead in a cerulean sky.

Callie followed his gaze. She was slightly disappointed that he didn't seem as curious about her relationship with Silas as she was about his.

She gestured toward the mantel. "I love that painting. I love all of his beautiful watercolors. Do you know who the artist is?"

"I painted them," Pinckney said simply. "I painted every one."

Callie was skeptical. "Really? The painter's name is May. Is your last name May? That's the name scribbled at the bottom. I thought you were a Pinckney."

He looked sheepish. "I took the name Pinckney when I met Betty. Her people are Pinckneys. Around here, that carries some real weight."

He sipped his coffee and then pointed to the watercolor over the mantel. "Mr. Roberts was generous with supplies and such. He wanted pictures of the sea, the marsh, and all the places he and William used to spend their time. That one was the first—when William was about ten. I sketched that one out while they was huntin' for cowry shells and sand dollars in the surf."

"You're incredibly talented," Callie said. "You could sell your work."

Pinckney smiled. "Thank you. I always enjoyed paintin'. Haven't had the chance to paint pictures in a long while, though. I dabbled a bit when I was young."

"Where did you grow up?" Callie asked.

"I'm from everywhere and nowhere." Pinckney shrugged. He returned his gaze to the seascape over the mantel.

"I hope I'm not prying, but can you tell me more about your time with Silas?" Callie asked, her curiosity getting the best of her.

He shrugged. "He hired me at a time I needed work desperately. Worked from '05 until the war. I served in the Army," he said. "But I took a bullet in the leg in '17. That's how I got my limp." He patted his thigh.

"You're a hero then," Callie said.

"Nah. It was friendly fire. I was just too old and slow to get out of the way." He paused and sipped his coffee. "Mr. Roberts let me stay over the garage—free room and board until I could work again. That was the plan. But while I was healin' up, Mr. Roberts got word of William's death. He packed up and went back to Pickens. Told me he didn't know when he'd be back. But he didn't come back down at all. Not once. I stayed on for a few months after the war ended, to let my leg mend up. I kept the house and grounds tended for him, thinkin' he'd come back down or write. He'd been so good to me. Then the war ended, and white folks came sniffin' around, wanting to buy the place, and asking for the owner. Twice the police came and kicked me out—thinkin' I was a squatter. I was a veteran, and I'd worked here twelve years, but it didn't matter. I had no proof of employment. I was just a bum."

"So, what did you do?" Callie asked.

He looked at her pointedly. "I left and went to Chicago. I'd been up north once before. It didn't work out then, but I had hopes." He shook his head. "I thought I could get a good job. I'd been a machinist in the Army. I found work in the spring of 1919. A real good factory job. But I only stayed until that August. They called it the Red Summer."

"Yes," she whispered, wondering about her own father. "I'd heard about that. Awful. What did you do?"

Pinckney finished his coffee. The cup clattered as he set it in the saucer. "Some white folks burned down my apartment building. The factory fired all of the colored men. So, when a buddy was headed back down this way, I hitched a ride as far away from trouble as he'd take me—which was Charleston. I hired on with a house paintin' crew. That's how I met my Betty. Her cousin was on the crew and introduced us." He winked. "And how I became a Pinckney."

Betty appeared in the doorway, her purse hooked in the crook of her elbow. "Soup's ready, Miss Carrie. There's a pan of corn bread on the stove, too. We can walk home. The rain's stopped. I'm real sorry 'bout your grandmother. We'll look after your place while you gone. I hope she gets better soon."

"Thank you, Betty," Callie said, standing.

"I should look at that dripping faucet real quick." Pinckney stood and looked at Callie with such a sad expression that she wondered if she'd opened up some old wound with all her questions.

She was sorry that his chatty spell was over. "Oh. The faucet. It can wait until I get back. You go on. You need to get into dry clothes. Next week, we can chat about the oddities in this quirky old house and what needs what in the yard. I'll be back in a few days."

"I'm sorry. Sorry 'bout your grandmother," he said.

"Thank you," Callie said. "I should have gone to see her before now. I've been so busy. But I should have gone home . . ." Her voice trailed off.

"Say, what's your grandmother's name? We'll say a prayer for her," Betty offered.

"Her name is Seeta. Seeta Young. I'd appreciate your prayers."

Betty smiled. "Seeta. That's a pretty name."

Callie was surprised to see the glimmer of tears in her eyes.

She was about to ask Betty if she was alright when Mr. Pinckney spoke. "*Clementina Carboneri*," he said. "The name of the tea roses out back."

Chapter Twenty-Seven

Upstate, fields and horse pastures appeared utterly vanquished as Callie drove toward Greenville. Her tires spun up clouds of red clay dust behind her. Sere and dusty roadsides devoid of spring wildflowers told Callie that her home was in a dry spell. She prayed it wouldn't be like the drought in '25. It cost farmers millions and sent an already fragile farm economy close to the brink. And how odd, she thought, to be coming from the wet and humid Lowcountry, where daily storms had turned her garden's tomatoes and squash into mush, where mildew grew on the sides of her house and mushrooms popped up in fairy rings around her yard.

But as she veered off the highway into Greenville and headed toward Zeke's neighborhood on the outskirts of town, she realized how much she missed the cooler climate, the plants, trees, and the blue hills of Upstate South Carolina.

It was a Sunday evening, and Callie watched people stroll down the sidewalk, maybe heading to evening church services, or returning from a meal at a neighbor's. Several down and out men sat on a curb, and as she passed, she watched them lift up tin cups, hoping for a handout. She averted her eyes and sped up, embarrassed that her shiny automobile proclaimed her good fortune in the midst of an economic catastrophe.

Her heart ached as she thought of Seeta. The guilt was nearly unbearable. She had found a grandmother and then had spent only months with her before running away. They had exchanged letters at first, until Seeta's spidery handwriting had become nearly illegible from her arthritis. Callie missed her grandmother. *But she wanted me to go to the coast,* Callie reminded herself. *To get away.*

At dusk, she neared the neighborhood of middle-class homes owned by better-off black families. Nearly a mile away from the last white neighborhood, two streets of neat frame houses sat at the county line. It was probably their separation that kept the homes intact. If they'd been any closer to the white areas of town, there would have been troubles, Callie suspected.

The cracked and broken sidewalk in front of Zeke's house was dotted with pedestrians walking slowly toward the large white house. Callie pulled her car to the side of the street. The flashy new Ford stood out against a backdrop of two older models, with their rusted fenders and dented doors, and the horse-drawn buggy tied to a pine tree. The stream of folks dressed in Sunday clothes approached the front porch of the house, where a small knot of people congregated by porchlight. Callie swallowed hard. *Am I too late?*

Callie regarded the suitcase on the floorboard and decided against bringing it in. Maybe she wasn't expected to even show up, and to stay here would be out of the question. She hadn't even been able to telephone Zeke. She'd find a hotel room in town later. She lifted her navy cloche from the passenger seat and settled it over her hair. She exhaled slowly and opened the car door, ready to join the apparent queue of mourners.

She soon fell in line behind two women, each carrying a covered dish. They both looked at Callie strangely. Trying not to panic, she pressed forward and stepped onto the wide front porch of the home she'd purchased. Callie was surprised to see the pink tea roses that Seeta loved had been planted in front of the porch skirting. Small buds dotted the shrubs, and Callie knew that in just days, the fragrant blossoms would be open, like their cousins in the Lowcountry, the scent perfuming the front porch.

The women in front of her walked easily into the house, where a group of people milled about. Callie hesitated. A man on the porch nodded and stepped aside at the sight of the nicely dressed white woman in her fashionable navy suit. A few women put their heads together behind gloved hands and whispered quietly.

Callie blushed and continued into the house. Eyes turned her way and stared. Suddenly a woman's voice shouted, "Callie! Is that you?"

Callie turned to find Mattie rushing toward her with extended arms. Callie felt a flood of relief and sadness all at once. The woman enveloped

Callie in her ample grip and hugged her tightly. "Oh, your granny missed you so. We all did. She be so happy to see you!"

Sudden tears trickled down Callie's cheeks. "Oh, Mattie! I should have come sooner," she said softly. "How is everyone?"

The murmur of the curious crowd resumed and left the two women alone.

"Delia's fine. Baby Rose is fine. She's two months now." Mattie held Callie close and stroked her back. "Don't come here feelin' like you let us down. Your granny never wanted you fussin' over her in any way."

"What happened?" Callie asked as she pulled her handkerchief from her purse.

Mattie shook her head. "Oh, Lawd. She got pneumonia real bad, an' her fever won't break. I put her under a poultice, and she sleepin' now."

"Wait. She's alive?" Callie dabbed her nose and a wave of relief passed over her. "Thank God. I thought she had died!" She glanced around and lowered her voice. "Then—who are all these people?"

"Oh. You thought—" Mattie leaned in and chuckled. "No . . . This is my Sunday School class. We havin' Bible study an' desserts here tonight."

Callie exhaled and felt herself relax. "Thank God. I would have called first—"

"But Zeke cut the phone," Mattie said. "He didn't like havin' it, an' we had to let some things go. Delia ain't workin' because of the baby, an' I lost my job house-cleanin' for Mrs. Jones." Her expression brightened. "Oh, wait till Zeke sees you came. He didn't think you would. He'll be home soon. And my, look at you!"

Mattie took in Callie's appearance from head to toe. "The Lowcountry is treatin' you right. You look good enough to eat! And you is about to be an official nurse?"

Callie grimaced at Mattie's effusive praise. "May I look in on her?" she asked.

Mattie nodded. "First door on the right upstairs. Delia is gettin' Rose to sleep in the next room so be kinda quiet."

Callie walked slowly up the stairs and stopped at the first door on her right. She knocked softly and was flooded with relief when she heard Seeta's voice crackle softly, "Come in."

She opened the door. The sliver of light from the hall was the only light in the room. "Granny, it's me," she whispered.

There was the sound of shifting in the bed and then Seeta's voice. "Callie girl?" she rasped. "Come over here. Turn on my little lamp!"

The room reeked of onion and garlic, prime ingredients in Mattie's poultice. Callie felt her eyes well with fresh tears, and she rushed toward the bed. She fumbled for the small lamp until she found it, and then turned the knob. The dim bulb flipped on, and Callie stared at the wizened face of her grandmother. She appeared little more than a skull with brown flesh draped over it, and her bony chest heaved with each crackle of breath. Callie couldn't believe how tiny Seeta had become. Shrunken.

"Oh, Granny, you're so sick. I should have come sooner." Callie pressed her pale hand against Seeta's sharp cheekbone, and then removed it quickly. Seeta was burning up.

Seeta fumbled for her glasses and set them on the bridge of her nose with a shaking hand. "My granddaughter. My beautiful girl," she said. "It's good to see you."

Seeta sighed. But her sigh led to a cough. Then another. Callie could hear the crackle in Seeta's lungs after each exhalation. She placed two fingers against Seeta's tiny wrist. Her pulse was thready and weak. "Has the doctor been out?"

Seeta nodded. "But you the best medicine."

Callie lifted the onion poultice from Seeta's chest with a grimace and sprang into action. She pulled a small medical kit from her bag and soon had a thermometer under Seeta's tongue. She peeled back the heavy quilts and massaged Seeta's cold feet. "We're going to do the warming socks. I've got cotton and wool ones in my suitcase. It'll pull the fever down." She removed the thermometer and squinted at the results.

"Granny, your fever is 102." She poured a glass of water and gave it to Seeta in small mouthfuls.

"I know I had a supply of butterfly weed root tincture that I left here last summer. Where did Zeke and Delia stash my crates? It should still be good."

Seeta whispered, "Your boxes are in the bedroom at the end of the hall. Under the bed in Cal's room."

Callie turned and tiptoed down the darkened hall, twin emotions of anger and guilt rising in her chest. *I should have come back at Christmas–at the very least.* She slowly turned the knob on Cal's door and quietly entered the room. The toddler lay asleep in his bed, face down, his bottom scrunched up high in the air. He clutched a blanket in his chubby fist and snored softly. Callie leaned over her nephew, smiling. *He's grown.*

She longed to stroke his head and kiss his plump cheek, but instead, squatted and felt under the bed for the wooden box that held the last of the tinctures made before she'd gone to the Lowcountry. She dragged the box out slowly and lifted it to her chest. She turned and quietly left the bedroom, pulling the door closed behind her.

When she returned to her grandmother's room, Seeta's eyes were closed, but opened when Callie perched on the edge of the bed. "Granny, we're in luck. I found it." She held a small brown bottle in front of her. "I'll give you ten drops now. I may come back around midnight and dose you again."

"You made this from dried root, like you know to?" Seeta asked. When Callie nodded, Seeta opened her mouth, and Callie dribbled the tincture between her lips.

Seeta swallowed the medicine and regarded Callie. "The very hour you were born, I gave you a dose of milk thistle tincture because you was yellow. Dropped it right in your mouth, and you took it like a baby bird."

Callie replaced the dropper in the bottle and regarded her ill grandmother. She reached out tentatively to touch Seeta's gnarled hand, ropey with raised veins. "Granny. I'm so sorry," she whispered. "I was afraid. Will you forgive me?"

Seeta squeezed Callie's hand. "I'm glad you went away. And you need to go back," she rasped. "Get that certificate. That piece of paper that says you is a real nurse."

"Soon, it'll be official."

Seeta beamed.

"Granny, I do love it there," Callie said, leaning closer. "Maybe someday, I can take you down to see the coast."

"Did you find out why Silas wanted you to see it?" Seeta croaked.

Callie nodded. "I think so. It's a beautiful place. It's quiet. Far from here. And the nursing school is there. It seems a perfect place to hide away. Everyone thinks I'm white."

Seeta frowned. "I don't think he meant you to hide away. You have too many gifts, girl."

Callie gently squeezed Seeta's hand. "It doesn't matter, really . . . The old caretaker said he'll keep up the place for me. His wife cooks and cleans. She is a dear. That's a huge help to me, and they need the money."

When Seeta's eyelids drooped, Callie stood and pulled the quilts back up to her grandmother's hips. "You try and sleep now. I'll go on downstairs and prep the socks and then check on you later. Mattie is having a Sunday School meeting downstairs, and when I walked in, you should have seen the looks on people's faces," she said.

"Givin' the good Christians of Mountainview African Methodist Episcopal somethin' to talk about besides the book of Romans," Seeta said with a chuckle. "A white girl in Sister Mattie's house!"

Callie kissed Seeta's fuzzy head and then left the room. Mattie appeared at the bottom of the stairs. "How she doin'?"

"Her fever is high. I took the poultice off and gave her some pleurisy root tincture I'd saved. It'll make her sweat. I'll dose her again around midnight." She glanced toward the living room where ten people sat in a circle, chatting over chocolate cake and cups of coffee. "I hate that I came during your meeting. Where is Zeke?"

"He should be home real soon," Mattie said. "He's the night janitor at the white school. Had to take another job because the automobile shop cut his hours. He works evenin's cleanin' the school."

Callie's stomach tightened. They were barely getting by. Zeke had cut the phone out and was working two jobs. Mattie and Delia had lost theirs, and Callie had been blithely unaware of the downturn in her family's welfare.

"Mattie," she began. "I can give y'all money. I—"

"No!" Mattie hissed, before looking past Callie to her company. "You've done enough. Zeke wouldn't hear of it. I got to go back in now, or Sister Sylvia gone take over. But we talk when they leave. There's some fried chicken and coleslaw in the ice box. I saved some for Zeke, too. Go get some dinner and then put your things in my room. You can stay with me." She gave Callie a quick hug before returning to her guests.

Callie went into the kitchen and opened the ice box. She pulled out a platter of chicken drumsticks and a cold jug of buttermilk.

"Well, look what the cat drug in," a man's voice growled behind her.

Callie turned with a ready smile. The man in front of her had a few more lines on his face, some new gray at his temples. He wore dirty overalls over a flannel shirt. "Zeke!" she said affectionately, taking a step toward him.

Zeke smiled but made no move to come closer. "So, you got my telegram."

"I did. I've already checked on Seeta. Granny. I had some pleurisy root tincture. I'm hoping that will turn the fever around . . ." Her voice trailed off.

"If you can't heal her, no one can." Zeke ran his hand across his rough chin, a day's worth of stubble also peppered with early gray.

"Here. Sit down and I'll make you a plate. Mattie has her Bible class here, and Delia is putting Rose to sleep. I can't wait to meet her," Callie said.

Zeke removed his hat and sat down wearily. "She's a pretty baby. Cal's real fond of havin' a sister."

She busied herself plating chicken and slaw for them both. After she poured two glasses of buttermilk, she sat down across from her cousin. "How are you, Zeke?"

Zeke bit into a chicken leg, then chewed and swallowed the mouthful before answering. "Times are hard."

"Let me help out. I want to."

"You already bought us this house. I have to support my family on my own," Zeke said. "Mr. Green cut my hours at the shop. I'm only there one mornin' a week now. He says he has to save the hours for white men who need work. Unskilled white men who don't know what they're doin'." He wiped his mouth with his napkin. "He knows that I know cars. I'm the best mechanic he has."

He looked at Callie with hard eyes, daring her to question his skills, and continued. "Silas Roberts' old Ford? It had its problems, and it had been dunked in the river, but like I said, I'm a good mechanic. Runs like a dream now." He slid a forkful of slaw into his mouth and nodded toward Callie. "We glad to have that car. Thank you for that too."

"Mattie said you're working at the school. As a janitor?" Callie tried.

Zeke nodded. "For pennies."

The pair ate in silence for several minutes before Zeke leaned back in his chair, studying Callie.

"You look like a rich Charleston lady now," he said. "I see them silk stockin's and that fine suit. Them fancy shoes. I guess the Lowcountry agrees with you."

He means that I look white.

"They know you're half-colored?" Zeke smirked.

Callie put down her fork. "Zeke, I said I would help you. And I meant it."

Zeke's expression softened. He leaned forward again. "I'm sorry, Callie. I'm grateful for this house, the car, all of it. You been nothin' but kind to my family. To Granny. You saved Delia's life. I'm just so—frustrated." He clenched his hands into fists. "We barely keepin' it together. With Granny sick an' a new baby, I want to be able to pay our bills . . ." He leaned his head in his hands. "But a black man can't get a good job."

Callie nervously sipped her buttermilk. The clink of cups and saucers and the chatter of Mattie's guests in the next room seemed completely out of sync with her cousin's despair.

"Zeke, I'll stay to see Granny better, if that's alright. If you'll let me. I don't want to make people talk."

"Stay as long as you want, Callie," Zeke said wearily. "But I ain't takin' no handouts. No one here knows about you. If you want it known that you're more than just Seeta's white friend, you'll have to tell it."

— • —

Around midnight, Callie padded up the stairs in her robe and slippers to check on Seeta. The house was completely still, save the creaking of her feet on the old treads. She saw a light under Seeta's door and knocked quietly.

"Come in," Seeta murmured softly.

"I brought the warming socks." Callie stepped through the door and saw Seeta sitting up in the bed. "I worried when I didn't hear you coughing." She pulled back the covers and gently lifted Seeta's left foot. "The socks are quite cold from the ice box." She rubbed Seeta's right foot briskly, fitted the icy cold and damp sock on Seeta's foot, and then worked a warm woolen sock over the cold, wet one. She repeated the process on the other foot. "There. Keep those on all night, and it'll help draw out that cough." She held up the small bottle of pleurisy root tincture and added, "Time for another dose."

"You comin' back to see me is the best medicine," Seeta said. "Now I can die happy." She patted the edge of the bed.

Callie sat down. "Don't talk like that." She dribbled another dose of pleurisy root between her grandmother's lips.

Seeta swallowed the medicine. "Are you goin' to Pickens while you're here?"

"Why on earth would I do that?" Callie asked.

"Have you heard anything from Dr. Sam?" Seeta tried again.

Callie's shoulders sagged. "Why bring him up? Why bring up any of it? I'm trying to put the past behind me. Let's focus on getting you better."

"What you're doin' is runnin' away." Seeta continued before Callie could respond, "Dr. Sam's been on my mind lately."

Callie sighed. "Mine, too. I'm sure he went back to Atlanta. Probably has a rich Jewish city girlfriend—maybe a wife—by now. Someone he can show off at society parties."

She placed her palm on Seeta's forehead. The fever was down. Not gone, but definitely down. She handed her grandmother the tall glass on her bedside table. "Here. You'll sweat a lot tonight. Drink some water and then try to sleep."

Seeta crossed her thin arms defiantly. "You think I don't know about butterfly weed? Girl, I was dosing folks with it for pleurisy and coughs before you was born. I know to drink water. I'm toleratin' the tincture well. Let's go to fifteen drops tomorrow."

"Yes, ma'am," Callie said playfully.

Seeta pointed a finger at Callie. "He loves you. I know he does. I saw the way he looked at you."

Callie lowered her eyes. "Granny, he doesn't know that I am half Negro. Remember? In this world, that won't work. You know it. You said the same thing about my mother and father. He'd probably drop in his tracks to find he'd kissed a mulatto girl. He thought I broke things off with him because he was Jewish. I want to keep it that way. Let him think I'm a snobby racist. Now, enough of Sam Epstein and going back to Pickens and—and all of it." She stood. "I'm going to let you rest."

Seeta took Callie's wrist. She looked at her granddaughter with tears welling in her dark eyes. "You listen to me. You can't carry this load."

"What do you mean?" Callie asked.

"This fear. This hate. I see it in yo' eyes. You got to let it go. It's weighin' on you."

Callie tried to step back, but Seeta maintained her hold on Callie's wrist. "Don't let them win. Remember what I said. Keep climbin' to the sun."

Callie grunted, exasperated with her grandmother. "They've already won, Granny. They took both of my parents. They took my house. My livelihood. My cat. My peace of mind. And Sam. If Silas hadn't given me money and a way to escape, where would I be?"

"No!" Seeta said, giving Callie's arm a good shake. "They only win if you don't forgive them and move on. The fear and the hate will seep into your bones and rot your own life, otherwise. You have to forgive them. That's the only way to free yourself. Don't let them steal your joy." She dropped Callie's arm. "The Lawd has promised good to you. Trust Him."

"Is that a Bible verse?" Callie asked sarcastically. "Is that supposed to keep me from being afraid? And angry?"

Seeta huffed. She leaned back into her pillows. "The Lawd didn't give you a spirit of fear. No, ma'am. He gave you a spirit of power and love. And a sound mind. That's a Bible verse." She paused. "How you think I've lived this long after everything that's happened to me?"

A hot flush of shame crept into Callie's cheeks. "I'm sorry, Granny. I don't know how you could ever forgive these people for the things that they did to you. And here I am unwilling to forgive something that's a trifle compared to that . . ." She pulled a tiny bottle from her dress pocket. "Lavender oil. Let me rub a bit into your forehead. You'll sleep better."

Seeta leaned back into her pillows, closed her eyes, and let Callie massage the sweet-smelling oil into her temples. She rasped, "I trust that God'll take care of me, and then just let the rest go. An' He has. Would you be down in Charleston—in a house given to you—and at nursin' school, unless He was takin' care of you, too?"

Callie had to admit there was much truth in her grandmother's words. "I surely missed you, Granny."

Seeta opened her eyes. "You have to promise me. I need to know you won't let those men take your joy. Promise me." Seeta took Callie's hand and stared up at her, waiting.

Callie felt like her heart would rip in two. "I promise."

Chapter Twenty-Eight

Callie woke with a start. Bright sunshine streamed through Mattie's open curtains. The smell of coffee and frying ham wafted into the room. She squinted at her wristwatch. 8:40. She flipped the quilt back and dressed quickly, ashamed for having overslept.

The twin bed next to her own was empty, its owner already well up and about.

"Good morning," Callie said, entering the sunny kitchen. Mattie stood at the stove. Little Cal sat in his highchair, playing with the scrambled eggs on his tray. He grinned and pointed when he saw Callie.

"Mornin'," Mattie said. "I checked on Seeta about an hour ago. She was asleep." She turned and smiled at Callie. "Her forehead was still warm, but she seemed comfortable."

"I'm glad." Callie squatted in front of Cal. "I'm Auntie Callie. My, how you've grown, little man. Where is your new baby sister?"

"Hi!" Cal responded with an egg-filled grin. He reached a chubby palm toward Callie's cheek.

Mattie inclined her head toward the living room. "Rose is in there. She likes to look at the sunshine playin' across the wall in the mornin's. Delia walked into town to interview for a job doin' laundry for a white lady on Washington Avenue. It's Monday, so Zeke is goin' into the auto shop in a while. You can help me with the babies." She poured a cup of coffee and handed it to Callie. "Check on Rose, if ya will."

Callie grabbed the cup eagerly and padded toward the living room.

Baby Rose was laid out on a scrap quilt, gazing at sunbeams dancing across the wall. "Well, hello, little angel," Callie crooned. "I'm your Auntie Callie."

She sat down cross-legged and placed her coffee cup on the low table as Rose babbled a greeting. A book on the table caught Callie's eye. *The Weary Blues*. Her thoughts spiraled back to the first time that Zeke and Seeta had met Sam, and Sam had quoted lines from the Langston Hughes poem.

"I got the weary blues, and I can't be satisfied.

Got the weary blues and can't be satisfied—

I ain't happy no more and I wish that I had died."

She cracked open the cover and her heart flipped. A short message was scribbled on the first page.

To Zeke, my friend.

—Sam Epstein

Rose turned her little head toward Callie. Her large brown eyes gazed at her aunt, and she cooed a wet greeting. Callie felt the sting of tears. She ached for a baby of her own, and months of attending to infants in the Charleston clinic had sharpened the edges of her grief. Now, seeing a tiny baby felt like a heart-wrenching loss, not just a dull hope.

She swiped her eyes with her sleeve. Delia had these two lovely children and a husband. She had neither.

Stop it! Callie leaned closer to her tiny niece and sipped her coffee. The baby glanced at her and then resumed watching the morning sun play across the walls and bookshelves.

Callie's eyes followed her niece's gaze. Her attention was drawn to the familiar watercolor above the cabinet on the far wall.

"Mornin'." Zeke appeared in the doorway. Rose squealed with delight, and Zeke scooped up his daughter and nuzzled her soft skin. "I'm sorry about my behavior last night, Callie. I shouldn't have been rude to you. We gonna be fine. This janitor job pays alright. I just don't want to be cleaning toilets when I could be fixin' engines. But I'm lucky to have work."

Callie stood. "It's all forgotten, Zeke. Your daughter is a little princess." She pointed to the watercolor, her pulse quickening. "That's Granny's Table Rock painting, right? It was in her bedroom in Liberia?"

"That's right. She wanted that paintin' to have a proud place in our new house. Since Uncle Marcus painted it, I mean. It's all she really has of him. Well, besides you," he grinned. "It had a old dime-store frame. I had it reframed all fancy for her last birthday," Zeke said.

Callie felt her heart beating wildly in her chest. She walked slowly around the table and approached the painting, already knowing what she would see. Of course. The same brushstrokes. The same style. She stretched out a trembling finger and touched the signature. Scratched into the painting was the word *May*.

"Zeke," Callie began, her hand shaking. "Please tell me. Why does this say *May*? Who is May? There are paintings at Silas's house by the same artist."

Zeke came up behind Callie. "That's not anyone's name. That's Uncle Marcus's initials," he said, kissing Rose on the head. "Uncle Marcus was Marcus Alan. Marcus Alan Young."

Callie turned to look at her cousin. The same round eyes, the long, broad nose. The gray at his temples. Zeke looked so much like Mr. Pinckney. How could she have not seen the resemblance right away?

"Zeke, you won't believe this. My father. I—I think Marcus is alive! At the coast! I've met him!" Callie could barely form words. "He worked for Silas! He's been the caretaker there all these years That must be why Silas wanted me to go there!"

Zeke looked at Callie with narrowed eyes. "I don't understand."

She stabbed a finger toward the painting. "At Silas's house on the coast—there are paintings like this. All with the same signature. May. The caretaker—Mr. Pinckney—still lives on the island. He worked for Silas and said he painted the watercolors of Silas and his son. They're signed the same way, Zeke! I think my father, your uncle Marcus—Marcus is hiding there!"

The baby began to fuss. Zeke bounced Rose in his arms and looked at Callie skeptically. "Nah. There has to be another explanation. Uncle Marcus went north. To Chicago. This man is just takin' credit for Uncle Marcus's pictures. Did he say he was from here?"

"Zeke, it's him. He said he'd gone north—to Chicago! Twice. Neither time worked out. The paintings prove it's him. And he looks like you!" She had a thought. "Granny had a picture of him as a young man up north—where is it?" she asked eagerly.

"I don't know what picture you're talking about," Zeke said, confused.

Callie sighed, exasperated. She thought of her grandmother, her frail body battling pneumonia. "I don't know how he ended up down there, but it's him. I can't tell Granny until I have him here, but it might turn her illness around! I have to get him back here. To see her. I told him her name. Told him she was sick and his face fell. I should have known!"

Zeke appeared confused. "What's he doing down in the Lowcountry?" Zeke asked. "If that's him? Why not come home and see his mama?"

"He's hiding," she said. "After what happened. I'm sure of it. But he's the right age. And he looks so much like you."

They heard a commotion in the kitchen. Mattie called out, "Zeke? Callie? Can one of you come get Cal down? My hands are in biscuit dough, and he done eatin'."

Callie looked at her cousin, silently pleading with him to believe her.

Zeke shook his head and turned to go. "This don't seem real. I think you imaginin' things, an' I got to get to work."

Callie glanced at her watch. "Zeke, I'm going to check on Granny, and then I need to be on the road. If I can bring him here to see her, think of how happy she'd be . . . That will surely make her well!" Her voice trailed away as Zeke left the room.

She lifted her hand and touched a finger to the signature at the bottom of the painting. May. It had to be him. A shockwave went through her body. *I told them Granny's name is Seeta Young.* And he'd handed her the mail addressed to Callie Beecham. The letter that she opened, as Carrie Smith. *He knows that Seeta is alive. That I am his daughter.*

Callie quickly took the stairs. She knocked tentatively on Seeta's door. "Granny?"

She heard a shuffling of the bedclothes and a small, crackled murmur.

When she opened the door and saw the small lump under the quilt that was her grandmother, there was no mistake. Seeta was not better. "Granny?" Callie sat on the edge of the bed and placed her palm on Seeta's brow. Hot to her touch. She peeled back the quilts and pulled off the socks. Icy cold. She rubbed Seeta's feet briskly to pull the circulation into them.

She picked up the small brown bottle of pleurisy root, removed the dropper, and leaned over her grandmother. "Granny, please open your mouth," she whispered. "I need to give you medicine. You're burning up."

Seeta turned away from Callie, tight-lipped. With every exhalation, Callie could hear the rattle of thick mucus clogging her lungs. A death rattle.

"Granny, please." Callie held the dropper, suspended over Seeta's mouth. "Please. I need you to sit up. I want to pat your back to break up that cough."

The woman only turned further away. There was a movement behind Callie.

"I brought up some tea," Mattie said.

"She's burning up again," Callie said softly. "She won't take the medicine. Can you bring me some cider vinegar and rags?"

Mattie set the teacup on the table and hurried from the room. Callie lifted Seeta's hand and kissed it. "Granny, don't give up. You've got to fight this."

She thought of Marcus and how the sight of him would send Seeta's spirits soaring. Her boy—alive. Her eyes scanned the dim room for the small, framed photograph she remembered.

There, propped on the dresser, Callie saw it. She crossed the room and picked up the frame. The man sat on the steps of a northern brownstone, casually smoking a cigarette. His eyes and his chin. His build. It was Mr. Pinckney nearly thirty years ago. It was Marcus. Still, she wouldn't dare say anything yet. She would bring him home. She set the frame on the bedside table.

Mattie soon returned with a basin of water, rags, and a bottle of cider vinegar. Callie set to work. She poured the vinegar in the bowl of water and then wrung out a cloth. She draped it across Seeta's brow and then wrapped each foot in a vinegar-soaked rag.

"She's given up," Mattie murmured.

"Don't say that," Callie whispered. "She can't go. Not yet."

"Callie, she's ninety."

"She can't go," Callie repeated.

Mattie sighed and sat down in a rocker across from Seeta's bed. "Girl, your granny loves you so much. She real proud of you, an' you only brung her joy. Never sadness."

"And have the bad people left you alone here? Have you all been safe?" Callie turned to look at Mattie.

"Look around you, Callie," Mattie said easily. "It all a chain of goodness. Seeta watched over Mr. Roberts' wife at childbirth. Mr. Roberts watched over you, because Seeta was good to him all those years ago. She got to see you again. You watched over Seeta—and us. And we have this beautiful home because of you an' Mr. Roberts and Seeta. With runnin' water an' lights. My family lives under one roof, and your granny is safe. She has two beautiful great-grands downstairs. Here you is, her granddaughter, tendin' her in this fancy new bed. What more could

Seeta ask for at the end of her life?"

Callie bent to smooth Seeta's hair. *I could give her back her son.* Seeta had lapsed into sleep again. "Mattie, I just don't want her to go yet. I have someone I need to bring here. Someone who needs to see her."

Mattie patted Callie's shoulder and leaned close. "Oh, baby. Sit with your granny as long as you can. Tell her all the things you want to tell her now. I don't think she'll be with us much longer."

— • —

Seeta died later that morning, with Callie nestled next to her, reading out loud from the worn Bible Seeta kept by her bed. Callie had just finished reading Psalm 91, Seeta's favorite, when she knew. Seeta's spirit vanished—just left the room so suddenly and completely that Callie inhaled sharply at the pain of it. She lay still, watching Seeta's chest for another rise or fall, hoping to give lie to the knowing.

Outside, a bright cardinal chirped from his perch in a cedar tree. Callie smiled through welling tears because a cardinal's appearance at a loved one's death always meant that the deceased was happy and at peace, looking out for their loves on Earth.

"You've reached the sun, Granny." She kissed Seeta's brow. "You'll get to meet your mama, Ona. And reunite with your beloved husband, John. Be happy."

Callie and Mattie had washed Seeta's wizened body, sponging the stick-thin arms and legs tenderly. They dressed her in her Sunday best, a sky-blue dress now much too big for her spent frame.

When the doorbell rang later that day, Zeke opened it to two dark-suited men from the new funeral home for colored people of means, Westside Funeral Parlor. Zeke scooped up his grandmother's body and carried it downstairs. He lay Seeta in the satin-lined casket that the funeral home employees had placed on a bier in the living room. Mattie rearranged her dear friend's hair and her clothing before crossing her gnarled hands at her breast. The two men spoke quietly with Zeke and then let themselves out the front door. The funeral would be held the following afternoon.

Callie and Zeke sat together on the sofa late into the night, welcoming a steady stream of mourners from the Mountainview AME Church and even a few from Liberia. They came and went during the "settin' up," bringing plates and covered dishes late into the night.

Delia had gone to bed hours ago—a tired young mother with two babies and a new job as a laundress starting the day after the funeral. She could barely be expected to sit up all night.

Mattie dozed in a rocking chair nearby. It was past one in the morning, but seven guests obviously had no plans to leave. They took their job of "settin' up" seriously. There had been prayer and hymns, and Liberia friends had shared their tales. Old remembrances and stories of Seeta's kindness rose into the ether that night. Seeta Young had been a good woman, a skilled midwife, and healer—a kind friend.

Callie stifled a yawn and closed her eyes as three men sang the final verse of "Swing Low, Sweet Chariot." The trio harmonized beautifully; baritone, bass, and tenor voices melted together in a tender homage to their friend.

Zeke leaned close to Callie and whispered, "I just don't get it. Why would Uncle Marcus hide down there? And why wouldn't Mr. Roberts have told you?"

Callie opened her eyes. "I don't know," she murmured. "But when I told Marcus her name, he looked stricken, like he'd seen a ghost." She looked at her cousin. "If you saw his face, you'd know it is him. He looks like you. But now, he won't have a chance to see her."

Zeke looked skeptical. "Callie, if that's him, he had more than twenty-five years to come home. To write. He never wrote her. Why would you want to have anything to do with him? I sure as hell don't."

The baritone singer started in on "Nobody Knows the Trouble I've Seen." The man's voice was deep and soothing. Callie's eyelids drooped, but Zeke poked her hard, and she sat up and rubbed her eyes. The mournful song reminded Callie of the horrible tale Seeta had told of her grandfather John's lynching at the hands of white farmers.

Seeta was strong. Impossibly strong. How could she have remained so kind, so at peace after witnessing such a thing? Maybe the thought of the same fate awaiting Marcus was enough for her to banish him away, never to see or hear from him again. Maybe Silas had stepped in yet again to save Callie's family by giving Marcus a job. Maybe.

The song ended. One of the old men in the room stood with the help of his daughter. Jonah Byrd was eighty himself and had driven his wagon from the hills east of Table Rock to mourn Sister Seeta. Seeta had saved his own wife and oldest child during childbirth in 1885. He was now a man with eight grandchildren and eighteen great-grands. He began to tell his story for the second time that night, taking breaks only to spit into his snuff bottle. His voice was like butter and soon lulled Callie to sleep.

Once again, Zeke's elbow in her ribs jarred her awake. "Callie!" he hissed.

"Miss Beecham, how is it you know Sister Seeta?" Jonah Byrd asked. "You the only white person here tonight."

Callie swallowed. *I can do this hard thing.* The roomful of mourners sat up, their interest piqued. "Seeta is my grandmother. Her son, Marcus, was my father."

Several women nodded as if they'd suspected as much. Callie watched Jonah roll the wad of snuff in between his cheek and gum thoughtfully, before spitting the liquid into his bottle. The habit was disgusting, and she sorely wanted to tell the man it increased his chances of oral cancer. But then again, he was eighty.

He stared at Callie for a minute, assessing her skin color, hair, and eyes. Callie knew that the man was weighing her worth. "You a colored gal, huh? You a pale little thing. Hard to think of you with a Negro daddy. You lucky you pass." He apparently had no more to say on that subject.

Jonah's daughter gave her father a withering look, leaned forward, and smiled at Callie. "I'm Mable, ma'am. I remember Marcus. He was a fine son to his mama. We was the same age, and I knew him at church when he was a boy. Then he was gone. Jes' up an' gone north."

Jonah Byrd sighed heavily and glared at Callie as though it was her fault. "He was chased away by white folks who woulda lynched him."

"Lots of folks left around that time, Jonah," Mattie challenged. "Lookin' for a better way. They still leavin'. Hopin' for better times up north an' out west. Anyhow, ain't none of it Callie's fault."

Jonah spit into his snuff bottle. "It no better any place else, is it?" Jonah Byrd looked directly at Callie. "Is it?"

Callie shook her head, chastised. "No, sir."

Jonah closed his eyes and began to hum. Callie wished that she could be anywhere other than in this room, thick with perspiration, sadness, and death.

— • —

Callie walked through the next hours as if in a dream. She had ordered a granite headstone, but until it arrived, a mound of freshly turned earth and an expensive bouquet of hothouse flowers would be all that marked her grandmother's final resting place under a spreading red oak. The funeral home had all details well in hand, but she fretted over making it fine for her grandmother.

She was relieved that she'd come to Greenville with her dark blue suit. It would have to do for the funeral. She laid it out and blocked it as best she could, in an attempt to appear crisp and pressed. She thought about sending a telegram to Dean Perkins but hadn't had time to ask about the nearest telegraph office.

The funeral was a simple graveside affair. The Reverend Lee gave the eulogy, and Mattie sang the hymn, "How Great Thou Art," one of Seeta's new favorites from the weekly radio gospel hour. Callie was so glad she had installed her Philco for Seeta before leaving for the coast.

There were perhaps several dozen mourners, and they dutifully lined up after the service to extend condolences to each member of the family. Callie stood at the end of the receiving line, a pale exclamation point to anyone who might wonder about Seeta's family. She was anxious to be going. Her only desire was to head for Charleston and find the man known as Mr. Pinckney. Her father.

As the last mourners filed past the family and out of the cemetery, Callie's eyes were drawn to a white man in a gray suit, standing outside the cemetery gate, smoking a cigarette and scanning a newspaper. He leaned against a shiny gunmetal blue Ford. His familiar hat was pulled low over his forehead, and at first, she assumed he was affiliated with the cemetery somehow. But it was a colored cemetery—and he was white. Her blood chilled when she smelled the aroma of the Chesterfield. *Impossible*, she thought.

Zeke came up alongside her. "You alright? That fancy funeral home car is leavin' and it's packed. Can I ride with you?"

Callie nodded but didn't take her eyes from the man in the distance.

"So, you going back tomorrow?" he asked.

"Yes," she said, her eyes not leaving the stranger. "Seeta didn't get to see that Marcus is alive. But I want him to know he has family. He should come home." She clasped her gloved hands together to steady their shaking. "At least for a visit."

Zeke snorted. "Well, unless he has a good reason for hiding all these years, I'm not much inclined to roll out a welcome mat for an uncle who ran away an' never wrote his mama."

The man in the distance sucked on the cigarette and then tossed it on the ground, grinding it into the dirt with a wing-tipped shoe. He blew a stream of blue smoke over his head and nodded at Callie.

Callie stared at the man. "Zeke, that man over there. That's Earl Davis."

Zeke followed her gaze. "Now what the hell does he want? Trouble?"

"With a capital T," Callie said. "But I'm damned if I'm going to let him frighten me anymore. Let's go." She hurried toward the cemetery entrance, Zeke at her heels.

As she neared the gate, she squared her shoulders and turned to her cousin. "Zeke, can you give me a moment? I'll meet you at the car."

"Callie, I—" Zeke began, worry etched across his face.

"I'll be only a moment," she said quietly.

He shrugged and headed toward her car.

Callie turned and walked quickly toward Davis. "What in God's name are you doing here?" she barked. She was relieved to find that she was more angry than afraid.

Davis removed his hat. "Afternoon, Callie."

Callie's brown eyes bored into his blue ones. "Earl, if you've come here to hurt this family anymore, so help me—"

The man raised his hands in surrender. "No."

"How did you know where I was?" she asked, her pulse thumping in her temples. She noticed that the man's face was thinner, haggard. *Good.*

"I saw the funeral notice in the paper," he said, lifting a folded copy of the Pickens newspaper in his grip. "I hoped you'd be here," he said.

"Well, here I am. At my grandmother's funeral." She crossed her arms defensively, silently thankful she'd heeded Cutler's advice to keep a Pinkerton on retainer. "What do you want?"

"I'm here to ask for your help," Earl said, tucking the newspaper into his suit jacket.

Callie couldn't help the laughter that bubbled up from her core. "Help? You've done everything in your power to ruin my life. You should be in jail. And you want my help?" She brushed past the man and hissed, "Go to hell."

A firm grip on her upper arm stopped her short. "Please. Give me a minute to explain," Davis said gruffly.

In the distance, Callie saw Zeke make a move to come help her, and she shook her head quickly. The last thing she wanted was for her cousin to tangle with this awful man. She looked down at Davis's hand clutching her arm and said, "Take your filthy hands off of me." Simmering with rage, Callie was still surprised when the man released his grip and backed up.

"Please," he said again, removing his hat. "Just give me a minute."

Callie felt her heart thumping like mad in her chest, but a strange sense of calm began to descend. "You have one minute, and then I am going to leave. I'll call my contact with the Pinkertons if you follow me."

Earl shoved his hands in his trouser pockets. "I'm not here to make trouble. It's Anne."

Callie's eyes narrowed at the mention of her former friend. "What happened to Anne?" She hadn't seen Anne Walton since the disastrous dinner date with Sam over a year ago. She did remember that Davis told her he was sending his niece to a Palm Beach surgeon.

She was surprised when Davis dropped his head. When he looked up, his blue eyes were rimmed with tears. "She had surgery last fall, and the doctors told her that they got it all. At first, she was getting better. But she's lost more than twenty pounds and refuses to see any more doctors. She's real sick." He pulled a handkerchief from his pocket and dabbed his eyes.

"I'm sorry to hear that. But it has nothing to do with me. Now, if you'll excuse me." Callie began to walk toward the car, aware of the vitriol in her voice.

"She wants to see you," Earl called. "She's Mildred's only blood kin left. I promised her that I would try to find you."

Callie swallowed hard and considered Davis's news. She turned. "Why on earth would Anne want to see me? I'm sure that you told her all about me."

Davis hesitated as if the words were difficult to say. "I did. But she remembers you as a friend. She thinks you can help her. She won't let me—or Mildred—remain in her life unless I can bring you to visit."

"Oh, I see. It's not Anne. Mildred's given you an ultimatum." Callie snorted. "You're standing here in the middle of a colored cemetery, where I just buried my grandmother, asking for my help? For God's sake!"

Davis eyed Callie, awaiting a response.

Callie lifted her chin. "Do *you* remember your threats, Earl? Do *you* remember that you vandalized and then took my home? Had my poor cat killed and me run off the road? Tried to harass my family and burn down my grandmother's shack of a home? You turned away sick people from your own practice. Kept a good doctor from treating folks who need medical care in Liberia. You're despicable. You're a disgrace to your profession."

Earl Davis crossed his arms defensively and stared at the ground but didn't say a word.

Callie felt the flood of angry feelings rising up at once, eager to spill out. They would have easily turned into hateful words, had she not remembered where she was standing. In the cemetery where her grandmother's body lay. Her grandmother who made her promise not to let anger and fear paralyze her. Destroy her.

At that moment, Callie sensed Seeta's presence. Her grandmother was right. She could wait forever for an apology that might never come. Or an insincere *I'm sorry* that meant nothing. She couldn't let Earl Davis win that way. She couldn't let him think his apology was necessary for her to go on with her life. To be free. Only she could let it go. Only she could break the chain that she forged, that threatened to add a new link with every fearful thought. Every angry word.

Callie glanced at her wristwatch. "Where is she?"

Davis looked up, surprise written across his face. He stepped forward, and Callie could see the hope in his expression. "She's staying at our house for now. Mildred is taking care of her. Would you see her?"

Callie chewed on her lower lip and tried to calm her nerves. She studied her watch. After some time, she spoke. "I will see her. I'll go this afternoon. I'm leaving town tomorrow."

Davis sighed heavily. "All right, then."

"Assuming you will let a colored woman into your house."

"Yes." Davis nodded.

"In one hour." Callie brushed past the man and strode toward her car, marveling at what had just occurred, and knowing that Seeta somehow had a hand in it. Even from the grave.

— • —

The ride back to Zeke's house was quiet. After hearing about Callie's encounter with Davis, Zeke let out a low whistle. "Damn. Why in the world would you agree to go back there an' see his niece?"

Callie shrugged. "Anne was my friend. And Granny's last words to me were about forgiveness. For my own sake. I'll let you know what happens."

"You goin' now? The ladies from church are expectin' the family to eat. There's probably more food in that house now than you've ever seen."

"I'm sorry," Callie said. "I have to do this."

Zeke shifted in the seat. "You gonna get a Pinkerton to go with you? That man has only tried to kill you is all."

She gave him a playful swat on the arm. "I'll be fine. I'm just visiting a sick friend. I wish you hadn't cut off your telephone service, Zeke. I've missed talking with you. Let me pay for it, hmm? So I can call if I need to speak to you? About your uncle?"

Zeke sighed. "I'm a proud man, Callie. But if it'll make you happy, alright. Go ahead and turn it back on. God knows Mattie'll be happy to hear it. The woman was on that thing all day. Every day. It was nice to have for emergencies though. Maybe if I get more hours at the auto shop, I can pay you back."

Callie laughed. "Zeke, no need. It was Silas's money. Not mine. I want to do this. And I don't know if I ever thanked you, but I'm thanking you now."

"What for?" Zeke asked, with a snort. "I should be thanking you—again. You paid Granny's funeral expenses." He pulled a cigarette and matches from his pocket and lit a cigarette.

"For taking me in as family." Callie frowned and waved the smoke from her face. "Those things will rot your lungs."

Zeke blew a cloud of blue smoke out of his open window. He looked at the cigarette in his fingers. "You're my cousin, not my nurse," he said with a grin. After some time, he loosened his tie and turned toward her. "So, are you a colored woman when you in Charleston? Or are you white?"

Callie was jarred by the direct question. She stared hard at the road, her cheeks hot. "Zeke, what a horrible thing to ask."

"You can't live with one foot in each world, can you? I'm wonderin' which world you chose?"

Callie sighed. "What would you do, Zeke? I don't fit in either place, really. Granny made me promise to live as a white woman. I look white, so it is easier."

"Must be nice to be able to switch like that. Go from one to the other." Zeke looked out the window. "Fit in everywhere."

Callie shook her head. "I don't fit in anywhere. Black people are as likely as whites to turn their backs on me. I'm a mulatto. I'm a half-breed—a betrayal on both races."

Zeke shrugged. "You say that. But I don't remember anyone in Liberia treatin' you bad."

Callie gripped the steering wheel hard, mulling the truth of Zeke's words. "I'm not welcome in white circles, and I'm not welcome in black circles either. Don't even try to understand what that feels like. But I know I have it better because I look white. It's true. Maybe one day it won't matter, but today it still does. And yes, I was able to get us out of something bad and into something better. But that, cousin, was all because of Silas. Not me."

"Then don't try to understand what it feels like to be a black man who can't feed his own family," Zeke huffed.

Callie nodded. "You're right."

"You gonna bring that man back here then?" Zeke asked, a chill still evident in his voice.

Callie answered firmly. "Who? Marcus? He's my father. Your uncle. He has some explaining to do, don't you think?"

Zeke tossed the cigarette out the window and muttered, "That's for damn sure."

Chapter Twenty-Nine

Pickens had not changed, and Callie found herself missing her pretty hometown. She drove past Mable Keith's dress shop and Flora's House of Beauty. The churches raised their steeples into the air and signs in the hardware-store windows advertised fertilizer and canning jars. The wooden benches in front of the filling station were the place to sit and watch cars come and go. The maple trees along Main Street waved in the breeze and the mighty Blue Ridge Mountains hovered over it all in the distance.

Despite her courage in front of Zeke, she was scared. Driving down Main Street, all of Davis's threats came rushing back. How many people here knew about her now? Did Dr. Davis tell the whole town? Callie pulled the car up to the curb in front of the Davis home on Mountainview Street. It was hard to believe that she'd been welcomed at Thanksgiving dinner here less than two years ago. She found her courageous mood spiraling downward, and when she parked the car, she sat for a few moments, willing her hands to stop their trembling.

After a quick prayer, she opened the car door and stepped out. She smoothed the skirt of her suit and adjusted her hat before squaring her shoulders and heading resolutely up the walk. To visit a sick friend. And then she'd be off to Charleston. To confront her father. To live her life. Begin an exciting new job as a nurse. She knocked on the door and waited.

From behind the screen door, footsteps hurried down the hall. The door hinges squeaked loudly, and Mildred Davis appeared in the doorway, twisting a handkerchief in her hands. "Callie Beecham!" she exclaimed. "Earl said you'd come. And you have!" She peered outside nervously in both directions before she stepped back and added, "Please, come in."

Callie stepped into Mildred's foyer. The place reeked of Chesterfields, and she remembered that Mildred did not smoke. Earl was probably somewhere in the house. "How is Anne?"

Mildred smiled nervously. "I'll take you back. She'll be so glad to see you." She paused and eyed Callie's expensive suit and heels. "Callie, you look well. I-I heard about your situation. From Earl."

"And what situation is that?" Callie asked crisply. "The one he caused?"

For a moment, Mildred fumbled for words. "Y-you lost your business . . . moved away."

"Hmm. Yes." Callie resisted the urge to say more. "May I see Anne now? I have a long drive ahead of me."

Mildred nodded and beckoned Callie to follow her down the hallway. She stopped at a closed door and knocked lightly. "Anne dear? You have a visitor. It's Callie Beecham. Uncle Earl was right." She opened the door and allowed Callie to enter first.

Callie was stunned. The frail wraith of a woman in the bed in front of her wasn't Anne Walton. It couldn't be. Her angular cheekbones jutted from her wan face. Shoulder bones rose up through a thin bed jacket. Her disheveled hair was no longer a Marcelled platinum blonde, but a dishwater mess of frizz. Her blue eyes were dull and sad, jaundiced, although they brightened by the merest degree when Anne saw Callie.

"Callie." Anne smiled. "My friend." She looked past Callie and said crisply, "Thank you, Aunt Mildred. You may go."

Mildred closed the door. The sound of her footsteps receded down the hall.

Anne reached for Callie's hand with an outstretched arm. "Callie, come sit."

The sudden memory of her introduction to John Walton in the speakeasy made Callie ignore Anne's gesture, and she sat down in a nearby chair. "Anne, what happened?"

Anne dropped her hand and rolled her eyes. "It's a long and sad story. But first, what happened to you? You vanished into thin air. And now you reemerge—looking fabulous, I should add." Her eyes scanned Callie from head to toe before she announced her verdict. "You look like the divine Norma Shearer. Your bob is terrific, and I adore your suit. Quite stylish. And do I detect kohl around those luscious brown eyes of yours?"

Callie recognized the stare of someone who was trying to assess the amount of "colored" in her appearance. Steven Cutler had done it. Old Jonah Byrd had done it. All of Liberia had done it. Mildred had just done the same thing at her front door. And now Anne. No wonder Sam had gone back to Atlanta. No one could handle it.

"I've just come from my grandmother's funeral. This isn't my usual attire." Callie began to remove her gloves, one finger at a time. "I'm here because your uncle found me at the cemetery after the service."

Anne nodded, chastened. "Callie, I am sorry. Sorry for your loss. And I'm sorry that I introduced you to John. I feel like everything that happened to you after that was my fault."

"It was your uncle who caused me so much grief," Callie said.

Anne lowered her voice. "I've known about Uncle Earl's... affiliations... for some time. John supports that cause. I do not. John couldn't wait to get home and telephone Uncle Earl after that night in the speakeasy. To tell him that you and Sam were there."

"Your uncle is a Klansman." A righteous indignation burned in Callie's chest. "We must have been the talk of the club. A Jew and a mulatto walk into a bar... It sounds like the beginning of a very bad joke," she said crisply.

A small flush of color bloomed in Anne's cheeks. "I am so ashamed. I never meant to hurt you. Or Sam." She tilted her head and added, "You don't look colored at all."

Callie ignored the comment. "How long have you known?"

"Maybe a few days after we saw you at Michel's. John didn't tell me. Uncle Earl did. He exploded when I mentioned coming to you for treatment. He told me that you had a colored father. That I could never ever step foot in your home again. He set me up with Florida doctors, but I went by your house to see you before I left town. You'd moved out. Your telephone number was disconnected. I went to the office and asked Sam. He was shocked to hear you'd moved, but said you'd broken up."

Callie just stared at her friend.

"I didn't say anything to him about your—your paternity," Anne offered.

"Well, I am surprised to hear that you tried to reach me. Thank you. But your uncle made me leave town."

Anne gazed dumbly at Callie from jaundiced eyes.

Callie continued, enumerating Davis's crimes with gloved fingers. "He had someone toss a bag of dead kittens on my porch, along with a threatening note. They killed my cat. Broke my front window. He made threats against me and my family. Threatened Sam. He came to my shop—my home—and made me sign the title over to him."

Anne dropped her head. "Oh, Callie. I am so sorry. And to think that you still came to see me . . ."

Callie nodded. "Enough of Earl Davis and his mouth-breathing cronies. I missed you, Anne." She finally extended her hand, and Anne squeezed it gratefully.

"I want to be your friend," Anne tried. "I told him that if he couldn't find you and make amends, I would cut them both out of my life."

Callie shook her head and sighed. "Don't do that. They're your family. You'd regret it one day." To her surprise, Callie knew that she meant it.

Anne beamed. "Always the good soul . . . I have missed you. Where did you run to?"

"I'm living in Charleston now. James Island, actually. About to finish nursing school," Callie said, coming to perch on the edge of the bed.

Anne brightened. "A woman of independent means. I'm impressed. And a little jealous. Everything I have is because of John. When I get better, I'll come see you. We're on King Street."

"I'd like that." Callie frowned. "What is going on with you? Why are you in this bed and not galivanting somewhere exotic with John?"

Anne's expression changed abruptly. "John and I might be on the outs. He can't handle my infirmities. I'm no fun anymore."

"But you had surgery?" Callie began to remove her silk jacket, keenly aware of how the scene had flipped. Here she was, stylish and smart, while her once-beautiful friend languished in the bed, pale and sickly.

Anne began to chew on the fingernail of her once-manicured hand. "Uncle Earl insisted I go for the surgical consult. It was two against one after the fancy Palm Beach doctor convinced John that I would still be able to have children."

Callie leaned forward. "That doesn't sound ethical. Or factual."

"I know." Anne sat up. "But do you know what? They did another x-ray prior to surgery and the tumor had shrunk. Callie, all I had done was what you'd started—the strange diet, the teas, and no smoking and drinking. And it had shrunk by half!"

Callie smiled. "That's good news. It means you should have had a better recovery from surgery. A good prognosis. What did they do?"

Anne's shoulders sagged. "They took out everything."

Callie knew that a full hysterectomy meant that Anne could never have children. She wanted to remain positive for her friend. But she sensed what Anne was thinking.

"Was I a fool to let them operate on me, Callie? I knew that John wanted children. I knew that a hysterectomy meant that could never happen. I don't think the doctor lied necessarily, but he got John's hopes up, and now I'm left . . . like this." Anne sighed. "Would the tumor have dissolved completely if I'd seen you for treatment?"

Callie squeezed Anne's hand. "Anne, don't go down that path. Who knows what might have happened?"

Anne shrugged. "I will never let another doctor near me as long as I live. Even Uncle Earl. Although he did draw blood when I arrived last week. I am anemic."

Callie frowned, her mind already assessing symptoms.

"Uncle Earl thinks they didn't get it all. That I still have the cancer."

"Why does he say that?" Callie asked, exasperated. "Do you have the physician's report?"

"John had it. I never saw it." Anne shrugged. "I have no energy. The anemia, I suppose, is responsible for that. I have fevers that come and go. Chills. I've been this way for weeks. Maybe a month. John left me in Palm Beach with a nurse and went back to Charleston. He's not good with such things. I decided to come here and let Aunt Mildred baby me—which she is so good at. But I wanted you."

Callie's mind searched through a litany of questions and clues. "When was the surgery?"

"Early December."

"And you've had the fevers and chills, the yellow eyes, since then?" Callie asked. She picked up Anne's wrist and began to take her pulse.

Anne thought for a minute before answering. "No. I was told to rest for six weeks, and I did. I felt good through the winter, actually. My incision healed nicely. We even managed a trip to Cuba in April. Mexico in May. John said it would be a second honeymoon."

"Oh, how nice," Callie said, feeling a touch envious.

"It wasn't. John drank too much and stayed out late playing poker. The weather was rainy and humid, and we tromped about in absolute jungles looking at sites where he and his business partners might put in a golf resort. When we came home, I could tell something was wrong with me. I was sick. Pains in my gut. Nausea and vomiting. Intermittent fevers and chills. I was an emotional wreck."

Callie cocked her head and made a mental map of the symptoms. "Anne, I don't recall you ever telling me that you had fever and chills before. Or pain. Other than the small tumor I saw on x-ray, you were healthy as a horse."

"But if it has spread? Wouldn't that cause my symptoms?" Anne asked. "That's what Uncle Earl said."

Callie sighed heavily. "I don't think so. And I would discount anything your uncle has to say."

Anne dropped her gaze and picked at her fingernails again. "But he said he could find you—and he did." She looked up at Callie and added in a voice barely above a whisper, "In another time and place, will you tell me what happened? All of it?"

"No." Callie tried to muster a smile for her friend, but the idea of Earl Davis looking for her was revolting. "Anne, my wise grandmother told me to forgive him. I'm trying to do that. Let's not talk about him anymore. Ever."

"Of course. I'm just so glad that you came."

Callie's mind was racing, diagnosing. "Back to your case. Have you had nightmares? Strange hallucinations even?"

Anne nodded eagerly. "As a matter of fact, I have. A few months back, when it started. I was quite feverish. I had some vivid dreams."

"Anne, I don't think this has anything to do with the tumor spreading. Obviously, you'll want to follow up with a reputable surgeon in Charleston. I do know a few I can recommend. And take back the pathology report left with John. It's your body. Your report." She paused. "But this is not that."

"Really? Callie, you don't know how relieved I am!" Anne said eagerly. "So, what is wrong with me?"

Callie stood and removed her jacket. "You, my dear, probably have malaria."

— • —

Callie placed her medical bag in the passenger seat and walked around to the driver's side of the car. Behind her, she heard the loud complaining of the screen door and turned to see Earl standing on the front porch, the ubiquitous Chesterfield dangling from his lips.

"Thank you," he called gruffly. "For seeing Anne."

"Anne will heal," Callie said stiffly. "She'll need quinine pills from the druggist as soon as possible. She has malaria. I left a tincture of boneset and some wormwood tea. I've instructed Mildred in what to do.

If you can get tonic water with quinine, that wouldn't hurt."

"Malaria?" Earl muttered incredulously.

Callie bit her lip to keep from saying more. She had seen enough malaria in Charleston patients to recognize its lingering symptoms in her friend after her trip to tropical Cuba. After explaining the treatment, and extracting a promise from Anne to visit her at Turtle Island when she had recovered, Callie wanted nothing more than to get back to Zeke's and pack for her early morning departure for home. There were so many things she wanted to say, to spit from her mouth in an angry rant.

Forgive him. Let it go. The quiet voice in her mind could have been hers or Seeta's or even God's, for all she knew. But it was clear. *Let it go.*

She started the ignition, nodded toward Earl Davis, and eased the car down the quiet street.

— • —

The Ford sped down the two-lane road toward the coast, the thin tires spewing dust and gravel behind them. As she drove, Callie recounted the events of the past week. Still reeling from Seeta's death, she was in awe of the truth in her grandmother's words. Forgiving Earl, visiting Anne, had taken some huge weight from her shoulders that she hadn't even realized was there.

The sun was bright, and wildflowers waved from along the roadside refreshed overnight by a summer shower. The world seemed a better place than it had just a week ago.

She made a mental list of questions to ask Marcus. Why did he come back to South Carolina? Why didn't he write Seeta? And why did he remain silent last year when he saw the envelope from Zeke addressed to Callie Beecham, the name of his own daughter?

Since he agreed to stay on as caretaker, she hoped he wanted to get to know her, to explain himself. She weighed the idea of having a father for the first time in her life. *What do you think, Callie? You'll hire him as a convenient caretaker, and then keep him around as your—secret—biological father?*

She glanced at the fuel level. *Blast. Almost out of gas, and I missed my turn,* Callie realized with consternation. She didn't recognize the road she was on at all. A filling-station sign on her right advertised cold drinks, boiled peanuts, and gasoline. Callie quickly pulled into the dilapidated station. Two elderly black men sat on a bench in front, munching on peanuts from a shared paper sack. They eyed Callie suspiciously as they tossed peanut shells to the ground.

A young man came trotting out of the small white frame building, brown eyes wide. He was shirtless and barefoot, dungarees cinched tight with a rope belt. He whistled when he saw the sleek Ford.

"Fill it up, please?" Callie asked. The man nodded and set to work filling the car's gas tank. Callie stepped out of the car nervously and headed toward the store, wishing to God she'd packed simpler clothing. Zeke's comments about what color she tried to be in Charleston unnerved her. In her fashionable suit and kid-leather heels, she looked too fine for this part of the world.

She pushed open the door and entered the building. Wooden shelves lined the left wall, and a variety of canned and dry goods sat waiting for purchase. A swollen pickle barrel was off to the right. A large black woman wearing a faded gingham dress slumped behind the counter, her eyes focused on a battered copy of the *Saturday Evening Post* she held in her hands.

Callie blanched when she realized she'd kept that same November 1927 issue, with its cover art entitled *Hat Shop*. It depicted a young white woman in blue seated in front of a mirror, trying on a smart cloche. At that minute, Callie resembled the art so much that she wondered if some cosmic joke was playing out at her expense.

The woman looked up from her magazine, and straightened, eyes wide. "He'p ya?"

Callie pointed to the car. "I'm getting gasoline. It was so low, I was worried that I wouldn't make it another ten miles." She smiled. "I'm dying for a Coca-Cola. Can I get an ice-cold one from the bottom of the cooler?"

"We ain't got cold drinks no more, ma'am. Got a pump out back though. I can give you a cup fo' water. It's clean." The woman slid a spotless tin cup across the counter.

Callie picked up the cup and exited the building. She found the old pump easily enough and pumped the handle a few times. Clear water gushed into the bucket hanging over the pump, and she dipped the cup and then drank deeply.

She turned and saw a whitewashed outhouse at the rear of the property. With a grimace, she yanked open the door and went in to take care of her personal business. Despite the horrible odor, the privy was neat and fairly clean. Old catalogs sat in a neat stack at her feet, along with a hand-lettered sign; "*Use only 3 pages a visit.*" When Callie stepped outside after a few minutes, she came face to face with the woman wringing her hands, her expression one of shock.

"Lan' sakes! You use the privy? I'm so sorry, ma'am. We use to had a white bathroom inside, but we ain't got water to it no more," she exclaimed. "We don't have a privy fo' whites." She explained, "This here is Salters. It's a colored town now." She motioned for Callie to follow her back inside.

"Salters?" Callie swallowed. She'd never heard of it. *Where am I?*

"Yes, ma'am. Used to be lotsa white folks in Salters. Mr. an' Mrs. Jones owned the fillin' station. Use to have lights an' water. When they moved away, it all got turned off—an' no one gone turn it on fo' the likes of me." She glanced at the rusty drink cooler, its lid wide open, empty.

"You own the store now?" Callie asked. "Good for you!"

"I do," the woman answered proudly. "My name's Susannah. Susannah Walters. I bought it from Mr. Jones. I didn't know he'd cut the services off. I'm glad I can get gasoline and canned goods delivered. Not many places will deliver to a colored store. My daddy an' my husband farm. We barely make it some months, so when Toby saw you drive up, we was hopeful you'd buy somethin'."

Callie nodded. "Mrs. Walters, I had a small business. I know how hard it can be." She sighed. "And I might have run out of gas if I hadn't found your store. May I also buy a map, please?"

Susannah shook her head.

"No maps?" she asked weakly.

"No, ma'am," the woman said. "I got pickles an' boiled peanuts. Got some homemade strawberry jam. Best you'll ever taste."

"Then a jar of jam, a bag of peanuts, and a pickle for the road," Callie said.

The station attendant opened the door. "Ten gallons, Mama," he called.

The woman nodded and looked at Callie, her wide smile revealing even white teeth. "Two dollars, ten cents fo' the gas and another thirty cents fo' the snacks. Thank ya so much fo' the business."

"We working gals have to stick together." Callie fumbled in her purse for cash and produced the right amount, which she laid on the counter.

The cash register rang, and the drawer opened. The woman placed the cash in the drawer and slammed it shut, causing Callie to jump. "You alright, honey?"

"Not really. I'm lost. I'm trying to get to Charleston." Callie tried to quash the rising panic in her voice, doubtful the woman could help.

Susannah began to put the purchased goods into a paper sack. "You ain't lost. You wantin' to go outta here back the way you came and then take the left at the sign fo' Bonneau. It's a big white sign. That'll get ya back on the right road, an' then look fo' Monck's Corner signs. You get there and then you back on the road straight to Charleston. Monck's Corner got stores and services fo' whites. You be alright."

Callie wanted to leap across the counter and kiss the woman on the cheek. Instead, she thanked her and turned to leave.

"Ma'am?"

Callie stopped and turned. "Yes?"

She eyed Callie's clothing, taking in the velvet-trimmed cloche, the finely tailored suit, matching shoes, and silk stockings. She leaned her large frame against the counter and pointed one meaty hand toward Callie. "Is you a movie star? 'Cuz you look jes' like this magazine cover."

Callie looked down at her clothing and laughed. "No. I'm nobody special. I saved that same issue because I loved that outfit. When I saw it in the store, I just had to have it."

Susannah grinned. "Huh . . . Well, I'm nobody special, too. If I ever can fit into clothes like that, I'll buy me a suit jes' like it. I'll wear it every day. With the velvet bow on the hat an' everything. It looks real nice."

Callie smiled broadly. "Thank you. And I think it would look lovely on you, too. Good luck with your store. Don't give up!" She pushed through the door and into the bright sunshine, suddenly feeling better about the world as it might be one day.

— • —

The headlights played across the yard, and oyster shells crunched under tires as Callie pulled the car into the circular drive at Turtle Island. She was beyond weary, and the late hour meant she couldn't track down Marcus until the following day. *I should have sent him a telegram*, she thought. And Seeta was gone. She wouldn't be able to reunite mother and son, to give her grandmother an incredibly precious gift.

She'd been away only five days, but it seemed an eternity. She grabbed her suitcase and climbed out of the car, dejected. Immediately, a sultry breeze caressed her cheek, welcoming her back to the Lowcountry. She smiled.

Spring peepers chirped in a happy chorus from the marsh. The house was dark, and only a sliver of moonlight illuminated the walk to the front steps. She fumbled for her key but found the lock with little trouble. Callie turned the doorknob and entered the house, grateful to be back. She dropped the suitcases and switched on the light. Home.

She stepped out of her shoes, peeled off the suit jacket, and removed her hat. *Tea.* Too nervous to sleep, she padded into the kitchen to make a cup of chamomile tea. She flipped the light switch and put the kettle on to boil. When she turned, a milk glass vase of pink flowers on the table caught her eye. Betty or Marcus must have come by and cut some of the roses. The ones that reminded her of Seeta. She smiled. Then, something else caught her attention.

There was an envelope tucked under the vase. It was addressed to her. To Callie. Not Carrie. With a shaking hand, Callie lifted the vase and picked up the envelope. *He does know.*

She quickly tore the flap and pulled out a single sheet of paper.

Dear Callie,

I knew it was you when you stepped out of the shed that day. You looked just like Kizzy, with that cloud of wild hair and your big brown eyes. And then last week when you said my mama's name, I thought my heart would break. I am Seeta Young's son, Marcus. You called her your grandmother, so you must know your family story. You are my daughter and I'm sorry about that. I hope that when you see this, it means my mama is better.

In this world, a black man can't have a daughter that looks like you. And a woman who looks like you can't have a father like me. They'd kill me and they'd never let you be anything good. Stay here and be a nurse and help people.

I won't write or let on where me and Betty end up. Somehow it would get out and you'd have to run again. And so would I. It's why I can never go back home to Seeta. There's always someone waiting to take us down.

This house is your home now. I wonder if Silas sent you here to find me. I made him swear he'd never tell you and Mama. But tell Mama I love her.

Marcus Young

The tea kettle whistled. Callie sank to the floor, her cries almost as loud as the steam shrieking into the ether.

Chapter Thirty

The Calhoun Street Clinic was especially busy that rainy October morning. Callie had already stitched up an elderly man's lacerated calf, tended a child's hand burned in a woodstove accident, seen to a young postpartum woman with severe mastitis, and dosed three malaria patients with quinine.

She'd gotten a letter from Anne just that morning. Her friend was feeling much better, up and about and back at home, getting her strength back after the debilitating bout with malaria. She thanked Callie profusely for healing her and mentioned nothing of Earl. She had reconciled with John, she wrote, and wasn't sure what would come next. His fortunes had diminished considerably after the Crash, but, indeed, these were hard times for everyone. She promised to make a date for lunch soon.

Callie's feet throbbed, and she longed for a moment to sit down, but there was still a patient waiting to be seen in Room One. Dr. Drake and Nurse Graves were currently finishing up in Room Two. She glanced at her watch. It was eleven thirty. At noon, she would wolf down a sandwich and then join Dr. Drake at one to interview a new doctor who hoped to join the busy practice. The clinic really needed another nurse. It couldn't afford to add one of those, too, though, so Callie's days would continue to be very long, but rewarding.

She adjusted her crisp white nurse's cap and inhaled deeply. She still found herself nervous before meeting each and every patient. She exhaled slowly, before knocking on the door of Room One. A woman's faint voice answered, "Come in."

Callie pushed open the door and regarded the well-dressed young woman seated before her, looking glum.

"Good morning. I'm Nurse Beecham," Callie said. "Your name?"

"Melton. Grace Melton." The woman crossed and uncrossed her legs nervously.

Callie wrote the woman's name on her chart. "Age?"

"I'm eighteen."

"What seems to be the problem, Miss Melton?"

"I have a pain. Here." She placed her palm on her right lower abdomen. "It's especially sharp when I press in."

Callie jotted notes on her clipboard. She looked up. "How long have you had it?"

The woman thought for a minute and said, "Two days. I'm feverish, too."

"Hop up on the table, and I'll feel around on your abdomen. Dr. Drake is in the other room with a patient, but we can get started."

"I don't need to see him. I'm fine with a nurse." Miss Melton stood and climbed onto the examining table.

"We'll see," Callie said. She noted no facial expressions or body movements that revealed pain when the woman moved.

"Say ahh." She placed a thermometer under the young woman's tongue. After a few minutes, she removed the thermometer. "Normal. Please lie back and I'll have a look."

The woman lay down against the pillow, her blue eyes darting from her abdomen to Callie and back.

Callie palpated the woman's entire abdomen, being careful at the junction of the small and large intestine. The woman didn't flinch or make a sound. She picked up the woman's thin wrist and took a pulse. Normal.

"Hmm. Does it hurt now?"

"Y-Yes, it does. Is there some medicine you can send home with me?" Miss Melton asked.

Callie pressed on the area between the right hip and pubic bone.

"It's not my time of the month, and it's nothing I've eaten."

"Could you be pregnant?" Callie asked.

The woman blanched. "Gosh, no!" she whispered.

Callie sensed fear in Miss Melton's voice. Indeed, her eyes shifted to the door, the window, and then back to Callie several times.

"Miss Melton, are you really ill? Or is there someone else you are here for?" Callie asked softly. These days, it wasn't uncommon for people of means to try and procure medicines for down-and-out friends and family.

The young woman lowered her voice. "It's my—friend. He's in the back alley. He's very sick—but he can't come inside."

Before Callie could ask why not, she knew.

Grace shook her head. "Please don't say anything to the doctor. Dr. Drake knows my parents. Can you help my friend? Please? He's burning up. Doubled over. I didn't know what to do. Or where to take him. I can pay you."

Callie suspected acute appendicitis. She thought for a moment. "You're my last appointment before lunch. Check out at the front desk and then go on out. I'll meet you in a moment in the alley."

Grace hopped off the table easily and grabbed her purse.

"Miss Melton, you're a terrible actress," Callie said softly.

"Thank you so much!" Grace grinned and hurried from the room.

Callie tossed some aspirin, a sphygmomanometer, and a thermometer in her purse. She stepped into the hall just as the head nurse stepped out of the second exam room.

"Everything alright, Nurse Beecham?" asked the nurse, eyeing Callie's purse suspiciously.

Callie nodded. "I'm through until one, Nurse Graves. Taking my lunch break."

The nurse nodded and continued down the hall.

Callie quietly headed for the back door and let herself into the alley.

A slight drizzle cloaked the already poor visibility in the dark alley, although it appeared clear toward the street, except for the rusty and overflowing garbage cans stacked outside of the various businesses with alley access.

"Nurse!" a voice hissed from the opposite direction. "Over here!"

Callie hurried to a small alcove tucked out of sight from the street. Grace was crouched next to a young black man who lay doubled over against the brick wall, his face drenched with sweat or rain drops, she wasn't sure. He was in obvious pain.

Grace wiped the man's forehead tenderly with her handkerchief. "Robert, this is the nurse from the clinic. She can help you." She looked at Callie with desperation in her blue eyes.

Callie knelt by the young man. "Robert, show me where it hurts."

Robert pointed to the midpoint between his right hip bone and his groin. "Hurts like the devil, ma'am. Been like this for nearly two days, but this morning, I can hardly bear it." Indeed, he spoke through clenched teeth. "I been vomiting, too."

Callie put a hand on his damp forehead. The man was burning up.

"I thought this was the place that would see colored people," Grace said. "He said it started with a C or a K... But when I got Robert here, he said it wasn't the right place. That's why I tried to act like it was me that was sick."

Callie frowned. She ticked off the clinics she knew of in the city. Most were strictly off-limits to colored people. She had heard Betty once mention a cousin who had been sick and gone somewhere downtown... Not Calhoun. Not Columbia...

"Cannon!" she said. "Grace, you have to take him to Cannon Street. He has appendicitis, I think. He'll need emergency surgery."

Grace began to whimper. "That's blocks away! I can't hold him up. I could barely get him here. Can you help us, please?"

Callie gasped. "I can't leave the clinic!"

"Cannon. That's the one. Please?" Robert whispered through a grimace. "Please—help me."

Callie glanced in both directions. "My car is parked out front. Give me ten minutes, and I will come for you."

Robert nodded. Grace mouthed a silent "thank you," and Callie stood. She pulled open the heavy door and disappeared inside.

— • —

Callie pulled her car up to the three-story brick building as the rain began to come down in earnest. A large sign read *Cannon Street Hospital and Training School for Nurses*. The idea jarred Callie and excited her at the same time. She looked again. *Cannon Street Hospital and Training School for Nurses*.

Stunned and elated that the place even existed, she hurried toward the building's entrance. Her white skirt and stockings were mud-streaked from the alley. Her hair was beginning to come unpinned in the rain, but she merely pushed it out of her face.

A uniformed orderly opened the door, his face as dark as Seeta's. "Can I help you, nurse?"

"I have a young man in my car with what I think is acute appendicitis," Callie said.

The orderly motioned to someone in the lobby, and a second orderly appeared in the doorway with a metal gurney. The gurney rattled loudly down the cracked sidewalk as the young men followed Callie to the car where Robert lay in the back seat, curled in the fetal position.

Grace stood by the car, wringing her pale hands.

Callie bent to speak to Robert. "Robert, you're at Cannon Street Hospital. These men will take good care of you."

"I—I don't have money," he gasped. "I don't want Grace to pay."

"Don't worry about that, now. Let's go," she directed.

The orderlies gently helped Robert from the car and onto the gurney. They began to wheel him back toward the building, Callie at their heels. She turned to see Grace standing helplessly by the car, her sodden dress clinging to her frame.

"Grace! Aren't you coming in?" she called.

The young woman clutched her jacket around herself tightly. "I can't," she wailed.

"Why the hell not?" Callie snapped, wiping her wet hair from her cheeks. "He's your friend. You've come this far."

"If my father finds out I was here, he will kill me."

Callie resisted the urge to scream at the girl, to berate her for her fear. But she checked herself. The woman clearly cared about her friend and had tried to help him.

"Very well. Get yourself home then. Thank you for getting him to me." Callie turned and jogged after the gurney as it entered the hospital. Immediately, several members of the staff surrounded the gurney.

The spacious lobby surprised Callie, as did the bustle of hospital staff around her. She'd had no idea the place existed. Clean and bright. Full of people of all colors.

"Ma'am?"

Callie turned. A middle-aged nurse stood there, clipboard in her white hand. "Did you bring in Mr. Barnes?" Her badge read Nurse Scott. The woman took in Callie's soaked and mud-stained uniform and waited for an answer.

"Who?" Callie asked, confused.

"Robert Barnes?" The nurse pointed toward the gurney, now being hustled through a set of double doors.

"Y-yes. Well, his friend brought him to the Calhoun Street Clinic. She came inside and told me about him."

"Oh. I see. Calhoun Street." The nurse jotted something in the chart.

Callie wanted to die of shame at how it appeared. Racist. Hateful. Why hadn't she had the courage to bring him into her own clinic when time was of the essence?

"Did you check his vitals?" the woman asked.

Callie shook her head. "No. I—I hurried to get him here by car. I think he has acute appendicitis, and I knew we needed to get here—to a hospital—fast."

"Next of kin?"

Callie thought of Grace and shook her head. "I don't know. Just put me down for now." She touched her badge and added, "Nurse Callie Beecham."

"Very well," the nurse murmured. "He's headed right to the doctor and then possibly to surgery. Will you stay to get a diagnosis from the doctor before he goes in?"

Callie looked at her watch. She had thirty minutes until her lunch hour was over, and Dr. Drake would expect to see her back in the office. She swallowed hard. "Yes. I can wait."

Nurse Scott nodded and turned to leave. Callie looked around the lobby and wandered toward the waiting area rimmed with metal folding chairs. She sat down wearily across from an elderly black woman winding a ball of red yarn.

"You here to get a job, ma'am?" her small voice asked. She continued winding the ball of yarn, but her brown eyes stared at Callie through thick glasses.

Callie was cognizant of her own disheveled state. She waved her hand in dismissal. "Oh, no! I brought in that young man who just went back. I'm waiting to hear from the doctor as to surgery."

"Too bad. They could use more nurses here. They have white ones and colored ones. They treat me like a person. My husband Willis is in there." She pointed toward the double doors.

"I'm sorry," Callie said. "I'm sure that the doctors will take good care of him."

The old woman leaned forward. "They always do. Me an' Willis is old. We come here a lot." She chuckled. "An' you know what else? They'll let me pay the bill sometimes with fruit an' things I've canned. Lawd, what would folks do without this place?"

"I had no idea it was here." She looked around at the staff coming and going. The orderlies had been black. The receptionist white. The nurse was white. She'd seen two patients so far, both black.

Callie began to assess the Cannon Street lobby. On the wall, her jaw dropped when she saw a large poster for an upcoming reception honoring a black nurse named Anna DeCosta Banks. The quote under her photograph read, "*I have found that when a person is sick or in need, it does not make any difference to them who you are or what. If you have come to help them, all are gladly received."*

A hand-lettered sign propped on an easel proclaimed, "No one will be turned away from this clinic because of their race or their ability to pay." The thought made her pulse quicken. *No one is turned away. White or black.*

At the Calhoun Street Clinic, it was implied that the office was for whites only. Indeed, Ida Crouch, the elderly receptionist, scowled at everyone who entered, no matter their station, and would surely drive away any black person who dared step into Dr. Drake's plush lobby.

There were no signs, no explicit instructions from Dr. Drake, but Callie had never seen a colored person enter the building. They wouldn't dare. The only other businesses on their stretch of cobblestoned Calhoun Street were two attorneys and a dental practice. The office was surrounded by large homes with manicured gardens, walled off with elaborate wrought-iron gates.

This place felt different. Warm. Welcoming. Callie cleared her throat and pointed to the poster. "Do you know Nurse Banks? There is a reception coming up for her."

The woman grinned knowingly. "Nurse Banks? Why sure, honey. She been here thirty years. Nurse Banks is the kindest, most carin' woman. She was the head nurse, and she trained the other nurses who came up. At the school."

"Mrs. Green?" A door opened, and a young mulatto nurse stood in the doorway, waiting. Her skin was almost as pale as Callie's, but her features and hair marked her as mixed.

The elderly woman tucked her yarn ball into her bag and stood. "I'll say a prayer for that boy."

Callie smiled. "Thank you. And I'll say one for your husband." She watched the woman totter across the terrazzo floor toward the smiling nurse. "Hello, Nurse, how is he?"

The young nurse put an arm around the elderly woman and spoke quietly as she steered her through the doors.

Callie found herself wondering about this Anna DeCosta Banks. What kind of woman was brave enough to become a nurse at the turn of the century? And a black woman at that! What must she have seen and dealt with along the way?

I've been a coward. I've been living in hiding for far too long, just like Marcus. I'm tired of hiding. But she had to admit it—so much beauty had come from the ashes. She'd been given great gifts: the love of a grandmother she never knew, an extended family she didn't know she

311

had, Silas's friendship, and then his entire estate, which led her to meeting her father, a home on James Island, and nursing school. And that was something.

A white nurse chattered amiably as she pushed a black teenage girl in a wheelchair across the hall. The girl burst out laughing at something the nurse said. The desk receptionist welcomed a young black couple into the lobby, the woman visibly pregnant. They took their seats across from Callie, eyes only for each other.

This place. *This place could be a soul-satisfying place to work*, she thought. And maybe Callie could be herself. Not white. Not black. *Both.*

The double doors opened again, and a caramel-skinned nurse appeared. "Family of Robert Barnes?"

Callie stood slowly. The young couple stared at her as she crossed the lobby.

"Are you kin to Robert Barnes?" the nurse asked skeptically, taking in Callie's appearance.

"There is no family here," Callie apologized. "A friend of his brought him to Calhoun Street Clinic, but she left." *Or fled.*

The nurse looked at her clipboard, at Callie's badge, and back to her clipboard. "The doctor wants to speak with family," she said, exasperated. "Mr. Barnes will need surgery right away. They're prepping him now."

Callie thought of Grace Melton. "I don't know his family. But I can speak to the doctor if you wish. And then I'll find his friend. She's a patient where I work. She'll know where to find his family."

The nurse sighed heavily and jotted Callie's name on her clipboard. She motioned for Callie to follow her. They went through the double doors and down a long corridor, before entering a small waiting room.

"Wait here. I'll tell the doctor you're available." The nurse left quickly, and Callie sat down to wait. She tried to brush the dried mud from her skirt. Her white stockings had started to run at both knees, and her hair had frizzed dramatically in the rain. She checked her wristwatch. Ten minutes until one. She could lose her job. What had she been thinking?

She dropped her head into her hands. After some time, she heard the door open.

"Callie?"

Callie raised her head quickly. "W—what? What are you doing here?" she gasped.

Sam Epstein smiled incredulously. "Oy. I should ask you the same question."

Epilogue

She'd never known such pains—strong and regular, hard muscle clinched tight around the baby, and pushing downward with every contraction. She grimaced and held her breath as her abdomen tightened yet again. She blew out a low moaning breath between pale lips and willed the inescapable process to slow down, before leaning over and bracing herself against the bed rail.

"Sam!" she called weakly. "I want Sam."

"I'm here, Callie. I'm here." Sam leaned close to Callie and mopped her damp brow with a cloth.

"I can't do this." Callie panted.

"Of course you can. Our baby is coming soon and you're doing great. I love you."

Callie reached for Sam's hand and gripped it tightly, unwilling to let him go.

The young midwife leaned over Callie, her dark face lovely and kind. "You're almost there." She reached for Callie's arm and wrapped the blood pressure cuff around her upper arm. After a minute, she said, "Everything looks good, Mrs. Epstein. One more push should do it. This will be a special baby—it's not every day that we have a Cannon Street doctor and nurse having their baby here." She glanced at the clock on the wall. "And guess what? It's midnight. Happy New Year!"

Sam bent down and kissed his wife on the cheek. Callie closed her eyes and grimaced as another contraction began to rise like a cresting wave.

"Alright," the midwife said. "This baby is ready to meet the world. One more push and the little one will be here—Cannon Street Hospital's first baby of 1932. Here we go!"

Author's Notes

The research for this fictional story took me down new and interesting paths. I wasn't familiar with many events from the time of the Jim Crow South, and I've learned a lot about that sad era in our nation's history. *Climbing to the Sun* is based on stories and events that took place across the country nearly one hundred years ago during the Great Migration, one of the largest migrations in US history. For a truly fascinating and well-researched book on the migration of Black Americans out of the Jim Crow South, I urge you to read Isabel Wilkerson's *The Warmth of Other Suns*.

The small community of Liberia, South Carolina, is very real. And very beautiful. It began as a community of freed slaves after the Civil War. The original Soapstone Baptist Church was lost to arson, but a new church was built on the same site. The small congregation has, according to their website, "relied on and been blessed by financial contributions literally from around the world." For more than twenty years, a monthly fish-fry, open to the community, raised additional funding to help support ongoing needs. Those funds allowed the congregation to pay off their mortgage in December 2020 and still help maintain the property. To help support Soapstone Baptist Church's mission, go to www.soapstonechurch.com.

For more information, you'll want to read John M. Coggeshall's book, *Liberia: An African American Appalachian Community*.

To read more about the tragic summer of 1919, I recommend *Red Summer: The Summer of 1919 and the Awakening of Black America* by Cameron McWhirter.

Cannon Street Hospital was one of the only African-American hospitals in South Carolina during the nineteenth and twentieth centuries. Due to segregation laws at the time, black doctors and nurses could not see patients in white hospitals. The hospital is no longer standing.

Anna DeCosta Banks was the first head nurse at the Hospital and Training School for Nurses in Charleston, South Carolina, located at Cannon Street Hospital. She became the Superintendent of Nurses there, a position she held for thirty-two years. Throughout her career, she focused on seeking more equitable health care for black patients. Banks had such a significant effect on nursing within the state of South Carolina that the Medical University of South Carolina named a wing of their hospital after her. In 1930, she passed away. She was the oldest nurse working in South Carolina at the time. "All ages, classes, races, called her blessed."

Acknowledgments

Thank you, Mama, for getting us back into the Smoky Mountains. Thank you for introducing me to the *Foxfire* books, for mountain laurel, for your clear creek to fish from, and the "boar woods." Thank you for growing your own food and for your reverence for the old ways of plant medicine. I wish I'd caught on sooner.

Thanks to my family for being the first readers of my early drafts and for giving me moral support. And thanks for suggesting I not kill off the evil characters—but, instead, forgive them.

I would like to thank the many readers of *The Earth Remains*, who knew that Ona's story wasn't over—but had to convince me that this was so.

Thank you to Angie Chatin of JC Picture Cars for patient explanations and corrections to my understanding of how to drive a Model T. I am sure that driving one is hard, but writing about driving one was challenging enough for me!

Thank you to Mayor Fletcher Perry, the first Black mayor of Pickens, South Carolina. His inspiring stories about growing up in segregated Pickens County have stayed with me.

About the Author

Shelley Burchfield is a writer, mom, and former teacher with deep Southern roots. She enjoys writing "what-if" fiction that flips notorious events upside down. She lives in the beautiful South Carolina Upstate with her husband and a menagerie of cats and dogs.

Also by this Author

In a time when humans owned other humans and a nation was torn by war, doing what was right sometimes meant being on the wrong side of the law.

www.shelleyburchfield.com